THE ARYAVARTA CHRONICLES
BOOK 1

GOVÎNDA

Krishna Udayasankar is a graduate of the National Law School of India University (NLSIU), Bangalore, and holds a PhD in Strategic Management from the Nanyang Technological University, Singapore, where she presently works as a Lecturer.

Govinda is Krishna's first published novel. She is currently working on the second and third books of *The Aryavarta Chronicles* and a collection of prose-poems entitled *Objects of Affection*.

A resident of sunny Singapore, when she's not busy writing and teaching, Krishna loves to watch Rajinikanth movies first-day, first-show, complete with applause and whistles, and to go on long drives with her husband, Jai, and two Siberian Huskies, Boozo and Zana.

THE ARYAVARTA CHRONICLES
BOOK 1
GOVÎNDA

Krishna Udayasankar

hachette
INDIA

First published in 2012 by Hachette India
(Registered name: Hachette Book Publishing India Pvt. Ltd)
An Hachette UK company
www.hachetteindia.com

1

Map on p. ix illustrated by Priya Kuriyan

Author photo on cover by Alvin Pang

ISBN 978-93-5009-446-4

Hachette Book Publishing India Pvt. Ltd,
4th & 5th Floors, Corporate Centre,
Plot No. 94, Sector 44, Gurgaon 122003, India

Typeset in Arno Pro 11/13.2
by Eleven Arts, New Delhi

Printed and bound in India
by
Manipal Technologies Ltd., Manipal

Author's Note

Aryavarta, circa second millenium BCE

In a large glen somewhere in the verdant forests of Naimisha, a sattra, or conclave of scholars, has been convened by the sage Saunuka Kulapati. Here, in what is described as a sacrifice lasting twelve years, the finest scholar–seers of the land, the keepers of knowledge, have gathered to discuss the knowledge of their times and give final form to its codification as the Vedas, Books of Knowledge. At the centre of this conclave stands Ugrashravas Sauti, the bard, traditional keeper of the ancient narratives known as the Puranas. The story he tells them, however, is their own, the tale of who they are and how they have come to be there.

He calls it *Jaya*. Victory.

To the gathered scholars at Naimisha, that story was neither ancient nor mythological. It was itihasa, or history. *Jaya* was undeniably a tale of its time, and just as posterity elevated the great men of that time and saw them as gods, so too was the story's context adapted and its reality turned into metaphor. In order to go behind the metaphor, and to tell the tale as mytho-history rather than mythology, the essential question that came to my mind was: If Govinda and all the other characters of this grand narrative had walked the world as we know it today, bound by our languange and constructions, our common perceptions of physics, psychology and politics, what might their story really have been? Surprisingly, at its core it may not have been very different from the one that took form millenia ago during the conclave of Naimisha.

Like societies, stories are made up of two elements that I call (admittedly with neither theological nor philosophical expertise) moral *imperative* and moral *principle*. Moral principles are the relatively immutable values that guide human life, perhaps even underlie philosophical evolution, whereas moral imperatives are the derivative rules that are part of social structure, the behavioural norms embedded in everyday interaction. These norms are often context-specific and change as the structure of society changes. At the same time, for any social institution to survive, it must either adapt to these changing imperatives, or else justify defying them.

Through a process of re-interpretation and interpolation, even some aggrandization, the many unnamed narrators who have passed down such epic tales through the centuries have recast some events and explained others differently to make them not just palatable but also plausible and relevant to their audience. What remains constant, however, are the broad sweep of the story and the moral principles that underlie it.

There began the quest for the story that lay hidden beneath the larger epic tales of ancient India. The story that emerged as a result is the product of research and analysis based on both mainstream and alternative (e.g. Bhil and Indonesian Kakawain) narratives, the details of which are given at the back of this book.

Based on these works, ranging from Bankimchandra Chattopadhyay's and K.M. Munshi's interpretations in their books *Krishnacharitra* and *Krishnavatara* respectively to Van Buiten's critical translations of the epic's texts and Alf Hiltebeitel's scholarly research papers and books on their symbolism-rich language, and to alternative Bhil and Indonesian Kakawain versions, to name a few sources, it becomes possible to construct a story of why things may have happened as they did, a plausible narrative with reasonable internal logical consistency. Something that could well have been history, something that stands firm not just on faith but also on logic and science. In short, the story of why something might have happened.

And so, Aryavarta comes to life not as a land of demigods and demons in strife, but as an empire of nobles, commoners and forest-dwellers in socio-economic conflict. Kalas, Yugas and the Wheel of Time make sense as theories of revolution and renewal, and the terrible Rakshasas of legend can be seen as Rikshasas – Vriksha or tree-people – their horned heads and fanged teeth morphed back into animal-horn helmets and tiger-tooth necklaces. The mythical epic of old, a story of gods and all-encompassing divine will in action, then falls into place as the tale of a feudal, agrarian hierarchy based on natural law and religion, caught in the throes of technological and economic change. In fact, the moment we do away with assumptions of both preternatural and supernatural forces, of omnipotence and divinity, we find ourselves necessarily seeking out political, social and even psychological explanations – including theories of conspiracy and political intrigue.

We are the stories we tell. *The Aryavarta Chronicles* are neither reinterpretation nor retelling. These stories are a construction of reality based on a completely different set of assumptions – a distinction that is important because constructing shared reality is what links individual to society, however widely we may define the latter. To that extent, it no longer matters whether these events happened or not, or whether they happened in a completely different way, because the idea that such things have come to pass has affected the lives of many for a very long time now. There is a sanctity which has developed as a result of what people have come to think and do as they have interacted with the spirit of these epic tales and their characters, with the world of Aryavarta. At the end of the day, that spirit is much, much larger than any story, or a book.

I am simply one of those innumerable bards who passes the story on, contexualized and rationalized but not lacking in sincerity or integrity. It is you, the reader, who shall infuse it with meaning and bring it to life as you will.

narayanaya vid mahe
vaasudevaya dhi mahi
thanno vishnu prachodayaat

We shall know the divine spirit within
We shall meditate on the essence of all beings
Thus, the all-pervading shall blaze forth.

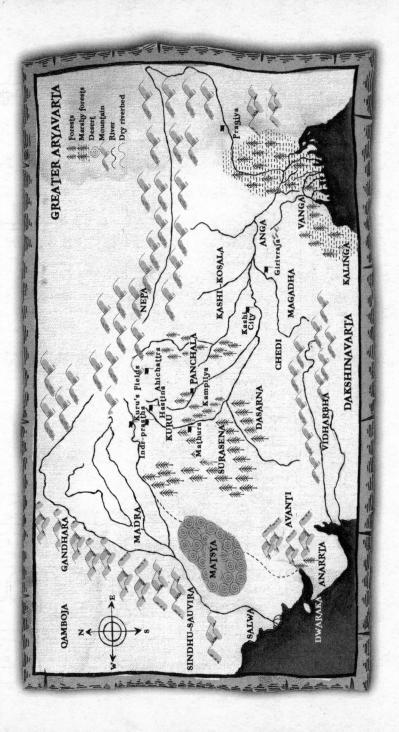

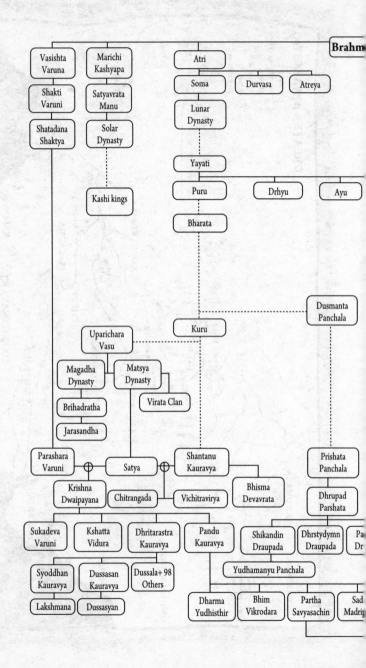

The Dynasties of Aryavarta

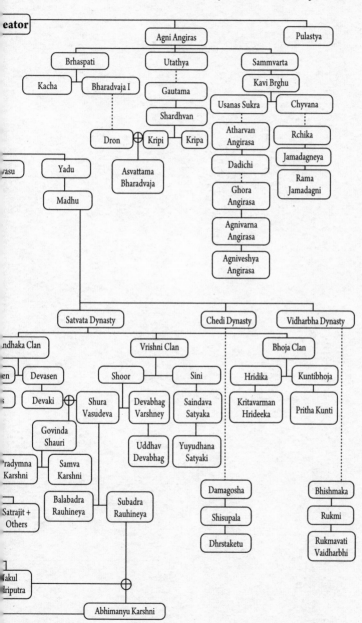

adi

The Beginning

THERE WAS NOTHING BUT THE BLINDING, BLAZING SUN. THEY moved slowly, every step forward an overwhelming effort as weariness overcame their will to live. The brightness was beyond bearing; all they could see was an endless golden shimmer.

The young woman smirked, bitter. *Perhaps we're already dead, and in Indra's heaven.*

But then there were the vultures. The intense haze made it easier to ignore the scavengers, but once in a while she spotted a lone bird perched either on a dead tree or on some debris, watching them keenly. It took her some time to realize that it was the same creature following them, moving as they moved.

It's waiting for us to die.

She calmly met the vulture's gaze. The bird no longer inspired fear or revulsion, not since she had come to terms with all that had happened.

We brought this upon ourselves. We deserve this for trusting that scum, those godless magicians … A curse on the head of every Firewright!

Firewrights. The old order of scholar–seers had promised a great revolution, a time when man and his harvest would depend on the fickle gods less and his own will more. The river's course, they said, could be made to move, to feed the lands, turn the most barren earth into verdant bounty. It would be, they had promised, an era of unrivalled prosperity for the whole empire of Aryavarta. An age when humans would defy the might of the gods.

We deserve this for our blasphemy.

The lands the two travellers crossed had once been seasonal but fertile. Now, they lay fallow and the earth had splintered in patterns of horror. The vast river had slowed to a trickle, the skies had turned stark and cloudless and the furrows on the land had deepened further till it had all become the same – one endless desert, with neither a drop of water below nor a cloud above.

Tears welled up, unbidden, and as her vision blurred she stumbled. The man walking behind her rushed forward to help. 'Princess!'

She waved him back. *Princess! Hah!* She, Satya, was the daughter of the mighty Emperor of Aryavarta, a woman destined to be a queen. And now it had come to this. She was nothing more than a refugee. Like the rest of her people, the few who still lived, who were now trying to flee the forsaken land that had once been their bountiful home.

The man passed her the small waterskin that hung from his shoulder. She took it with a grateful smile and drew a careful sip. The water had to last them all the way till their destination, an insignificant village of fishermen far enough across the desert to remain blissfully unaffected by their tragedy. It was the one place that her father believed she could be safe. Perhaps he had hoped that under the care of his old friend she could somehow begin a new life.

The princess made a solemn promise to herself, renewing it as she had every day for what had been a short while, though it now felt like years: She would live. And she would have her revenge. The need to destroy those who had destroyed everything she had ever held dear – her people, her home, her very belief in human goodness – burned in the pit of her stomach. She closed her eyes and savoured the feeling, letting it fuel her tired limbs.

That night, she and her guard made camp under the stars. They needed protection neither from the cold nor from wild beasts. Nothing had survived the drought. The princess wrapped herself up in her tattered cloak and lay down, while the guard sat a few feet away, keeping watch. She slept, and dreamt she was running across endless green fields, laughing and playing, while a great river gurgled along at her side wherever she went.

The next morning she woke to see the guard keeled over. With a sigh, she went closer, knowing exactly what she would find. He had died without a whimper. The princess suspected that he had not let a drop of water pass his lips for over three days, saving it all for her.

You won't be forgotten, my friend. She picked up the dead man's waterskin and resumed her journey.

The vulture would now be her only companion. She looked out for him eagerly, as if he were a friend. She did not dare sleep that night and kept moving, using the stars to guide her. It felt warmer in the dark than it had during the day. Sometime during the moonlit night, the water ran out. She could not see the vulture in the darkness, but knew he was waiting. She pulled out her knife and resolved to walk as far as she could before using it on herself.

A little before dawn, the moon set. In the ghostly light, she heard the sudden flutter of wings and panicked. It was only for a moment and she quickly pulled her wits together, but it was enough to make her lose her footing. She stumbled and fell, bruising her knees on sharp pebbles. Despite her terror, she recognized the irony of the situation – she had fallen on the dry bed of what had once been a strong, swift river. The rocky shoals that had dotted the river's course had become dark islands in a sea of white sand. For an instant, she imagined she heard the gurgling of water. Then darkness took her.

The princess stirred at the soothing touch of a cool, wet cloth on her lips. She heard someone calling to her, but the voice was vague and distant. With great effort she opened her eyes and realized that it was sometime in the afternoon. A stranger – a young man – was looking down at her with concern. He was tall and hardy, his long, matted hair was pulled back into a coil, and he wore simple, ochre robes.

A sage! Disgust welled up in her, and instinctively she pushed him away.

The man looked surprised, but yielded with grace. He held out his palms in a conciliatory gesture and took a few steps back to perch on a rock.

Slowly, she sat up, her eyes on him all the while.

'I won't hurt you,' he assured her in a kind, sincere voice. 'Don't worry.'

She did not look convinced.

He glanced around, uncertain, wondering how best to handle the young woman. At length he said, for a momentary lack of imagination, 'I'm Parashara, the son of Shakti in the line of the great Elder Vasishta. What's your name?'

She stared at him, incredulous. 'A Firstborn?'

He laughed. 'Yes, that's what they call us. Our ancestor was the first son of the Creator, and our order has carried the title ever since.'

'What ... what are you doing here?'

He pointed upwards. 'I saw the vultures swoop in, one after another. I ... I suppose I wanted to make sure that their quarry was really dead ... not ... You know what I mean.'

'Thank Rudra!' the princess exclaimed. As an afterthought she added, 'Thank you.'

'You're welcome. Now, if you'll tell me who you are and where you are from, I can see you safely home.'

She thought quickly. 'I'm Chief Dasha's daughter.'

'Dasha? Of the fishermen?'

She nodded, and waited for the inevitable question as to how she had come to be here. To her astonishment, Parashara accepted her averred identity without demur.

He said, 'We're not very far from your village. But you're tired and it's only another two hours to sunset. I suggest you eat such food as I have with me, and then sleep and get your strength back. We can leave in the morning.'

Though wary and suspicious, the princess agreed. She tried to stay awake, but eventually drifted off. Faint but seductive tendrils of hope flashed through her jumbled dreams.

The next morning they set out westward. Parashara headed in a different direction from the one the princess had been taking so far, but she followed him without question. Soon, jagged blue peaks came up on the horizon, low but running on unbroken as far as one could see.

'But …' she started to protest.

'Don't you know the way to your own country?' Parashara teased. 'There's a small path that leads up one of the cliffs. It's not easy, but it'll get us out of this damned desert,' he hissed out the last few words with venom. As if needing to vent his anger he continued, 'Those meddling Firewrights; heretics, the lot of them! The river Saraswati hides from Indra's wrath while the people of these lands pay the price …'

'I take it you don't like the Firewrights?'

'No, I don't.'

'Then we have something in common.'

Parashara's voice was a restrained sneer. 'Whatever have the Firewrights done to you?'

The princess gave a slow, firm shake of her head. 'Whatever they did here, to the people of this land, it was wrong. No one with a conscience can dispute that.'

'In that case, I won't.'

By afternoon, they were nearly at the base of the cliffs. Already the air was cooler, and the princess found herself laughing with relief. Parashara guided her with familiarity, occasionally pointing out some marker which he used to find his way. They rested for a short while at the foot of the cliffs and then began their upward climb. The narrow path, if it could be called that, was nothing more than a precarious series of outcrops and ledges that formed a stairway of sorts. But the sheer relief of leaving the desert behind gave the princess strength.

It was still light when they reached a tiny stream that flowed out from a small fissure in the ground, but the two decided they had walked enough for the day. They drank of the clear, cool water to their hearts' content. Parashara quickly doused himself from head to toe and left the princess to bathe in private while he stepped away to pray and meditate, assuring her he would remain within calling distance if she needed him.

By the time he returned, she had picked a few fruits and berries from the surrounding trees to make a sparse meal.

'We should be there by noon, tomorrow,' he said as they ate.

She did not reply, lost in thoughts of the future. The rest of their meal was quiet.

Soon after, he settled her into a thick, soft patch of grass that made for a wonderful bed and stretched himself out some distance away. He was lost in pleasant contemplation of the night sky, gazing at the stars as they emerged one by one, when he heard the soft rustle of leaves. He turned to see the young woman walking towards him and greeted her with a confused look. She knelt next to him, her eyes bashful, and placed a gentle hand on his chest to stop him from getting up.

A smile played on the scholar's lips, but he seemed to reconsider. He shook his head, his eyes shadowed by regret. 'There's nothing I can offer you, my dear. Like my father before me, I'm sworn to my order, to the Firstborn, and now, after all that has happened, the rest of my life will be devoted to just one thing – the fall of the Firewrights. There's no room for a woman – or a family – in my life.'

Her eyes mirrored his sadness. 'We share a common goal and that has already tied our destinies together. Still …'

She made to stand, but Parashara reached out and grabbed her wrist. Tilting his head back, he looked up at the stars. 'Destiny is a dangerous master,' he softly told her, his eyes fixed on the sky. 'It'll bind us beyond just this one night, for better or worse …' He turned to her, meeting her piercing gaze. 'Bear me a son, conceived in the fire of our common hatred. A son who shall destroy the Firewrights, shatter their sect and uproot it from its foundations. Let that be what we share.'

The princess nodded. Both of them remained still for a while, unsure of themselves. Then, as though they were of one mind, they moved closer.

It was nearly noon, a few days later, when they arrived at Chief Dasha's village on the River Yamuna. The princess burst into tears at

8

the sight of the wide expanse of flowing water, the mighty currents a memory of all that she had once loved and had now lost, not swept away by the tides of time but slowly dried and shrivelled by human ambition. She cried for what her home had once been and could never be again, for all that was irrevocably gone.

Parashara placed a consoling arm around her. 'Our son will avenge you, Princess.'

She looked up at him, surprised.

'I've known who you are all along,' he said. 'But when I speak of you in future – and believe me I will – I'll refer only to Chief Dasha's daughter, the beautiful fisherwoman who moved me to desire … Goodbye, my dear.'

The princess never saw Parashara again. Not when her son was born, not even when he was sent away to his father to study and to learn of the great destiny that awaited him. She held on to no memory, nor to any regret, but an excited, uneasy hope simmered constantly in the depths of her heart.

It would take decades, but she would have her revenge.

Part 1

1

THE TALL MAN SHOOK HIS HEAD. HIS EYES WERE COLD, BRUTALLY calm, as he told his companion, 'We both know that this is how it must be. The Secret Keeper must die for another to take his place. That is the law.'

The two men considered each other in silence, all emotions suspended in the face of inevitability. A sharp knife flashed in the dark, its metal cutting through skin and flesh in a single, deep thrust. A bloodcurdling scream of pain ripped through the silent night, desecrating the tranquil haze of fragrance from the night-jasmine trees that surrounded the small cluster of huts not too far away and stunning the inhabitants out of their sleep.

The first to tear out of his modest hutment was a young scholar. Almost immediately, he saw the prone figure at the edge of the woods. Calling to others for help, he ran towards the fallen man.

'Oh Varuna!' the scholar exclaimed as he took in the scene before him.

The victim was old and shrivelled with age. He wore the ochre robes of an ascetic, but they were worn and tattered. A grizzly white beard covered most of the man's face; his hair was matted, and messy to match. The shining blade that had pierced right through his feeble, emaciated chest was not a long one, but then the old man was as thin as a parchment. Blood pooled on the ground, dripping off the tip of the blade that emerged from his back.

'Who did this to you?' the scholar urged.

'... doesn't matter ...' the old man gasped. He closed his eyes and drew a pained breath, willing his body to hold on to mortal existence or just a little longer, till his work here was done. When he opened his eyes again, an irrepressible light shone in them.

A hum of frenzied activity slowly enveloped the two hunched figures as the other residents of the huts milled around, holding torches and braziers. The man looked at the gathered crowd, but gave up as his vision blurred and then darkened altogether.

'Dwaipayana. Dwaipayana, the Vyasa …' he wheezed.

'This is his hermitage. But the Vyasa isn't here. I … I'm Suka, his son …'

The injured man tried to focus on the speaker, but failed. With great effort, he raised his right hand and placed it on the scholar's head in a gesture of blessing. 'Tell your father,' he said in a trembling voice, 'for so long we have been sworn enemies, and now there's no time to set right the past.'

He paused and gestured feebly at the anxious crowd. At a nod from the young scholar the residents of the hermitage moved a respectful distance away. The scholar then raised the old man's head and placed it in his lap.

The dying man spoke again, but this time his voice was surprisingly strong. 'We, the line of Agni Angiras, were born of Fire. Firewrights, they call us. Ours was the charge to purify and renew Aryavarta, the land of the noble. But the fire of change has failed and my failure haunts us all. When the Age of Kali dawns, the world as we know it will come to an end. The end is the beginning, and the beginning is hope …' His strength ebbed, and he descended into a rasping cough.

'Acharya, please,' the scholar tried to calm him. But there was more to come.

'You're the Vyasa's son? His heir?' the old man asked.

The scholar nodded.

'You'll be Vyasa after your father?'

Again, he nodded.

The old man laughed softly. 'Who remains, then, to be Secret Keeper after me? But that is no longer *my* burden. There are no secrets left in my keeping, not any more. Tell your father that the

Firstborn have won … Tell him that I, Ghora Angirasa, died here. Tell him that it's over.'

The young scholar was frantic. 'In Varuna's name, Acharya … '

The Firewright's tone was suddenly consoling and his eyes held neither confusion nor uncertainty. 'May the Fire burn bright within you, my son. Be at peace, for I go happy, to the timeless future that awaits me. I leave Aryavarta in good hands.' No longer was he aware of the man cradling his head, or the crowd standing around them. Instead, he gazed into the distance. His very being glowed with peace. 'Narayana …' he called out. Then he closed his eyes and smiled for the last time as a mortal being.

Birds began to twitter softly in the woods surrounding the hermitage. Soon, the sun would rise.

2

'AND SO, IT BEGINS …'

Govinda Shauri, Commander of Dwaraka, ran his fingers through his wavy, almost curly, hair before throwing both arms up and out in a languorous stretch. He looked with longing at the endless blue sea that extended far beyond the crystalline towers of the island-citadel that was his home.

Dwaraka stood proudly facing the oceans of the west, the entire length and breadth of Aryavarta behind it. From a distance, it looked like a magnificent mountain of crystal and silver, its tall spires a bridge between the blue of the ocean below and the skies above. A bridge between the heavens and the earth, some called it. Govinda knew better than to spend too much time looking skywards, all the more so from where he stood now, on the tallest tower of the city. His eyes sought the far distance across the never-ending expanse of the dark blue-green waters. The seas were their future, one he longed to throw himself into. The day was clear and inviting and a warm breeze had replaced the monsoon winds that had brought him home over the sea some weeks ago.

Another three weeks, and the winds will be right for us to set out once more.

'I don't see you sailing away anytime soon, Brother,' a tall, fair-skinned man intruded on Govinda's thoughts.

Balabadra, Govinda's half-brother, looked every bit the wrestler he was. He drained the goblet of wine in his hand, and twirled it around in his large grip for a while, before finally getting up to refill it. On impulse, he offered the brimming goblet to Govinda and raised his brows in surprise when it was not refused. He poured himself another cup of wine and returned to his seat.

The third man in the room took things in with a slight smile. Ayodha Dhaumya's long hair was pulled away from his face and held in place by a small scrap of ochre cloth that matched his renunciate's robes and he wore a string of polished wooden beads around his neck. The short, well-trimmed beard he sported made him look older than he was; nevertheless it added to his charm.

'In less than a week,' he ventured, 'Emperor Jarasandha will have more than ten full divisions of men at Mathura.'

'Hmm …' Govinda examined his wine, pensive.

'It's all too neatly timed!' Balabadra glowered. 'After years and years, Ghora Angirasa finally emerges from hiding, only to die a mysterious death. And just days after that Jarasandha moves his troops to strategic positions throughout the empire. Maraka!' he swore. 'A damned plague is upon us!'

'The Eternal Universe doesn't work through coincidences,' Govinda said. 'It's simple cause and consequence. The Emperor rose to his current position of power by hunting down and wiping out the Firewrights. But where most were killed, a few, Ghora Angirasa most notable among them, went into hiding, and the possibility of their retribution has held many a monarch, the Emperor included, in check. Ghora's death means that Jarasandha now has nothing left to fear.'

Balabadra remained sullen. 'And the mighty Emperor of all Aryavarta – ruler of all that lies south of the Great White Mountains right up to the borders of Dakshinavarta – plans to turn it into a new beginning. One that might spell the end for us too.'

16

Govinda shrugged lightly and said, 'Well, not quite Emperor of all Aryavarta. The east is his, no doubt – his own kingdom of Magadha makes an exceptional spot for an imperial capital. Coupled with the garrison he has in the west, at Mathura, his empire is a strong one. However, between the east and the west lie the powerful kingdoms of central Aryavarta.'

'They're hardly powerful, trapped between the two garrisons,' Balabadra pointed out.

'True, but you must admit they've remained fairly independent. They've accepted Jarasandha as Emperor in name and they pay their share of taxes and tributes, but their internal affairs remain their own. This is not the great dominion of old that legendary emperors once ruled over. Two things stand undeniably in Jarasandha's way. First, the terrain – the most direct route to the north-western regions of Old Aryavarta, the land that extends till the natural borders formed by the River Sindhu, is cut off by the desert lands of Matsya. He'd risk losing control over eastern and central Aryavarta if he tried to get his armies through the forests and mountains of the north around Matsya.'

'And the second?'

'Us.'

Balabadra roared with laughter at the bold declaration.

Govinda watched him indulgently for a few moments before adding, 'I mean it. As things stand, the quickest way for Jarasandha to get to, and command, the north-east is by travelling along the coast from Dwaraka to the kingdom of Salwa, and then north towards the frontier. That way, he can avoid Matsya altogether.'

'Except, of course …'

'We won't let him. Not unless he asks nicely,' Govinda finished with a snide grin.

'But …' Dhaumya began, and then paused as his breath caught in a silent gasp as the other man suddenly met his glance.

Govinda's eyes both begged and defied description. They seemed always to hold many secrets, but they also contained a promise of utter honesty that made the scholar reluctant to pry. Settling at that moment for silence, he studied the young man before him with a thoughtful frown.

Govinda had the strong, chiselled build that even the most sporting noblemen would not manage to acquire, for it took a childhood spent in tough labour and simple, outdoor living. His wavy hair formed a dark halo around his head and was unfashionably short for a nobleman, falling just to his shoulders. He wore a white silk antariya – a length of cloth tied around the waist, passed between the legs, pleated and tucked in at the back – that fell in elegant folds around each leg till the ankles. He had cast aside his scarlet upper robe before stretching out on the couch, but had kept on the sash-like leather belt that held his sword. But for his weapons and his fine clothes, he looked just as he had fifteen years ago. Only, Govinda had then been a simple gwala, a cowherd.

The cowherd who defied a king, Dhaumya mused, his eyes flitting over the mark on Govinda's chest. Set close to his heart was an artistically traced circle, resembling a stylized lotus. Inside the circle, in proportions so precise and symmetrical as to almost defy human ability, were set nine interlaced triangles in a symbol known as the mark of Sri. It looked like, and was often mistaken for, a birthmark, though undoubtedly it was a tattoo or even the result of a brand. None but the keenest of eyes, or one who knew it was there, could make out the tiny scar left by a sword point on one of the dark triangles – the reminder of a test of Govinda's true identity.

Govinda's grandfather had been the king of Surasena till the tyrant Kans, also Govinda's maternal uncle, had usurped the throne and imprisoned Govinda's parents, the true heirs of the kingdom, in their own palace prison in Mathura, Surasena's capital. When Govinda was born, his parents had managed to smuggle their infant son out of prison, an act of desperation and hope for his future and the future of their land. Govinda had been sent to live in hiding where no one would think to look for the Crown Prince of Surasena, among common cowherds and peasants.

Dhaumya, then an acolyte under Surasena's royal priest Gargya, had been there when the seventeen-year-old Govinda had been discovered and wrested by Kans's soldiers from his home in a small, quiet village and brought to Mathura to be beheaded in public. He had come to know and love Govinda then, as the young man reclaimed his throne against many odds. But, before long, his rule had been threatened by a new enemy – Jarasandha, Emperor of Aryavarta. After a few short but difficult years in which Govinda and Balabadra had defended their kingdom against Jarasandha's many onslaughts, they had led their people, the Yadus, to withdraw to their new home on an island off the western coast of Aryavarta. Here, they distanced themselves from the tumultuous affairs of what had then been Jarasandha's rising empire.

Dwaraka, the new city-state of the Yadus, was an island in more ways than one. Set off from the rest of Aryavarta by the surrounding region Anartta, a daunting mix of mountain and marshland, it had, at first, offered little hope to foster a new nation. The land simply could not support the agricultural and herding activities that were the backbone of all of Aryavarta. But Dwaraka's founders had remained undaunted. They had eked out what they could from the harsh, barren land to survive. To prosper, they traded. And so began Dwaraka's slow but inexorable rise as a sea-faring nation with a huge trading port and an impressive navy. Today, it was one of the commercial gateways to the huge expanse of land that was Aryavarta.

All that had been over fifteen years ago. Still, Dhaumya did not find it difficult to believe that it was the same Govinda who sat before him now, one arm casually outstretched on a bent knee.

'Don't you see, Govinda,' the scholar pleaded, 'it's exactly as you two said. The end of the Firewrights means a new beginning for Jarasandha. Unlike the older kingdoms, he has no qualms about whom he rallies to his cause – rogue vassal, remnant Firewright, or some foreign power. His enduring dream of expanding his empire to the old borders of Aryavarta, and perhaps even beyond, is closer to reality than it ever was. More important, he hopes to solidify his control over the domain that's already his in name. War, alliances, the affairs of the state – all of it have remained at a standstill of sorts for the past some years. But now, with Ghora's death, the balance is broken and brute strength is all that matters. Jarasandha's control, nominal as it may seem to you, will soon become absolute. The very same autonomous central kingdoms that have stood directly and indirectly between the Yadus and the Emperor ... if they were to join forces against you, or even just get out of the way, it would mean disaster for ...'

Balabadra cut in, 'How much time do you suppose we have before Jarasandha sets out against us?'

'Not much,' Govinda replied. 'He'll strike hard and fast. This is a matter of power, vengeance and pride. Any one of the three is motivation enough to raze us to the ground.'

'So, unless the central kingdoms – the Kurus and the Panchalas – help us ...'

'We're doomed,' Govinda cheerily finished.

'You're close to the Panchalas ...' Dhaumya pointed out.

'Yes, I am. The prince is one of my dearest friends, but he's also a prince. He can't escape his nation's politics.'

The scholar sighed and stood up, brushing off the non-existent dirt from his robes as a force of habit acquired from sitting on bare ground. He adjusted his upper robe thrown diagonally over his torso, passing it over his left shoulder, under his right arm, and over the left shoulder again.

'What, leaving already?' Balabadra asked.

'I came here to deliver news of Aryavarta to the Commander of Dwaraka, as is my duty. As for what happens next, that's up to Govinda Shauri. Strange and difficult times lie ahead. If you can impose on your friendship, then there's hope ... Though, I suppose, it's too much to ask for. You should prepare for war.'

'True,' Govinda agreed as he turned to Balabadra. 'Start organizing the armies, Agraja.' He tempered what was undoubtedly an order with the respectful term used to address an elder brother.

Balabadra was unimpressed. 'And you?'

'Our friend here is right. I'd better find some way of slowing down Jarasandha, preferably through diplomatic means. I'll leave tonight for Panchala, maybe talk to some people there and find out what the other kingdoms are planning.'

'The Council …'

'We can't afford to wait for their permission. Besides, they know as well as we do that we can't risk war against the Emperor.'

'Why not? We can defend Dwaraka. We have our trade. We have the sea. We can survive. We've *always* survived!'

'Not without an empire, we can't. That is our dilemma, Agraja. We're dependent on the empire – unless the empire prospers we cannot! Our well-being is linked to its trade and commerce, even its politics. If it collapses, if Aryavarta goes back to being a bunch of small kingdoms squabbling with each other over land and water, there'll be no trade, and no one will have any use for us anymore. We *need* the empire. What we don't need is an angry and ambitious Emperor determined to destroy us.'

'What do we do? What *can* we do?' Balabadra sounded angry.

'This thing isn't going to solve itself by sunset. While we try to find some other solution to this mess, I'll try to see if Panchala can help us.'

'It's too dangerous, Govinda,' said Dhaumya, disapproving. 'The only thing Jarasandha hates more than your nation is you. This is his chance to get rid of you without too many questions coming up, and he won't want to lose it. His spies watch Dwaraka day and night; he'll anticipate your every move. Trust me, you can't cross into central Aryavarta without running into his assassins. They'll be waiting to hunt you down.'

'In that case, I'd better get going. I'd hate to disappoint Jarasandha or his generals.'

The scholar clucked his tongue in exasperation and looked to Balabadra, hoping he would dissuade his younger brother.

Balabadra looked far from discontent, but made a show of grumbling. 'As always, you're going to get us into trouble, Govinda!'

'What's new?' Govinda retorted. The look he gave his brother was one of great affection, but his eyes held some other veiled emotion. The two men had fought many battles together; together they had overthrown Kans, built a mighty city and led their people to this new nation. Balabadra had always been there with him, playing the part of a responsible older brother and running things with crisp efficiency.

Someday, Govinda promised himself, *I'll tell him everything, I'll explain it all. Just, not yet …*

3

EVERY MORNING, DEVAVRATA, REGENT AND PATRIARCH OF THE Kuru kingdom, known to all as Bhisma the Grandsire, woke to the heavy tread of Jarasandha's soldiers as they marched with impunity through the capital city, Hastina. Every day, he was reminded that his kingdom was less than a day's ride from Mathura, where the Emperor's huge garrison prepared itself for war, and that Emperor Jarasandha would soon trample over them all.

Devavrata considered himself in the burnished mirror. His silver-white hair and his wrinkles only served to make him seem more authoritative as he aged. But then, he noted with satisfaction, he did not remember looking any different from the way he did now. He was as strong today as he had been forty years ago, still able to defend his reputation as an unbeaten warrior. It was the greatest honour any Arya could hope for. Yet he saw his reflection stoop just that much, as he came to terms with the truth: His notions of honour would soon mean little. Being Arya would soon mean little. Kali, the age of darkness, drew near.

As a child, Devavrata had asked his father, King Shantanu, why the Creator had filled the land with vile commoners when He was capable of creating exalted beings, such as the Aryas.

His father had been direct in his response. 'It is destiny, my son. They're meant to serve us, just as we serve the gods. In return, we rule them with a balance of authority and benevolence. It's what the gods have ordained. An Arya's duty is to fulfil the destiny that has been chosen for him by the gods.'

22

How much longer before their ambition, and our kindness, doom us? Bhisma wondered. *Perhaps, it is already too late.*

Even now, Aryavarta was overrun by Sutas – children of Arya fathers born to concubines and slaves. They were neither truly noble nor base commoners. Many were raised as playmates to princes and grew to be counsellors to kings, and Sutas born into scholarly lines became bards and administrators. But no matter what the kinship, or their position, these children were not Arya. They could train, but they would never be true warriors. They could learn, but they would never be scholars. To be born Arya was a blessing from the divine; it was destiny. It was as immutable as the gods. It had to be.

Yet, as things stood in Aryavarta today, it was not. The Emperor of Aryavarta, Jarasandha, saw no reason to live by these rules, especially since allowing Sutas to serve as his saamantas – vassal lords – increased the sheer number of his armies fourfold. No Arya king, however skilled, could survive an attack by the Imperial Army, which left most kings with the eventuality of diluting his own reign with Suta vassals. It was that, or to give in to Jarasandha and become what was politely termed a 'loyal ally'. This was exactly what the last of the old kingdoms, including Kuru, had done. Better to be a mere saamanta with honour, than to rule with none. And this was, very simply, why Jarasandha of Magadha was Emperor.

Bhisma clenched his fists in despair. Once, his ancestors had been Emperors of Aryavarta; his grandfather had ruled a sprawling Kuru kingdom. Now, the ancient kingdom was effectively nothing more than a common vassal to an undeserving overlord, lying in the shadow of the Emperor's largest garrison. What was he, Bhisma Devavrata, to do when the kingdom was threatened? When their way of life, righteousness and morality were all threatened?

Why did it have to happen in my lifetime? Why me – when I've spent my entire life protecting these very ideals? The answer came to him, soothing his troubled thoughts like a summer shower or a spring breeze. The gods had chosen for him a life of great deeds, of great responsibility and even greater sacrifices. He was Bhisma, the blessed one. This was his destiny.

With a sigh, he brought his attention back to the moment. An attendant knelt before him respectfully, his head bowed low with the privilege of serving his superior, awaiting instructions.

'Show him in.'

The attendant withdrew. Bhisma tried to quell the discomfort that stirred in him at the thought of his guest, the rising disgust that had instinctively surfaced since his very first meeting with the man.

Sage Krishna Dwaipayana of the Firstborn. *My stepbrother.*

Devavrata had been in the prime of his youth when his father had fallen in love with Satya, the young and exceptionally attractive daughter of a fisherman. He dutifully set about seeking her hand in marriage on behalf of his father. Satya had agreed to marry the king, but on one condition – the prince would have to forgo his right as heir to the throne and further ensure that the Kuru kingdom passed on to Satya's line in perpetuity. It took Devavrata many years to understand why she had imposed that condition. At that moment, however, he had reflected joyfully on divine predestination, on the fame that would be his forever because of his noble actions. He not only gave up the crown, but also swore himself to a life of celibacy. He would have no descendants who would compete for the throne with Satya's children. The oath had earned him the title of 'Bhisma', one who undertakes a terrible and insurmountable task. It was now his name.

When Shantanu died, Bhisma installed Satya's elder son as king of Hastina, but the young King Chitrangada died soon after. Right away, Bhisma crowned Satya's younger son, Vichitravirya, in his stead. But the boy was just that – a boy – and Bhisma had no choice but to become Regent of Hastina. Under his rule, both the new king and the kingdom grew strong. When the boy became a man, Bhisma secured for him eminently suitable wives – two of the three princesses of Kashi. The princesses, Ambika and Ambalika, turned out to be very attractive, both politically and aesthetically, but perhaps a bit too suitable for the young king. The might of Hastina continued to grow, but its king soon lost himself in the pleasant company of his wives. After a short life of royal indulgence and over-exertion, he, too, died. More to the point, despite his untiring efforts to procreate, he died without leaving a single heir. A sliver of hope remained, for he had left behind two fertile and attractive wives, the queens of Kuru.

It was at this time that Satya had called on Bhisma to break his vow of celibacy for the sake of the Kuru dynasty and future of the nation. He refused.

'It's nothing new or abhorrent, my son,' Satya had pleaded. 'Our scriptures clearly sanction it. When a king is unable to produce heirs, his wives may join with his brother or a man of great nobility and virtue to have children and so ensure the continuity of the royal lineage. These children are raised as the king's own and have incontestable claims as his heirs.'

'In that case, mother,' Bhisma argued, horrified, 'why don't we marry our women to many men? We encourage our kings to take more than one wife to make sure that the dynasty lives on. Why not do the same with our queens?'

'Sometimes,' Satya had wistfully said, 'I think you're still the same, innocent Devavrata who has learnt nothing in all these years. You still believe that the world runs on duty and piety, not on politics. Our dynasties are traced through the man. The problem with polyandry is the question of identity. The only way we can ensure the identity of the child's father, is by excluding the possibility that another man could have sired the child. Imposing chastity on a man may seem morally attractive, but it serves little purpose. A woman's chastity, however ...' she trailed off, a disdainful look on her face.

'Mother?'

'Which is why women like me keep their secrets well, Bhisma. I have another son. He was born before I met your father.'

And so, Bhisma had sent for Dwaipayana, the great scholar–seer and Satya's son by Parashara of the Firstborn. The line, as Satya had unfailingly pointed out, of Vasishta the Elder.

Vichitravirya's widows had begged him and Satya not to force another man upon them. Ambika cried, while Ambalika argued.

'When your brother married us,' she said, 'it was with the sacred fire as witness. By that holy fire he pledged to protect us. Now that he's gone, you think you can force any man you choose on us? We loved our husband. Can't you honour that devotion by allowing us to mourn in peace and live with his memory?'

'Daughter,' Satya tried to explain, 'when you married my son, you also agreed to share his responsibility as king. It's that duty that one of you must now fulfil by producing an heir to the throne.'

'Responsibility!' Ambalika spat, standing tall, while her sister hid behind her, sobbing uncontrollably. 'That's something your son should have thought of, *Mother*, before he turned the whole of Hastina into his personal playground. Besides, does this responsibility rest only with my sister and me? I don't see anyone forcing the esteemed Bhisma to fulfil his duty. What makes his vow greater than the vows of fidelity that my sister and I made to our husband? Isn't it enough that the great Bhisma forcibly brought us here from Kashi, destroying our city and our people to satisfy your son's lust? Isn't it enough that we lost our sister Amba? Must he now destroy the two of us with his vows as well?'

Her arguments had been in vain. When Dwaipayana arrived, Satya's instructions to him were clear: He was to take the women at all costs, against their will, if required. He was to impregnate them without fail. Bhisma had shuddered and struggled in torment when he heard the queens' fervent pleas to Dwaipayana to spare them. Their screams had pierced the walls of the palace as they were forcibly ravished. All Bhisma could do was remind himself that destiny was ordained by the gods and its intricacies were intelligible to few.

So it was that the seed of the reclusive ascetic achieved what the strength of the Kurus could not. Ambika gave birth to Dhritarastra, blind but virile, who would be King of the Kurus and father of a hundred and one children. Ambalika had brought forth the younger prince, Pandu. It later emerged that in his enthusiasm to fulfil the duty assigned to him, Dwaipayana had also impregnated the queens' loyal friend and handmaiden. She, too, brought forth a son – Vidur the Wise.

That was a long time ago, Bhisma told himself, though it did not make him feel any better.

Now, Syoddhan, the eldest of Dhritarastra's sons was heir-apparent and had been so for the past six months – ever since Pandu's five sons and their mother Pritha had disappeared. The six had been at the summer retreat of Varana when a fire had broken out, supposedly killing them all. The charred bodies of five men and one woman had been recovered, but Bhisma did not believe they were the corpses of the princes and the queen any more than he believed that rumours that the fire was part of Syoddhan's plan to kill his cousins.

Would this have been the state of affairs if the true blood of the Kurus – my father's blood, my blood – had continued the line, Bhisma wondered. It did not matter. As long as he lived, he would do whatever it took to protect this kingdom, and the glory of the Kurus. And right now he needed Dwaipayana. Willing himself to remember that, Bhisma turned to welcome the man who entered the room.

4

KRISHNA DWAIPAYANA, THE VYASA, WAS A DARK, DIMINUTIVE man. His white beard was not as well-groomed as Bhisma's, but its unruliness was becoming in its own way. His manner seemed docile, cheerful almost, like that of a good-natured, gentle grandfather, but his pitch-black eyes sparkled with the fiery intensity of an intelligent, even youthful, mind. Despite his physical appearance, the Vyasa was not, by any reckoning, a man one could ignore. He was the head of the Firstborn, the one who received First Honour at any gathering of nobles, the most respected man in all of Aryavarta. And the most powerful.

Bhisma was unimpressed. He came directly to the point. 'Can I trust you, Dwaipayana?'

Dwaipayana took no offence at the question. He replied, 'If you're asking me whether I had anything to do with Ghora Angirasa's death, the answer is no. I'd have the decency to protect a man who stood in my home, even if he was my enemy. Besides, if I were involved, I hope I'd have the good sense to avoid even a hint of suspicion. That Ghora was killed in my hermitage is unfortunate, but it serves rather well to exonerate me of all doubt.'

'Then who ... ?' Bhisma countered.

'Who *doesn't* stand to gain from Ghora Angirasa's death?' the old scholar sneered. 'For one, an old warrior like you, one of the few ever to be trained by a Wright, who now has no equal. Isn't that a strong temptation?'

Bhisma could feel his breath quicken, but he said nothing. Consciously, he adjusted the glittering crown that adorned his head. He may not be king, but he was still a prince of the Kurus and had served as Regent for over fifty years. He would not be treated with impunity and accused of murder.

Dwaipayana was unaffected by the blatant display of grandeur. He thought the Regent looked overdressed in his silks and wore far too much jewellery. For his own part, he wore only the mandatory strings of beads around his neck and both his wrists. His hand moved to adjust the former as a matter of habit, but he stopped himself. It would seem insulting to point out the contrast between them, and tempting as it was, it would not do to provoke Bhisma.

He spoke softly, but his voice held a clear note of bitterness. 'Perhaps that's the smallest of the prizes, and the worst of our current troubles. We call them "heathens" and "those meddling Firewrights", but in all fairness they were also a great line of weapon-makers. Unfortunately, they also had the arrogance and ambition that goes with such ability, and we all know where that left us. My father spent his whole life ridding our lands of their kind, but his success brought with it a peril of another kind – I've lost count of the number of Wrights and Wright-impostors who've sold themselves to the highest bidder, even to would-be foreign invaders. At least, the name of Ghora Angirasa, the fear of the Secret Keeper, kept these mercenaries and their masters in check. With his death … You realize this changes the situation in Aryavarta completely?'

Bhisma nodded. 'This is the kind of weak ambivalence Jarasandha has been waiting for. He'll use this opportunity to solidify his hold over Aryavarta. Most likely, he'll try to make us all fully-subjugated vassals, rather than amicable allies.'

'My sentiments exactly. The Emperor has little allegiance to any cause. Firewright, Firstborn – all are the same to him.'

'The fault is yours! If the Firstborn had not stood so firmly behind him, Jarasandha would never have risen so quickly to become Emperor. He only had to promise to rid Aryavarta of every living Wright and you and your father were more than eager to see him rule. You did not even realize that he owed you no loyalty, nor did he do you any favours. The Firewrights were the reason why the previous Emperor, the King of Matsya, was reduced to nothing, and Jarasandha knew better than to make the same mistakes as his predecessor. At the same time he is not above using the Firewrights for his own gain and, indeed, he has brought some of them into his service under the pretext of destroying them. Now he is unstoppable, and it is the kings of Aryavarta who must pay the price for the Firstborn's folly!'

'We did what we had to then, as we need to now. But, yes, you're right. The Emperor is not above using the Firewrights he took in. We need to hunt down any Wrights who may be left – whether in Jarasandha's custody or otherwise – before he can put them to use. And I have just the man for the task.'

Bhisma paused, realizing whom Dwaipayana was referring to. 'Do you trust him?' he asked, frowning.

'He's the best his father ever trained, the princes of Hastina included. And I suppose there's something to be said for his blood and ancestry after all. He's a dangerous man, one of the few who can find the last few Wrights who remain unaccounted for, no matter where they hide or who protects them. As for us, we need to turn our attention to more refined, though equally important, issues. There still remains the matter of Jarasandha's huge armies. This kingdom has neither the money nor the military strength to defend itself, particularly if we're attacked from both the east and the west. Nor do we have enough political leverage, or the right kind of alliances, and we certainly can't presume on the Emperor's kindness, no matter how good a friend of Syoddhan's he claims to be. The Kuru kingdom is in a precarious position. We must act at once.'

'We need Southern Panchala on our side,' Bhisma said. 'Dhrupad's armies are formidable and his treasuries brim over.'

'So take Southern Panchala! Or do you need me to teach you how?'

Both men stared at each other in the silence that followed, each angry with the other for being able to provoke such emotion. They knew they had little choice but to trust each other, yet there was the childish need to gain the upper hand and put the other down. At length, an unspoken consensus settled in, and the conversation continued.

'I trust Dhrupad,' Bhisma pointed out. 'But his children, his sons … they're grown men now. Is it really possible to rely on their loyalty?'

'True. Diplomatic ties alone won't suffice, not in times such as these. When Dhrupad gives his daughter in marriage, she must be brought into the house of the Kurus.'

'I didn't hear she was to be married …'

'You soon will. I intend to go to Kampilya right away and remind Dhrupad of a father's duties towards his daughter. When all else is in doubt, it's the simple, familial ties we must trust. Even those who would throw their lives away on a whim will stop to think if the well-being of their children is at stake. We must bind together the futures of the two nations. We cannot depend on diplomacy and friendship alone.'

Dwaipayana placed a hand on Bhisma's shoulder. To his surprise, Bhisma did not flinch, his expression remained stolid. The diminutive scholar leaned forward, bringing his mouth close to the tall man's ear. 'Dhrupad won't refuse us what we ask him. He can't afford not to see reason ... But Dhrupad isn't the only one with secrets, is he? Surely you haven't forgotten, Devavrata? I know it's been many years, but I'm sure you still carry the guilt, just as he does?'

Bhisma stared, wide-eyed with disbelief. 'Why you ... !'

Dwaipayana's whisper was a hiss, as he said, 'We both know how they screamed that night. I'm sure you remember every excruciating moment, don't you? But, it was done for the good of this nation and by the will of the gods. Or, did you perhaps do it because deep inside you regret, even resent, your forced emasculation? It still bothers you, doesn't it, that there was a third woman, who didn't scream after all?' Bhisma gave a roar of anger, but Dwaipayana was not at all affected.

He straightened up and continued, 'Sometimes, for the greater good of a family, an individual must be sacrificed. An individual for a kingdom is a very fair trade. We are in this together and I, for one, won't fail. Please don't let your self-indulgent sense of virtue get in my way.'

Bhisma sat gripping the arms of his throne in festering rage. He shuddered from the effort, but did not dare look at Dwaipayana for fear of losing his composure. His face had turned red, in striking contrast to his silver hair and beard, and his breath hissed from his nose, as he tried hard to ignore the throbbing pain that rose to his head. 'How can you justify what you did, Dwaipayana?' he asked in a hoarse voice quite unlike his own. 'How can you answer to the gods you worship; you, who are learned and enlightened? You who claim true devotion to the Divine? How do you answer to the judgement of your conscience?'

A lesser man would have quailed before the Regent's fury. The Vyasa, however, remained unperturbed. 'I answer to the most fundamental of truths,' he replied. 'What we call the world is sustained by the Creator, and we are just a pale reflection, a tiny spark of the Great Divine. This, our kala-kalpa, the cycle of existence, is but one day and one night for Bramha; one day in the fifty-first year of His life. Within this single kalpa are a thousand aeons, of which we

31

are in the twenty-eighth. Each such aeon, my dear Devavrata, spans over four million human years and is spread over four epochs. Kali, the fourth of these ages is almost upon us. Does that give you some sense of who we are and what our destiny is? We're the servants of this greater power; to understand this duality is to see the earth transformed into heaven itself. As there are heaven and earth, there are rulers and the ruled; there are gods and there are kings. To lower our heads in reverence is our duty and to accept destiny is the greatest worship. Only heretics and demons seek to question their roles, the way of life that has endured for millennia.'

The words only heightened Bhisma's confusion. Dwaipayana regarded him with sincere sympathy, feeling sorry that the old warrior struggled so hard with his conscience to do what was indisputably right.

'Don't let your conscience bother you too much, Bhisma. There's much you don't fully understand, and there's much more that you don't know.' He added with a smile, 'But, don't you worry. I am Dwaipayana, the Vyasa of the Firstborn. Aryavarta is in my charge.'

5

A LITTLE BEFORE DAWN, GOVINDA LEFT DWARAKA, HEADING EAST. His silver-white Qamboja stallion, Balahak, blazed across the mist-covered fields like a ghost, and by the time the sun came up they were a good distance from the city.

They pushed on, crossing the Raivata mountains and then turning northward, to ride alongside the River Charmanvati. Around noon, man and horse sought refuge from the burning sun in a shady glen, but were back on the road before long. They stopped again in the evening, when Govinda caught a little sleep, and shortly after moonrise the two set off once more, galloping over silver-blue plains as a wild happiness took over them. At their current pace, Govinda was three days' journey from his destination in central Aryavarta. Balahak, named so for his strong legs, would make short work of the leagues that took the common warhorse nearly a week and a packhorse much longer. Balahak's speed, coupled with Govinda's exceptional skill with his beloved steeds, made him one of the fastest riders in Aryavarta, and when he yoked all four of his temperamental silver-white stallions to a chariot, few could keep up with them.

In the misty darkness before the second dawn of his journey, he realized that he was being followed. Even before he saw or heard the riders behind him, he sensed them. Closing his eyes, he focused on the faint hoofbeats. *Three riders*, he concluded, chuckling softly as he guessed who they were. Slowing down, he whispered a few calming words in Balahak's ear and let out a slow, long-drawn whistle. It rose in a reedy, quavering note before he cut it short. Within moments, he heard the horses behind him rear. Govinda stopped and, wheeling Balahak around, waited.

'Watch out!' a familiar voice cried through the mist.

Another protested, 'I am, I am!'

'Mih!'

'You oaf. Oww!'

'No! Not that way! That's me, you cross-eyed paayu! Look out!'

'Steady, steadyyyy! Dumb horse!'

'Stop butting me, Muhira! You idiot! Arrgh.'

'Oh Rudra!'

'Oi! Oi! Ohhhhhh …'

The neighing, and jostling of horses and human expostulation, reached Govinda, followed by the sound of a deep, rich laugh. One of the pursuers seemed to have fallen off, for a riderless horse emerged through the mist at a light canter. It trotted up to Balahak with the relief of familiarity and the two horses nuzzled each other in greeting. Govinda reached out to stroke the newcomer, a brown stallion with a trident-like white marking on its forehead.

'Are you hurt?' a young voice called out.

'No, I'm dancing with the nymphs of heaven, you imbecile. Help me up!'

'You think he heard us?'

'Vathu! Hush!'

'Of course he heard us,' a third man said, before bursting into more laughter at the antics of his companions.

Unable to resist any longer, Govinda guided Balahak back along the path, the brown stallion following alongside. He could not help but smile at the scene that greeted him. On the ground, his feet still tangled up in a mess of stirrup and reins, lay Govinda's young cousin and adopted heir, Pradymna. Standing over the youth, trying without success to unravel the tangle, was the dark-skinned Samva, the second of Govinda's adopted sons.

'Aah! Not that way, you idiot. You're going to kill me!' Pradymna shrieked, as Samva tried to help the struggling youth out of the jumble that bound him.

'I'd do a better job of killing you if you'd shut up,' his brother exclaimed.

Both men noticed Govinda and fell into silent sulks.

Govinda paid no heed to them. Instead, he led his horse towards the third rider, a fashionably dressed man of his age, who still remained comfortably astride his horse. 'Yuyudhana,' he nodded in greeting.

'Cousin,' the man inclined his head. 'I left as soon as I saw you weren't present at the Council meeting. Couldn't let you have all the fun, could I?'

Govinda said nothing, but he was far from displeased. He trusted Yuyudhana implicitly and was glad of his company.

'Those two,' Yuyudhana continued, with a nod towards the squabbling youth, 'came along at the last moment. Impetuous brats!'

'Hot-headed, impetuous ... I'd love to call them a few other things, too,' Govinda noted. 'Pradymna's nearly twenty-one, but by Rudra, can he act like a child! And Samva ...' he let the phrase hang as his face broke into a wide grin.

'Oi! We're right here, you know. We can hear you,' Pradymna protested.

'Indeed, your presence might be more notable and respected if you could at least stay astride your horse!' Govinda retorted.

'Or follow the instructions of your elders,' Yuyudhana wistfully added. 'In any case …,' he turned to address Govinda, 'shall we?'

'Of course.' Govinda set off along the path at a slow amble, Yuyudhana riding alongside.

'Wait! What about us?' Samva cried, leaving Pradymna behind to run after the two departing men.

'Next time!'

'If you learn to ride, by then,' Yuyudhana quipped.

'And you're any smarter,' Govinda added.

'Which alas is …'

'Impossible?'

Laughing, the two riders tugged at the reins, urging their horses into a gallop. With a great deal of shouting and cursing, the two youths followed.

The four horsemen made good time during the day, and it was a little past sunset when Govinda veered away into a small forest abutting the riverbank. He proposed to set up camp there for the night. In the morning, Pradymna and Samva could head back to Dwaraka, while he and Yuyudhana forded the river, crossing over into the region commonly known as central Aryavarta. Govinda knew his sons would not be happy with his suggestion that they return, but they would not disobey his command.

Ignoring the matter for the moment, he and Yuyudhana hunted some jungle fowl and cooked it, while Pradymna and Samva let all four horses drink from the river, then removed their saddles and rubbed them down before setting them free to graze. The men then washed up and threw themselves down on the ground, by the fire. Soon the fowl was done and eagerly consumed. Their upper robes serving as cushions, they stretched out on the soft grass in a well-nourished stupor. For the time being there was no need to keep watch or guard. In these territories, their instincts would suffice. As the dying fire crackled a soft lullaby, Govinda's eyes closed in an invitation to sleep. He was vaguely aware that Yuyudhana was speaking, addressing the two youngsters.

'…Aryavarta wasn't always as we know it, nor were its people. Some talk of simple hunter-tribes who lived in peace and had a great spiritual connection with their natural surroundings. Others still believe that it was full of ruthless fiends who practised human sacrifice and cannibalism. You see, what we today call the beginning of civilization is really only the beginning of recorded history. The further back we go in time, the less we are certain about. Different people then begin to interpret and understand things differently. Some of these stories become indestructible myths and even acquire a supernatural tinge, because we start taking literally what might have been merely symbolic.'

'You mean things like Bramha the Creator giving life to the first of beings, his sons?' Pradymna intervened.

'Yes and no. I don't question that Bramha did give life to us all, including the very first of us. But we know nothing about who or what existed before the five brothers our scriptures name as Bramha's sons. The eldest of these, Vasishta, was the ancestor of the Firstborn. Marichi's children live on today as the Solar Kings, and Atri's son Soma founded the Lunar Dynasty. Pulastya's descendants chose Dakshinavarta as their home. Angiras, the youngest, was the progenitor of the Firewrights.'

With an expression of great humility, Samva said, 'Uncle, just because Pradymna here is an absolute blockhead, there's no need to tell us what we've known since we learnt to crawl … I want to hear about the Firewrights, about Ghora's line.'

'That's Acharya Ghora to you, young man,' Yuyudhana corrected Samva. 'He was a teacher – show him that respect!'

Pradymna grinned, enjoying watching his brother get rebuked. Samva made a show of ignoring them all, and waited with a look of polite anticipation for Yuyudhana to resume his tale.

'It's kind of simple if you know your history,' Yuyudhana complied with shake of his head. 'A long time ago, the Firewrights were well-respected, revered even. In fact, it was their skill at weapon-making and metalcraft that kept Aryavarta safe from many invasions and led to the evolution of an empire – a reasonably cohesive region, set off from the rest of the world by the seas and the Great White Mountains. At the same time, the Firstborn concerned themselves with temporal and spiritual affairs. I suppose we could even say that the Firstborn and the Firewrights complemented each other in their own ways. But you know the old saying – you can't have two swords in one scabbard.'

'But wasn't whoever held the title of Vyasa considered the most powerful?' Samva asked.

'No. That happened over time. As the empire grew, so did its knowledge. Some generations ago, the Firstborn began gathering and managing the collective knowledge of Aryavarta, creating an intricate system of scriptures and rituals. That's when the head of the Firstborn order took the title of Vyasa, or Record Keeper. The Vyasa, however, was more than that. Since he controlled the scriptures, the rules of life handed down to us by the gods, he became the man who determined what was right and wrong, moral and immoral.'

'And the Wrights?' Pradymna chipped in, intrigued despite himself.

'They assumed that their knowledge of warfare made them indispensable, that the kings of Aryavarta – the Solar and Lunar dynasties – would take their side. But, at the same time, the kings were completely dependent on the Firstborn to legitimize their rule, to keep them in power. Chaos was inevitable, as was war – not just between the two orders, but also the different kingdoms that supported each of them.'

A short silence followed as Pradymna and Samva thought over what they had just learnt. Hesitantly, Pradymna began, 'What about us, our people? Whose side were we on?'

'Us …? I'll leave it to you to decide whose side we are on. And whose side we *should* be on. But our people, the Yadus, have never really had the same kind of hatred for the Wrights that some of the central kingdoms do. Perhaps because our clans were too busy fighting each other we somehow stayed relatively neutral when it came to others' squabbles. In fact, one of the largest Firewright settlements used to be near Mathura …'

'And that's where Ghora … I mean, Acharya Ghora used to live,' an excited Samva said.

'Yes. But the settlement was abandoned almost two decades ago. Ghora Angirasa, then the leader of Firewrights, or Secret Keeper, as they called their head, went into hiding. He wasn't seen again in Aryavarta till the day of his death. Many believe he was the last of their order.'

Pradymna was surprisingly mournful. 'Then it's over? The Wrights are really gone?'

Yuyudhana glanced at Govinda, who lay still, his eyes closed. He took a deep breath and let it out. 'We don't know. Yes, spurred on by the Firstborn, many other nations heartily joined in the scourge, hunting down and killing the Firewrights one by one. For a while it seemed the Wrights might rise again when Jarasandha tried to rally them to his side. When that didn't work the way he expected, the Emperor simply found it more expedient to wipe them out and ally with the Firstborn instead. Rumour goes that the few Wrights who swore loyalty to the Emperor were spared, but they remained little more than prisoners and slaves.'

Samva frowned. 'But is the rumour true?'

'Not too long ago Firewrights filled the prisons of every kingdom in Aryavarta. Few men could've resisted the temptation to exploit their skill, Jarasandha included.'

'So that's how he became so powerful! I knew it. And today, he rules over Aryavarta with an army of butchers and mercenaries. His men are bound neither by loyalty, nor by a code of honour. His army is …'

'A force to be reckoned with,' Yuyudhana finished. 'Sleep now. Enough storytelling. It's been a long day.'

With silent nods, the two youths complied. Yuyudhana sat staring at the fire a while longer. Then, with a tired sigh, stretched himself out. Like his younger companions, he too was asleep within moments.

Govinda opened his eyes and turned to lie on his side, looking at the fire. He mulled over the conversation for a while and slowly let his thoughts wander to the past. He had been about Samva's age when he had first met Ghora Angirasa. The Firewright had led him into the deepest, darkest hell there could have been – a perpetual state of nightmarish mindlessness, before Govinda had found his way back to the light. His life had never been the same again.

All that, all of his life before Dwaraka, was like a dream whose memory had faded but the feelings that had been aroused remained, fragile like a mirage, sometimes insubstantial, sometimes so real that he could mistake them for being the here and now. Govinda shut his eyes and let the swirling sense of being half-awake take over him. Often it was the closest he got to sleep.

The four men woke, as a matter of habit, just before dawn, and plunged into the cold, refreshing waters of the river. What should have been a quick, purposive bath turned into a water fight, with Govinda and Yuyudhana acting every bit as childish as their younger kin. The sun had already cleared the first of the trees by the time the four, still caught in the throes of laughter, broke camp. Their horses saddled and ready, Govinda turned to Pradymna and Samva, ready to order them back to Dwaraka. The two youths, however, had already anticipated it and were ready to return.

'You'll have to manage without us. We've decided to go back. Our own decision, mind you!' Pradymna said, with every bit of his famed cheekiness.

Samva added, 'We ought not give two old men competition. The ladies would hardly notice you if we were around …'

Yuyudhana rolled his eyes in mock exasperation. 'Might I suggest we all shut up and be on our way. Words don't fill an empty stomach, nor do they hasten a horse's strides …' He turned to Govinda, inviting affirmation, only to find that Govinda had already set off down the road. Shaking his head, Yuyudhana followed.

6

A GUST OF WIND HOWLED ITS WAY THROUGH THE FOOTHILLS AND disappeared with a shriek into the snow-capped mountain peaks. Krishna Dwaipayana Vyasa took in deep of the cold air and released the snow pigeon from his tender grasp, watching it fly to its cote on the hillside. The place he called home, his hermitage, lay at the foot of the Great White Mountains, the Himalayas. He took in the white-crested mountains in the distance and the crisp green-blue foliage that dotted the nearby cliffs with a content heart. His wanderlust had earned Dwaipayana many a nickname since his youth, but few had understood his desire to travel far and wide. To him, it was not the going away but the coming home that mattered. Now, even home was no longer the same, he dully reflected. The one sanctuary in all of Aryavarta, the holiest of places, had been defiled by violence and blood. Ghora Angirasa's blood.

Dwaipayana found it disconcerting on many levels. *Why would a man who has lived in hiding, who has been an exile for so many years, return all of a sudden, courting death?*

It was not a question with easy answers.

Once, the legend went, Firewright and Firstborn had toiled side by side to raise Aryavarta to unparalleled glory. Now legend was all that was left. The Firewrights had been doomed, run into oblivion by their own. Ambitious, fearful and crafty, they kept secrets from those of their own order, even as they shared – no, *sold* – their warcraft and weaponry in return for power. Their other skills – healing, astronomy and the like – had ceased to be important or profitable. It had been a slow, almost imperceptible, decline, but each generation of Wrights had left behind less than what they had inherited. Most of it was now lost. The dilution of their knowledge was, Dwaipayana believed, the ultimate evidence of their decay. Indeed, most of the so-called Wrights he had met in his lifetime had known nothing more than the formula for a mild antidote or the design of a better wick-lamp. And then there had been Ghora Angirasa. The Secret Keeper of the small, reclusive group of scholars who strove, hidden, to preserve and extend the knowledge of their ancestors. Perhaps, Ghora would have been the man to bring the Wrights back to their former glory.

But not after what had happened at Matsya, Dwaipayana noted, bristling with rage at the memory. Not after the Firewrights turned the verdant, blooming land that had been the heart of a mighty empire into barren nothingness. The scourge that had followed, as retribution against them, had been bloody but essential and completely justified. Eventually, the last-known settlement of the Wrights had been found and destroyed and Ghora forced into hiding, a fate better than what had befallen the rest of his kin. Most of them had died, and not painlessly.

Dwaipayana had, for many years, nursed the secret dread that Ghora Angirasa, the Secret Keeper of the Firewrights, would die in the anonymity of some far, foreign land. It would have been the seed of yet another legend that kept their memory alive. In a way, he was thankful that Ghora's death, tragic as it was, had been less than dramatic.

The fault is ours. We made them out to be monsters, magicians, in order to destroy them. That reputation won't fade easily. Especially now ... The age of Kali is upon us.

The scholar set little store in the fears of some dark age that lay ahead. To him Kali was a different sort of blackness. It was the heavy, black iron that Aryavarta, and much of the world, still used. The Wrights had tamed this blackness, tempered it in fire, to make a light-weight silver steel, or Wright-metal, as it was commonly known. It had made for the best weapons, giving the Wrights their reputation. It was why they had been revered and feared.

Perhaps, Dwaipayana noted, he could put the panic, while it still lasted, to good use. Ghora's death would serve to heighten the mutual distrust and fear among the rulers of Aryavarta, Jarasandha included, making it the perfect political climate to set his own plans for the future of the realm into motion.

Acknowledging the greetings from the residents of the hermitage and their families with a polite nod, he walked towards the secluded group of huts meant exclusively for him and his acolytes. He entered the enclosure to find someone waiting for him.

41

The man was thin and angular, but also distinctly regal in his stance. At first glance he could easily be mistaken for a monarch rather than one of the ruled. He sported a moustache and beard, and his hair fell below his shoulders, in keeping with fashion. In all, he lacked the general air of self-deprivation and strict discipline that one would associate with the disciple of a great scholar. But that was exactly what Sanjaya Gavalgani was. The son of an Arya soldier and a slave-maid, despite his birth as a Suta, Sanjaya had risen to the rank of a minister in the service of the Kuru kings. He was also Dhritarastra's favourite counsellor and most trusted advisor. Rumour even named him as the next Prime Minister of Kuru. Despite his significant success, the young man had remained disconcertingly humble. It suggested, Dwaipayana observed, an enormous ego well-concealed at the insistence of an even more astounding intellect.

Sanjaya greeted Dwaipayana on bended knee, remaining that way till the scholar urged him to stand.

'Welcome, my son. I didn't hear you arrive. I really must be getting deaf in my old age.'

Sanjaya chuckled at the statement. Seers were, in general, rather long-lived. Some attributed it to their piety, others to their simple, healthy lifestyles. Sanjaya simply found them to be resilient. Dwaipayana, he estimated, would be less than ninety years old. The Elder had a good forty more to go, by the average lifespan of his kind.

'Well?' Dwaipayana enquired. 'I know it must be a new development and one of some importance, else you wouldn't have hurried here ...'

Sanjaya knew better than to be astonished. The preceptor was both observant and astute, and put the qualities to good use. Dwaipayana had been at Kampilya just days ago and Sanjaya could have easily met him there. That he had not, showed the matter was a recent one. And that he had then made the journey to these remote parts, foregoing discretion in favour of speed, showed it was also a matter of some weight. The conclusion was obvious.

'Govinda Shauri ...' he declared, a note of contempt in his voice.

'Ah yes, Govinda Shauri,' Dwaipayana was mildly amused. 'Commander of Dwaraka. The gwala boy who defended Mathura against Emperor Jarasandha's forces. Not once, mind you, but many times.'

With a respectful familiarity that had not been painless to earn, Sanjaya pointed out, 'There is such a thing as too much credit, Acharya. Govinda held Mathura for just four or five years. Despite his supposed ancestry and all his efforts, he surrendered the city to Emperor Jarasandha and retreated to the western shores, claiming to have founded a new nation. If it weren't for your support, I doubt he'd even have emerged from obscurity.'

'Well, I hear he's become a full-grown man, and a fairly intelligent one at that. Some claim the new city of Dwaraka is unrivalled for its splendour in all of Aryavarta. And, of course, their armies, the specially-trained Narayaniyas, are feared even in foreign lands.'

'Acharya, I ...' Sanjaya paused and then continued with determination. 'You favour him too much ... He's a charismatic flirt, a swordsman of some repute and I know he has been outspoken against the Firewright menace, but is that reason enough to ... ?' He stopped, realizing he had touched a chord.

'Why does he bother you, Sanjaya?' Dwaipayana asked. 'Why have you come all the way here to speak of him?'

'Jarasandha has been amassing forces at Mathura. Sooner or later, he will attack Dwaraka. Isn't it likely that Govinda intends to somehow ward off such an attack?'

'Indeed, it is what any sensible commander ought to do ...'

'To have a man running around Aryavarta making his own plans ... Grandsire Bhisma feels it puts our entire strategy at risk.'

Dwaipayana did not miss the hint of a smile on Sanjaya's lips. 'And you? What do you feel?' he asked.

'I don't like it either. But I can't indulge him, or ignore him the way you do.'

The Vyasa considered his disciple in silence. It struck him that his own son, Suka, could not have been more different from Sanjaya. Yet the two men were the closest to him and also the most committed of his disciples. It was ironical that Ghora Angirasa had died in Suka's arms. Dwaipayana had wanted nothing more than to leave his son with the holiest of legacies, a realm free of Wrights, of their power-mongering and intrigue. Undeniably gifted though Suka was, he had neither the aptitude nor the training to deal with a political morass and Dwaipayana did what he could to keep it that way. There were few people he trusted and none as much as he did Suka. Where the Vyasa was the conscience-keeper of all of Aryavarta, Suka was the minder of *his*, and Dwaipayana sought his son's advice on every matter of import. Except, of course, when it came to matters of politics. Such things were best left to men like Sanjaya.

'Govinda has never been unfaithful to me, or to the Firstborn order,' Dwaipayana pointed out. 'He could have had all that the Wrights had to offer, he could have protected them, used their skill to defend his throne. Instead, he chose to surrender Mathura, give up his kingdom rather than embrace the unrighteous path.'

'Ah, but he's no faithful follower of yours, either. You could have raised him to even greater heights if he'd agreed. He's a man without ambition, and such a man is always dangerous. When you don't know what moves a man, you can't foresee his actions ... I'd sooner trust someone who's selfish or greedy, for I'd know what drives him. I'd know the limits of his faithfulness. But, Govinda ...' Sanjaya ended with a shrug.

Dwaipayana laughed. His eyes were wistful as he said, 'True. Govinda Shauri is a very different kind of man. He's brave, valiant and his intelligence is far from bookish. The problem is, he's also elusive – what you have just called a man without ambition. He questioned his own right to rule Surasena, rather than submit to the gods that could've given him legitimacy, unquestioned authority over his own kingdom, perhaps even Aryavarta. Instead, he refused to be what we – the Firstborn – could have made him. It doesn't mean he's beyond control or any less useful. When you meet him, you'll see what I mean. Or, maybe, you'll see through him where I've failed to. Either way, you'll soon get your chance ...'

Sanjaya looked surprised, but before he could seek an explanation

Dwaipayana continued, 'The girl – Dhrupad's daughter – is to be married. She is indeed the loveliest of Bramha's creations. I think the Creator must have laboured over even the drop of sweat that rests on her smooth skin ...' he paused, noting with mild amusement that he could still find room for such youthful diction if not desires. With a self-recriminating shake of his head he went on, 'There's no weapon in existence as deadly as a beautiful woman, Sanjaya. We can use her in our favour. Generations who come after us will blame her or praise her for much that happens, whether she had anything to do with it or not. As for the present, who knows how many will bend to our purpose, lured by her kingdom's wealth and might, or simply the prospect of winning such an attractive woman as a prize. Govinda Shauri will come to Kampilya, as will many others. You can study him to your heart's content then.'

'And if he wins, Acharya?'

'I thought you found his reputation unwarranted?'

'With all due respect, I've heard he's rather fond of the girl. Her brothers are his friends and they'd be happy to have him as their brother-in-law.'

'Fond? My dear boy, he has a fondness for all pretty women. Indeed, weren't you the one to point out that particular distinction of his?'

'As a matter of fact, Acharya, it has been rather instrumental in influencing my opinion of him. As you'd once taught me, reputations of excess are often ways of hiding deficiencies or even the total lack of accomplishment. Particularly, those famed for their romantic prowess are cowards of the worst order ...'

Dwaipayana laughed. 'You've decided not to like him. Well, I won't bother changing your mind. But remember this – Govinda won't think twice before throwing away a woman's affections for greater political gain. As long as the threat of Jarasandha remains over his head, he won't interfere with our plans. He's quite harmless. He wants a Kuru–Panchala alliance as much as we do!'

'And then? After the wedding?'

The scholar did not answer the query. Instead, he questioned, 'What do you know of the training of wild beasts, Sanjaya?'

'Acharya?'

'When a tiger is first captured by trappers,' Dwaipayana said, 'it'll refuse to eat when fed in its cage because the beast is driven by its instinct to hunt. Some tigers eventually starve and die. Others break; they begin eating the meat that is fed them. Once that happens, even if you release the animal from its cage it won't hunt. Instead, it'll wait to be fed. Only then is it fit for use in a carnival, for it is tame and domesticated, and the hunter within has been lulled into impotence. It can't hunt anymore, or inspire terror or awe, and it becomes nothing more than a pet, a joke even. And so it is with men like Govinda. If he is to be of any use to us, we must let him and everyone else believe that he acts of his own will.'

The Elder sat down in his customary place on the large porch that fronted his hut. He slowly crossed his legs into the lotus posture, relishing the simple pleasure of sitting down on the well-worn mat that was his own. 'Does it amaze you, my son, that I can be so cold, so ruthless? Do I seem like a vengeful old fool to you?'

Sanjaya looked at his teacher with undisguised adoration. 'The enlightened, civilized man rears animals, treats them with kindness and tends them as best he can. Scholars and rulers nurture the common man the way he nurtures his herds. And just as man decides what fodder must be given, what ploughing must be done and even purges the herd of sick beasts, so must men such as yourself herd us all towards the divine light.'

He knelt down, bringing himself face to face with Dwaipayana. In a soft voice he urged, 'Such is your sacred duty. If the very animal that you tenderly raised from a youngling threatens to destroy the herd with its sickness, it can't be spared. It must be killed. And sometimes it is the best of beasts that must be offered as a sacred sacrifice. But I still have one last question ...'

'Hmm?'

'The matter of Ghora Angirasa's murder ...'

Dwaipayana's smile was mysterious. 'The Wrights had a law, Sanjaya. They said the Secret Keeper had to die for another to take his place.'

'So whoever killed Ghora …'

'Is a deadly enemy. One we can't afford to ignore. If Govinda Shauri is what it takes to divert this man's attention or perhaps to stand between us and all these dangers,' the Vyasa solemnly declared, 'then so be it.'

7

GOVINDA SAT UP WITH A START IN HIS MAKESHIFT BED, PRODDED awake by some deeper intuition, and looked around the small, misty clearing. He and Yuyudhana were in the forest bordering Surasena, the kingdom that had once belonged to Govinda's forefathers. It was now in the hands of Emperor Jarasandha, who used it as a base to control the central and western reaches of his Empire. But Govinda knew it took more than just being in enemy territory to induce the prickling sensation on his neck. The peril was much more immediate. He remained still, listening to the muted jungle sounds around him. Soon, he heard the soft but unmistakeable tread of heavy boots.

Soldiers! Govinda was on his feet at once. Yuyudhana was missing, but the horses were still where the men had tethered them, trained to be as silent as spirits.

He must have headed towards the road, Govinda surmised, noticing his companion's light tracks. But the soldiers, he judged, were approaching from the other direction. With a quick check on his sword-belt, he went deeper into the forest, moving stealthily. Soon he spotted his quarry, thanks to the light of the still-resplendent setting moon. Three soldiers, of the Emperor's Western Battalion by their uniform, were trying to trace the tracks he and Yuyudhana had left the previous night.

There was something else, too. Not danger, but something pleasant, familiar almost. He grinned, recognizing the person standing right behind him without having to look. For once, he had been caught by surprise.

'Panchali,' he said, and turned around. The young woman acknowledged him with a nod and a smile. She raised a finger to her lips, indicating to him to remain quiet.

Govinda heard the soldiers as they followed his trail into the thicket. Panchali nodded a signal, and on the silent count of three the two of them moved, Govinda throwing himself onto the path with his sword drawn and Panchali disappearing into the thicket behind her. It took them little time to fall upon the unwary soldiers, from opposite directions. One of the soldiers stepped forward to engage Govinda, while the other two teamed up against Panchali, whom they judged to be the weaker quarry. Govinda finished off his opponent with cold efficiency and made to help her, but found that it was unnecessary. Both the soldiers lay dead. Panchali, for her part, was breathing hard from the exertion but was otherwise unhurt.

Govinda studied the attractive woman, a smile dancing at the edge of his lips. She was dressed in the androgynous attire typical of the central kingdoms – a pleated antariya, like the men wore, and a wide band of leather branded with intricate patterns covering her bust and midriff, fastened at the back with silken strings. Her upper garment was a long robe that went over her left shoulder in gathers and fell till her knees in front and at the back, almost like a long tunic. Her dark skin set off the thick cord of gold around her neck and she wore delicate gold rings in her ears as well as a thick amulet on her upper arm. Instead of bangles she sported leather gauntlets, her only concession to fashion being that the gauntlets were trimmed with gold studs and the leather matched her vest in colour. Over her right shoulder was a baldric-like device that strapped a quiver of arrows and her scabbard to her back. Panchali returned her sword to its sheath with practised ease. Her warrior's attire and her lack of elaborate coiffure or clothing served to enhance her fiery beauty.

Panchali was not tall, barely coming up to Govinda's shoulders, but carried herself with grace and confidence. Her piercing black-brown eyes were housed in large, rounded lids fringed by thick, luxurious lashes and her face was sculpted yet soft, with full, rosebud lips that were now curved in a smile. Save for the dark kohl that lined her eyes and extended outwards from the edge of her lids in intricate patterns, and the small designs drawn on her chin and arms in fragrant sandalwood paste, her skin bore no embellishment. Long, jet-black hair had been pulled into a thick fuss-free braid that hung down her back, falling below her waist.

Central Aryavarta was much more conservative than the northern or western kingdoms, and it was unusual, though not unheard of, for a woman to join or lead soldiers in battle. Govinda knew, though, that as far as Panchali was concerned the issue was not personal. She found the status of women to be one of the many ways in which society had failed and drew on its personal relevance as inspiration to fight for a greater cause. Yet, as she would often admit to Govinda, her defiance was flawed. She was an elite product of their elite society, talking of others' travails while she dressed in fine silks and slept with a full stomach. It was this self-realization that inspired her brothers to take her with them on their adventures, despite their father, King Dhrupad's, constant protests.

'Govinda?' her voice was a pleasant intrusion on his reverie.

He quietly met her gaze.

Eyes flashing bright, Panchali laughed and said, 'My, my! How a great warrior like you can get into such trouble was beyond me! Now I know ...'

'Well, Princess,' Govinda bantered, 'I'm a simple gwala boy, a cattle-herder, and know nothing of fighting, armies or warfare.'

'Then I'll have to see you to your destination, safe and sound.'

'I'd be honoured.'

'Come,' she said, 'my brothers will be so happy to meet you. We knew you'd turn up, sooner or later.'

Before Govinda could ask her what she meant, she undid Yuyudhana's tethered horse, intending to lead the stallion towards the road. Govinda quickly rolled up his saddle bag and Yuyudhana's, threw them both on to Balahak's back and followed. He stepped out of the thicket and onto the main road to discover Yuyudhana in conversation with an old friend.

The man cut a strapping figure, standing half a hand above Yuyudhana. His simplest movements contained the suggestion of restrained power, a mysterious mix of strength and grace as though he were both fighter and dancer. He sported his taut muscles and battle scars with an unassuming air, and his grey-brown eyes held a dangerously feline glint, reminiscent of a wild panther that watched and waited for the perfect moment to kill.

Like Panchali, the man wore an antariya of dark grey linen and his black upper robe was wrapped as a sash, around his waist. A wide leather baldric went across his chest and back, leaving his sword hanging at his left hip. He wore a short string of tiny, intricately engraved metal beads strung together in the form a thin chain – the only piece of jewellery on his tanned body. Most remarkable about the man was his long hair, set into many tiny braids, all pulled back and tied together at his neck. It gave him his name: Shikandin.

With a roar of affection, the man stepped forward to embrace Govinda, slapping him on the back with familiarity.

Govinda returned the embrace with gusto, saying, 'I can't tell you how good it is to see you, old friend.'

'As usual, we're in time to save your stiff Yadu neck!' Shikandin teased.

A small cohort of well-armed, fierce-looking cavalrymen came up the road, led by a young man of regal bearing. Dismounting, the man pulled Govinda into a friendly grip. Every gesture of his screamed of royalty and privilege.

'Yuyudhana,' Govinda made introductions. 'This is Dhrstyadymn, the Crown Prince of Panchala.'

Yuyudhana politely acknowledged the other man, but said nothing. He noted that the prince was far more handsome than artists and minstrels visiting Dwaraka made him out to be. While it was not unusual for bards to use their talent to embellish royal features that were otherwise plain, Dhrstyadymn's reputation for his statuesque looks was well merited.

'The young lady here is his sister, Panchali,' Govinda continued. 'And Shikandin, their elder brother, you already know.'

'Who doesn't?' Yuyudhana quipped. 'I also know of many gorgeous women back home, from princesses to courtesans, who pine for his company.'

'I trust you've personally consoled them, you rogue!' Shikandin bantered, as the five descended into open, hearty laughter.

'I'd love to catch up on all the gossip,' Panchali said as she pulled a thick cloak off her horse and bundled herself up in it, 'but the horses tend to cool down far too much standing around, and so do I ...'

'You woke me from my sleep, Mahamatra,' Yuyudhana good-naturedly complained, 'and now you want me to ride in this cold, misty weather. Well, since you come so well-mustered, I have no choice but to obey you.'

'You have no choice but to obey if you'd rather keep your head on your neck! There's more where those three came from,' Panchali said, nodding towards the depths of the forest behind her. 'Damn those murderers!' she added, suddenly angry.

Shikandin explained, 'There's an entire unit of these soldiers on your trail and more waiting along the way.'

'How did you ...?' Yuyudhana was surprised.

'I have a very reliable source inside Jarasandha's garrison at Mathura ...'

'Shikandin has a knack for finding the best of spies in the most unlikely places,' Govinda added.

Shikandin nodded. 'Truth be told, I was expecting you, Govinda. Ghora Angirasa's death has thrown Aryavarta into complete disarray. Magadha's moving troops all over the empire and, as a result, so is every other kingdom. Armies are being mustered, and every soldier has been ordered to report for duty. Seems to me like the kind of hornets' nest you like playing with so much.'

Yuyudhana said, 'Jarasandha won't let Dwaraka be. I can only hope that when war does come to our doorstep, it is of an honourable kind ...'

'Then, in your interests and ours, we'd better get moving,'

Panchali cut in. 'They won't dare follow us into Panchala. If we ride fast, it'll save us some needless fighting. When there's battle, friend or enemy, it's still human life that's lost.' Even as she said it she seemed to realize that the statement sounded incongruous coming from her, for she softly added, 'That's what I've learnt from Shikandin ...'

Her innocent but fervent zeal was nothing short of charming. With a smile of submission, Yuyudhana swung on to his horse and readied himself for the ride ahead. In a habit born of long use, he took off his quiver and made sure that the arrows were neatly stacked inside. He then refastened the quiver across his back, pulling the belt tight to bring the edge up high on his right shoulder. The Panchala soldiers watched him, impressed. Yuyudhana was one of the fastest archers in Aryavarta and the best bowman of the many Yadu clans of Dwaraka. He could, in fact, as the old saying went, shoot faster than one could blink.

Soon all of them were back in the saddle. Shikandin whistled a signal to his soldiers and the cohort set off in perfect unison.

'I still haven't thanked you for your timely help, Panchali,' Govinda said, as they rode side by side. 'As always, I'm left in your debt.'

'Must we play games like adversaries or, worse still, strangers?' she asked him in a low voice. 'Why don't you speak to me plainly? You come and go at a whim; sometimes you sail away for months on end. Every day I wait to hear from you, but ...' She breathed out hard and added sharply, 'And now, you finally turn up, but it's taken a dead old man to bring you here. I demand no explanations, but won't you at least be honest with me?'

'I have no honest words to explain my actions, Panchali, not at this moment.'

'Then keep your mouth shut!' she snapped.

Govinda nodded meekly as Dhrstyadymn called to him above the thud of hooves, 'There's no arguing with that one, don't even bother!'

The company had been riding for only a short while, when the sound of galloping horses closed in on them from behind.

'Keep going,' Shikandin ordered. 'We're at the border. Cross the stream, and we'll be in Southern Panchala.'

They emerged from the woods onto a short, open stretch that led to the stream. As one, the riders urged their steeds on as fast as they could. Hardly had the first horse set foot in the water, when imperial soldiers poured out of the forest behind them. The first of the enemy's arrows fell short, but by the time Govinda and his companions were halfway across the stream the distance between them and their pursuers had decreased. With a whistle and a dull thud, an arrow caught one of Shikandin's men in the arm.

'Go!' Shikandin urged the others, as he went to help the wounded soldier. 'Go! Don't engage! Just go!' The last thing he wanted to do was make a stand in the middle of a stream.

Arrows began falling around them as they urged their horses on through the strong current. Fortunately, the stream was narrow and soon they were all across. They kept going till they were within the first of the woods of Southern Panchala, then slowed their horses down to a gentle trot. Barring the soldier who had been hurt, there were no casualties. They stopped and slid off their horses, letting the animals catch their breath.

Yuyudhana cast a look over his shoulder. 'They're not crossing ...' he pointed out.

'They'd better not,' Dhrstyadymn said fiercely. 'This is Panchala. We're its princes!'

'And,' a confident voice interrupted, 'Lord Jarasandha is its Emperor.' More imperial soldiers emerged from the surrounding thicket to form a circle around the companions and their men.

Dhrstyadymn growled at the speaker, a man they recognized as one of Jarasandha's generals. 'Emperor he may be, but how dare you stop the Crown Prince of Panchala in his own realm!'

'I have no quarrel with you or your men, Prince,' the Magadhan replied. 'It's just that some of your companions fit the description of much sought-after spies.'

'I can vouch for my friends, soldier! These aren't the men you're looking for.'

'Unfortunately, I'm duty-bound to take them in for questioning. I'm sure you'll have no objection to that if these men aren't really traitors, or the lovely woman there isn't a spy ... You wouldn't want us to interrogate *her*, would you? What say you, Prince?' he turned to Shikandin, ignoring the look of pure rage that Panchali cast his way.

'I say you talk too much.' Before the man could react, Shikandin's slender wooden arrow had pierced the man's throat, running right through his neck.

The Magadhans watched, stunned, as their leader fell to the ground. Then, with a blood-curdling yell, they rushed forward. Govinda and Dhrstyadymn drew their swords, as did the Panchala soldiers around them. Yuyudhana was ready with his bow, the man-high weapon poised on the ground in front of him. Arrows flew from the string at an impossible speed.

The enemy, however, had the advantage of numbers.

'Mih!' Govinda cursed, as he heard them shout to each other to 'take the woman alive'. He glanced over at Panchali and could not help but chuckle as he saw her kick an enemy soldier, coming up from behind her, in the groin without a second thought. Then she turned and drove her sword right through the man in one fluid move.

Reassured, Panchali's companions fought on with a fury that stunned their enemy.

The skirmish was bloody, but it was soon over. 'We'd better get out of here, and quick,' Shikandin instructed, panting slightly as he looked around. 'I just hope those fools on the other side haven't heard anything ...'

He moved around checking on everyone, and spat on the ground when he found that nearly half their men were dead. Panchali had a huge red welt on her forearm, where her leather gauntlet had taken most of the blow from a heavy sword. The rest of them, thankfully, were unhurt.

Setting off at once, the company rode till noon, at which time they stopped for a while to tend to their wounded with greater care. Although exhausted, they still trudged on. Kampilya was not too far away.

'The King, how can he … How can your father stand for this?' Yuyudhana asked Dhrstyadymn, as they rode alongside.

'What can he do? Unless Hastina defies Jarasandha, Panchala can't. Panchala won't.'

'But surely your saamantas and your …'

Dhrstyadymn interrupted, his voice a low rumble, 'This isn't your democratic island on the sea, Yuyudhana. Panchala is a monarchy, one of the oldest in Aryavarta. Here, all land and all life belongs to the king.'

8

THE MAN WAS TALL, AND HE LOOKED TALLER STILL FOR THE WAY he held himself, rigid and unyielding. The black upper robe he wore as a shroud flapped around in the wind, giving him a frightening, unreal appearance. An alabaster hand held a stained sword, from which dots of crimson slowly dropped at his feet, as if in adoration. He strode over the burnt remains of man and beast alike, unaffected by the gruesome scene around him, the wails and shrieks of those who were, as yet, painfully alive.

A woman, bruised but otherwise unhurt, dragged herself away from him in ineffective desperation. The man noted that she was attractive, as a point of information. Women, wealth, power – all these things were at his beck and call; they did not interest him in more than a mundane way. He glanced around at the charred remnants of what had been a small, happy village. This was what he lived for: The perfection of death. The pinnacle, the ultimate purpose of life, was the dying, for it was a journey into the truth, into the darkness that dwelt inside every human being. The very notion sent a shiver of pleasure through him.

He stepped past the crawling woman, kicking away, without breaking his step, some debris she weakly threw at him. She drew a breath of relief as he walked on by, but perhaps too soon. For in one effortless move he turned around, grabbed her by her hair and slit her throat. The fear on her face delighted him beyond any pleasure she could have possibly given him. His eyes blazed, a reflection of his inner fire, as blood spurted out of her neck onto his light-skinned hands. He waited till the woman's life ebbed out of her and let her fall to the ground.

Enough distraction, he reminded himself. It was time to finish what he had come for.

A small hut still stood at the edge of the village, its walls cracked but still intact. The man walked up to its entrance and paused, savouring the momentous occasion.

He entered.

'So you've finally come,' a low, tired voice greeted him. 'Good. I'm tired of waiting.'

The man paused, amused. The speaker seemed to think that he had come to rescue him from captivity. He would regret his words when he saw the death that awaited him.

It was dark inside the hut, and the man used his sword to hack away part of the thatched roof, letting in the sunlight. The beams fell on a wizened figure within, withered not so much by age as by tragedy. He wore the ochre robes of a scholar–sage, but had neither the tell-tale matted hair nor the rosary of rudraksha beads.

The scholar turned, unseeing, toward the light his visitor had let in through the roof, feeling its warmth on his face. Suddenly, he smirked. The action made the tall man recoil. It was an impossibly joyful action, by smooth, almost young, lips on a face that had been partly burnt and completely blinded.

'Well? Are you going to save me or kill me?'

The visitor responded, 'Whatever I do, I won't do it just yet. But I can make it sooner than later.'

'Ah, so you want information,' the blind man was inordinately cheerful. 'Well, then I won't trouble you much. Ask me all you like and I'll answer.'

Doubt flickered black across golden-brown eyes. 'And you'll tell me the truth?'

'If you know who I am then you know very well I'm sworn to

the truth – a rather unfortunate arrangement, as many of us have since realized. But I suppose speaking the truth is a shortcoming in your line of work.'

The warrior drew an arrow from the quiver on his back. Instead of fitting it to his bow, he placed the tip at the maimed man's neck. 'You're blind, but surely you can smell this. You know what it is … I've used it on the villagers outside. Didn't you *feel* it?'

'Yes, I felt a little of it. It's not too badly made. I'll admit you're good, but not *that* good. There's a difference between knowledge and enlightenment. You have only the former.'

'Not that good? Why, you useless imbecile, I'm the best there is!'

'If that's the case then there's nothing you need from me, is there?' the blind man said, softly. 'No matter, I'm ready to die.'

The warrior lost his haughty manner and withdrew his arrow. He bent down, bringing his face close to the other man's. 'There's another weapon, isn't there? One better than this? More dangerous than this?' he asked gruffly.

'Better? There's nothing better than this astra. That's why it's called the weapon of Bramha, the Bramha-astra. But I thought you were the best among its makers,' the scholar mocked.

'I am. But the ingredients are rare these days …'

'And men who can use them well, rarer still.'

The warrior hesitated, then reached out to lay a hand on the man's fragile shoulder. 'Uncle,' he called out, carefully watching the disfigured face for the slightest reaction, 'it is I … your very own Little Rudra. Don't you remember the old nickname you gave me?'

The blind man laughed. 'So it *is* you, all grown-up and now the most feared man in all Aryavarta. And still you skulk around, nameless, like a common assassin, wreaking death and terror. Tell me, *Little Rudra*, whom do you serve?'

'I am master of my own self,' the man bristled.

'Really?' the unseeing eyes bestowed a knowing look. 'How is he … my old friend, Dwaipayana? I knew him once, when he was just Dwaipayana, before he became the Vyasa. He dreamt, even then, of ruling mankind, body and soul. I wonder what tiny scrap of a kingdom he has promised you in return for your services …'

'The legacy of the Angirasas will be back in my hands.'

'The legacy of the Angirasas! Hai! There is no legacy,' the blind man hissed, with surprising rage for one so feeble. 'We, the rebels, those whom *you* call Firewrights and piss on, have been the last defence for generations! Once, five great dynasties ruled Aryavarta, each founded by one of the sons of Bramha himself. Today, three of the five lines are as good as dead and the fourth flounders. I once believed we would rule these lands. But now I see that we shall not last long.' He chuckled at an unspoken thought, but the sound grated in the warrior's ears.

For the first time the warrior felt a twinge of doubt and discomfort. He nearly lost his temper, but resisted out of sheer will. Then he remembered that his momentary lapse was his own secret – the other man could not see. The thought brought back his cold, heartless equanimity, and he smiled.

'There's no reason I should help you,' the blind man continued. 'You can go ahead and kill me. That's what you were ordered to do, isn't it? To kill me? Or was that just something you wanted to do anyway?' He thrust his chin up. 'I was a young fool who believed that the Wrights alone could save Aryavarta. I didn't see it would come to this.'

'But it has. All this … for what …?'

'Vathu! Is your contempt for your own so deep that you judge us like this? You're more one of us than you care to admit! Look inside you, Rudra, inside the Firewright's heart that you hide away from your father's scrutiny and you will see how dearly I have paid for my beliefs. My children are dead, the order lies shattered, and I … I'm nothing more than a scarred fool who has spent his last years hiding from power-hungry men. I'm of no use to you, young one. Tell Dwaipayana that I'm no danger to him, either. I serve neither Emperor, nor any Firstborn. My allegiance lies with the Secret Keeper of the Firewrights.'

The warrior stared thoughtfully at the withered man for a while before he declared, 'Then you serve nothing and no one. The Wrights are finished. Ghora Angirasa is dead. The Secret Keeper is dead.' He began moving towards the door, intending to leave the old Firewright alone with his torment.

'Wait!'

The departing visitor complied, a little surprised.

'Then it's time. Come here.' The scholar forced himself to stand up on trembling, unsteady legs. He reached out and ran his hands over the younger man's face and chest, smiling at the picture his fingers painted. 'Ah, how you've grown! You're a handsome man and your shoulders are strong. Your father must be so proud of you. If you can pretend for a moment that you're still the same precocious little boy with a weakness for sugar candy, I'll give you a small gift, as I used to. I'll leave you with one final secret. In return, rid me of my guilt ...'

'Uncle ...?'

The blind man nodded and reached out to embrace the other. Pulling the strapping warrior down a little, he whispered, 'There's hope, Little Rudra. A Secret Keeper lives. There's hope.'

The warrior stiffened for a moment, completely taken aback at the revelation. He shook his head slightly as he said, 'That plan fell apart decades ago. Like you, I too had great expectations of the one whom Ghora had hoped to make Secret Keeper. I thought he could perhaps put an end to this madness once and for all. But many things have changed over the years, as has the man on whom our hopes rested. He ...'

'He is the Secret Keeper. Some plans are made to succeed when everything falls apart. Don't you see, Little Rudra?'

He did. Comprehension finally dawned in his eyes and a new kind of serenity filled him.

As if he too could see, the blind scholar laughed at the man's reaction. 'Now you understand me, don't you?' he said. 'Now you see why I've held on to these beliefs for so long. Narayana!'

He tightened his feeble embrace, throwing all that was left of his strength into the moment. The gesture was affectionately returned. With soothing words, the warrior held the old man close, like he would a lost child. He used his other hand to pull out the knife from his belt and, with a silent prayer, slit open the scholar's neck. The dying man's head lolled forward to rest on the warrior's chest, still-warm blood staining his skin in blessing and debt.

The two of them remained that way for a long time, till one was free of his pain. The warrior then carried the scholar's body down to the nearby river, where he built a pyre and consigned the remains to its flames. He waited till the flames began to die down. Then he bathed in the river and made his way home.

9

YUYUDHANA WOKE UP TO THE MELLOW CARESS OF SUNLIGHT ON his face. It took him a moment to realize that it was not morning, but late in the afternoon. They had reached Kampilya a little before sunset the previous day. King Dhrupad, a portly man with inherited pleasant looks and a carefully-cultivated diplomatic manner, had made an exception to protocol and come forward to personally welcome Govinda. It had been a small, informal affair involving only the important officials of the kingdom, among them Satrajit, Dhrupad's eldest son by one of his secondary wives. Satrajit's valour and dedication were widely known and he served his nation faithfully as commander of Panchala's armies as well as an able administrator of the kingdom's affairs. Yuyudhana had felt a slight pang of discomfort as they were introduced. He had met enough men like Satrajit to know well that the prince would, in all likelihood, die for his country or even his father's pride and arrogance, but history would not remember his name. His unease had grown when he realized that Satrajit was not the king's only offspring with due cause for displeasure. By right, Shikandin ought to have been standing where Dhrystydymn was, in a place of honour by Dhrupad's side. Yet, it had seemed that the apparent anomaly caused more concern to Dhrystydymn than it did to Shikandin, who had merely fallen in next to Satrajit without complaint.

Yuyudhana had been on the verge of commenting to Govinda on these subtle undercurrents when Dhrupad had begun his warm speech of welcome. The monarch had been brief, but ended with the promise that a more fitting reception would be held later, after the travellers had rested and refreshed themselves. With that, the visitors were guided to well-furnished rooms.

The sight of a comfortable bed with its soft silk sheets, and the pleasant fragrance of incense in the room, had made Yuyudhana realize how tired he was. He had allowed the attendants to help him wash up, particularly enjoying the feeling of clean feet after days of travel. By the time Govinda had come to fetch him for a drink with Shikandin, he had been fast asleep.

Trying to muffle a violent yawn, Yuyudhana realized he had slept straight through the evening, the night and most of the next day. He gradually began to note the soft but unmistakeable sounds of life as the occasional person passed by. Faint sounds of laughter came floating on the breeze and were quickly gone, but the fragrance of jasmine that followed lingered. Groaning in mild protest, he forced himself out of bed, waving back the omnipresent attendant who ran forward to help. He tucked in his sleep-loosened antariya around his waist and shuffled groggily to the huge doorway that led to the narrow balcony that was attached to his room and ran all the way down the length of the building. Leaning against the red stone walls, he took in his surroundings.

The sprawling green lawns of the palace at Kampilya were well maintained, but lacked the contrived look that royalty usually favoured in their gardens. The undulating land had been only partly cleared and small copses dotted the entire landscape, shading it in old and new hues of green. A small stream flashed out of a particularly thick copse and wound back into a large wood that looked untouched and pristine. Many kinds of jasmine, and a red flower Yuyudhana did not immediately recognize, were in bloom on some of the trees and shrubs. To the north he saw the blue sparkle of the River Ganga as she flowed eastward beyond Panchala towards Kashi, Magadha and Anga before turning south to meet the sea. The river marked the border of the woods surrounding the palace and of the realm of Southern Panchala. Beyond the sparkling waters was the 'other' Panchala, as Yuyudhana had heard Dhrstyadymn refer to it – Northern Panchala, the land of kinsmen and enemies. Not so long ago the two kingdoms had been one, a great realm spanning from the lower Himalayan ranges in the north to the source of the River Charmanvati in the south. Now things were different. Very different.

Reflecting on the vagaries of life, Yuyudhana turned to look at the city of Kampilya, which spanned from the western wall of the palace out into the distance. It had every mark of a bustling trade city – right from the dense cluster of buildings with their multi-coloured awnings that formed the central market to the more spacious and less bustling residences of the nobility. Like the palace, the city walls as well as the public buildings and official residences were all built of a rich, red stone, but towards the northern part of the city, close to the river, it gave way to a less porous, more resilient grey rock. A variety of boats were docked along the river, the arrangements ranging from a seemingly chaotic mess of barges and small paddle boats at the point closest to the marketplace to the orderly calm around the immaculately maintained royal sailboat and smaller leisure craft. Here and there, spires of smoke rose to the sky in evidence of daily human activity, but the palace remained pleasantly secluded from the smells and sounds of the city.

Though he could not see it from where he was, Yuyudhana knew that a huge garrison lay to the south of the palace, shielding it and the rest of Kampilya from the lands beyond. The armoury and the officers' quarters were closest to the royal palace, while the soldiers' barracks and stables ran the entire length of Kampilya, till both garrison and city ended at the huge structure known as the Western Gate, the main entrance into Kampilya. Beyond the city, coloured flags dotted the landscape, fluttering in a strong breeze. These marked the Great Road that spanned Aryavarta from west to east.

Or so it's claimed, a sardonic Yuyudhana noted. The Great Road, for the most part, served only the old kingdoms, which barely covered half of what was Aryavarta today. From Panchala the road ran west and north through Surasena into the Kuru kingdom. There it came to an abrupt stop at the edge of the desert. Only when that harsh nothingness had been traversed did the road suddenly blossom out of the earth again, as a short stretch that ran through parts of Salwa.

In stark contrast, the eastern part of the Great Road was long, well-laid and also well-defended. It ran past the capital of Magadha almost to the borders of the empire. A series of small but adequate roads branched off from the Great Road into the various vassal kingdoms of Anga, Kashi–Kosala and others. With small towns, inns and resthouses dotting the countryside, these roads formed an alternative route that ran parallel to the Great Road, though much further south.

But, of course – it's Jarasandha's lifeline, his passage to Aryavarta.

The Southern Roads, as they were called, came as far west as Vidharbha but went no further. Not into the tract of rocky deserts that was part of the Anartta kingdom. Not to the western coast of the empire. Not to Dwaraka.

Yuyudhana sighed, and returned to tracing what he could see of the Great Road. Only then did he realize that what he had supposed was a cloud was really dust, dust that only a huge convoy could raise. He dismissed the idea of an army – he would have seen the glint of armour, perhaps even felt a slight tremor from the marching of elephants before he had noticed the dust. This was, beyond doubt, a civilian convoy. He looked on in disbelief as the procession progressed along the road. He could see the faint outlines of slow bullock-carts, men and women walking alongside them herding pitifully small and most likely starved herds of cattle and sheep.

'By Hara!'

'Refugees,' a voice explained.

Yuyudhana turned as Govinda walked in from an adjoining room, shutting the connecting door behind him. He came to stand alongside his cousin and continued, 'That's the latest flood of refugees, from the northern and north-western frontiers of Aryavarta. Rather, what used to be the frontier. It's now under the control of

Yavanas and soon to legitimately become their lands. Shikandin's men report that this lot,' he gestured toward the oncoming cloud of dust, 'are all that's left of nearly four hundred villages. For each person that has made it this far, at least three have died, either fighting to protect their homes or, worse, while crossing the desert.'

Govinda raised a disdainful eyebrow at the expression of shock on Yuyudhana's face. 'Does it really surprise you? The Yavanas, the Huns, the Pahlavas, have all realized that if we can cross the mountains and conquer them, they can do the same to us. Drawn by the allure of Aryavarta they'll find a way over the White Mountains or around it. And here we are, an empire in name but really just a fragmented bunch of petty rulers ready to squabble with each other at the slightest provocation. But that's how it'll be as long as there's only so much fertile land to till and many mouths to be fed, and, of course, many coffers in each kingdom's treasury to be filled.'

'I didn't know that Panchala offered sanctuary.'

'Not sanctuary. But in a city like this there are nobles who need slaves, attendants, prostitutes. I believe even the Chief Attendant of the palace has ridden out to get an early pick ...'

Govinda tried to keep his tone casual, but it betrayed his acrimony. 'Sometimes people stay willingly, believing that life may be better here than elsewhere. Most of the time they're sold one by one, by their own families, for food. In the cities, it's mostly women. Along the farms and pasturelands it'll be the children ...'

'But where ... Where are they headed?' Yuyudhana asked.

'Magadha. They go to join Jarasandha's teeming armies. All the men, without exception, and even some of the women are willing to serve however they can ... What else can they do? They're not safe in their own homes, nor are they welcome anywhere else. So they'll join the Emperor's forces, and when the *real* invasion of Aryavarta does happen they'll be the ones to die first. But they probably believe they have that one chance to fight back for their families, for what they've lost. It almost makes me wonder if it's really worth defying Jarasandha ...' Govinda muttered the last few words before he trailed off.

Yuyudhana, however, did not miss a word. He knew well what was on his cousin's mind and had no stomach for it.

'Yabha! So that's your excuse then, Govinda? We should defer to Jarasandha? We should hide and run from him because he's not above using desperate men, not above throwing their lives away to feed his ambition? We should let him destroy us just because he offers us the semblance of a united empire? You wouldn't face him before, and even now you hesitate, don't you?'

'Who's "we", Cousin? Is that the royal "we", or "we" the common people?' Govinda snidely quipped. 'Only the royal "we" find the notion of an empire, any empire, disconcerting. The common people need it. Small nations don't have the resources to do more than survive. To maintain a great army, one capable of defending a realm the size of Aryavarta, we need an immense agrarian base and, also, the capacity to match the army's requirements for weapons, land, transport, sustenance and whatever else they may need. In effect, the functioning of an empire takes coordination and efficiency, not just with the army but also across other essential activities – settlement, irrigation, pasturing, mining and production, all have to be efficiently guided.'

'Hu!' Yuyudhana dismissively waved his hand. 'This is just the kind of dung-pile answer that I'd expect from one of the Faithful, the Firstborn-loving spineless monkeys that the empire is full of! If your empire works, shouldn't it have brought us specialization? But, no, instead of learning to be excellent at various skills, we find the same, mediocre replication of mundane activities in each village, hamlet and city – the same old medics, the same old smithies, the same old priests and scholars, the same old stagnation. What else do you expect, Govinda, if you rely on common peasants to provide the solution? It is arguments like yours that have brought us to this pathetic state!'

'And you kings have the answer? Indeed, you do, but it's not a solution you like too much, is it? Why not learn, why not trade? But no! As far as the kings are concerned, wealthier vassal lords mean more tax, but wealthier peasants usually mean trouble … So, we'll let the people struggle to earn every grain of rice they eat, even though the royal granaries may be full of paddy. Keep them hungry and dumb, and we can stay noble! Isn't it? What a conundrum ...' Govinda's voice brimmed with sarcasm. 'Aryavarta is both attractive and indefensible. We've fallen into the dregs of mediocrity and sloth, yet are so knowledgeable, so prosperous, that foreign invaders find us to be a very desirable conquest. Indeed, what do they want from us? Our corrupt and greedy rulers have already sold them the very weapons they use to attack us.'

'Just as it's a conundrum,' Yuyudhana glibly replied, 'that our rulers are power-hungry, corrupt tyrants, but we need them to form an empire and rule us for our own good? Then what you'll get is what you deserve – a vengeful fiend who lets half his empire rot and fall into ruin while the other half prospers and flourishes!'

'Perhaps my expectations of an emperor are lower than yours?' Govinda offered. 'I'm willing to settle for a human emperor. Not some god-like half-celestial buried under a mound of legend and mysticism, but someone who talks to his people more and to the seers and their gods less. But the fact remains that our approach to dominion is flawed – an emperor, any emperor, who tries to reduce the differences among the nations of Aryavarta does so at the expense of his own dominion. By enhancing the prosperity of other nations, he sets the stage for one of those kings to rise up and take *his* place. Surely, that's something you'd understand, *Prince*?'

A moment of silence followed, as Govinda recognized he had been unusually scathing. It was not often that he let his ire get the better of him. He looked at his cousin and could tell that Yuyudhana was desperately fighting to keep his temper. Even among the hot-blooded, impetuous Yadu clans, Yuyudhana had a reputation for being easily provoked. Few people, family included, would ever speak to the man this way.

'Silly of us to argue, you know,' Govinda continued lightly. 'We're both agreed on the problem. You know and I know that the perfect empire is an impossible dream. It's our solutions that differ. You'd rather not settle for an imperfect resolution, while I think it better to try and make do …'

Yuyudhana made a strained effort to smile. 'It's gone from afternoon to evening and all I've done today is listen to you prattle on,' he complained. 'I haven't had even a drop of water, on my inside or outside. First, I need a bath and then some food. Perhaps some drink too, if we can find the stuff …'

'Find the stuff? My dear Yuyudhana, you can have all the drink you want, all the wine in Panchala if you like! Don't you see the flares being set up all around the palace? A grand wedding is in the offing. Just this morning, Dhrupad announced that his daughter is to be married in less than a month. All the royals of Aryavarta have been invited to Kampilya to compete for her hand. A tournament is the plan, I think …'

'Panchali?' Yuyudhana gasped.

'Yes, Panchali!' Govinda laughed. 'A relief, isn't it?'

'A relief?'

'But of course! A tournament and a grand wedding. It will be *the* diplomatic event that will determine Aryavarta's future and Dwaraka's with it. At the very least, Jarasandha won't start an unnecessary war till the new political landscape becomes clear. It gives us time, and it gives us a huge opportunity. The king is hosting a banquet tonight to mark the announcement. Be a good diplomat and get dressed up to look important, will you? There are three attendants waiting outside …'

Yuyudhana studied Govinda for a few moments, trying to decipher the inscrutable emotions that showed in the man's eyes. With a shake of his head, he gave up. 'Looks like you need their help more than I do.' He gestured towards Govinda's simple cotton robes.

With a reluctant groan Govinda said, 'You're right. I'd better get changed too. I think I'll borrow one of Shikandin's silk tunics …'

Yuyudhana watched his cousin leave and then set about his routine. As a purple darkness spread over the sky, the Great Road and its travellers disappeared into the horizon. In and around the palace, a dazzling array of lights flickered to life.

In a shadowy room, not too far away from where Yuyudhana stood lost in contemplation, King Dhrupad ambled around in an attempt to keep anxiety at bay. Braziers set into the many pillars that ran down the length of the hall panelled the floor in light and shadow, now throwing the monarch's face into relief, now hiding his thoughts. He came to stand, pensive, in front of a portrait of his father, the previous ruler of Panchala.

The memory of his father made Dhrupad swell with pride and, at the same time, bristle with rage. Within moments those emotions changed to shame and disgust, as other thoughts flooded over him. Half their territory and all their honour had been lost because of that weakling, his wastrel of a son. With a shake of his head, he resumed pacing, flinching as loud laughter erupted from the banquet hall, where the feast was still in progress. He would have to join them soon. But before that he had to see to an unavoidable task.

'You sent for me, Father?'

Dhrupad turned around. Shikandin looked every bit the prince he was. His hair was no longer wild and matted; instead, it fell sleek and straight down his back, in sharp contrast to the white linen tunic he wore over his pleated lower robes. He had no sword, as was the etiquette expected at a banquet, and so had swapped his baldric for a belt, which he wore over his tunic.

Dhrupad felt neither happiness nor pride at the sight of his son. A grimace was all he had to spare as he coldly declared, 'The alliance we'll make through Panchali's marriage can secure the future of this kingdom. Dhrstyadymn finally has the chance to rule a great nation, perhaps even a unified one. I won't have his destiny compromised by your folly or your treachery. Is that clear?'

'Yes, Father.' Shikandin's eyes shimmered their usual green-brown; his face remained impassive. It irked Dhrupad no end.

'I have recalled Yudhamanyu, the boy you claim to have fathered, from his training. Henceforth, he'll stay here under my watch. If I sense even a hint of betrayal on your part, even a whisper of your past treason, he'll suffer the consequences more than you will. It may be too much to bear for a motherless son …'

Dhrupad looked at the younger man with expectation. Surely, he would show some emotion. But all Shikandin said was, 'Yes, Father.'

The brief interaction between father and son would have ended there, but for the small glint of metal that escaped from under the high neck of Shikandin's tunic. Dhrupad felt his heart speed up as he realized what it was. Before he could help himself, the images came flashing, hard and strong – the desperate princess at his doorstep asking for his help, the rage in her eyes at being turned away, the curse she had spewed before leaving, never to be seen again ...

He drew in a deep breath at that thought, even as more memories followed, filling his mouth with a bitter taste. Shikandin, all of seven years old, saying, 'But, Father, they are people, too,' staring wide-eyed as those heathen Firewrights had been executed in public, and then the day he had found the fine beads and brought them to Dhrupad, saying excitedly, 'Father, look what I've found ...'

Dhrupad felt a fresh surge of anger rush to his head. The wretch of a boy had not done one right thing as a youth and certainly nothing as a man. His folly had been somewhat bearable when he was a child, for Dhrupad could give vent to his anger with a few well-chosen strokes with the flat of his sword, but Shikandin was a grown man now. A part of Dhrupad toyed with the idea of ordering his guards to take his son down to the dungeons and whip him, just to see pain, any emotion really, in those stone-cold eyes. The temptation passed, pushed out of his mind by the thought of the banquet that was on, of his daughter's imminent wedding and its political implications, all weighed by the same ambitious pragmatism that had guided Dhrupad's every decision as a prince and as a king. He settled for barking out, 'And take that damned thing off! How many times have I told you not to wear it! Now, get out!'

Shikandin bowed, stiff and formal. Then he strode out of the room and did not stop till he was a long way from Dhrupad's private audience hall. Pausing for a moment, he tucked the chain of beads into his tunic so that it did not show, but he did not take it off. He knew better than to waste time on trying to please his father – that was something he could never manage to achieve no matter what he did. He also knew better than to feel hurt. His father's offences against him paled in comparison to what others had suffered at Dhrupad's orders.

A burst of merry laughter from the direction of the banquet brought Shikandin out of his solemn thoughts. He recognized the voice as Dhrystydymn's and smiled. *The sins of the father shall lie heavy on the son ... Better me, than my siblings.* Turning around, he headed directly for the quarters that had been assigned to the Yadus. He found Govinda in the middle of pulling on a borrowed tunic. Govinda paused and gave him a questioning look.

'The usual,' Shikandin replied. 'Don't bother getting all dressed up. We'd better get going while the banquet is still on and no one notices. One of my spies just sent word ...' he remained cryptic, knowing that there were many hidden ears listening, even within the royal palace.

Govinda nodded and followed Shikandin out of the room. Soon the two men were riding into the night. Behind them, the celebrations continued.

10

PANCHALI HAD REFUSED TO ATTEND THE BANQUET. SHE SAT ALONE in her room, dazed, and thankful that no one was around to notice. Ever since the news of her wedding had been broken to her, she had been overcome by a sense of foreboding. She felt angry, desperate and, as she ultimately admitted to herself, terrified.

Govinda had greeted her father's announcement that she was to be married with the diplomatically expected degree of enthusiasm, but nothing more. He had displayed no emotion at all, not even surprise. Worse still, he had taken the news that she would be married away to whoever won the tournament without a stir. She had been made a prize, an object, a *thing*, and it had not seemed to bother him in the least. That had hit her hard.

All these years Govinda had been privy to her deepest secrets and passions, the anger she felt against the world around them, her joys and sorrows, hopes and dreams. She was brutally honest with him, always. He, on the other hand, had many secrets, secrets she often never knew he had. Their differences, their similarities made little sense by themselves, but it all came together when they were together. They were two halves of a whole – equal yet opposites, similar yet complements. They had never spoken about their relationship, or put a name to what they shared. It was sometimes perfect, sometimes imperfect, but far from mundane and normal. Or was it?

Watching him as her father had made the announcement, Panchali had no longer been sure of what to say, or if she ought to say anything at all. She had cut short her ineffectual protests and meekly assented. Somehow, in that single moment, her usually fiery will lost some of its effulgence. She had often been accused of trying to emulate her brothers, of assuming an air of masculinity – something she had vehemently denied. But now she wondered if the emotions had been borrowed, after all.

Panchali cringed as raucous laughter blasted into the night from the banquet hall. With some effort, she willed herself to be patient, to wait for the festivities to end. At last, when the bustle of activity slowed down and then stopped as everyone retired for the night, she made her way through the silent corridors of the palace, to Dhrstyadymn's room. She waved aside the guards on duty at his door and knocked on it. Knowing her brother well, she kept knocking till she heard sounds of movement and wakefulness from inside.

The door opened, and one of her mother's many lovely personal attendants stepped out. The sairandhari looked back and smiled at Dhrstyadymn before disappearing down the dark corridor.

'Well, come in then,' Dhrstyadymn invited his sister in.

Panchali stepped in and seated herself on a cushioned bench next to a window overlooking the balcony. Her brother moved around, lighting up a few of the brass lamps that hung suspended from the ceiling. That done, he sat down next to her and studied her for a while.

'This had better be important, Panchali. I was having a rather good time.' He tried to feign irritation but his tone gave him away.

Panchali remained serious. 'Do you remember anything from, you know, before ...?' she asked him.

Dhrstyadymn regarded her critically. 'What does it matter?'

'I need to know,' she confessed. 'I need to know if I am even half the person that I long to be. Don't you wonder?' Panchali keenly considered her brother. Their stark resemblance had earned them the label of twins, but she was the younger of the two by a couple of years or so. As best as they could tell, Dhrstyadymn was hardly twenty-three or twenty-four, but right then he looked so much older. Older and tired. Or, perhaps, she wondered, she just felt that way because things were no longer the same between them.

Once, Dhrstyadymn had been her best friend. These days, though, he had grown distant. Panchali could not understand whether he was trying to protect her from the many burdens she knew he carried, or if they had truly grown apart. She had thought many times to ask him directly, to force him to share his life with her for his own sake. But to her that was the ultimate admission of estrangement. Her brother would have to bare his soul of his own will or not at all.

'What time is it?' Dhrstyadymn suddenly asked, looking out of the window at the stars. The skies of Aryavarta served well to keep track of the sidereal day, which all its nations followed. The day, which began and ended at sunrise, was divided into thirty periods, or muhurttas. As though looking for a way to ignore what he would soon have to do, Dhrstyadymn allowed his mind to abstractedly ponder the significance of the number thirty, which so dominated chronology: Thirty kashtiha made up one kala, thirty kalas made one muhurtta, of which there were thirty in a day, and, finally, thirty days made a month. Each kashtiha itself comprised fifteen nimisha, or blinks of the eye. The measurements then went into factors, rather than multiples, with three lava making up a nimisha, three vedha making a lava. A vedha was measured as a hundred thruti, a thruti being the time it took to integrate three trasarenu, or molecules, each made as a combination of six celestial atoms, the most fundamental unit of existence itself.

Oblivious to her brother's ruminations, Pancali followed his gaze and noticed that it was late. 'Six muhurttas to sunrise,' she estimated.

Dhrystydymn thought for a while longer and then said, 'Come with me.'

A trusted attendant brought them their horses, discreetly saddled and retrieved from the stables. The two set out, leaving Kampilya unseen through an inconspicuous gate between the palace wall and the army garrison.

Panchali kept quiet till they were a fair distance from the city and among open fields. She then pulled on the reins, making her horse rear up and whinny in challenge. 'Care for a race?'

'Go!' Dhrstyadymn instantly cried out and spurred his horse into a gallop.

'Not fair!' Panchali shouted and set off after him, laughing.

Their melancholy dispelled by the magical stillness of the moonlit night, the two rode at a steady pace, heading south-east from Kampilya. They occasionally stopped to let their horses catch their breath or slowed down to a serene canter in the moonlight as they conversed, but for the most part they rode in silence. Panchali found herself enjoying the unspoken companionship that she had regretted as lost just a while ago and felt happier than she had all day.

A little before dawn, Dhrstyadymn turned due south and into the large forest tract that formed a border with their westward neighbours, Kuru and Surasena. Panchali followed without question as he led them into the deepest part of the woods. The soft twitter of birds and the gentle susurrus of awakening forest life helped dispel the heavy, somewhat ominous, air. Beams of sunlight shone through the occasional gap between the trees, trapping eddies of fresh mist and forest-dust in fragile sculptures of light and shadow. For the most part, though, the forest was still dark and the horses carefully picked their way through the thick undergrowth.

Without warning, the dark canopy overhead gave way to a burst of white brightness, and the thick air felt lighter. They stood at the fringes of a clearing. Blinking, Panchali urged her horse into the open space. The semi-circular glade was filled with stone debris and the remains of what looked like a lined pit or shallow well. The grass underfoot was young and green, but grew only in patches. Some of the older trees overhead bore signs of charring.

She gasped. 'Hai! Is this … ?'

'Yes. Father brought me here once, hoping it would stir my memory. It didn't, though I tried. Rudra knows, I tried.'

Panchali looked around, suddenly feeling weak and frightened. Her life as she knew it had begun here, with fire.

Fire. It had spread from the crumbling walls to the thatched roof in moments. Panchali remembered every detail, as if it had happened slowly and she had been an engrossed spectator. She had not screamed. She was terrified, but some instinct had told her to get out because she had to live. Fumbling around in the smoke, her vision hazy, her hand touched another's. Her brother's. She knew, somehow, that he was her brother. She clung to him in relief, the will to live no longer just her own.

They did not speak, not a word, but both of them knew what had to be done. She found her thick, woolly cloak on the floor and tried to wrap it around them both – ineffectively, for she was too short and her brother too tall. He bent down to pick her up in his arms and bundled her close to his chest. She covered them both as best she could with the thick material, letting it fall over her brother's head and around them in a protective mantle, which she held shut with her hand. With whispered words that might have been a prayer, her brother stepped through the fire towards the faint patch of light and colour, which they hoped was the doorway.

After that all she remembered was a blurred flash of images. The two of them laughing, breathing deep of the clean, smokeless air, glad to be alive. People milling around, trying to put out the fire. A couple moving toward them, the man embracing her brother as though he were a gift from the Divine, while the woman cried at their pitiful state – blackened faces, mild bruises and burns, and a fair amount of disorientation and shock, all of which could easily be set right.

'Welcome, my children. Welcome, Dhrstyadymn, the future of Panchala, and its saviour,' the man had declared. 'We're your father and mother, my children. We have been praying incessantly to the gods, the Benevolent Ones who've brought you to us.' At that moment, the statement had sounded no less believable than the suggestion that anyone could escape alive from that infernal blaze.

Right away, the two siblings had left with their newfound parents and their royal retinue for the capital of Panchala, Kampilya. That night, and for many after that, they stayed in one of the smaller palaces on the way, although, as Panchali later found out, Kampilya had been but half a night's ride away. A few hours after they arrived there the man who had declared himself their father, King Dhrupad, asked to see them in private. He greeted them with warmly and served them wine himself. No attendants were present, nor was the queen. Even though she had still felt bewildered by all that had happened within the past day, Panchali knew, with an instinct that she could not explain, that all of this was most strange.

After some awkward small talk, to which Panchali and Dhrstyadymn had simply contributed with silent nods, Dhrupad had gently but pointedly asked them, 'Tell me, what can you remember from before the fire?'

The siblings had confessed that they remembered nothing, not even the names they may have had. All they knew was they were brother and sister, and that too was a feeling rather than the certainty of knowledge. Dhrupad, however, had been relentless in his questioning, asking if they recalled where they used to live, whether it had been warm or cold there, their dwelling large or small, whether they remembered any of their kin, if they spoke any other languages, how old they were, where they had been schooled, and many such details, in an attempt to kindle their memories. At the end of the night the two had remembered nothing that could point to their prior identity. It nevertheless took many such nights of inquisition before their father had been satisfied.

At length, he had smiled and declared, 'You are born of my penance and the sacrificial fire. You are blessings from the Divine.'

At that moment Panchali had hesitantly inquired, 'What's my name?'

Dhrupad was taken aback, as if the thought had not crossed his mind in all these days. Flippantly, he declared, 'Panchali.'

It was bland, but fitting, Panchali had decided. After all, she had neither memory nor identity. She only was, as her name meant, a woman of Panchala.

The very next day, they had left for Kampilya.

Hardly had Panchali settled into the royal palace than Queen Gandavati sent for her. Panchali had rushed over, driven by respect and a dutiful stirring of affection for the woman who was now her mother.

The Queen came straight to the point. 'We're hardly mother and daughter, Panchali,' she began, 'but we share this much, that our lives shall never be our own.'

She gave a hollow, chilling laugh, and continued, 'I told Dhrupad that we should have picked up orphaned infants, that you are both too old. Whether you remember your past or not, you are who you are, and it's too late to mould your characters, your nature. But then, when did my husband ever listen to me? Yes, there were times when I could have sworn he almost felt love, especially in those months that I carried the Crown Prince in my womb – the same Crown Prince whose right you and your brother have now irrevocably taken away. Nevertheless, I am thankful to you both. You may not be aware, but it's an open secret, and one sanctioned by scripture, that kings in need of an heir may ask other men … men of nobility, such as great sages, to sire children in their wives …'

Panchali had felt a sense of dread creeping up on her as, for the first time, she saw the larger implications of their adoption. She never would forget that moment when she had finally brought herself to meet Gandavati's gaze, for it was then that she had been gripped by an indescribable fear, despair at the notion that her life as a whole was about to be reduced to nothing.

The queen's tone had become disturbingly sweet. 'As a token of my gratitude, let me give you some advice. Not as your mother, but from one princess to another. Like it or not, no matter how much you fight or what you say, you can't change the decisions that are made around you, for you. You cannot even begin to alter the life that's laid out for you. All you can do is choose whether you'll resist the occasional happiness that comes your way and be tormented by your own hatred and self-loathing, or you'll spare yourself your own judgement at the least and take what you can get.'

Those, possibly, had been the most maternal emotions Gandavati had ever shown her.

The moment the queen had swept regally out of the room, her old nurse had entered. The woman had been kind and gentle in her examinations, but much to Panchali's discomfiture, also obedient to the orders she had been given. That the nurse had reported to Dhrupad, with some relief, that his new daughter was in all objectivity an attractive woman of unblemished beauty had brought no comfort to Panchali. But it had irked her just a little that he had treated the news with the same decisiveness he had shown when the training commander had informed him that Dhrstyadymn was an exemplary soldier for his age: Dhrupad began making his plans.

After that, Panchali had quickly understood the deeper truth behind Gandavati's words. Day after day, she and Dhrstyadymn had been amazed by their own abilities, things they had not known they could do. They could read and write, which placed them as being of somewhat noble, if not royal, origin. Their knowledge was broad, ranging from astronomy to geology and the basics of medicine. Whoever had taught them had taught them well.

It was then that the idea had struck them. Perhaps they could find out their former identities, after all. The siblings turned to their tutor – a young Firstborn scholar on his very first assignment as a full initiate into the order. Despite his youth the scholar was a learned man and enthusiastically engaged Panchali and Dhrstyadymn in discussions on such works of knowledge as the Vyasa permitted to be shared outside the confines of the Firstborn order. With his help the two siblings made a list of all the topics and premises that they were able to recall and tried to match them with a place of learning where they were commonly taught. In this way, Pançali hoped, they could identify their teachers, maybe even the hermitage where they had been educated. But it was what they had not known that had defined their fate. Most astonishingly, Panchali and Dhrstyadymn both found they had never heard of Firewrights.

Their tutor's reaction had been one of disbelief. He had sent immediately for his senior colleagues and as a group they had yet again expressed their dismay at the ignorance of the two youngsters. The matter was then referred with the utmost urgency to Dhrupad.

Whether Dhrupad was concerned or offended at their ignorance, Panchali never did find out, but he had immediately sent for her and Dhrstyadymn. He led them down into the deepest levels of the castle that housed the dreaded dungeons. There, as screams rent the air, and the smell of blood and decay hung heavy over them, Dhrupad had proudly explained to his children the strict laws that Panchala had against the Firewrights, those ruthless fiends who questioned the system of divine law and order set by the gods; tricksters who beguiled commoners, sometimes even kings, with their false promises of magic that could pervert even all-powerful destiny.

He had then made them watch while a suspected Firewright was interrogated.

Panchali had flinched, though she did not turn away, as the young man was painfully, brutally, blinded right in front of them. The memory still made her want to retch but, more important, it secretly kept alive the anger she had felt at that moment. For many nights after that, she had lain awake, tormented by what she had seen. No matter how evil the Wrights and how much hatred she could rile up in her heart for them, she still could not reconcile herself to the brutality of her own kind, of the noble, enlightened rulers of the land. It just did not make sense. But she had kept her thoughts to herself.

The incident had been their last trial, and from that day Dhrupad began to lavish great affection and pride on them both. They had become his children, without question, shadows of his own soul. Soon their lives were no different from that of any other prince or princess of Aryavarta. Their tutor was recalled to the service of the Vyasa and the siblings were forced to abandon their research into their past. Instead, they were guided towards activities more suited to their new station in life. Panchali was taught to sing and paint, and Dhrstyadymn was put into intensive military training. Their spirits were tamed and lulled into submission and the two of them became nothing but prisoners held in luxury.

Then, Shikandin had returned home to Kampilya from his post near the Eastern Forests. The palace had filled with rumours of a dark past, of how he had driven Dhrupad to hatred and shame. Panchali and Dhrstyadymn, however, had neither time nor thought to spare for such gossip, filled as they were with guilt at the thought of the Crown Prince they had dethroned. Their fear had been as ironical as it was redundant, for Shikandin was nothing like they had expected him to be. Only after his return had the two siblings dared to laugh and live and feel – it was he who had truly made them the prince and princess of Panchala.

Dhrstyadymn's voice brought Panchali back to the present. 'Do *you* ever wonder who we are, Panchali?'

She was momentarily taken aback by the question. 'Every single day,' she finally confessed. 'I … I feel terrified, Dhrstyadymn.'

'Why are you afraid, dearest sister? What are you afraid of?'

'What am I afraid of?' she screamed out loud, giving vent to emotions suppressed for so long. 'What is there to not be afraid of? An exiled Firewright returns to Aryavarta after decades and dies. Within days, armies are mustered and moved all over the empire, long-lost friends return, bringing death and danger on their tail, and it's decided that I am to be married within weeks. What in this do you *not* find disconcerting?'

Dhrstyadymn threw his arms around her in an encouraging

embrace. 'Oh, Panchali! It's only natural that you're afraid, I suppose. I should have realized. But don't worry, more than half the contest has already been played out, across assembly halls and private audience rooms, at dinner feasts and in courtesans' beds … not just in Kampilya, but all over Aryavarta. Many will come, but not compete; and many will compete, but not win. This was instigated by Bhisma, the Grandsire of the Kurus. In fact, Dwaipayana, the Vyasa, came here straight from Hastina and settled everything with our father. You're to be married to Syoddhan, heir to the Kuru throne.'

'What? But …'

'Trust me, Panchali, you've got nothing to fear. Everything has been arranged. You, my dear, will be Queen of Hastina!' he joyfully concluded.

Panchali longed to retort, but the happiness on her brother's face made her hold back. *Our lives are not our own.* Once again, Gandavati's words had been nothing less than prophetic.

'Come,' she said, forcing cheer into her words, 'we ought to head back. I'm famished. Besides, Shikandin will worry when he finds us missing.'

Dhrstyadymn shot her a strange look. 'He and Govinda left, not long before we did, I suspect. The attendant found their horses gone when he went to fetch ours. No one can tell where they were headed to.'

Panchali sighed. 'And what's new about that?'

11

'WHOEVER DID THIS …' SHIKANDIN BEGAN AND THEN FELL SILENT, his knuckles white from his tight grip on the hilt of his sword.

'… had no choice. He has his loyalties as we have ours. We can't hold it against him,' Govinda declared, calmly surveying the carnage around him. It had taken them one night to reach the Eastern Forests that lay on the border of Panchala, but they had spent the better part of the next day searching for the first of the destroyed villages. From there on, the trail was unmistakeably clear. 'Still, we're too late to save anyone,' he dully admitted.

The two men walked past the still-smouldering debris to the hut at the edge of the village. Tethering their horses to a tree-stump outside the hut, the two stepped in and looked around.

'He was here,' Shikandin remarked, his nostrils flaring ever so slightly as though he could still smell the previous visitor's scent. His eyes took in the clean cut in the thatching where the warrior had slashed at the roof, and he reached up thoughtfully to pull at a loose straw. Letting it drop to the ground with a quiet sigh, he came to join Govinda, who was perched on one knee, examining a dark stain on the ground.

'Hardly a day old,' Govinda said. Standing up, he fixed the other man with a steady gaze. 'You still have your men posted in these parts?'

'Yes.'

'Trusted men?'

'Of course.'

'Then how did he get through? Why didn't anyone stop him? I can understand someone slipping past the Emperor's ring of spies and guards, but how did they get past yours?'

If Shikandin saw the least offence in Govinda's questions, he did not show it. He stared at the blood-stained floor, then moved back slowly, step by step. 'Come on,' he called out, heading outside. The warrior they were following was adept at hiding his trail, and once outside the hut his tracks all but disappeared. It took Shikandin every bit of his skill to find a dislodged pebble, or the slight dent in the tender bark of a young tree – signs that their quarry had gone that way. It was slow work, but by nightfall they reached the river. Despite the dim light they could make out the smoking pyre, the last few embers still shining in the dark.

'I can't track any further in the dark, Govinda. We'll have to wait till morning,' Shikandin said.

Govinda said nothing. He simply nodded and drew his sword, a long, flat blade with a straight hilt and open grip that spanned nearly

81

four feet, from hilt to tip. The two-sided blade was inflexible, but strong and unusually bereft of the markings that narrated the lineage and victories of the sword and its owner. It bore only its own name as inscription, a strange one too for a sword – Nandaka, that which brings bliss.

As unconventional as its name was the use to which Govinda now put the sword. In a move that most Arya nobles would have squirmed at, he stepped up to the pyre and used the blade to go through the ashes. Looking around, he picked up a dry branch from the ground and unceremoniously thrust it into the depths of the pyre. The heat trapped inside was enough to set the dry wood ablaze.

He pulled out the branch and handed it to Shikandin. 'Light a fire, will you.'

'With this?'

But Govinda had already walked away, toward the river.

Shikandin sighed, looking down at the flame. 'Oh well, I suppose death follows life, and all that …' He walked for some distance along the riverbank till the fragrance from the night-blossom trees cleaned his nostrils of the ashen smell of death. Then he started a small campfire and led both their horses to the river, where he washed them and let them drink, before diving in for a cooling swim. By the time Shikandin had returned to the small campsite, Govinda was already there. From the looks of his wet antariya, he too had indulged in a bath.

'Hungry?' Shikandin queried.

'Are you joking? Are you?'

Shikandin said nothing as he sat down next to Govinda. 'First Ghora, now him – Agniveshya Angirasa, Ghora's own grandson …' he began. 'Dwaipayana certainly doesn't leave things to chance.' His tone was soft, but held an unmistakeable edge.

Govinda said nothing. Without another word, they both turned in for the night.

Shikandin woke up well before dawn. He saddled both horses and put out the campfire before he gently awakened Govinda. It was still dark as the two men led their horses back to the pyre but the smell of dawn was already in the air. The misty freshness of the forest was pleasantly invigorating and they felt light-hearted despite the task that lay ahead of them. As the outline of the bier loomed ahead, Govinda stopped and took the reins of Shikandin's horse as well. He waited as Shikandin walked ahead and crouched down on the ground. The sun soon broke from the unseen horizon, and the forest came alive with light and sound.

Govinda watched with a smile as Shikandin became one with the forest, keenly aware of every bent blade of grass, every broken twig and twisted leaf. Shikandin, he knew, was more than just a good tracker. He was a true hunter, a creature of the wild. Few men could see the forests as he saw them, a living tapestry of life and death. Still crouched on the ground, his eyes closed in concentration, Shikandin heard the territorial rumble of a tiger as it prowled the opposite bank; he noted how the wild hog ran, grunting, it's scavenging complete; and watched as the smaller game began their day's journey, heading downriver. All these signs told him that their quarry had gone upstream, to the north. Almost reluctantly, he pulled himself back into the world of men. Taking back the reins of his horse he began to lead the way. Govinda followed wordlessly, unwilling to defile the serenity around them with speech.

They stopped for the night but did not light a fire. Govinda was about to suggest they take turns to keep watch, but Shikandin pre-empted him. 'Sleep. I'll take the first watch.' He fell asleep, knowing well that Shikandin would not wake him till morning. In any case, with Shikandin around, no creature of the wild posed any threat.

By afternoon, the next day, Shikandin began to look downcast. 'We're almost at the northern end of the forest. We'll soon emerge onto the last plains before the White Mountains begin.'

'Perhaps we can still find out which way he went before that.'

'And of what use is that?' Shikandin grumbled.

It was a little before sunset when the two friends emerged through the last of the trees, onto the edge of a small hillock. Below them lay the rolling plains of Northern Panchala. In the distance, almost at the foothills of the lesser Himalayas, was the hazy outline of Ahichattra, its capital city.

The two men trailed their quarry down to the edge of the plains, but the tracks were soon lost in the ploughed consistency of the farmlands.

'Mih!' Shikandin swore out loud. 'He's gone over the freshly tilled land and not through the fields which are yet to be harvested ... It's almost as if he knew he'd be trailed!'

'Trailed through the Eastern Forests, and that too for two days?' Govinda was incredulous.

'What are you saying Govinda? That he knew I'd be trailing him?'

'Possibly,' Govinda's voice took on a strained timbre, 'and that he surmised I'd bring you here. Strange, isn't it? It's almost as if someone wanted me to know that Agniveshya had been killed and who had done it. As if any of it would make a difference to my decision not to compete for Panchali's hand.

'And it won't?' Shikandin was terse.

'No,' Govinda shook his head. 'Come,' he continued, in a lighter tone. 'You'd better get back to Kampilya quickly. They'll be wondering where we've disappeared. I too need to meet Balabadra and the others near your borders.'

Shikandin nodded. For a moment he hesitated, as if on the verge of saying something, but then decided against it and rode on in silence. His thoughts rested on his sister and his eyes held a pained regret.

Govinda did not notice.

12

HASTINA, THE CAPITAL CITY OF THE KURU KINGDOM, LAY AT A unique junction of the Great Road and the River Ganga. Large crowds moved incessantly from the Great Road in through the city gates and out again.

Inside, a medley of smells and sounds, the endless bustle of life. Canals from the river ran through the city, the veins of its flourishing commerce. Small boats plied to and from the larger barges moored on the river, carrying various goods and occasionally people to the large marketplace that had sprung up along both banks of the largest of the canals. From this point, a series of narrow, cobbled streets branched off into various parts of the city, their haphazard pattern a stark contrast to the well-laid-out canals. Both close to the canals and in the more distant parts of the city, the streets were packed with residents and visitors alike, and many more people occupied the stone buildings flanking the narrow pathways. These structures were built over three, sometimes four levels and could house close to twenty large families. Some of the slightly more affluent buildings had a small inner courtyard with a common well. It was said that to find a piece of bare land in Hastina was impossible. Unless, of course, one was a king or a prince. Then the crowds would easily part despite the packed streets, and heads would bow in unquestioning obedience despite their many everyday cares.

As they did now for the tall rider. The hushed whispers that ran through the crowd, however, held more than habitual servitude. Those who knew him spoke of him with warm respect, and those who did not stared at him in admiration. His eyes were a warm, molten brown and his chiselled face sported a distant but pleasant expression, quite unlike the disdainful looks nobles readily bestowed on commoners. The flaming jewel he wore on his forehead hung between his brows like a third eye. Men stopped in their tracks, awed by his presence and manner, while women of all ages fawned over his pale, flawless complexion, which they said shamed even the white silk of his robes.

The rider left the narrow streets and entered the vast stone courtyard that separated one part of the city from the other. He headed straight for the huge edifice that dominated the cityscape – the golden palace of Hastina, home to the royal dynasty of the Kurus. The palace was a low-lying structure that occupied a small part of the grounds that it was set in. Built in a complex symmetry to house the many immediate and distant members of the royal family as well as a large part of the kingdom's administrative offices, it looked all the more amazing for its garden-like surrounds. The grass underfoot was velvet-soft, a carefully maintained species that was not native to the sometimes inhospitable climate of Kuru, but the shrubs and trees were native to the region. The flora had been arranged to form many smaller parks – areas discreetly enclosed by shrubs and bushes to offer privacy for the many undoubtedly pleasant uses the members of the royal household had for them.

At that moment, however, the general air of stillness around the parks and the entertainment podiums told the warrior that the hundred princes of Hastina, their courtiers, and their lackeys had already left for the tournament at Kampilya. The city was but a day's ride away, but the brothers would no doubt stop to hunt or be otherwise entertained on the way, and it would take their convoy at least three days to make the journey. Their absence did not bother the rider and, in fact, he relished the feeling of orderliness and calm that reigned over the palace grounds. The Crown Prince, Syoddhan, was his friend, but there were many in that lot of brothers that he thoroughly despised, for he had little patience with those who did not treat him with the respect he deserved. He came from an old and powerful line of scholar–warriors and was one of the best fighters in the empire. His father, Acharya Dron, had been teacher to all the Kuru princes and many nobles from other kingdoms too, and there were many assemblies across the land in which the acharya would be shown First Honour and recognized as the best of men unless, of course, the Vyasa Dwaipayana himself were present. Above all, he, Asvattama Bharadvaja, was not only the son of such a man but also a king in his own right, and his realm of Northern Panchala was one of the most prosperous and verdant in all of Aryavarta.

Asvattama left his horse in the care of an attendant and walked through the gilded halls as though he ruled the place. His hard sandals clacked loudly against the pristine, polished stone floors. He found the sound pleasing; it affirmed the idea that he would leave his indelible mark on the palace. *We should rule here*, he thought to himself. *Instead, Father has us remain servants with his talk of outdated morals and codes of duty and loyalty.*

In truth, Asvattama lacked no comfort that the kings of the realm had. As Dron's son, as a man who had served the Kurus faithfully time and again, he knew he was more than welcome to stay at the palace, attended by his own retinue of servants and soldiers both. Still, he felt different. After all, he was one of those who had given in, one of those who had traded the sacred, secret knowledge of his former order for gain. To live in Hastina would be too stark a reminder of his choices, and his guilt would condemn him to live in servitude – a privileged and honourable one, no doubt, but still servitude.

Bristling slightly at the thought, Asvattama entered the opulent central wing of the palace that housed the famed assembly hall of the Kurus as well as minor offices of the administrative machinery of the nation. It was to one such office, unremarkable in its location and appearance, that he now made his way, walking right in without announcement.

Sanjaya stood up on seeing him. 'Asvattama, welcome!'

Asvattama did not return the greeting. He did not need to; Sanjaya was a lowly Suta.

'Agniveshya Angirasa is dead,' he declared.

'But ... you ... are you sure ... it was him?' Sanjaya looked far less pleased than Asvattama had expected.

'Have I ever been wrong?'

'No ...'

'Surely, the Vyasa would be happy to know that his enemies are destroyed?'

'Yes. Yes, of course,' Sanjaya tried to show enthusiasm. 'But I must confess, I didn't expect this – I've been quite worried that a man like Agniveshya, a man who could rise to claim the title of Secret Keeper, was still at large, but now ... It is good news indeed. And I thank you for it, Asvattama.' He paused and fixed his visitor with a piercing look, 'This means, then, that you are all that's left of the Wrights, doesn't it? I sincerely hope you don't become the very danger we asked you to eliminate.'

Asvattama's voice was cold. 'It's true that I am of the lines of Bharadvaja and Gautama, descendants of Agni Angiras through his first and second sons respectively. But make no mistake, Sanjaya. I am not a Firewright. My father pledged allegiance to the Vyasa many years ago.' The emphasis on the last few words was unmistakeable.

Sanjaya spread his hands in what might have been an apologetic gesture, but said nothing.

Asvattama continued, 'As for whether any other heathens remain alive, both you and the Vyasa know what the situation is. Agniveshya, my uncle, is dead and only his children, if they're still alive, are of any consequence. But pretty much anyone who would know their identity is now gone. All I've heard was that Agniveshya's older child was sent to Dakshinavarta to study, while the younger one remained with Ghora. But I've never seen them, not even as a child; or, perhaps, I have seen them and didn't know who they were. My uncle used to say that both his children were as skilled as he was, that they had all the makings of warriors. One powerful Firewright is enough to be noticed; surely we wouldn't miss two of them? Of course, if you want to believe every madman who rants on about the order never dying out ... Well, what can I say?' He finished with an indifferent wave of his hand that hid nothing of his contempt.

Choosing his words with care, Sanjaya asked, 'So you're convinced that this is the end? Some claim that Agniveshya's father – Ghora's son – is still Jarasandha's prisoner in one of the Kashi kingdoms. It might be best to get rid of him, too.'

'What do you think I am, Sanjaya? Your servant? Or your deputed assassin?'

'I think you're a man who has much to gain from the death of these men. The Vyasa, on the other hand, wants them gone because they are a danger to Aryavarta.'

'Surely a man of learning and nobility such as the Vyasa doesn't place faith in childish tales of magic and sorcery? Or have you been sharing your commoner's superstitions with him?' Asvattama was intentionally insulting, but Sanjaya remained unfazed.

'The Vyasa encourages independent thought, even disagreement, in his students,' he slickly replied. 'I'm fortunate to not have to serve as a sycophant to some prince or some decrepit Regent ...'

'Pity! Such a calling is exceptionally suited to those with some ability and no nobility whatsoever. You'd have done well as a lackey to more than just the Kurus. Perhaps you could reconsider; it's never too late to bend further than you already have …'

Sanjaya tried to keep a rein on his temper, reminding himself that he acted on Dwaipayana's behalf. Asvattama was an important element in the Elder's plans, an element that could not be compromised. He was only partly successful, and his voice held just a trace of smugness as he said, 'Speaking of bending – I suppose, Asvattama, you won't vie for Panchali's hand …'

It was a statement, not a question; an order that clearly came from Dwaipayana himself. Asvattama hesitated a moment, wanting to disobey the Vyasa just to prove a point, but decided to settle for the satisfaction of knowing that not a single Kuru prince could hope to win against him if he chose to compete. Panchali was nothing more than his charity to them, a scrap for stray dogs. Keeping his thoughts to himself, he calmly replied, 'You can assure the Vyasa that the Kurus have my support. I'm sure one of them will make him proud.'

'It's your father, Acharya Dron, who will be made proud. He is, after all, their teacher and yours. A Kuru victory at the tournament is to your father's advantage in many ways … and yours. The resulting alliance will serve to keep Northern Panchala an independent state. Or would you rather be Jarasandha's vassal?'

Asvattama grimaced. There was no need for Sanjaya to drag Dron into it. 'What more do you want?' he rudely snapped.

Sanjaya held out his hand. 'Not I, Asvattama. I'm merely a servitor.'

His eyes boring into the other man, Asvattama reached into his waist-sash and pulled out a small, well-wrapped bundle.

Sanjaya took it, with a cautiousness marked by reverence. 'You made it stronger this time?'

'Yes. Don't break the damned bottle,' Asvattama warned, almost gleefully. 'A whiff of this can damage your nerves and even a single drop of it will leave you a blathering idiot for the rest of your life. Though I doubt we'd know the difference.'

Ignoring the temptation to retort, Sanjaya said, 'Thank you.'

His face set in its characteristic expression of cold contempt, Asvattama walked out of the room.

Alone, Sanjaya smiled to himself, revelling in the simple satisfaction of serving a greater cause. He was ready. If Govinda Shauri or, for that matter, anyone but the right man tried to wed the girl, they would rue their decision for as long as they lived.

13

THE PREPARATIONS FOR PANCHALI'S WEDDING HAD REACHED A feverish pitch.

All of Kampilya had been brightly decorated with flowers and creepers, and the streets rang with the sounds of festivity. Over the past few days, scores of Panchala's subjects had been pouring in from every corner of the kingdom to witness and celebrate the marriage of their beloved princess to the hero who would win her hand. Just when it looked like the city would burst with revellers, the royal guests began to arrive. Convoy after convoy marched toward the city in slow ceremonial processions designed to show off wealth and power. Gold-laden elephants, massive horse-drawn chariots and bejewelled attendants pushed through the already-packed streets of Kampilya in a grand spectacle as the crowds looked on in wonder.

Panchali watched discreetly from a balcony in the royal palace as wheels trundled through the palace gates in a solemn, boring, rhythm. Most of the central kingdoms used horse-drawn vehicles, the term chariot itself implying the ornately designed ceremonial monstrosities that rattled along slowly on special occasions. Compared to the simple, unshielded military rigs that were used in battle, the ceremonial chariots that now made their way towards the palace were covered on most sides, heavy and highly ornamented.

Not unlike their occupants, Panchali snidely noted as yet another bejewelled suitor descended from his vehicle and was welcomed in state by a member of the royal family.

Her face lit up as she spotted the people she had been waiting for. A small, boisterous party made its way through the gates. Conspicuously absent were the hosts of soldiers and war elephants. Instead, the group was escorted by a small retinue of guards and heralds. The heralds moved aside and raised light trumpets to their lips to let out a short, merry trill that announced the arrival of the leaders just as four blazing silver-white stallions led in a light two-wheel rig.

For a few moments Panchali indulged in fantasies of escape, of being carried to the farthest corner of the world by the fastest horses in Aryavarta, away from this honourable prison of red stone walls, this palace where every brick and pillar seemed to stand as a testament to the duty and gratitude she owed her father, her family. She finally managed to pull her attention back to the present and stepped off the balcony and through the adjoining room to emerge onto a corridor. She sprinted lightly down the corridor and up an open stairway to the huge terrace that connected the various buildings that comprised the palace. Running across the burning mid-day stone, she took her place in a corner overlooking the royal courtyard. She was just in time.

The rig entered the courtyard and came to a stop. Shikandin and Dhrstyadymn stood ready to welcome the Yadus on behalf of their father, and Yuyudhana stood with them to receive his kinsmen. Balabadra dismounted and was welcomed formally by Dhrstyadymn. Behind him came two young men, who Panchali guessed were Pradymna and Samva. The two of them politely greeted Dhrstyadymn and Shikandin, but the men pulled them into a delighted embrace and indulged in light banter. Govinda remained at his place at the reins, taking in the flurry of excited greetings and exchange of wishes. Quite suddenly, he looked up, as though he had known Panchali would be there, watching. She managed a tentative smile, her eyes revealing the storm of thoughts that swept across her mind.

In response, Govinda gave a discreet nod to say he understood.

The purple-red night sky seemed to have been coloured by Panchali's mood. Lightning flashed in the distance, teasing with the promise of a cooling downpour that would provide comfort from the sultry heat. She stood at the window of her room, but it was of little avail. Soothing incense burned in the background to keep nocturnal insects at bay. The smoke gave her a heady feeling but the fragrance was far too sharp for her to relax.

'Mih!' she swore in exasperation.

'Careful, Princess. Your father will have to empty his coffers to meet your dower if you're heard using such language,' a familiar voice teased from the dark doorway.

Panchali held her breath as she turned, forcing herself to remain impassive. 'About time,' she said. 'What took you so long? Such impoliteness doesn't become the Commander of Dwaraka.'

Govinda laughed. 'Am I to be held to task for remembering you and coming to see you, Panchali?'

'I'll forgive you on one condition, Govinda,' she offered. 'Tell me, what am I to do?'

'About what?'

'About my wedding, you miserable …'

Govinda sat down on a cushioned swing that hung on brass chains from the ceiling in the middle of the room. He pulled Panchali down by her hand to sit next to him. She pointedly refused to meet his gaze, and fidgeted with the wrought brass fastenings of the swing absent-mindedly.

'Your father is a powerful man,' Govinda began, 'and this kingdom is one of the mightiest in the entire land. You may not like it, but this makes it a rather complicated political situation. Your wedding could well determine the future of Aryavarta. Surely that's flattering?'

'Don't provoke me, Govinda. I feel like … like …'

'An animal at a sacrifice?'

'An animal at a village auction,' Panchali snapped. 'And not just any animal. I feel like a cow, because that's what I am supposed to do – stand there and chew cud till someone grabs me by the tail and takes me home.'

'Wouldn't you rather be a cow than a sacrificial bull, Princess?'

Ignoring the bait, Panchali continued, 'Dhrstyadymn mentioned Syoddhan of the Kurus.'

'Hmm. He's a good man.'

Panchali felt anger flood her insides with such venom that it frightened her. She did not understand her rage, but knew she could no longer resist it. 'Be that as it may, I don't want to marry him,' she stated, feeling very much like a stubborn child.

'Why not? He's a very handsome fellow ...'

'Hah! More handsome than you, Govinda?'

'No one's more handsome than I am, Panchali!'

'Then, I shall marry you ...'

'But I'm a bad choice. Don't you know? The people of Dwaraka are mere cattle herders, our vagrant chiefs not the least. You'd be treated like a cud-chewing cow. You should marry a brave warrior. Don't you love some warrior, Panchali?'

'Only you, Govinda. Only you.'

'Careful, I'll hold you to that,' he said, beaming joyfully at their interchange.

Panchali longed to reach out, to touch him, to feel the warmth of his skin. She laughed at her own thoughts, her dark eyes sparkling, and impulsively took his hands in a friendly grip. Govinda grinned at the sight of her small, graceful hands wrapped around his much larger ones. She was dark-skinned, just as he was, dark and alluring as the night. But where her skin was the sultry copper glow of a storm-clouded sunset, his was the cool, translucent obsidian of moonrise.

Slowly, he pulled his fingers out from between hers. She reacted with a look of surprise, but quickly hid it. Standing up, she began to pace the room, trying not to let her embarrassment and disappointment show.

Govinda smiled in his characteristic way, a slight curve at the edge of his lips, as if both amused and sad at some private, secret thought. Leaning back against the cushions with an exaggerated sigh, he said, a hint of the smile in his voice, 'Ah, Panchali. Have mercy on your suitors ... What man could resist you, resist his desire for you? Do you know how many hearts you'd break if some crownless cowherd were to steal you away?'

Panchali did not stop pacing as she glared at Govinda. Her

supposedly impeccable beauty meant little to her beyond the evaluation of her value as a breeding animal – eyes, ears, nose, all properly set and working well; slender fingers on strong hands to wait tirelessly on a husband; childbearing hips that curved wide from a small waist; and firm breasts to suckle children. She was beautiful, yes, but surely there was more to her than just that.

Meanwhile, Govinda continued in a dramatically lovelorn tone, 'Like Ahalya of old, the Creator has made you peerless. Truly, your beauty knows no bounds.'

Despite herself, Panchali laughed at his choice of words. Ahalya was a woman cursed to turn into stone for her passion. Only Govinda could speak of her with such reverence, she reflected. Putting on a coquettish expression, she petulantly complained, 'How would I know? I'm only what you see me as – the childish, useless princess of a powerful nation. Besides,' she said, feigning an offended pout, 'it would make for very dull gossip if the princess of Panchala were anything but attractive.'

Govinda laughed. 'You foolish girl! Have you never seen yourself in a mirror that you need me to tell you this? Don't you have any idea how exquisite you are? Whether you like it or not men will yearn for you to the point of being driven to madness.'

'I don't care,' Panchali shouted, as her patience snapped. Exhaling hard, she lowered her voice and repeated, 'I don't care. I don't want to marry any of them. I don't love any of them. I know that's the whim of a spoilt girl and has little merit for reasons of state. But I just don't care, Govinda.'

'You don't care, or you won't care?'

'Damn you! You could milk a bloody bull with your words.'

'I *am* a cowherd, Panchali.'

'Fine!' she said, furious now. 'I don't and I won't. Does that please you?'

'It's rather simple then, isn't it?'

'Is it?'

Govinda gave her an exaggerated look of bewilderment. 'You don't care, do you? So why should it bother you?'

Panchali ignored the jibe. 'Please …' she said. Coming closer, she knelt down on the floor before him in a gesture of earnestness and trust. 'Please, Govinda. I know you can.'

'You know I can do what, Panchali?'

'Marry me, Govinda.'

There was no levity in the suggestion, only unabashed innocence and stark, painful sincerity. Govinda studied her for some time, gazing deep into her eyes. Then he reached out to place a hand on her head. It was an incongruent gesture, one that held far too much tenderness to be a benediction or a patronizing pat. But his voice was cold as he told her, 'I can't, Panchali, my love. You know I can't.'

'Why not?' she asked him, adding, 'and do me the courtesy of telling me plainly, Govinda. Don't insult my intelligence or my respect for you by bothering to lie.'

Govinda leaned forward, resting his elbows on his knees. He took her hands gently in his and said, 'You must know that I care immeasurably for you. But if I married you, it would put far too much at risk … After a long time there's a chance for stability in the realm, a chance to create alliances of trust rather than arrangements based on political intrigue. I owe it to my people and to those who've placed their trust in me to do what is best for us all.'

'And what of me? Do you owe me nothing?'

'Ah, Panchali. You …you're a wondrous dream, a dream that fills me with purpose. You have fire in your soul and radiate hope in a world where everyone is resigned to a life of defeat … You are why I make this choice, don't you see? '

Panchali stared at him, incredulous. 'Why must I be your dream, your purpose, when you won't be mine? Do you not see …the very hope I feel is because of you?'

'Why must you always respond with a question?'

'Why do you never answer mine, Govinda?'

'Is that what you want?'

'Is that what you'd willingly do?'

'Will you stop?'

'No. Will you?'

Govinda said nothing, and a strained silence followed. Finally, he spoke. 'I can't give you what you want, Panchali,' he softly confessed. 'I can neither fulfil your dreams nor protect you from your fears ...'

Panchali stood up in a single graceful move. 'I understand,' she said, her face taking on a polite distance. 'Govinda Shauri always has a plan, doesn't he? And now his plan involves using me as though I was of no consequence at all ...'

'You amaze me. Surely you'd know by now what is of consequence to me and what isn't?' '

Panchali opened her mouth, intending to say something extremely nasty but gave up in disgust. 'What about me?' she simply asked.

Govinda burst out in a short, incredulous laugh. 'Aren't we both guided by the same belief that a family is more important than the individual, the village more than the family, the nation more than the village, and a federation of nations, an empire, greater than a single nation?'

'What does it matter to you what I believe in?' Panchali snapped.

'Because we have to give up certain things to stand by what we believe in. Emotions, affections – these things just get in the way of what needs to be done. The question is, are you willing to make the sacrifice it'll take?'

'By Rudra,' Panchali said in a horrified whisper, 'what kind of a man are you?'

Govinda's lips curved in a noncommittal gesture. 'I'm just a calculating instrument, Panchali, an unbiased measure of the greater good.'

'Why would you do that? Why become this ... thing, this horrible, insensitive thing?'

'Ah, Princess, what you call inhuman is just dispassion. Without dispassion, we cease to be creatures of reason, and that's the worst thing we can be. But this isn't what you want, is it? I know what goes on in that pretty little head of yours. You want fame and glory; you want to be part of such great deeds that minstrels will sing of you for centuries to come. But I can't offer you that. You'd be rather unhappy with me, I think.'

Panchali regarded Govinda with an unfathomable expression.

He stood up and started to say something, but she snatched her hands out of his grasp and sharply turned away. In a cold, regal tone she said, 'You'd better leave. I'm to be married very soon.' Scathingly, she added, 'Go away, Govinda. The sight of you disgusts me.'

Panchali willed herself not to show any emotion, even though all she wanted to do was spin around and slap Govinda hard for rejecting her in such a callous manner. Shaking with fury and pain she began to walk away, but Govinda reached out and grabbed her wrist. She resisted, refusing to look at him. He laughed at what he saw as petulance, and stepped closer. Panchali tried to ignore his touch, his warm breath on her shoulder, the sensation of having him so close to her. She closed her eyes, unable to understand whether she cherished or hated every moment that they stood this way.

Govinda let go of her wrist, and Panchali almost gasped out loud at the loss. She felt his fingers pull gently at the jewelled pin on the crown of her head. Ever so carefully, he undid the tight, complex braids into which her hair had been set that morning, his fingers weaving through the dark waves of her hair, soothing, comforting. Panchali soaked in every sensation, as he combed each long strand gently with his fingers. She revelled in the very smell of him, mingled with the faint aroma of flowers from her hair. There was something indescribably intimate about the moment. It would be her secret to keep, she decided. He need never know what she felt.

Her eyes fluttered open and her dark, thick lashes glistened with a hint of tears. She studied the lines of his face, etching every curve, every angle into her memory. His eyes were constant, a deep, dark ocean of endless existence. She teetered, suddenly dizzy, and let herself go limp, dreaming of drowning in that eternal ocean, praying silently that it could be so.

Govinda quickly held her, hissing in surprise at her childlike surrender as she let him take her weight. With a wistful shake of his head, he steadied Panchali back on her feet and let go. Instinctively, she reached out to him. He took her hands and squeezed her fingertips in reassurance. Looking steadily into her eyes, he took a couple of steps back, letting her fingers slip out of his grasp till his hands were empty.

They stood in quiet stillness. Somewhere in the palace a gong sounded loudly, announcing to the various guests that the evening's festivities were soon to begin.

'I must go,' Govinda said, gesturing with his head in the direction of the banquet hall. 'I've strained your father's goodwill enough by coming here tonight.'

Panchali dully nodded. Govinda placed a quick, light kiss on her forehead and left. She heard him start whistling a tune as he walked down the corridor, as if he did not have a care in the world.

14

'IMPOSSIBLE!' DHRSTYADYMN EXCLAIMED IN A HUSHED VOICE.

He stood on a dais that commanded a full view of the huge arena. Every pillar and alcove had been decorated with flowers. Golden statues, each the size of a man, gleamed as sunlight streamed in from the circular opening overhead, and auspicious symbols drawn in fragrant pastes on the floors and the walls filled the space with a heavenly smell. Rows of seats for the contestants and royal spectators rose step-like along the walls and the King's ornate throne had been set at the highest level, facing the dais. A pool of crystalline water sparkled in the middle of the arena. From this pool rose a towering pole, on top of which revolved a wheel set with five spokes. At the outer edge of each spoke was the metal sculpture of a fish, hardly larger than the palm of a hand. Despite the minuteness of each statuette, the metal fish had been wrought with immaculate attention to detail, right down to the black orb inside the eyes. Five arrows, one each to pierce the five fish-targets, were arranged on a velvet-lined tray that rested on a low table near a massive, unadorned stone slab, now empty. A powerful iron bow, crafted in the purest of fires and wrought on the hardest of stones, rested askew on the marble floor of the arena.

Next to it, Syoddhan of the Kurus lay in a stunned daze. The rest of the hall was still.

The silence broke. The air filled with shouts and yells. Competitors and spectators alike sprang from their seats and clambered towards the fallen man. Vasusena, the King of Anga and Syoddhan's dearest friend, pushed through the unruly crowd and ran forward to help him. Syoddhan waved him back and slowly stood up. His fingers were still wrapped around the bow. With resigned steps he walked up to the stone slab, set the bow back on it, and returned to his seat. Many of the other contenders, who milled around awaiting their turn, tried to ask him what exactly had happened. He did not even look up.

Panchali was as astonished as everyone else, but she remained as she was on the dais, next to Dhrstyadymn. She tried hard to show no reaction, staring instead at her henna-decorated hands, the fine golden weave of her silk robes, the heavy bangles on her wrists. They proved to be of little use as distractions. Closing her eyes, she tried to focus on the less pleasant sensations she felt – the mild irritation of her large, round earrings brushing against her cheeks, the way her heavy waist-girdle seemed uncomfortably constricting and, above all, the many eyes boring into her, evaluating her usefulness in more ways than one.

Finally, she gave in and glanced at Govinda, sitting on the balcony with Balabadra and the others of their family. He did not seem in the least taken aback and was whispering something to his brother, the expression on his face pleasantly ambivalent. He caught her looking at him and winked cheekily at her before continuing with his conversation.

Panchali turned away at the touch of a hand on her arm. Dhrstyadymn apologetically met her eyes. 'Panchali …' he whispered, not knowing what more to say or do.

'Hush. It's not your fault. We've all been misled …'

Her quiet acceptance cut Dhrstyadymn to the core. He felt sick, enraged even, and wondered if perhaps he ought to do something, anything. Image after terrifying image flashed through his mind, of what might happen next. He tried to think, shutting out the sounds around him – the rising tumult, Panchali calling to him, her touch as she desperately clawed at his arm. Then he heard the twang of a bowstring. Before he could look, the bow sang again – not once, but four times. A stunned silence filled the hall yet again as high above them all the wheel softly creaked to a stop. The five arrows were still embedded in their targets, the metal heads piercing the eye of each wrought metal fish.

The arena exploded with enthusiastic applause and roars of rage. Near the target stood a man dressed in the coarse linen robes of a scholar–sage. His hair had been pulled back into a knot, and a thick beard obscured most of his face. The man's forearms, however, had the tell-tale scars of a professional archer. As ordered, the bards and musicians in the arena had already struck up a victory song, but the atmosphere was far from the jubilant gathering they lyrically described. Insults and jeers rained down on the dubious victor, who was joyfully embracing four other men, all dressed like him in rough ochre robes.

Dhrstyadymn turned to Panchali. She remained expressionless. Even more anxious than before, he looked to King Dhrupad for guidance, but the monarch was sitting with his head in his hands. He somehow found the words, saying them out loud to his sister as though he needed to hear them himself. 'You're bound, upon your honour and mine, to marry that man. To marry whoever wins this tournament.'

'I know,' Panchali evenly replied.

'But … I … we …'

The sounds of dispute, of heated words, began to intrude on their strained conversation. Slowly, the two siblings realized that they were not the only ones who found it strange that some unknown, bedraggled scholar could have succeeded where a mighty prince like Syoddhan had failed at the task.

The disgruntled suitors began to hurl accusations of Panchala trickery and sabotage, their rage rising as the full extent of their humiliation slowly sank in. The musicians stopped playing, as Satrajit gave them an angry shake of his head. The murmur of discontent grew louder still, taking on the trappings of an argument. Some of the gathered nobles gestured towards Panchali. Others strode angrily towards Dhrupad, demanding, rather violently, an explanation for the turn of events. Royal guards instantly got into formation and stood in the way of the angry suitors.

'By Hara! No!' Dhrstyadymn exclaimed as he emerged from his shock. He jumped off the dais and began to make his way towards the centre of the confusion, Panchali right behind him.

'Stay here!' he instructed, over his shoulder.

'No, I'm coming with you!'

'Panchali ...'

Before he could finish the clang of metal rent the air, followed by loud cries of pain. The nobles had attacked Dhrupad's personal guards and three of the men already lay dead. More suitors now joined the fight, though some others, including Syoddhan, watched, uncertain what to do. Hopelessly outnumbered, the guards fought on, even as Dhrstyadymn shouted frantic orders to his soldiers. He bounded across the arena towards his father, as did Satrajit, but both of them knew they were too far away.

More soldiers fell and two of the attacking nobles retired, wounded, but many others took their place. The small space at the foot of the stairs leading to Dhrupad's throne had turned into a battlefield. Panchali winced as she heard the whiplash of a blade descending and the soft, sickening sound of it renting through flesh and bone. 'Father!' she cried and ran towards the throne. She was pulled back by a firm hand around her wrist.

'Let go of me,' she hissed at the bearded man, the supposed victor of her calamitous wedding contest.

'It's not safe,' he cautioned.

Panchali continued to struggle. 'Let go of me, or by Rudra you will not leave this place alive!'

Astonished, the man complied.

Panchali glared at him and his four accomplices, then ran forward to where Dhrstyadymn stood. 'Father ...' she began, and then gave a sigh of relief.

Dhrupad stood by his throne, a little ashen but otherwise unharmed. His would-be assailants were on the ground a few feet away, one of them alive, but barely. Two more had been cleanly beheaded. Towering over them stood Shikandin. He held his bloodied sword casually, resting its tip on the ground, as he glared at the others who thronged in front of Dhrupad's throne. 'We can talk, or we can fight,' he announced matter-of-factly. Panchali wanted to laugh with relief, but settled for squeezing Dhrstyadymn's hand.

Meanwhile, two of the five scholars, such as they appeared, had come up behind the two siblings. The other three had used the moment of confusion to discreetly leave the arena.

'Shikandin!' one of the scholars softly exclaimed.

Panchali was filled with an inexplicable ire. 'That's Prince Shikandin to you!' she snapped.

A loud chuckle punctuated the moment, followed by a familiar voice. 'Ah, you have a tough task on your hands with this tempestuous young woman!'

Panchali turned to see Govinda standing right behind her. His eyes remained on her, as he softly said, 'Take good care of her. She's my life, my very soul.'

'Your Highness, rest assured, I shall.'

Govinda laughed. 'No, I'm no king or prince, for you to address me so. I'm just an ordinary man.'

The archer exchanged looks of surprise with his bearded companion, even as Dhrstyadymn studied them intently. With a polite nod, Govinda walked away.

Panchali now noticed that Balabadra and Yuyudhana were standing next to Shikandin, and the three men were trying to resolve matters. Syoddhan stood listening respectfully as Balabadra spoke to him at length, a familiar hand on the man's shoulder. None could hear the words that passed between them, but Syoddhan first looked amazed, and then confused. Eventually he turned to the angry mob of noblemen and began to act as mediator.

Many of them, including Syoddhan's brother Dussasan and Vasusena of Anga, were not persuaded. They clamoured around and began arguing loudly with Balabadra. It was all the man could do to keep Yuyudhana and Shikandin from striking again. Just as another skirmish seemed imminent, Govinda appeared in their midst. He patiently dealt with each enraged nobleman, meeting their anger with warmth, responding to their insults and their offensives with reason. Soon, the other nobles too were nodding in agreement. But the damage had been done, and little remained of the mood of jubilation expected on such an occasion.

The guests began to disperse, a few of them glaring at Panchali as they passed her. She met their gaze without flinching.

Finally, when the arena was near-empty, she turned to Dhrstyadymn with a determinedly bored expression. 'What now?'

It was the archer–sage who answered, 'Come with me.'

Seething with quiet, cold anger, Panchali silently complied.

To her surprise, the man first led her to one of the small ante-rooms nearby. 'Here,' he thrust a set of rough linen robes in her hand and looked at her haughtily, waiting for her protest. Without a word she began to remove the heavy jewellery she wore. The man went outside to wait while she changed.

A little while later Panchali stepped out of the room, looking surprisingly at ease in the rough attire. The red silk robes she had worn earlier were now neatly folded. Her ornaments – the necklace set with the largest and finest of gemstones, earrings, bangles, anklets and the heavy musical waist-girdle – were placed on the robes. She held out the bundle to the archer. Taking it from her, the archer walked over to where Dhrupad and his sons stood, watching anxiously. He held out the robes and the jewels to Dhrstyadymn, who stared at them, aghast. Reassured by Govinda's firm nod, Shikandin stepped forward instead to take the bundle.

With a defiant nod at them all, the archer took Panchali's hand in his and walked out of the arena. His companion followed them out.

15

PANCHALI'S ESCORTS LED HER QUICKLY AND DISCREETLY THROUGH the city's less frequented alleyways to a small, unremarkable hutment at the edge of the city.

As they approached, a man emerged from inside, exclaiming joyfully, 'Ah, there you are!'

She stared uncertainly at the dignified figure in front of her. He looked to be in his late thirties. His bearing was noble; he had a gentle voice and a countenance that could pass for pleasant. His dark hair fell straight to his shoulders and was slicked back in the style that was common among royalty.

'Welcome, my dear,' he greeted her warmly. Then he addressed the two men who had brought her there. 'Go on, Brothers. I'm sure you'll be glad to look normal again.' The two disappeared into the hut.

So, Panchali noted, these were disguises after all. A sixth man came out of the hut to join the group. She considered his immaculately trimmed beard and his ochre robes sceptically.

'No, that one's genuine!'

Panchali felt her heart skip a beat. Pretending to be unaffected, she casually admonished, 'Really, Govinda! You've got to stop sneaking up on me this way.'

The new voice brought her escorts running out from behind the hut. They too had finished shaving off their ascetics' beards. The five stood side by side, warily looking Govinda up and down.

Moments later, more footsteps were heard, and Balabadra came striding through the undergrowth, looking back at something on the path behind him. He came to stand next to his brother and looked at the five with curiosity. 'By Rudra, Govinda, you were right after all!'

Govinda stepped forward. Bowing low to the first of the men, he introduced himself formally. 'Your Highness, I am Govinda Shauri, your kinsman by birth.'

'What ... how ... How did you know?'

'Ashes don't hide fire, Cousin. I had no doubt that you are Dharma, son of King Pandu of the Kurus and my aunt, Queen Pritha. These, of course, are your renowned brothers, and the scholar–sage there is my old friend, Ayodha Dhaumya of Utkochaka.'

Dharma regarded Govinda and Balabadra uncertainly for

a moment and then broke into a smile. He nodded to the others, and all four of his brothers stepped forward to greet Balabadra, their elder.

Panchali looked on in surprise as each of the brothers introduced themselves – Bhim, a tall, broad-built man with a round face. Partha, dark, with high, chiselled cheekbones, was the archer who had won her. Nakul and Sadev were twins, with handsome, friendly faces. And, of course, the man who had greeted her when she had arrived – Dharma, the eldest and once heir to the Kuru throne.

With a mix of irritation and astonishment she realized that this was probably another part of Govinda's grand scheme. Syoddhan had been nothing more than a means to distract other potential suitors. Partha had been meant to win all along. She didn't bother with anger, and stood there, benumbed, as around her excited greetings were exchanged.

Govinda and the archer were face to face for the second time that day.

'So we meet again, Cousin ...' Partha exclaimed, pulling Govinda into a friendly embrace. If Govinda was bothered by the exuberant display, he hid it well.

With the introductions done, Balabadra declared that it was time for them to leave. 'We don't want to draw undue attention to you ...' he noted. 'But from the look of things I'd say you were preparing to reveal yourselves. About time too.'

'So I'll see you both at the wedding?' Partha asked.

Panchali noticed that Govinda paused for just a moment, searching out Dharma's reaction. He replied, slowly, 'Probably not. I have some matters to attend to ... at Hastina ...'

This time, Dharma's reaction was palpable. 'Thank you, Govinda,' he said softly and sincerely.

'It's my duty, Cousin. The princess here is very special to me. It's the least I can do for her.'

With that, they left. Dhaumya accompanied them, promising to meet with Dharma later.

Govinda nodded at Panchali as he walked past her. It took every bit of self-restraint she had to not scream at him right there. Then he was gone, and Panchali felt inexplicably alone.

'Well ...' Partha looked enquiringly at his eldest brother.

Dharma was lost in thought, a look of consternation on his face. Govinda's declaration that he was headed for Hastina had suddenly opened a whole new world of possibilities. It made Dharma remember something that Dwaipayana and his mother had once told him. Strange, that he should recall such a thing at a moment such as this. But then, he observed, such were the intricacies of destiny, the workings of fate. The opportunity and the justification both lay before him. It was his sacred duty to act.

As a tense silence descended over them all, Bhim gently prompted him, 'Agraja?'

With a sigh, Dharma declared, 'Forgive me, Partha. But as your elder, it is my duty to save us all from sin. You're not conversant with the scriptures on this point, but it's a terrible offence for the younger brother to marry before the older. And so, I must ... I mean, I know it is unconventional that I marry the woman you've won as a prize, but for all our sakes this is how it must be.'

He paused, anticipating much discussion and debate. There was none.

Partha stared at him, eyes burning with fury. Bhim looked as though he wished to say something but could not. Nakul and Sadev spoke volumes with each other through glances they exchanged, but remained silent to the rest of the company.

'As always, Agraja,' Partha finally said, his voice strained, 'we shall obey you. It shall be as you say. Panchali will be yours.'

Dharma spontaneously embraced him, relieved that it had been so easy, surprisingly easy, in fact.

Sadev frowned. He could not hide his concern. 'Agraja ...' he hesitated, and at a nod from Bhim, continued, 'the custom is that the bride marries the victor of the tournament and, in effect, that marriage has already been consecrated. Partha took Panchali's hand

106

in front of the entire gathering. He walked out with her, hand in hand. If she now marries you it makes her wife to the both of you. It would be deemed immoral by most. At the very least, it's not right …'

Dharma responded, 'Morality is subtle; even the gods can't say for sure what is moral and just. I've earned by my word and deed the name that was given to me at birth. I am Dharma.' His pride resplendent, he continued, 'By my own life, I uphold that which is righteous and good. It's impossible for me to think an unrighteous thought, or speak an untruth. That I have considered this idea and come to this conclusion implies that it must be righteous and true.'

'But it's not fair to Partha!'

Dharma clucked his tongue in mild remonstration. 'My dear Sadev, whether it's you, or Partha, or Nakul, or Bhim, nothing is more important to me than your happiness. Our ancestors had a practice, almost a law, I think, where every brother has a right over the wife of his elder. In any case, anything that's mine is yours. If Panchali married two of us, or if she married all five of us … even that wouldn't be against our customs. How, then, can this be improper?'

'But King Dhrupad …?'

'Dwaipayana Vyasa. He will convince Dhrupad to see that there is nothing inappropriate about this. In fact, it's to his advantage to become father-in-law to the future ruler of the Kurus.'

Bhim intervened, 'Are you saying that you plan to go back to Hastina? But our uncle, Dhritarastra …'

'Bhim, think! How can our uncle deny us our birthright? Especially since we're now bound by marriage to one of the most powerful kingdoms of Aryavarta. All the more reason for me to marry the girl, don't you see? And then, there's that man … Govinda …'

The name swept over them like a hopeful gust of wind. One by one, the brothers nodded their silent assent. 'I'm sorry, Agraja,' Sadev softly whispered. Dharma nodded graciously to indicate he had taken no offence.

With that, the brothers dispersed. Dharma walked away with his head held high, trying to remind himself that this was a burden of duty he bore for his brothers, perhaps even a burden of sin.

Nevertheless, he felt jubilant with anticipation. The gorgeous Panchali would be his.

Panchali stood silent, as she had through the exchange between the brothers. The entire conversation had taken place in front of her. Yet, not once had one of the five men glanced at her, leave alone asked what her wishes or desires might be. She was furious; she felt a wrath so terrible that she feared it would burn her. Then, the cold light of reality, of helpless acceptance dawned on her.

My wishes were forsaken long before Partha won me. I was abandoned much before this. All that remains for me to do is to breathe in and out, for whatever time is mine.

Numbed, she stood where she was, till eventually Queen Pritha came bustling out of the hut to lead her inside.

The next day, a little after dawn, Dharma and his brothers were received with respect by Dhrupad and Gandavati at the palace gates. The five now looked the part of the fabled princes of Hastina. The gathered crowd greeted them with warm applause, of which a fair part was genuine, not pre-arranged by Dhrupad.

Panchali was led away to be dressed in ceremonial red silks and then taken back to the arena, where Ayodha Dhaumya, the scholar–priest she had met the previous day, sat in front of the sacred fire chanting the wedding mantras. Dharma stood dressed as the groom, radiant with happiness. At Dhaumya's instructions the couple walked around the fire repeating the sacred vows of marriage. A proud Dhrupad occupied a place of honour, while Gandavati sat alongside a tearful Pritha. A confused-looking Dhrstyadymn and an impassive Shikandin stood to one side. Panchali did not look at them, nor did she search the room for anyone else. Govinda, she knew, would not be there.

The nuptial chamber was splendidly decorated with lamps and flowers. A knock, and then Dharma entered, shutting the door firmly behind him. Panchali rose from her seat and greeted him with the proper degree of hesitation and shyness that was expected of her. She smiled uncertainly as he studied her, a peculiar expression on his face. He slowly walked to stand in front of her, staring, almost breathlessly.

Panchali was no ignorant child, but she had expected a few moments of polite conversation, some small talk. Instead, without a word, Dharma reached out for her upper robe. Suddenly, he checked himself, like he were about to do something despicable. It was then that Panchali understood the emotions that he was struggling with. He was caught between his desire for her, and his hope for a life of near-renunciation, a life devoted to moral pursuits and not material pleasures. She felt disgusted, nauseated at the thought of her own unclean, irresistible, sinful self, which could lead a guileless man astray. To Dharma, she was a symbol of sin, of all that he longed to be free of.

Including politics.

With grim resignation, Dharma silently led her to the bed and they consummated their marriage in a rough, ritualistic way. The two of them did not speak a word after, or through the rest of the night.

The next morning, Panchali rose with the dawn and quietly left the chamber. A solemn calm surrounded Kampilya. The tired revellers of the city were yet to awaken. Thankful for the illusion of privacy, she rushed to the bathing chamber adjoining her own room. But no matter how long she washed herself or wept, every time Panchali remembered the expression on Dharma's face as he had reached out to touch her, she felt sullied all over again.

Dharma did not seek her out that night. Panchali speculated that it would be a while before the pressure to produce an heir overtook his self-imposed asceticism. She was glad. Her room, her bed and her sleep were still her own. Or so she could pretend.

In the early hours of the following morning, she woke abruptly, struggling yet again with the instinctive guilt, the sense of filth and shame that she had felt every moment she had been in Dharma's embrace two nights ago. For a moment, she had the strange feeling that she was looking at two shadows of herself, each caught in the throes of a different point of view. Each had to overcome, to destroy, the other shadow-self in order to survive. She watched as both forms struggled ineffectively, each doomed by its incomplete, hollow nature. Eventually, she gave up and fell back into a medley of dreams in which she laughed and ran through cool, fragrant forests, splashed her feet in the clear water of gurgling streams, danced to the soft rhythm of raindrops as they caressed her skin and hair, and played as a child by a river that flowed through a happy, serene village she had never seen before. She slept without a care, dreaming that she was in the strong arms of a faceless, formless man whom she had always known.

16

UNLIKE MOST OF HIS PEERS, SYODDHAN OF THE KURUS WAS AN outspoken man. Outspoken, but not hasty. The first quality stemmed from his natural inclination towards honesty rather than the moral injunction against untruth most Aryas followed. Ironically, this was why they spoke carefully or not at all. Silence was, for the most part, the accepted corollary to that essential art of the ruling elite: manipulation. In this, too, Syoddhan was rare, if not unique. His diplomacy, as well as his remarkable patience, came from a carefully cultivated apolitical temperament.

Growing up as the eldest among so many, Syoddhan had always been aware of the strong undercurrents, of tempers and politics, in the brothers' personal lives, especially since the time when Queen Pritha had returned to Hastina with his cousins, his uncle Pandu's five sons. Dharma, the eldest of the five, had been seventeen then, and Syoddhan a few months younger. Despite the competitive, even hostile atmosphere around them, Syoddhan and Dharma had become friends, drawn to each other by their need to stay aloof from the complex threads that connected their lives. They had never made an overt show of their friendship, as if both of them had known their brothers would never approve of it. As they grew older they turned into completely dissimilar people, but still remained friends. While

Dharma continued to wear the cloak of high nobility and eschewed all conflict, Syoddhan had changed. He had little choice but to change and become the man he now was – a man who kept honour within and valour without, at the cost of gaining a reputation for neither. It was, he reassured himself, well worth it. The last thing he wanted was to grow bitter, like Dharma.

As a young prince, Dharma had pined for a reputation of valour on par with his brothers and cousins, but refused to seek it. He enjoyed the rush of adrenaline and longed for the thrill of conflict as much as the next prince, but, Syoddhan came to realize, was always hemmed in by his so-called nobility, his loftier notions that left him talking of peace and piety. After a few difficult, even embarrassing incidents in their youth, Dharma crafted an unusual model of compromise that indulged his competitive spirit without compromising on his piety. He would send his brothers into absurdly dangerous situations, taking upon himself the moral burden of having made the difficult decision to do so. Theirs was the claim to courage, while his was the claim to leadership.

Dharma also had a strange way of flaunting his bravery, such as it was. He laid a wager on just about everything. What may have begun as a simple distraction soon took on ridiculous, even perilous proportions. He would bet on the weather, on the outcome of the training jousts between the cousins, on the speed of horses and the memory of men. He would dare his brothers, mostly the indefatigable Bhim, and his cousins to perform near-impossible feats, and then lay a wager on the outcome. It became a habit with him – to wager, and watch.

Not all his bets came off well, and then it was to Syoddhan that Dharma would turn for help. On those occasions, he had an exceptionally persuasive argument. Syoddhan's father was king and, sooner or later, the kingdom would be his, but all Dharma could aspire to was an unblemished reputation. Surely, he would point out, Syoddhan would not deprive him of that? Spurred on by a youthful mixture of guilt and pity, Syoddhan always obliged, sometimes even by assuming the blame for things that had gone wrong – especially in front of Dharma's brothers. And so it was that Dharma's four brothers grew to hate him with a vengeance, while Dharma was looked upon as the epitome of righteous behaviour and nobility.

He had made a mistake, Syoddhan now realized, in more ways than one. His own brothers had not understood what he did or why. They simply thought of him as weak and made up for what they perceived to be his meekness with increased hostility of their own. The blame for that, too, had fallen on him.

Syoddhan gritted his teeth. He knew no one had believed him when he said that he did not want the crown; at least, not enough to fight his own cousins over it. Even Bhisma, the only man to occasionally take his side, had deemed him a trouble-maker and declared him unfit to rule. At that point, Syoddhan had honestly expected Dharma to step forward and exonerate him of the weightier accusations. But Dharma had said nothing, merely taking on the mantle of Crown Prince with humility and grace. For the first time, that day, Syoddhan had lived up to his undeserved reputation, letting his anger get the better of him. He had declared his allegiance to the Crown Prince, but then stormed out of the investiture ceremony before it was over. After that, there was no turning back, no hope of ever convincing anyone that it was not about the crown. Nor was there any hope of keeping his brothers on amicable terms with Dharma's.

When the fire broke out at the palace at Varana, people instantly assumed that Syoddhan had tried to assassinate his cousins. His own brothers did not know that he had actually saved their lives by making sure Vidur found out about the planned attempt. Vidur and, through him, the Vyasa. The thought gave Syoddhan some satisfaction. At least, those who really counted knew the truth. Dwaipayana Vyasa, the eventual decision-maker on the Kuru kingdom's fate had always known what was what.

The role of the Firstborn in general, and the Vyasa, in particular, was something Syoddhan had learnt to accept a long time ago. It had not been a difficult lesson, for he truly believed that the Firstborn acted in Aryavarta's best interests. Dwaipayana, especially, made no secret of his kinship, his bond as grandfather to the Kuru princes, and showed them as much favour and affection as he could within the bounds of his role. For his part, Syoddhan had willingly lent himself to whatever it was that the Vyasa would have him do – including, giving support to his admittedly ageing father's long rule. This once, though, he felt the slightest bit of disappointment with the Vyasa. All Dwaipayana, or for that matter even Grandsire Bhisma, need have done was to command him not to vie for Panchali's hand. Not only would he have stayed away from Kampilya, he would have kept his brothers and friends away as well. The farce that had just played out, the humiliation and disappointment, all of it had been unnecessary.

It still doesn't justify your rage, Syoddhan told himself. *At least, not the anger you feel against Panchali.* He tried to put all thought of her out of his mind, and turned around as he heard someone at the door.

Vasusena walked into the room in a slow daze, his face missing its characteristic scowl. Ever since they had returned from Kampilya to Hastina, the man had remained oblivious to everything but his failure.

Syoddhan placed a hand on Vasusena's shoulder and shook him gently.

The burly king of Anga looked up, appearing incongruously like a disappointed child. 'Did you hear?' he blurted. 'Govinda Shauri of Dwaraka is coming here.'

'Yes, I did, Vasusena. I'm not surprised. You know the Emperor has his sights set on Dwaraka. The Yadus need every friend and ally they can get, especially us. We are, after all, in a position to intercede on their behalf.'

Vasusena did not seem convinced. 'I don't like the man. He's too much of a smooth-talker. I don't like the way he just shoved himself into the middle of things at Kampilya. But, then, I don't like anything that happened at Kampilya …'

Syoddhan cleared his throat. He knew, sooner or later, he would have to ask Vasusena the question. Now was as good a time as any. 'Tell me, what exactly happened back there?'

Vasusena went pale, an unusual reaction indeed for the hardy man.

Lips trembling, he confessed, 'I'm so sorry, Syoddhan. I managed to string the bow, fit the arrow. Then … then …'

'What happened?'

'I don't know. I'd prepared myself so well, there was so much riding on this tournament … I still can't understand how …' Vasusena said, breathing heavily from the sheer effort of recollection. 'It was like, Panchali … she was there, in front of me … The way she looked at me, that haughty, scornful look she gave me, as if I was dirt. Her eyes seemed to say that she'd die before she married me, they taunted me to defy her. I thought everyone could hear her speaking, but by the time I realized no one else could …'

'What did she say?'

'She said she was an Arya woman … she would rather die than marry a Suta … After that my aim … Yabha! I couldn't even see the target anymore.'

Syoddhan felt a pang of regret on his friend's behalf. Vasusena, he knew, had no idea of his lineage or parentage. Abandoned as a child, he had been found and raised by a charioteer, a Suta. If Syoddhan had not given him the vassal lands of Anga to rule, Vasusena would have remained a servant and never become a king. The contest at Kampilya had been his chance to prove that he was no less than those of noble blood, a chance he had now lost.

Vasusena looked at Syoddhan expectantly, his bloodshot eyes begging for reprieve. 'Did you hear her, Syoddhan? Did you hear her say this to me?'

Syoddhan regarded Vasusena with sympathy, not for what the man had endured but because a good man had been reduced to seeking false assurances, needing illusions and excuses behind which to hide.

'I heard her,' he confessed, 'but not what she said to you, only what she said to me …'

'You mean …?' Vasusena looked at him, wide-eyed.

'She called me the blind son of a blind king …'

'Oh Varuna! What sorcery is this?'

'This was no sorcery, Vasusena. It seems you and I were drugged. And, for whatever reason, our deepest fears of rejection and loss were brought forth in our minds. The few men who might actually have fought off the effects of whatever the hallucinogen was – Asvattama, for instance – either didn't compete, or ...'

'Or?'

'Or ... won. Partha, certainly, was meant to. The question remains, who meant for it to be so? Sorcery, as you call it, was once aptly the vocation of sorcerers ... But that's being silly! Such men don't exist anymore. This was probably the Vyasa's doing. After all ...' Syoddhan dismissed the chain of thought with a soft laugh.

'How can you be so casual about what happened?' Vasusena protested. 'Both of us will be the laughing stock of Kampilya, if not all of Aryavarta!'

'Laughing stock. Hah!' Syoddhan exclaimed, his contempt apparent. 'If a man's honour is made or broken by this one thing alone then his is a questionable honour indeed!'

'Maraka! *She* must have known! She must have known, and she watched as we made fools of ourselves. A plague on her head! I can't ever forgive her for this,' Vasusena spat out through clenched teeth.

Syoddhan still looked unconvinced. He was willing to concede that Vasusena deserved better than he had got, but to blame Panchali for what had happened bordered on unfair. 'Let it be, my friend,' he urged kindly. 'We have many feats of valour ahead for you to prove yourself. For the moment, let's turn our minds to the other skill all monarchs require – diplomacy.'

Vasusena sighed. 'Diplomacy ... Of course. So, what do you know about Govinda Shauri?'

'Not as much as I should! His brother, Balabadra, was the one who taught both Bhim and I to wrestle when we were in the Kashi kingdom. But he said little or nothing at all about Govinda. I know the two of them managed to unite the seven squabbling clans of the Yadu dynasty and establish what they call a Confederation of Yadu

115

Nations at Dwaraka. Imagine, a country governed by a Council of Representatives rather than kings and their vassals! Ridiculous and yet charming, I suppose.'

'Even so, bear in mind that our friends, Shisupala of the Chedis and Rukmi of Vidharbha, aren't part of the Confederation ...' Vasusena pointed out.

'And they're openly faithful to Jarasandha ... Like most of us. Which, as I said, is probably why Govinda is coming here – to affirm friendship and kinship with those allied with the Emperor, and build a few diplomatic bridges ...'

'You really think so? You think that's why he's coming?' Vasusena was unconvinced.

Syoddhan's expression was neutral. 'We'll know for sure once he gets here. When did you say he arrives?'

'The day after tomorrow.'

17

GOVINDA FOUND MOST THINGS ABOUT THE KURUS TO BE GARISH and overdone, as though they clung to some archaic past and its glory. For one, their manner of speaking and forms of address, which were rather formal, even during simple conversation. Then there was the way they dressed, the routines they followed and ceremonies they observed on the slightest of occasions. Everything they did seemed to require great preparation and effort. His sudden appearance at Hastina, ahead of his scheduled visit, Govinda knew, went against the established protocol required for an audience with King Dhritarastra. The reaction to his arrival was exactly what he had intended and would suit his purposes splendidly. Amused by the thought, he sat back and examined his surroundings.

The royal assembly hall of the Kuru kings was considered a marvel by many, but Govinda found the endless medley of marble and gold far too contrived and artificial. Especially since just on the other side of these walls were the vast and spectacularly verdant grounds of the palace, the many famed lawns and gardens that seamlessly spread into thick, wild woods. The assembly, he sadly noted, did not have even a window that looked on to the vast stretches of green outside. All ventilation was provided by well-designed skylights that cleverly admitted sunlight and air, but not rain.

The assembly had obviously been built in times when the kings of Hastina had ruled many vassals, for it could seat an extraordinary number of people. At the far end, on an ornate marble dais, was the great Elephant Throne, once the seat of King Hastin himself. The wide throne was meant for both the king and the queen of the Kurus to occupy. On the same level as the Elephant Throne but a little off to the side, was an equally grand seat meant for Bhisma Devavrata, the Regent–Grandsire of Hastina. Its mirror, on the left, was meant for the Crown Prince. Below the dais were austere-looking, but comfortably velveteen seats for the royal advisors and priests, the acharyas Kripa and Dron, and of course, when he visited, DwaipayanaVyasa himself.

The array of glittering seats, however, did little to overshadow the one hundred jewel-encrusted thrones meant for the one hundred sons of Dhritarastra. These were laid out in elevated rows along the length of the hall, on either side of the king's throne. Behind the princes' places were more seats meant for vassals and other dignitaries. At the lower end of the hall, right opposite the Elephant Throne, were a few well-placed seats meant for the king's honoured guests. Govinda had been led to the centremost of these seats when he had entered the hall. He noted with an inward smile that even though the rest of the hall was now full – nearly brimming over, in fact – the places next to him remained empty.

Overhead, the vaulted ceiling rose, dome-like. The fine, pale marble had been carefully chosen to reflect light that came in from small windows set at the base of the dome, and could vary in colour from a fiery dawn-orange to clear, still blue on a bright day. Set into the ceiling were immaculate carvings of gods, celestials and men, in various poses of approval and benediction. Even the residents of Indra's heaven, it was said, gazed down upon the great kings of Kuru.

Govinda was mulling over that particular distinction afforded to his hosts when Syoddhan entered. The smile the host afforded his guest was polite, but hardly effusive. It was, after all, less than a fortnight since they had met at Kampilya. Vasusena strode in close behind, positively spewing fire. Govinda simply returned the man's grimace with a gaze that held mild curiosity, as though Vasusena were an entertaining but assuredly tame pet.

Syoddhan caught the exchange of glances between the two and stifled a chuckle. Govinda's behaviour, though infuriating, betrayed a light-hearted self-awareness. It was impossible to not admire the man's calm confidence.

A trill from the heralds cut in and, immediately, everyone in the assembly stood up. King Dhritarastra entered, his hand resting on his half-brother Vidur's shoulder in a gesture that was now second nature. Blind at birth, Dhritarastra had spent most of his life being led by Vidur. When he had married, his wife, the sighted Queen Gandhari had chosen to bind her eyes and share in Dhritarastra's blindness. She walked in slowly, her hand on Dhritarastra's elbow. Vidur saw the king and queen to the throne and took his customary place behind them. In discreet tones, he would relay all that transpired in the assembly exactly as it occurred, without bias. Only when asked would the minister proffer his opinions. Of course, it was well-known that he was often, if not always, asked and his advice unfailingly followed.

Govinda bowed to the king and queen, to the key elders, and finally to the gathering at large. He smiled with genuine warmth at Vidur, who returned the gesture with an affectionate nod. The assembly was then formally commenced and an elaborate message of welcome was read out by the crier. Much as Govinda would have liked to get on with his business here, it was not the formal order of things. He sat back, thanked the attendant who served him honeyed liquor, and prepared to be entertained.

The court minstrels stepped forward and began by invoking the blessings of the ancestors of the Kurus and narrating their tales of valour. Then, strumming their instruments, they broke into a compelling performance – a song naming each and every one of Dhritarastra's one hundred sons and his daughter.

All hail the one hundred resplendent scions of Kuru,
Beginning with Syoddhan, Hastina's future king
Hail his faithful captains Dussasan and Dursahana
And the brothers Dursalan, Jalagandhan and Samana.
Sahan, Vindhan, Anuvindhan and Durdharshan of keen sight,
Subaahu, Durpradharshan, Durmarshanan of might
Durmukhan, Durshkarnan, Vikarnan and Saalan
Sathwan the pure, Sulochanan and Chithran.

Upachithran, Chithraakshan, Chaaruchithran, Saraasanan;
Great men all, and this kingdom's fortune.
Durmadan, Durvigaahan, Vivitsu, the wise.
Vikatinandan, Oornanaabhan, Sunaabhan of fiery eyes.

Nandan, Upanandan, Chithrabaanan the meritorious,
Chithravarman, Suvarman, Durvilochan the glorious
Ayobaahu, Mahaabaahu, Chithraamgan of strong arms
Chithrakundalan, Bheemavegan, Bheemabalan, of burly charms.

Vaalaky, Belavardhanan, all deserving great praise
Ugraayudhan, Susenan, fashioned with divine grace
Kundhaadharan, Mahodaran, Chithraayudhan, Nishamgy
Paasy, Vrindaarakan, each with the strength of an army.

Dridhavarman, Dridhakshathran, Somakeerthy, Anthudaran
Dridhasandhan, Jaraasandhan, Sathyasandhan
These brothers hold the land in their sway
For their victory we shall ever pray.

Sadaasuvaak, Ugrasravas, Ugrasenan the unvanquished,
Senaany, Dushparaajan, of honour untarnished.
Aparaajithan, Kundhasaai, Visaalaakshan, the valiant,
Duraadharan, Dritahasthan, Suhashtan, the radiant.

Vaathavegan, Suvarchan, Aadithyakethu, named after the Sun,
Bahwaasy, Naagadathan, Ugrasaai, Kavachy and Kradhanan.
Kundhy, Bheemavikran, Dhanurdharan, the peerless,
Veerabaahu, Alolupan, Abhayan, the fearless.

Dhridhakarmaavu, Dhridharathaasraya, brothers of stout heart,
Anaadhrushya, Kundhabhedy, of courageous part.
Viraavy, Chithrakunthalan, men of exceptional grace
Pramadhan, Amapramaadhy, the scions of their race.

Deerkharoman, Suveeryavaan, Dheerkhabaahu, of noble manner;
Sujaathan, Kaanchanadhwajan of the golden banner.
Kundhaas and Virajass answer the battle call,
As does Yuyutsu, beloved to us all.

Dussala fills the air with her laughter,
Sister to great princes and the King's sweet daughter.
Sing well, ye bards, sing of Kuru's lords –
Of the mighty warriors, who outshine the gods.

Govinda inwardly smirked at the performance. Dhritarastra, it seemed, found his virility some compensation for his blindness, and took every opportunity to flaunt the sheer number of his progeny.

At last, the entertainers retired and a herald stepped forward to announce the guest in sonorous tones. 'Govinda Shauri Varshneya Yadau. Govinda, son of Shura, of the Vrishni clan of Yadus.'

Suppressing the desire to chuckle, Govinda stood up. Adopting the formal tones expected of him in the assembly, he said, 'My king, I come as your friend and kinsman. As I am nephew to your brother Pandu, thus also do I share with you the very same bond. I pray you, welcome me into your home as your son. Queen, my respected aunt Gandhari, grant me your blessings as you would to your own child.'

Barring Vasusena and a few other disgruntled vassals, the entire gathering was impressed. Govinda had a way with words that made even the formal, overbearing speech of the royal assembly sound sincere and passionate. Syoddhan found himself smiling openly, and Bhisma and Dron exchanged appreciative glances. In a rare show of approval, Dhritarastra gestured to Vidur, and with his help began descending from the dais. Govinda rushed forward to support the blind monarch.

Dhritarastra grasped the young man by his arms, and said, 'Welcome, my son. You are always welcome here, as kinsman and ... Why, you were once our neighbour too!'

The assembled audience laughed softly at the remark. He continued, 'I'm an old man, so forgive me if I should lovingly chide you for not remembering your uncle Dhritarastra all these years. But then, you are young and wilful, as well you should be. I'm only too glad that you've chosen to renew old bonds. Crown or not, you are Arya, and our kinsman.'

Govinda inclined his head in graceful admission. He did not miss the barbs behind Dhritarastra's words, the subtle reference to the surrender of Mathura, Govinda's ancestral kingdom, which had shared a border and part of the woodlands known as Madhu with Kuru. He also did not miss the clear insinuation that the bonds of old no longer existed. Indeed, Dhritarastra had not shirked from hinting at the reason. By law and custom, Govinda was little better than a foot-soldier. To forfeit a crown, to surrender and become ruler of nothing – men like Dhritarastra would find it unthinkable. Govinda, however, did not take the slightest offence. In fact, he enjoyed the verbal sparring, admitting the monarch's talent with a deferential smile. In any case, he knew, his next little joust would take them by surprise.

'Uncle, I ask that you allow me to present you with a small token of my affections,' he said, in the standard prelude to the inevitable routine of gifting treasures to the host.

'Thank you, my son.'

Govinda nodded to a waiting attendant, and then personally guided Dhritarastra back up the stairs to his throne. Positioning himself a few steps below, he watched impassively while attendants brought in some trays and uncovered them to reveal heaps of gold and silver coins as well as precious gemstones and finely crafted jewellery. Vidur softly described the contents of each tray to the royal couple, even as the many noblemen present whispered among themselves.

It was a sizeable fortune, no doubt, but hardly remarkable. The value aside, none of the gifts were novel, nor did they inspire interest. The coffers of Hastina were full, not just with wealth but with many curiosities from foreign lands, truly astonishing items. Most monarchs saw the ritual exchange of gifts as an opportunity to peacefully assert their power and supremacy. While sheer wealth never failed to impress, it was often the souvenirs of their travels and conquests that were eagerly awaited by one and all. Never-before-seen creatures, sometimes captured alive, unthinkable gadgets and devices, and of course new weaponry – all these showed the extent of the monarch's influence, his pioneering vision and valour. Govinda's gifts were decidedly commonplace.

With just the slightest tinge of derision, Dhritarastra thanked him, 'These are more than merited on this occasion, Govinda. Your affection for us has caused you to be too generous.'

'But of course not, Uncle! Your son Dharma has brought home the first of your daughters-in-law – the princess of Panchala, no less. In fact, I'd hoped to find them here and give them their gifts in person. As it happens, I left Panchala many days ago to meet with my clansmen and conduct these trinkets here …'

Syoddhan was forced to admit that Govinda had played the move admirably. For the past two weeks his father had been ignoring the inevitable tides of change, the fact that the sons of Pandu were alive and well. Now, thanks to Govinda, they would be forced to invite Dharma home along with his brothers and his new bride. Once that happened, the issue of succession to the Kuru throne would arise yet again. Even if Dharma's position as Crown Prince was not in doubt, Dhritarastra would be pressed by Dharma's father-in-law, King Dhrupad, and *his* allies to step down and let the next generation come into its own.

Dhritarastra realized as much, for his face contorted into a grimace of disgust, which he tried, at once, to hide. 'Ah, yes,' he began, in a

122

dismissive way. 'Dharma and my daughter-in-law. For the lack of an auspicious day to welcome them I'm yet to send them an escort, as is customary when we Kurus bring our brides home. I'm sure that the moment a suitable alignment of the stars is found for such travel, the royal escort shall conduct them here with all speed.' His malice unspent, he turned on Govinda. 'I shall ensure that your gifts to the bride and groom aren't missed in the multitude of treasures that await them here. Rest assured that I will personally point out how generous you have been.'

The king words provoked a titter of laughter around the assembly.

Govinda waited for the crowd to settle down and then gently said, 'In that case, Uncle, I'd be happy to leave it all in your charge. But I'm afraid I'll have to trouble you further ...' He continued, answering the questioning look on Dhritarastra's face, 'If you and my dear aunt should care to step outside ... I apologize that my choice of gifts are not of an adequately dainty nature to be presented to you here.'

'There's more?'

'But *of course*, Uncle.'

Govinda took Dhritarastra's arm and led him to the large golden doors fronting the hall. Vidur and Gandhari followed. Behind them the courtiers scrambled towards the entrance, careful only to not precede Dhritarastra. The doors were opened and the audience poured out on to the sprawling steps out front. As one, they gasped and then broke into excited chatter.

'By Varuna!' Syoddhan exclaimed and, unable to resist, collegially clapped a hand on Govinda's back. He received a genuinely friendly smile in return.

Dhritarastra was shaking a flabbergasted Vidur's shoulder. 'Well?' The minister had to shout to be heard above the crowd and, even then, fumbled for the words to describe the scene that greeted them.

A procession was making its way down the wide sand road that stretched from the palace gates, across immaculate green gardens, toward the assembly hall. Where the grounds of the palace had been designed to impress, the host entering it was even more awe-inspiring. One hundred and eight massive elephants in rows of nine abreast, their heavy ivory tusks trailing the sand, pulled behind them what looked like a long wooden palace set on wheels. As the convoy neared, liveried men atop the houses let fall huge squares of silken cloth. Syoddhan laughed out loud with joy. The elephants pulled not one long structure, but a trail of three shorter ones.

'Barges,' he informed his father. 'They look as sturdy as sea-faring ships, but are much sleeker in design and smaller too. I suspect they're lighter as well?' the last query was directed at Govinda.

'Yes. It's possible to use a lighter wood for freshwater crafts. Unfortunately, these wouldn't last more than a season in seawater.'

'By Indra's white elephant, Govinda, this is a prize fit for an Emperor!' Syoddhan instinctively exclaimed.

Govinda did not reply, though he did notice the flash of anger that crossed Dhritarastra's face, yet again.

Behind the procession of elephants was a convoy of horses, enough to seat an entire cavalry battalion. The horses were of the Qamboja breed, the same as Balahak, though not one of these was the pure silver-white that Govinda's four steeds were. Each stallion carried on its back a trunk-like box made of either silver or gold. Govinda signalled to the attendants leading the horses to bring one each of the boxes closer for inspection.

A shrill cry of excitement arose from one of the gathered nobles, while another let out the happy shriek of a child, as the boxes were opened. The box of gold contained innumerable perfectly rounded pearls of the most translucent paleness; the silver box yielded many pieces of a dark blue gemstone that was not native to Aryavarta. In fact, some courtiers dismissed the stones as pebbles, opaque and rounded as they were, but it was only when Syoddhan raised a large piece to the light that what had looked opaque was seen to be a medley of striations in every imaginable shade of blue.

'They reminded me of the skies of Aryavarta,' Govinda casually commented, picking up one of the gemstones and handing it to Syoddhan.

'They're magnificent!' Syoddhan acknowledged. He passed the stone to Gandhari, who ran her hands over its polished surface and beamed, as though her mind's eye still held the memory of having seen it in youth or, perhaps, she could imagine its beauty.

'I'll have them set for you in a necklace of diamonds and gold, Mother,' he gently told her. 'One fit to grace a queen's neck.'

Gandhari laughed and reached out to pat Syoddhan lightly on his cheek. 'Thank you, my son. And thank *you*, Govinda,' she said.

Govinda merely bowed, his head lightly resting on Gandhari's hand for a moment so that she would know. He then signalled to another attendant. The man came forward bearing a nondescript wooden trunk, far smaller than the ones containing the jewels.

'What treasure is this, Govinda?' Syoddhan jested. 'Knowing you, I'd say the humble box houses the most valuable jewel of them all!'

'Quite so,' Govinda confirmed, laughing. 'But, I'm afraid I must disappoint you by requesting you to pass this on, with my best regards, to the Vyasa, Krishna Dwaipayana.'

'Of course. But may I take a look?'

'Please …' Govinda personally opened the box, to reveal many different-sized scrolls made either of thick parchment or animal hide. He nodded, at which Syoddhan reached in to pick out a scroll at random and unrolled it.

'What in Varuna's name …?' Syoddhan clucked his tongue in appreciation as it struck him. 'A map?'

'Yes,' Govinda replied. 'I had my mariners and scouts prepare maps of all the places that we've sailed to. Of course, as you can see, some of the further coastlines remain incomplete or lack fine details, but whatever is recorded is accurate. You'll have all the time you want to study them,' he added, as a look of longing began to spread across Syoddhan's face. 'I intend for these to remain here at Hastina.'

Syoddhan made no secret of his delight.

Over the next couple of days, Govinda earned for himself immense goodwill among the Kurus, to the extent that Dhritarastra arranged for the royal astrologer to discover a rather propitious change in the alignment of the stars. As a result, the celestial bodies now afforded for Dharma and Panchali to be brought home to Hastina much sooner than had been originally expected. An escort was despatched with instructions to bring Dharma, his mother, brothers and Panchali to Hastina as soon as Dhrupad permitted.

Govinda treated the news of the sudden fickleness of the immutable skies with due solemnity. He commented blandly on the mysteries of destiny and the will of the gods and ended by expressing his regret that he could not stay to welcome the bride and groom. He left Hastina and made straight for Dwaraka, though Kampilya was less than a day's ride away. Somehow, Govinda felt as if he was at the end of a long, tiring journey. For the time being, Aryavarta would have peace. Ghora Angirasa would be forgotten for some time, and it would take a while for the inevitable conspiracies to start all over again. Until then … He breathed in deep of the fresh evening air and threw all thoughts of the future out of his head. Soon he would be home. He would sleep well, one with the rhythm of the ocean.

18

IN THE WEEKS THAT FOLLOWED PANCHALI'S WEDDING, THE RAINS set in. By the time she, Dharma and the others were ready to leave Kampilya, the roads were flooded and in many places the River Ganga had spilled over her banks. In all, it would make for a slow, soggy journey to Hastina, especially since Pritha, Panchali's mother-in-law, would make the trip in a large palanquin. Such low-slung litters, which took anything from two to eight men to carry, made for a slow and restful ride on longer journeys despite the vagaries of the terrain. Carriages and elephant-mounted platforms could be bumpy and often went too fast for the occupants' comfort.

In addition to Pritha's palanquin, over fifty other litters were deployed to carry the array of precious, sometimes fragile items in Panchali's dower. The sturdier things were loaded on to well-decorated elephants and horse-drawn wagons, the animals themselves forming a fair portion of her generous dower. After all, Dhrupad had insisted, Panchali was his only daughter.

The scale of these events made Panchali feel all the more like a helpless puppet, and she took to acting the part of a childish, petulant princess because it was all she could be. She knew she would regret it later, but for now she found herself quibbling incessantly over trivialities, pausing only to curse Govinda Shauri and his infernal meddling. Her petulance turned out to be of some use, for an exhausted Dhrupad eventually gave in to his daughter on one count. He agreed to her bridal escort being unconventionally small, barring the ceremonial guard of honour who would travel to Hastina and then return to Kampilya.

Panchali also adamantly refused the huge retinue of handmaidens and attendants that had been placed at her disposal, insistent that she would not separate them from their families. Instead, she asked for volunteers from among her sairandhari and welcomed the two ladies who came forward. Finally, feeling terribly sad about leaving her brothers behind, Panchali set out for her new home, and her new life, both of which, she feared, would be insignificant and boring.

She could not have been more mistaken.

The surprises began from the moment Panchali entered Hastina. While thousands thronged the streets, crying out their welcome, the city itself had little of the festive look she had expected. But before she could dwell on it further, they had entered the palace. Unlike the undulating lands on which Dhrupad's fort at Kampilya stood, Dhritarastra's palace was set on level ground, which made the enclosure seem more sprawling than it actually was. It also appeared that there was no garrison, or even a small force, within the environs of the palace. Instead, most of the space had been given over to well-manicured gardens dotted with dazzling recreation pavilions. Panchali quickly learned from one of the guards in their escort that the armies were quartered at the far end of the city, just behind the royal enclosure, but it still shocked her that the palace was so obviously undefended. Clearly, the kings of Hastina took their pleasures seriously.

The group was shown directly into the assembly hall, which Panchali had heard so much about. Her attention, however, was drawn neither to its sky-like ceiling, nor to the huge gathering of royals it accommodated. Instead, her gaze fell immediately on a slight but majestic figure. The Queen.

Gandhari had to be the stateliest and most imposing woman Panchali had ever seen, and came across as a stark contrast to the homely Pritha. She was slender, with features that still showed traces of the beauty of her youth, but it was not her attractiveness that took one's breath away. It was the way she held herself, with a subtle pride that came partly from who she had been and mostly from what she had done. Panchali had heard how, as a young bride, Gandhari had chosen to forever cover her eyes the moment she discovered her husband was blind.

Had it been out of love, Panchali wondered. *Or was it spite?* The story, as she had heard it, went that the strong and valiant princes of Gandhara had refused to wed their sister to the blind Dhritarastra. Outraged by the rejection, Bhisma had laid waste to their country with his armies, personally killing all but one of Gandhari's many brothers. Shakuni, the sole survivor, now led an almost servile existence at Hastina as some unimportant functionary or the other – a rather dishonourable end for one who had once been a great prince. Perhaps brother and sister had both thought to be constant reminders to Bhisma and the Kurus of what they had done to the people of Gandhara.

Panchali turned her attention back to the assembly as Dharma formally introduced her. She gracefully saluted all those gathered with an elaborate bow, ignoring the hushed whispers that hurtled around. She knew they were mostly varied tales of her wedding, of how she had been won by the younger brother, who had led her home by the hand, only to be wedded the next day to his eldest sibling. Slander was inevitable with all that had happened and Panchali refused to be affected by it. The enigmatic smile on her lips did not fade for even a moment. She took her seat next to Dharma and feigned a polite air of disinterestedness as the assembly went through the affairs of the kingdom for the day. In truth, Panchali missed neither a single word nor the most subtle of gestures.

In what was to be the greatest surprise for her as yet, Dhritarastra very matter-of-factly conferred on Dharma the western half of the Kuru kingdom, with its capital at a place known as Kandava. Panchali felt elated at that, but she was also inexplicably disappointed. It was not that she expected such an announcement to be accompanied by great celebration or a vulgar show of grandeur, but she did think some degree of gravity was warranted. Dharma and his brothers, however, did not seem at all upset. Next to her, Partha and Bhim exchanged whispers, noting with glee how furious Syoddhan was. She glanced over at Syoddhan but saw nothing in his expression that suggested displeasure. True he was not jubilant, but he seemed far from jealous or irked.

It made sense, Panchali silently noted. By giving away a part of his kingdom, Syoddhan could ensure that he held on to Hastina. Rather, that his father did. Dhritarastra looked much older than her own father, and Panchali found it surprising that he had not installed his son on the throne as yet. Perhaps he did not think that Dussasana, the third of his sons, would let his brother rule in peace. Panchali had heard much about the younger Kuru prince, none of it complimentary. His behaviour served to immediately justify the reputation he had earned, for even at that very moment the lecherous rogue was alternating between looking her up and down and glaring at the five brothers. It took much effort on her part to ignore him, but she did just that.

After a while Pritha, the five brothers and Panchali left the assembly for the small palace that had been made over for their use. Dharma led Panchali out with obvious pride. She chuckled silently at the warmth he suddenly exuded toward her, realizing that she had perhaps finally garnered a little of her husband's respect as an individual in her own right. But she also knew that with Dharma things were always complicated. Equality was something that he would graciously bestow on her as long as she did not take it as her due.

19

Hardly had she reached the rooms set aside for her in the palace than she was swamped in a rush of visitors as the various royal ladies of Hastina came to welcome the eldest daughter-in-law of the Kurus. After nearly three hours of polite smiling and light talk comparing the weather and landscape of Kampilya and Hastina, Panchali had reached the limit of her patience. She found herself wondering, for the first time as far as she could remember, if things might perhaps have been different if she had been born to her role as princess and queen. She had been a misfit at Kampilya and felt all the more so at Hastina, and right then she was far too tired to be convinced otherwise.

Just as she had flopped down on a huge, cushion-lined seat in a decidedly ungraceful manner, there was a yet another knock on her door. Panchali assumed it was her sairandhari, coming to announce one more royal lady. Irritated beyond measure, she snapped out, 'By Varuna, Asila, if that's another one of those dim-witted cows who've done nothing in their lives other than reduce their country's coffers with their dower, I shall scream.'

She jumped as a man's voice responded, 'Dim-witted I surely am, Mahamatra, but hopefully not a cow. May I come in?'

Panchali stood up and turned around, more anxious than embarrassed, but felt instantly at ease at the sight of the kind, genial figure she saw standing in the doorway. She had heard of Vidur, the youngest of the three half-brothers, the sons of Vyasa Dwaipayana. Despite the common talk that he was born of a slave-maid, the man looked no less an Arya than his brother, the King. Like her father, Vidur was well-kept for his age and exuded great energy. His silver-white hair made him look rather distinguished and his bearing clearly marked him as a scholar rather than a warrior. Panchali found herself thinking that as Dharma grew older he might come to look something like the man now standing before her.

'Forgive me. Please come in,' she bowed respectfully.

Vidur clucked his tongue in gentle remonstration. 'No, my dear, don't ever bow to me. Remember, you'll be queen of these lands!'

'Everyone needs the blessings of their elders and betters. A queen more so than others.'

Vidur's eyes sparkled with amusement. 'Ah yes, he did tell me it wouldn't be easy to have the last word with you around.'

'Who …?'

'Why, my nephew, Govinda,' Vidur replied. He saw the confusion on Panchali's face and explained, 'I'm married to his aunt, one of Queen Pritha's cousins …'

If Vidur found Panchali's silence at this unusual, he said nothing about it. Instead, he came straight to the point. 'I was in the assembly this morning – Dhritarastra's court – as you may have noticed … Panchali, Hastina is not kind to women who believe themselves a man's equal. Our ancestry is rife with many examples, some of which I find, shall we say, regretful. We don't deal well with royal ladies in active roles, and those who choose passive roles are more than amply rewarded by being held up as ideals.'

Inclining her head slightly to one side Panchali asked, 'Are you here to suggest that I learn to do the latter?'

'Would you accept such a suggestion?'

'If Govinda has told you anything useful about me, then you know I won't.'

'In that case I won't waste my time and yours with futile suggestions …'

'But you *will* let me have the benefit of your wisdom, won't you?' Panchali said, letting the man know her intent had not been to offend him.

'Hmm,' Vidur was noncommittal. 'All I can suggest, my dear, is that you decide the price you're willing to pay for your beliefs.'

'If they are negotiable,' Panchali pointed out. 'Aren't principles supposed to be beyond question, beliefs that are worth every sacrifice?'

'Would you consider discretion a high price to pay?'

Panchali was puzzled. 'To pay for …?' she asked.

'For … let's say, the respect of the Kurus,' Vidur replied.

'I'd consider it a terribly high price. Because this is not an issue about women. This is about the underlying hierarchies, the very belief that a formal system of inequality is just and fair.'

Vidur was impressed, and he let it show. 'And you'd suffer on par with the others trapped in the system as a matter of principle?'

'The suffering is irrelevant. I don't see myself as a self-sacrificing do-gooder. To be honest, if I could extract myself from the system by my own efforts, I would. But I wouldn't do it by conceding my beliefs. All that will achieve is the creation of one more layer, or class, in the system. Either I do wrong, in which case perhaps I don't deserve such respect. Or I stand by my beliefs no matter how I'm treated.'

'Words!'

'No, not just words …' she protested.

Vidur looked at her with warmth. 'Dharma and his brothers are fortunate to have you with them, Panchali,' he said. 'You are indeed a daughter to be proud of and a counsellor to cherish. But an argument is an argument, and so I'll say this … There's one thing you will realize when you grow to be as old as I am; unfortunately, never sooner. To uphold one principle you sacrifice another; to preserve one notion of goodness and righteousness you destroy another. Where then is the question of an absolute, immutable principle?'

Panchali stared at the man, amazed. But soon she was frowning, thinking through the argument Vidur had presented, and a few moments later she demurely conceded defeat.

'Don't take what I say seriously, my dear,' said Vidur kindly. 'My notions are quite antiquated, or revolutionary, depending on your perspective.'

'Surprising you should think so. All of Aryavarta knows you as the wisest of advisors.'

'I don't know if that is despite my lineage, or because of it,' Vidur jested. 'But my unique position does have its advantages. Hastina has for long been a key centre for the Firstborn. Not only does it have the most impressive collection of scrolls and manuscripts, all lovingly tended to by a congregation of dedicated scholar–sages. Few other cities in Aryavarta can even claim to have a library.'

'A library?'

Panchali's excitement was palpable, for Vidur smiled and added, 'The manuscripts are in an underground vault, and only a handful of Firstborn scholars know the location. Fewer still are allowed inside, for it is also one of the sites of the Vyasa's great undertaking. He has, as you might have heard, set about compiling all the knowledge of Aryavarta, even our knowledge of the lands beyond the seas. Much of what was orally transmitted from scholar to scholar in the past is now being set down in writing. His students travel to the furthest corners of Aryavarta, even to foreign lands, to learn from scholars there, as well as to teach from our scriptures. Hastina is one such place where many come to share their knowledge. Of course, that such things happen here is not very widely known …'

'I hadn't imagined in my wildest dreams that Hastina would hold this particular surprise,' Panchali gushed. 'I was under the mistaken impression that the Firstborn believed in strictly controlling knowledge, that there were many parts of the scriptures they alone were allowed to learn. Indeed, scrolls and books – these aren't things one readily associates with them.'

'Ah! Then yes, you were mistaken, though perhaps not that much. Codification can be a way to control access to knowledge. The Firstborn believe in a method by which the obvious is obscured, and then permanently recorded, copied and circulated. That way it shall never perish, but will also remain safe from misuse. They can leave the object in plain view, as long as they hide the key to it.'

'Like a secret message or a cipher,' Panchali commented.

'Hmm … Something like that, though not so obviously secretive. As you know, even among the Aryas not everyone can read or write to a scholarly level, and it's very rare to find Sutas, like me, who can read. To achieve a level of understanding that can penetrate the mysticism the Firstborn douse all knowledge in isn't easy. This project was on even in Dwaipayana's father Parashara's time, but it has taken on a new lease of life in recent years. The Firstborn scholars have taken to collecting anything and everything they can, zealously hoarding every bit of useful knowledge they can get their hands on. For the past decade or so, Govinda has been travelling all over the world for this very purpose, collecting various records that the Vyasa deems important to the future of Aryavarta.'

'Yes, I see ...' Panchali faltered, as she understood what had kept Govinda on the high seas all these years. *If only he showed those who've always been loyal to him a fraction of the loyalty he has for the Firstborn ...*

'Panchali ... ? Are you all right?' Vidur asked, concerned.

She managed a smile. 'Yes, yes. I'm sorry ... I don't know where I lost myself.' To change the topic, she asked, 'Have you seen these vaults, Your Highness?'

Vidur leaned forward and in a hushed, conspiratorial whisper said, 'I'll tell you, on one condition ...'

'Anything you say,' Panchali affirmed.

'Stop calling me Highness, Panchali. I'm just the son of a slave-maid. It won't do to address me this way, especially in the presence of others.'

Panchali looked at the courtier with surprise. 'How does everyone address you? Dharma, his brothers, how do they all address you?'

'They all call me Kshatta, or Dasi-putra, the son of a female slave,' Vidur replied, 'it'll be fine if you call me Kshatta.'

Panchali pouted in disapproval. 'What about Govinda? How does he address you?' she asked.

Vidur hesitated, then said, 'He calls me Uncle Vidur.'

'Then,' she stated, 'I shall take the liberty of doing the same. And now, Uncle, since I've met your condition, you must answer. Have you seen the vaults?'

'Yes,' Vidur nodded, 'I've seen the vaults. And I can tell you that what's written down is just one-fifth of that great treasure hoard that still lies in the minds of those who are at work on this task. But in this lifetime or the next, this task will bear fruition.'

Panchali's eyes widened. 'Amazing!' she whispered. 'What passion, what great foresight the kings of Hastina must have had to create such a thing, a vault for the storage of books and manuscripts ...'

'Hastina's kings!' Vidur said, and then clucked his tongue in mock regret. 'I didn't know any king of Hastina in the last twenty generations who has had that kind of good sense. Nor did our dear friends, the Firstborn, have the ability to build something of that sort. The vault that houses the treasure-trove of the Firstborn was, as strange as it may sound, built by the Firewrights.'

'The Firewrights?' Panchali exclaimed. 'You mean the magicians? But I thought ...'

Vidur laughed out loud, amused by her reaction. 'My dear child, the Wrights were no such thing! They were great scholars, committed to logic, reason and scientific discovery. Only the ignorant see their work as magic, sorcery or evil. What today is the vault once used to be a great workshop, a forge.'

'What? But ...'

'Let me explain. The Wrights, in all fairness, were genius scientists. It suited the Firstborn to label them as demons and heathens, and denounce their science as magic. Needless to say, it also made it easier to then get rid of anyone who took their side – as many of Aryavarta's kings did, some generations ago, in their own interest, mind you.'

Panchali failed to hide her amazement. 'Unbelievable ...' she gasped.

'Ah my dear, I wonder how you will react to the next bit of unbelievable trivia that I am going to share with you ...' Vidur's eyes twinkled as Panchali looked at him eagerly.

In a low voice that held a faint touch of regret he began, 'They once had such workshops in each of the nations of Aryavarta. Not very long ago the Firewrights fuelled all the industry in Aryavarta, making us the mightiest empire in the world. But, like heat and light from the same lamp, the fire is now dim and the light fades. The order is broken and the last of the Wrights are dead. You see, the Wrights became far too powerful, their knowledge far too extensive and beyond understanding, and so for decades both seers and kings have worked hard to stamp out what they considered a menace and take control of all Wright knowledge. But they ... we ... have perhaps been too successful. For with the Wrights has died their vast store of knowledge. Some of it was destroyed by us and some of it lost by them. It leaves us in a far more precarious position than we're willing to admit. If ever we were attacked by foreign invaders ...'

'But surely,' Panchali argued, 'necessity would drive us to industry and inquiry. Great as the Wrights may have been, it is not impossible to emulate their discoveries, is it? Especially if, as you say, it's a matter of survival?'

'No, it's not impossible. Indeed, that is what prompted the Firstborn to begin recording all that is left of our knowledge, as well as add what we can that is new. But they have learnt from the Firewrights' mistakes, and so they do their best to control knowledge, cloak it, making themselves the all-powerful interpreters and arbiters of all access to this knowledge. They can never be wiped out the way the Firewrights were because we need them. Their survival is essential to ours.'

'Be that as it may, isn't codification and control a good thing? You said that we need knowledge and discovery to survive, and now we have the Firstborn to protect us, our knowledge ...'

Vidur gave a sad chuckle. 'That is what many believe. That is certainly what my father – Dwaipayana – would have us believe. Perhaps you're right, my dear, it is better to have something than nothing at all. But as far as survival goes ...' he shook his head. 'We stand on the shoulders of giants. It's one thing to build on the collective wisdom of generations, and another to survive but begin afresh. The first Angirasa was Fire itself, one who learnt that this mighty element could be worshipped and tamed to our use. It seems commonplace today, but imagine: What if we somehow lost that first discovery, the fundamental idea that we can create fire using flint? Why, the very moral fabric of Aryavarta would be threatened. We would be nothing but primitive animals – hardly the noble race that worships the sacrificial fire as a symbol of Divinity. And that is the problem. With the Wrights gone not only have we lost a line of inventors and philosophers, but we have also lost the huge legacy of knowledge that was in their keeping. Aryavarta may soon be in the dark. Few men ... or women ... remain, who would dare question the Firstborn, and with good cause. Time and again Dwaipayana has proved himself worthy of receiving First Honour at every gathering of Aryas and the entire realm looks to him as its conscience-keeper. It is my unique position – as his son and a man of no consequence, unlike my half-brothers – that gives me leave to say what I think.'

Vidur paused and then suddenly said, 'But enough. I'm an old man and I pontificate like one. Come, let's walk around the gardens and I shall show you where the best flowers in all of Aryavarta bloom.'

Keeping her thoughts to herself, Panchali silently followed.

20

IT TOOK A FEW WEEKS FOR PANCHALI TO REALIZE THAT DHARMA had no say whatsoever in the running of the Kuru kingdom. Not even his half of it. In fact, he showed little interest in participating in its governance and appeared to have no intentions of leaving Hastina. Though he received many, if not all reports on the political affairs of the Kuru kingdom, he seemed easily bored by them and mostly left to Panchali the drudgery of going through the scrolls or listening to the accounts of administrative functionaries. She paid meticulous attention to all that she read or heard because they helped her see many things through new eyes. Including, she noted with an instinctive frown, the harsh realities that Shikandin and Dhrstyadymn had protected her from.

'Are you all right?' Dharma asked, noticing her preoccupation.

She nodded to tell him she was. The two of them were walking back to their palace from the just-concluded session of the royal assembly. As was their habit, they headed for Panchali's chambers. Entering, Panchali threw herself on to what had now become her favourite cushioned chair while Dharma moved around the room with familiarity, pouring himself some wine from a cask. In a way that was difficult to describe or explain, the two had become affectionate companions, though they had not been lovers since their wedding night.

Dharma thoughtfully sipped his drink. 'You don't like this new edict, do you?' he began, having guessed already what it was that irked Panchali.

Panchali shook her head. 'No, I don't. I find it reprehensible. Don't you?'

'It's undeniably based on scriptures and good authority, a compilation of key prescriptions from the various records the Firstborn scholars have put together.'

'This is not law, nor meticulous record-keeping! It is a recasting of our very moral principles. Every fact is being quoted out of the context of the record it is actually a part of! String many such pieces together and it can mean something entirely different from what was originally intended.'

'Panchali, relying on authority to lend weight to one's arguments is an old practice. If it was so laid down by the wise elders, it must be with good reason. Why does this make you so angry?'

'My anger,' she snapped, 'comes from the fact that this "Dharma Shastra", a supposed compilation of codes of human conduct, suggests that women are weak and promiscuous by nature, that their monthly period renders them perpetually unclean and unfit to rule, or to learn the scriptures. As a result, they require the protection and supervision of father, brother, husband or son at all stages of life. In return, they owe their unquestioning servitude and loyalty to these men.' She looked at Dharma sharply as she added, 'You don't see this position as having political undertones? You don't think it sheer chauvinist rat-droppings, the ignorant rant of deluded old ascetics who resent their forced celibacy and desperately need to justify their self-denial by representing women as the embodiment of all that is bad and evil on earth?'

Dharma considered her pensively. Initially her outspoken nature had given him many an uneasy night, but now he found it rather amusing. With a smile he said, 'Well, all the rhetoric apart, what political purpose could something like this serve?'

'It's never a single, overwhelming purpose. In this case, the motivation is that if a woman is considered incapable of being her own person, it follows that she is also incapable of inheriting property.'

'And all this for property and power?'

'Of course!'

He looked into the distance, thinking over what they had just discussed. 'Isn't it a rather convoluted way of doing things?' he eventually asked.

'No act of discrimination or oppression is ever truly an isolated one. Each seemingly trivial distinction justifies the larger principle. It may begin with the notion that women are not equal to men, but very soon something will emerge to prove that not all men are equal. It's never about a specific instance or selective events. It's about what we believe in as human beings.'

'But we're not – equal, that is. There's a world of a difference between a prince and a slave. We, the noble Aryas, were meant to rule these lands and preserve Divine order. That order isn't served unless we remain true to the hierarchies. We owe our duty to our superiors and I see nothing wrong with that. It baffles me that you should call it oppression and discrimination.'

Panchali regarded Dharma with astonishment. 'So, you'd follow your liege-lord even if he led you wrong?'

'It's complicated, Panchali.'

'What could be complicated about right and wrong, Dharma?' she emphasized his name ever so slightly. 'How can you allow injustice in *your* realm? Speaking of which,' she finally poured out what had been weighing on her mind for a while, 'when do we leave for Kandava?'

He laughed softly at Panchali's irritation. 'Kandava ...' he sullenly added. 'We'll never leave for Kandava. There's nothing there. It is nothing more than a title to keep us quiet. We'll remain Dhritarastra's dependents, always. What right do I have over anything, after all?' He was suddenly quiet.

Panchali waited a while, hesitant. 'Dharma?' she eventually prompted, her concern getting the better of her anger.

Dharma sighed. 'It's an old and long tale. But it's time you heard it,' he said, sitting down on a couch and inviting her to join him.

'It was a complex matter,' he said, 'and one of dishonour for my father, when he failed to produce heirs despite having two wives. He abdicated the throne in favour of his brother and retired to a hermitage with his wives. And then we have the commonly accepted account that through the use of sacred chants and prayers both my mother and my stepmother conceived the offspring of celestial beings. No, wait a minute ...'

Dharma raised his hand at the incredulous look on Panchali's face. 'It's called niyoga, a practice by which heirless kings take the children of their wives by their brothers or by honourable men, such as seers, for their own. Such male surrogacy is much more common than you might expect, especially in the Kuru dynasty. It is no secret that Dwaipayana, the Vyasa, fathered Uncle Dhritarastra, my father, as well as the Kshatta, Vidur. But for some reason, in our case the true identities are ... well, neither hidden as such nor explicitly acknowledged. I'm said to be born of the God of Justice, Bhim of the Wind-God Vayu, Nakul and Sadev of the Ashwins, twin gods of Healing and Medicine. Partha is the son of Indra, king of the celestials. Legally, of course, we're all Pandu's sons.'

'Do you ever wonder ...' Panchali began. 'Never mind,' she said, as a wild conjecture about Dharma's father's identity took form, an idea she knew better than to dwell on.

Dharma appeared to be of the same mind. 'What's the point wondering, Panchali? There's no point placing bets if you won't cast the dice. The question has no conclusive answer. My life is what it is, and for all purposes I am the son of Pandu and Pritha. Does it really matter whether I can conclusively affirm or deny the version that was handed down? If something is repeated often enough it becomes the truth. Frankly, I'm grateful that it has avoided us the tag of bastards for the most part ...'

He grimaced for a moment at some memory, and then continued, 'We grew up in a hermitage in the White Mountains, since my father had already abdicated the kingdom. We came to live at Hastina after he died. I was nearly eighteen then. Syoddhan wasn't happy when we turned up, nor was Uncle Dhritarastra. I can understand their resentment. The throne was originally my uncle's as he was the older of the two brothers, but my father was crowned instead because my uncle was blind. My father then abdicated the crown in my uncle's favour.'

'So the question remains, who ought to be the heir?'

'Yes,' Dharma confirmed, 'and with good cause too. The Kuru kingdom is today half the size that it used to be. What we call Kuru is what was once Eastern Kuru, the land between the rivers Ganga and Yamuna. Beyond the Yamuna, on the other side of the river, is what used to be Western Kuru. The land that's now been given to me, as *my* kingdom, is a land that's not even ours anymore!'

'The land was lost?'

'The land was lost or usurped, depending on how you look at it,' Dharma stated. 'In any case it's now the realm of Takshaka, the Naga king. For the longest time it was the hiding place of the last of the Firewrights.'

'How ...?' Panchali stuttered. 'How can King Dhritarastra give us something that's not his?'

'Bhim thinks it is a trap,' Dharma admitted. 'Kandava is definitely no great treasure, other than for its old reputation. There's nothing but dense forest and craggy mountain all the way till the place known as Kuru's Fields. It's why the Wrights were sent there by the old kings in the first place. They supposedly had a method by which they could cleave rock, even mountains, in two. It was once planned for the Great Road to run beyond Hastina, right through the rock and stone of Kandava. But till today Kandava remains impassable. The heathen Firewrights may well have failed to build the road, but they sure did leave enough of their craft behind for the Nagas to be able to defend themselves well. Even Grandsire Bhisma hasn't been able to drive the Nagas out of Kandava. In fact, giving this land to me may even be a challenge, daring us to claim what is rightfully ours,' Dharma concluded.

'The Kuru kings sent Firewrights ...?' Panchali asked, astonished.

'Yes. A long time ago. Once, Kandavaprastha used to be the capital city from which my ancestors Bharata and Pururavas ruled the empire of Aryavarta. Kandavaprastha was known as the Throne of Indra on Earth. For long, many have believed that the royal sceptre of the Kurus is Indra's Vajra, the thunderbolt made for him by the Firewrights.'

'The Firewrights made the royal sceptre?' Panchali stuttered.

Dharma's surprise at her ignorance was less only than his concern. 'Are you ... ? You're asking me the most ... never mind ...' he trailed off, not wanting to hurt her feelings.

Panchali swallowed her ego and set her face into a composed expression. 'No, honestly, I didn't know that Firewrights once held such prominence in Kuru. I always assumed that, like Panchala, the Kurus too had laws against the Wrights.'

'Ah, Panchali,' Dharma gently clucked his tongue. 'It's not your fault. Perhaps your father thought it better for you not to know about the Firewrights at all. But the fact is, it is well-known and widely accepted that the Wrights were responsible for the rise of the central kingdoms, the glory and the prosperity we see today. Not just Kuru, but Panchala as well. Of course, little record remains of what they may have achieved. It's not uncommon for new rulers to take credit for good work done in the past.'

Panchali nodded. 'I know,' she said. 'It's a way of legitimizing the new rule by reaffirming past glories in their name. But, then, how did things come to this – this great animosity that the Kurus and Panchalas have for the Firewrights?'

Dharma's smile faded. He thought silently for a while and said, 'Human beings are creatures of duty, Panchali. The moment we neglect duty and start to question the workings of divinity and fate, we fall from grace.'

'You mean, power corrupts?'

'On the contrary, that's what the Wrights believed. But as long as the Divine order of things, the hierarchies set by scripture, are maintained, that power is the means of achieving great things. In fact, I'd say it is our duty as kings to seek power and prosperity – the notion that we, descendants of the gods themselves, can act contrary to duty is itself profane. We are Aryas, the noble. To us, virtue is victory and in victory is virtue.'

'I don't understand,' Panchali conceded.

'Morality is a subtle thing, Panchali. It often depends on what is considered moral by the prevailing voice, those in power. Right and wrong, I'd think, are relative, not absolute. This brings us back to why Syoddhan dislikes me so much. His absolute sense of honour tells him that it is the worst compromise to put me, a bastard son, on the throne.'

'And your relative sense of justice allows it?'

Dharma's voice lost the note of grandeur it had taken on. He sighed and said, 'I have a confession. I've often wondered what is the point of it all. I know you'll believe me if I say I've considered this matter as one of law and principle, and not out of my desire for the crown. I've often wondered who really has the claim, in law, as the king's heir. My father was the younger of two brothers and ruled only because Uncle Dhritarastra was born blind. Did it mean that my uncle's heirs had lost their right too? Or did the right revert back to Syoddhan, and his sons and grandsons, when my father abdicated? Maybe the line of succession is irrelevant and the eldest of each generation ought to be king. If so, Syoddhan can't rule because I'm the oldest of all the cousins, the sons of both brothers. It's a contentious matter, one fit to wager a kingdom on! But, as it stands, I'm nothing more than the titular ruler of a land that doesn't exist.' With a dry snigger, he added, 'As I told my mother the other day these are times when I wish I had an elder brother. It would be *his* problem then!'

To that statement, Panchali made no response. Much as she now shared a comfortable relationship with three of Dharma's brothers, she could not help think that one more might just have been too many. Especially since there remained a brother with whom things were far from comfortable.

21

DHARMA'S WAS NOT THE ONLY FRIENDSHIP THAT PANCHALI managed to cultivate as she settled into her new life at Hastina. She found the youngest of the five brothers, the twins, easy to get along with. Nakul and Sadev were not much older than Dhrstyadymn, and they made her feel at home with their casual banter and their jokes. Nakul was considered the most handsome of the Kurus, surpassing both Partha and Syoddhan, though Panchali knew from Dhrstyadymn's experiences that it was not easy on an Arya prince if he were exceptionally good-looking; in fact, it was far worse for him than if he had been plain or even downright ugly. Nakul had to constantly deal with the misconception that he was not much use as a warrior. Unfortunately, Sadev shared that reputation with him, for little reason other than them being twins, though not completely identical in appearance. Sadev was also acknowledged, though not as widely and as often as he deserved, for his intelligence and acumen. His reputation for being an excellent astrologer was, however, one of the few things that people actually knew about him. It served at least to open the door to conversation and he patiently engaged the sceptical Panchali in endless debates on the science and philosophy of prophecy. As she spent more time with the twins, Panchali also realized, for the first time, that she really was as good an archer as her brothers gave her credit for. She had always supposed that they were just being indulgent, but when she tried her marksmanship against Sadev and Nakul she found she more than held her own with ease. To her surprise, the twins ungrudgingly admitted her to their practice sessions and took her with them on their rides and hunts.

Bhim, Panchali could not help but like. For a man with his reputation for physical strength, Bhim was rather lean. He was big-built and broad-shouldered, as most trained wrestlers were, but there was nothing otherworldly about his size. He laughed easily and had a great zest for life and, as a result, many at Hastina tended to dismiss him as a boor, a brawny, coarse lout – all of which was undeserved. As Panchali found out soon enough, Bhim was a man of fine senses, who loved music and art. He often slipped out in disguise to watch the wandering minstrels and performers in the street corners of Hastina, and was glad to take a curious Panchali along. He was also a superb cook, a skill she completely lacked, as was expected of her stature.

She had never developed an interest in the activity; nevertheless, she loved to sample Bhim's culinary creations and would keep him company while he conducted his delicious experiments. Most of all, Panchali admired Bhim for his courage. He was outspoken, perhaps even a touch too frank, but it made for a refreshing change from the world around them. In Hastina far too much was politely said and cruelly meant. Here, the truth was always veiled. It was the sort of place where while, in principle, the five brothers were equals in every way, all of Kuru revered one of the five above the others.

Then there was Partha. Everything about the third of the five brothers was just like his name – unimaginatively ordinary but unmistakeably special. Of the three sons born to Pandu's first queen, he alone was Partha, the son of Pritha. Panchali hardly knew him beyond the endless talk that ran through the palace, most of which centred on one or both of his two distinctions – he was considered a superb archer and could shoot in the dark using sound alone to guide him. Equally superlative, Panchali heard, was his skill with and exploits involving women. He remained an exception to the easy camaraderie she shared with the other four, for he pointedly avoided her, to the extent that she had never even had an opportunity to ask him why. Not that she ever would, for it was not difficult to understand why he behaved the way he did. He had won her and for a short while she had been his, and now she was not. They were both acutely aware of that. The realization had already made their presence in the same room a near-impossibility and Panchali shuddered to think how uncomfortable a private moment of admission might be. In her heart, she was glad that he kept his distance.

It was, therefore, most awkward for Panchali when, late one evening, Partha walked out on to one of the many covered terraces of their palace to find her there, watching the thunderstorm that was in full swing, unmindful of the rain that splattered in through the open sides.

She rummaged ineffectively in her mind for something to say or do and, finding nothing, made a trite comment about the rain being lovely. Partha merely nodded. Thinking it best to give him some space, she turned her attention back to the elements outside. The evening storm had lit up the sky and the treetops in impossible colours of red and brown. The downpour was a sultry haze as it hit the dry, sun-parched ground, giving rise to a slight mist.

Panchali revelled in the feel of the light spray on her face, the smell of wet earth and the strong, steady breeze. *How good it is to be alive*, she thought. Closing her eyes, she soaked up the sensations – the rain, the wind, the touch of a hand on her shoulder, on her bare waist, the feel of a strong body against hers, of gentle lips, now warm on the soft skin of her neck, now whispering in her ear, 'Panchali …'

She felt her heart thudding wildly as he drew her closer, his words and actions leaving little doubt about his desire. Panchali had heard much gossip about his exceptional lovemaking skills and how he could seduce any woman into submission. Now he wanted her. Partha wanted her. Part of her felt a grim satisfaction at this proof that Dharma's disgust on their wedding night had not been her fault, but his own. In husky whispers and with promise-laden words Partha gently reminded her of how he had won her, of the way they had held hands in anticipation of a lifetime together – a lifetime that he wanted to offer her, still.

Panchali gasped with muted pleasure at his determined touch as he made her turn to face him. She wanted desperately to believe his reassurances, his declarations, the words of affection. She let her fingers slide softly up Partha's arms and as he pulled her closer still she wrapped her arms around his neck. Even as she instinctively responded to his attentions, the vague sliver of a reflection came to her mind.

Govinda.

The image jolted her out of her trance. Her eyes flashed open; panic, guilt, desire, rage, all coursed through her in a searing mix, leaving her weak and limp.

Weak? Never! She felt something inside her rise in rebellion.

'No!' she cried out, and pushed Partha away. She took a few steps back, until she felt the wall behind her. She turned away, resting her forehead against the wall, focussing on the sensation of the cold stone touching her skin.

The sound of Partha's rough breathing told her that he was still there but she could not bring herself to look at him. After what felt like an eternity she heard him say, 'I'm sorry.' She waited, unmoving, till she heard his footsteps fade away.

Slowly, Panchali turned around, glad for the way the raindrops stung her face. She did not understand why she had almost given in to Partha's touch. Or maybe, she admitted with a sigh, she did. Maybe she had just wanted to know that she was not detestable, forbidden or sinful, to Dharma, to anyone …

To Govinda.

Taking a deep breath, Panchali closed her eyes and raised her face to the sky, letting the rain flow down her cheeks as the tears she refused to cry. She had never felt so alone in all her life.

22

WHAT HAVE I DONE? WHAT HAVE I DONE!

Partha walked blindly around the open palace grounds in the rain. He did not understand why Panchali tempted him beyond reason, why her mere presence drove him insane. Her unassailable composure got under his skin, fascinated him and disturbed him no end.

Just like Govinda, he thought.

He wondered how, for all that he had seen in the world, he could be so short-sighted. *Not everyone is an impassioned, irrational Kuru.*

But was it just that? Was there not something much more primal, more irresistible?

He thought of the sairandharis who shared his bed, of their hushed confessions of how even they could not stop themselves from staring at Panchali, at her perfect form as she bathed, as she dressed, as she slept – all of it, they insisted, in innocent ignorance of her own beauty. Partha listened to their stories and then pleasured them with fury as his mind rested on Panchali alone.

How dare you! She's your brother's wife, his conscience reminded him. But even as he remonstrated himself, his anger at her, at his brothers, raised its head. *I am not the only one who wants her.*

Dharma's eagerness had been all but transparent that day in Kampilya. Partha briefly wondered if this were some ploy or trick to drive a wedge between the five brothers. After all, greater men had made fools of themselves over a woman. Striding even faster through the rain, he dismissed the idea. No matter what, the five of them would remain undivided. But what about Panchali?

She's mine, his mind argued. *I won her with my skill and valour.*

Do you love her? A voice inside his head asked, tentative at first though it grew stronger: *Or do you just resent the fact that your righteous elder brother enjoys the fruits of your toil?*

No! I won't think that way. My duty is to my elder and I will die for him if need be.

Indeed, you will, the voice seemed to say, before disappearing. *But don't forget that you wanted her as your own.*

Partha found himself running to Dharma's room. He burst in without knocking, surprising his elder brother, who benignly sat at his desk, reading.

'What happened?' Dharma asked, rising quickly to throw a warm blanket over the shivering Partha. 'Are you all right, Partha?'

'Panchali ...' Partha gasped.

Dharma started making for the door, when Partha caught him by the arm and stopped him.

'She's all right,' Partha said. 'She's all right, Agraja, but I ... I ... I couldn't stop myself. Please – please forgive me, I'm so terribly sorry.' Partha fell to his knees as Dharma stepped back, shocked.

'Is she ... did you ... did you force yourself on her Partha?'

'No,' Partha replied. 'I came to my senses before that.'

A moment of silence, and then Dharma sighed in relief. 'Go, get some sleep. We'll talk about this tomorrow in the sane light of day. Come on, stand up.' He raised Partha off his knees.

'I've failed you, Agraja. I've failed us all,' Partha said.

'Vathu! That's enough, Partha! I understand you're upset, but we *will* get beyond this misunderstanding. Things will be all right.'

'No, Agraja,' Partha argued, 'don't you see … how can she feel safe again under our roof after what I've done?' He coldly regarded his brother, stating the truth that he knew Dharma would not accept. 'Each one of us wants her. How can she trust us?'

Dharma did not respond.

Partha continued, 'There's only one way to make up for this. You must punish me for wanting her. Panchali must realize that *you*, as her husband, will protect her. That you won't permit such behaviour.'

'Come now,' Dharma said. 'This talk of punishment is silly. She may be married to me, but you do know that anything that's mine is equally yours. Am I supposed to punish you for being my brother? What would you have me do? Imprison you? Order you whipped? Really, Partha!'

'I shall go away as an exile,' Partha stated, unconvinced by Dharma's arguments. 'I'll go away from Hastina and journey to hermitages and holy sanctuaries. There, I'll pray for forgiveness and guidance.'

Dharma had the feeling that this was not about penitence alone. His gaze was firm, though his voice misleadingly soft. 'Partha, it's for you to realize and answer for yourself whether or not you truly seek forgiveness. Personally, I believe that you want to leave because you don't trust yourself to be around her.'

Partha began to protest, but Dharma pre-empted him, 'There is no need for you to convince me or explain to me, Brother. But I don't want you deluding yourself that you are paying for your mistake, when the truth is that you are as much a victim of your desires now as you were earlier this evening. I hope that through your prayers you find the courage to be honest with yourself.'

The younger man nodded. He stared out of the window for a while, and then, with a final look at his brother, left.

Dharma did not hear him ride away, but he knew where Partha would head, sooner or later. He would go looking for the same answers that Dharma wanted. Perhaps he would solve the puzzle that perplexed them both. What sort of a man could flippantly throw away a wonderful prize like Panchali? What sort of a man, really, was Govinda Shauri?

23

THE RAIN HAD STOPPED BY THE TIME PANCHALI REACHED THE stables in the late hours of the night. The lone stableman was asleep and she did not bother to wake him; instead, she saddled her horse on her own and headed out to be in the open for a while. Heading southward, she exited from the palace grounds directly onto the open fields, avoiding a journey through the sprawling city. The river ran alongside on her left, its clear waters reflecting the stars above in its dark blue depths.

Panchali rode along the bank at a brisk pace, enjoying the cold wind in her face. She had been riding for a while when she noticed the sky lighten ever so little as dawn drew nearer. Soon enough, the cacophony of birds filled the air with energy and a bend in the river ahead shimmered to life. Here, the waters curved away to run eastwards, forming in effect the border between Northern and Southern Panchala. She slowed down, taking in the scenery. She had not realized Panchala's border lay so close to Hastina, or perhaps she had ridden too fast, she thought.

A pang of homesickness washed over her, more because she so missed her brothers' company. Not that Dharma and his brothers had not gone out of their way to make her feel at home in Hastina, but it was not the same. She felt that she moved from one mildly entertaining situation to another, but no meaningful thread connected the activities that made up her day. And now Partha had done what he had done.

This isn't me. This isn't my life, Panchali told herself. *It doesn't matter what led to this state of things. I must choose whether I shall be passive or act to change what I can. The responsibility is mine.*

Feeling light at the realization, she drew in a deep breath, filling her lungs with the crisp morning air. It was now light enough to make out the rolling hills in the west, which gave way to the luxuriant green plains that stretched till the eastern horizon. Copses of trees and patches of tilled land occasionally dotted the landscape. Everything around her was alive and brimming with energy. The feeling was contagious, and despite all that had happened Panchali found herself smiling.

The shrill cry of a hawk rose to a magnificent crescendo. Panchali looked up to see the majestic bird swoop down and rise again as it hunted. She stared with admiration at the way the bird glided, turning effortlessly with a light sweep of its wings, its every move precise and graceful. The bird dived again and, this time, kept diving. It was going for a kill, a lone grey-white pigeon. Panchali turned in her saddle, eagerly tracking the chase between hunter and prey. The hawk was now nearly on the pigeon, which fluttered its feeble wings in a desperate attempt to escape. Talons outstretched, the seasoned hunter waited for the right moment. Suddenly, the twang of a bowstring rent the air. A speeding arrow gleamed as a metal barrier between hawk and pigeon. The hawk wheeled away, confused – perhaps even frightened – by the pigeon's unnatural protector.

Panchali whipped around to see the archer, a tall figure on a horse, on the opposite banks of the river. The archer had another arrow ready and was following the retreating hawk. Determined, she pulled her wood-and-metal rider's bow from her horse's side, where she usually kept it strapped. Fitting an arrow from the quiver on her saddlebag, she waited, the string drawn back. Whoever the man was, he had to be one of the most flawless bowmen Panchali had ever seen. The angle of his arms, the delicate way he gripped the arrow and his patience as he followed the target, waiting for the perfect opportunity – almost a hawk himself, she noted.

The moment she heard the second twang from his bow, she released her arrow. The archer turned, surprised by the sound, and realizing what she had done looked up at the bird. Just before his arrow hit its target, it was deflected by Panchali's shaft. The hawk gave a long, shrill cry that could have been a call of thanks or of amusement and then soared high, well out of arrows' range.

Satisfied, Panchali readied to face her chance adversary. She smiled tentatively, hoping that the dim light was enough to convey the apologetic look on her face. Meanwhile, the archer had urged his horse forward, right into the river. She recognized him the moment his horse clambered up the slightly sloping riverbank, though he was missing the jewel he wore on his forehead instead of a crown whenever he was present in Dhritarastra's court. As he drew closer she noted that he appeared more amazed to see her than she him.

'Mahamatra,' he said, nodding politely.

'Your Highness,' she returned the greeting.

The man chuckled. 'That has to be the first time any of Dhrupad's kin have called me that,' he said.

Panchali was unfazed. 'Rightly or wrongly, it is your title, Your Highness,' she said. 'What you've won is yours to keep … till I win it back, that is.'

The man laughed uproariously, looking different when he did. His otherwise icy demeanour, his haughty manner, momentarily disappeared.

Settling down to a smile, he told her, 'In that case, let's keep it simple. Why don't you just call me Asvattama?'

Panchali considered him for a while and then said, 'I'm sorry about the hawk … It's just that he was such a magnificent creature, I couldn't stop myself. In any case, I was just lucky …'

'Yes,' Asvattama admitted, 'he was a beautiful creature. I wouldn't have shot at him if he'd taken another go at the pigeon. I suppose it was his immediate retreat that disappointed me. Perhaps it's just as well that you stopped me from killing him – I might've regretted that a little later.'

Panchali had no response to that. In an unspoken consensus both of them urged their horses forward and began making their way north, towards Hastina.

The sun soon cleared the horizon, filling the vastness around them with light. On either side of the river, the plains came to life with farmers, herdsmen and their animals, and an assorted bustle of various activities. Panchali could now see all that she had missed during her ride earlier, and was amazed at the verdant surrounds and the rhythm of human activity.

A small, sturdy bridge appeared ahead. Two liveried guards

stood on two sides, one dressed in the colours of Kuru and the other representing Northern Panchala. Their function, however, was purely ceremonial, for Panchali had seen the common folk openly ford the river where it ran shallow.

'Have you ever been in Northern Panchala?' Asvattama suddenly asked.

Panchali shook her head to say she had not.

'Would you like to ride on the other side of the river?'

She paused for a moment, wondering what her brothers would have to say about it, but politeness got the better of her. 'Yes, please,' she replied.

Asvattama turned and led the way across the bridge, the soldiers on both sides snapping to attention and saluting him. Once they were in Northern Panchala, he guided Panchali a little further inland to a narrow but well-paved road that ran alongside the river.

'We can't ride too close to the river on this side, because of the canals,' Asvattama said by way of explanation. 'Northern Panchala is much drier than Kuru or Southern Panchala. The soil here is sandy – it can't hold water. Those canals alongside the river,' he pointed, 'run inland for a fair distance. Of course, these fields right here get about as much rain as Kuru does, but once you head further east the winds from the mountains deflect the rain southwards. Without these canals ...'

'Impressive,' Panchali conceded. She did not know whether Asvattama was intentionally showing off or not, but that did not change what she saw before her.

To her surprise, he took no credit. He said, 'It's not new, and certainly not of my doing or design. Of course, I'll admit that keeping them in good shape takes some administrative effort, but that's about it.'

His casual tone made Panchali voice the question that had long perplexed her. 'Forgive me for asking, but when you fought my father, when you attacked us, why did your father take Northern Panchala for his bounty? You won the war, defeated my father, so why not take the southern part with its verdant fields and the capital, Kampilya?'

Asvattama seemed surprised by her query. 'There was no question of choosing,' he stated. 'We fought for Northern Panchala.' He paused for a few moments, watching a perplexed frown gather on Panchali's forehead, and then gently asked, 'How much do you know of what happened before ... before you came to Kampilya? How much do you know of our battle with your father?'

'I know the version that's told in Kampilya. But I also know that it isn't the complete story ...' Panchali confessed.

Asvattama said nothing. The two rode ahead in silence until he said, 'Are you hungry? It must be a while since you ate anything.'

Without waiting for her to answer, he turned his horse abruptly towards a small stone garrison, comprising a building and a stable, all of it surrounded by a high wall. 'Come,' he added, as an afterthought.

Confused but tremendously curious, Panchali followed.

24

THE GARRISON WAS QUITE SIMILAR TO A FEW THAT THEY HAD passed earlier, and Panchali wondered why so many guards were stationed in such close proximity to each other. She found her answer the moment she stepped inside.

On the left was a small stable meant for no more than two horses. An even smaller store-house and rudimentary sleeping quarters for a few guards occupied the corner on the same side. Another room, built of the same stone as the walls, was set a little off the middle of the enclosure. The main purpose of the garrison, however, was something Panchali had not expected at all.

A metal sluice at the far end carried water from the canal outside and fed it into a stone-lined tank about ten feet long and as high as her shoulders. At the near end of the tank a wide, paved conduit had been set into the ground. The water fell from the tank into the conduit, pushing past a row of four cogged wooden wheels set on a single, stationary axle that was attached by two short wooden arms to the outer wall of the tank. The wheels rotated continuously against a corresponding set of larger wheels set on a wood and metal beam that was held up by two wooden pillars. Unlike the other axle, this one turned in tandem with the wheels, its ends rotating within hollowed-out recesses carved into the supporting pillars. The recesses were abundantly coated with some sort of oily substance which, Panchali supposed, made it easier for the rotating piece to turn on the groove. Stepping closer, she observed the last and central piece of the mechanism – the rotating axle pushed down on a broad wooden beam nearly the girth a man, driving it with considerable force into a pit-like receptacle, which was filled with ears of grain.

'A pestle!' she exclaimed, and did a quick estimation. 'I guess it does the work of fifty men in a day?'

Asvattama nodded. 'A pestle that rises and falls on its own, without any human intervention. Would you call that magic?' he asked.

Panchali studied the mechanism with wide-eyed delight. 'I call it genius,' she declared and looked expectantly at him.

'We can talk while we eat,' he politely offered.

Handing the reins of their horses to an attendant, Asvattama paused to give instructions to the soldier in charge, while Panchali quickly washed up at a smaller tank behind the main building. The two then went inside the stone building, which comprised just one room, with windows set into all four walls. A section of the wall near the door had been cut into recessed shelves, on which were neatly arranged an assortment of scrolls and parchments of various sizes. Simple reed mats and cushions made of rough linen were laid out on the floor. On a low table in the middle were an earthen jar and a few cups.

Asvattama sat on Panchali's right, facing the wide doorway. He said, 'I've sent a message to Hastina, letting Dharma know you're with me. I've said that you were out watching the sunrise when I ran into you ...'

'Thank you.'

Asvattama did not reply, waiting silently as an attendant brought in some bread and fruit. Only then did Panchali realize how hungry she was, her appetite whetted by the early morning ride. Neither of them spoke till the meal was done and the attendant had cleared away the remnants. Asvattama then rose and walked over to the stone shelves. He sifted through the stacked parchment rolls till he found what he was looking for.

'Here,' he said, unfurling a large hand-drawn map of central Aryavarta on the table.

Panchali eagerly leaned forward and Asvattama knelt down next to her. He reached for a piece of smooth charcoal that lay on the table and used it to mark a spot on the parchment.

'Ahichattra,' Panchali identified. 'The capital of Northern Panchala. *Your* capital.'

Asvattama marked a point north of Ahichattra, along the course of the Ganga, very close to its source, and said, 'This is where I grew up – the hermitage of the Barghava or Brghu sages, those of the line of Rama Jamadagni. My father was a student of Barghava Rama the Fifth.'

'But I thought your father and mine were fellow students at your grandfather's school.'

'Yes, they were,' Asvattama confirmed. 'That hermitage is in eastern Aryavarta, in the Kosala kingdom. Many years after that, my father came to study the science of weapons under the Brghus. We then continued to live in the Himalayan foothills and I was brought up there.' He paused and then added, 'I was trained by the Firewrights.'

Panchali started, but said nothing. She simply nodded, trying hard not to betray any emotion.

Asvattama smiled to himself at her efforts and continued, 'Coming to what happened, it's easier to understand why we fought against your father if you consider the geography of the region, especially the two rivers, Ganga and Yamuna. The Ganga lies east of the Brghu hermitage and the Yamuna to the west. The courses remain parallel for a long time – both flow south and then turn east. We met this morning at the eastern bend of the Ganga. The river flows through Panchala, past Kampilya, and ultimately converges with the Yamuna near a city in the Kashi kingdom, to the south-east of Kampilya.'

Panchali nodded again, her eyes on Asvattama's finger as it traced the course of the river on the map. 'Eastern Kuru,' he pointed, 'lies partly in fertile alluvial tract between the two rivers. This land has made the Kurus and the Panchalas the most powerful kingdoms in Aryavarta for many centuries. Hastina lies on the Ganga, while the old capital, Kandavaprastha, used to be on the Yamuna. You probably know the place better as Kandava forest.'

'Yes,' Panchali affirmed.

'The Yamuna bends from its southern course to an easterly direction near Mathura in the Surasena part of the alluvial tract. Just beyond this lies another fertile region. Where the two rivers join to run as the one mighty Ganga, is the vast feudal kingdom of Magadha.'

Panchali's eyes lit up as she began to see where Asvattama was going with this. 'So,' she ventured, 'the lands that are in the alluvial tract between the two rivers, or fed by the Ganga, are the most verdant and prosperous, are they not? And the part of Northern Panchala through which the rivers run is actually mountainous terrain. I suppose it's impossible to grow crops there?'

'Correct. The region south of Ahichattra has fairly fertile soil, but …' He used the coal to mark out a few of the main tributaries of the two rivers. 'It is fed only by rain of a rather seasonal and whimsical nature, serving really as a catchment area. Most of the water drains into either of the two rivers, but the tributaries, as such, don't run through here. Between the seasons and the ferocity of the rain, farming has always been near impossible. The solution to the problem is not a difficult one, as you've seen.' He nodded to the mill-pond outside. 'Reservoirs can be built to trap water and there's plenty of water in the Ganga that can be diverted through canals. This hurts no one.'

'So you built these canals?'

'No, we didn't, Panchali. I certainly lack the skill to build these machines. They've been there a long time. But it was prohibited to use them. The machines, the canals, all of it was made by the Wrights of long ago. We could only hope to repair some of the better ones, and clean up the canals and reservoirs. My father thought that given his old friendship he could convince yours to do what was right by the people. But Dhrupad's hatred of anything even remotely linked to the Firewrights was beyond all reason …'

'So this is what it was all about?' Panchali frowned. 'What I heard in Kampilya was that your father asked mine for half the kingdom!'

Asvattama grunted disdainfully. 'He did, to tell you the truth. He did say to Dhrupad that if he lacked the courage to do what was needed for his citizens he should hand Northern Panchala over to its people, who would then determine their own future. And, yes, my father did presume that his friendship with yours gave him the liberty to advise him on his duties. If this offends you I …'

'It doesn't offend me,' Panchali was firm. 'It doesn't offend me at all. Please continue.'

Asvattama drew in a breath. 'Once Dhrupad refused, we had no choice but to seek help from the Kurus – both in terms of legitimizing the use of these old Wright creations as well as military help. My father's students – the Kuru princes – led the war against Panchala. It wasn't easy to defeat the Panchala forces, especially your brother Satrajit's men, but it was done.' He hesitated, then gently added, 'Your husband and his brothers, the five sons of Pandu, managed to take your father prisoner. Partha, I remember was the one who … Anyway, your father was, of course, set free, but I imagine it dented his pride quite a bit. He tried negotiating with the Kurus for many years, asking Bhisma to order my father to return Northern Panchala to him. But it was of no use. That's when he took to the forests and conducted a great sacrifice, after which he came back to Kampilya with you and your brother. I hope he finds some poetic justice now in seeing you married into the same house that defeated him …'

Panchali gritted her teeth to keep herself from cursing out loud. *Govinda must have known. He knew it, and he used me.*

'And Shikandin?' she asked.

Asvattama considered her yet again, wondering whether her ignorance was just pretence. He apparently decided it was not, because he went on, 'Your brother was a young man when this war happened. He'd have been … seventeen or eighteen, I suppose. Why, *I* was hardly your age at the time. In any case, Shikandin knew well what the situation was in Northern Panchala. He tried hard to get Dhrupad to change his mind, but failed. Finally, he refused to fight, hoping that his actions, his shame, would make your father relent. But all it did was bring Shikandin dishonour. Trust me, at that young age your brother was a much more capable ruler than your father will ever be. Even today I hear that Satrajit pretends to follow your father's instructions, but he really takes his orders from Shikandin. Those canals out there? Those fields, those people? But for your brother's actions they wouldn't be there.'

Panchali felt proud and moved at the declaration, but also a little bewildered. 'They do you as much credit,' she offered sincerely.

Asvattama indulged in a cold smirk. 'No, Mahamatra,' he declared, with a shake of his head. 'I'm not half as principled as your brother. Unlike him, I found it easier to trade in my beliefs. Or, perhaps, that is the inevitable fate of those of my line ...'

'I don't understand ...'

'Everyone has their price, Panchali. Once, when Northern Panchala stood on the brink of imminent destruction, my uncles – the Bhrgus – made their deal. Bhisma was trained by Barghava Rama Jamadagni, the fourth of that name, and knows of every weapon, every astra there was. My father's price, my price ... Well, let's just say that in return for what we now have, my father has shared even the secret of the terrible Bramha-weapon with his best students among the Kuru princes. And I ...? King I may be, but most of my actions are the result of the Vyasa's orders. I'm not a Wright, Panchali, but I *was* trained to use their weapons. For all the Vyasa goes on about the Firewright menace, he has no complaint with their knowledge – as long as it remains in the hands of those *he* trusts and it serves *his* purposes.'

'Firewright knowledge? Does that mean you – you can actually ...?'

Asvattama smiled at her question. He murmured a few words and held up his right hand in a fist. Then, in a quick, smooth move, he flicked his hand over and opened his fist. A drop-like tongue of flame burned steadily at the centre of his palm as if he was the very source of the fire.

Panchali stared, speechless. Asvattama laughed softly. 'So you've never seen this before?'

'No,' she said in a hushed whisper. 'I've heard of it, but I've never … How do you do that? Or is it a secret? I mean, is it really magic?'

'Do you believe in magic?'

Panchali resolutely shook her head. 'No,' she said, 'not in this sense of the word. The method you use may be a secret and not easily understood, but it's not inexplicable in reasonable terms, is it?'

'It can be very easily explained and understood. As for magic, I've heard that the Wrights of the ancient past were capable of using subtle energies, the power of their finite minds, and that Wrights before them could tap into the energy of the Universe, the very source of the life that flows through us all. But they weren't magicians. They were inventors, scientists who were more interested in applying their knowledge for the benefit of others. They say that the first Angirasa was none other than Agni, Fire himself – a composite of light and flame, knowledge and action – both are equal principles of the primeval waters. Only by combining the two can human beings aspire to the Truth.'

Asvattama flicked his hand once more, making the flame appear, and then just as quickly turned his hand over to make it disappear.

Panchali asked, in an awed whisper, 'Do you believe it? Do you believe that the ancient Wrights had such powers?'

'I believe that divinity and science are not opposites,' Asvattama replied. 'Somewhere in the vastness beyond human comprehension the two merge. A lot that seems supernatural to us then becomes real, but that doesn't make it any less rational. What I do find unbelievable is the sheer apathy of people, their blind ignorance, and their aversion to understanding why or how something works. Over time, and as knowledge is lost, the simplest of mechanisms are transformed into magic, and either feared or revered.'

A pleasant quiet followed his words. Panchali could hear the far-away bustle of the world around them, as men and oxen tilled and ploughed the land. Closer still, the sound of horses in the stables, the soft pounding of the pestle punctuated by the gurgling flow of water and the occasional call of a bird or insect, lazy and languorous in the shimmering heat of the day. The calm rhythm of life was reassuring and Panchali felt her body instinctively relax. It only served to heighten the eddy of questions in her mind, the whirlwind of realization and answers that in turn birthed new questions. Finally, as the debate in her mind came again and again to rest on the one thing she still could not bring herself to accept, she said out loud, 'It doesn't make sense! Why? Why would my father refuse to use the canals just because they're built by the Firewrights? Why would any reasonable person throw away the power to do what is right and good, for his people? Why would he …?' she trailed off, unable to say the words.

Asvattama understood. He said, 'Why? Because he had no choice.'

'No choice?' Panchali bristled. 'The sovereign of Panchala had no choice?'

'Not if he is sovereign by the will of another. Have you heard of Ugrayudha?'

'The usurper? But of course! My great-grandfather ousted him from the Panchala throne and reclaimed it.'

'Usurper? Ugrayudha was the legitimate ruler of Panchala! He was your great-grandfather's cousin, his uncle's son.'

'What!'

'Perhaps, I'd better tell this story, too, in its entirety,' Asvattama said. 'It is said that when King Shantanu of the Kurus died, King Ugrayudha of Panchala openly declared his lust for the widowed queen, Satya, and asked for her to be sent to him. Bhisma, then a young man, took offence to this. He marched against Ugrayudha, killed him and installed your great-grandfather on the throne. Your line owes its rule to Bhisma. Specifically, to Bhisma's campaigns against the Firewrights.'

'And my father would let his own people die for that reason alone? Never!'

'It's not so simple, Panchali. One thing led to another. After Ugrayudha's death, his son, Kshemya, fled to Kashi. It took many years, but Bhisma eventually got him too. You've heard, haven't you, the tale of how Bhisma nearly razed Kashi to the ground when he brought back the three princesses of Kashi to marry Vichitravirya? Kashi – the famed stronghold of the Firewrights. Don't you see a pattern? These wars weren't fought for women and their honour alone. They were wars against the Wrights. Just as your family owes its allegiance to Bhisma, he in turn has pleadged loyalty to DwaipayanaVyasa and the Firstborn. When the Firstborn decided to get rid of the Firewrights once and for all Bhisma gladly marched against them, and your father emptied his country's coffers to send men and money to support Bhisma's campaigns. Northern Panchala paid the greatest price, for we were left neither with money nor with the means to survive.'

Panchali frowned, looking for the least inconsistency in Asvattama's narrative, anything she could use to escape the inevitable conclusions that formed in her mind. She finally found one. 'I see what you mean ... but weren't there *two* princesses of Kashi? One the mother of Dharma's father and the other who bore King Dhritarastra?'

This time, Asvattama was visibly reluctant to go on. Eventually, he cleared his throat and said, 'There was a third. Amba. Like many in history, she paid a heavy price for her defiance. She refused to marry Vichitravirya and came to Panchala, seeking justice against the man who had taken her and her sisters from Kashi by force. It was a really long time ago, though. Your father had been king only a few years. Obviously, he turned her away ...'

'What happened to her?'

'No one really knows. Your brother – Shikandin – is familiar enough with these stories. Perhaps you ought to ask him ... A long time ago, your father used to send him out on raids against villages suspected of harbouring Firewrights. Ask him, sometime, what used to happen on these raids; the stories they used to tell before they were burnt alive. Ask him what horrors he'd seen and heard of before he finally stood up to your father.'

Panchali felt sick. *The Firewrights were hunted down, relentlessly.*

In my own country. By my own kin. And, most important, at the cost of my people's well-being.

She finally understood, though a part of her had always known, why Shikandin held their father and even their grandfather in quiet contempt, why he remained a defiant and stubborn rebel though he lacked nothing by way of a sense of filial duty. Reaching out for the small urn on the table before her, she took a long drink of water, letting the cool sensation soothe her from the inside. The canals were there, as were the water wheels, she reminded herself. A part of her wanted to believe that the Firewrights too remained, just as their creations did. She wanted to believe that Ghora had not been the last, if only to deny the guilt of knowing that her kind, her kin, had destroyed his people.

'Why didn't anyone do anything?' she burst out, fists clenched in anger. 'Did no one care? How could they all just watch while such horrors came to pass? By Rudra, is there no honour left in our blood that we …'

'We'd better leave.' Asvattama was terse. Without waiting for Panchali's response, he moved to the doorway and gave instructions to prepare their horses. He turned back to her, and said, 'I'll wait outside. Whenever you're ready …'

Panchali seethed in silence for a moment. Then she stood up, straightened her robes, and walked out of the small room to join Asvattama.

He was gazing at the water-mechanism. Without looking at her, he said, softly, 'You ought to be careful, Panchali. It's best you don't speak of this conversation once you return home to Hastina – I mean never. It wouldn't do to upset the Kurus.'

'I meant no offence …'

As though he had not heard her, Asvattama casually went on, 'Dharma is no less faithful to Dwaipayana than Bhisma is. He wouldn't tolerate the least interest in, leave alone sympathy for, the Wrights.'

'You don't really like the Firstborn, do you?'

'I like the prospect of grovelling before Jarasandha even less – a fear that would have been completely unnecessary if the Firewrights had still been around. And such is the irony of life that our destinies are often forged by those whom we'd rather forget – as with you and the Kurus. You don't know what a critical role the Wrights of old have played in bringing you to Hastina. Dwaipayana may well have orchestrated your wedding, but it is Wright-craft that defined your fate ...'

'You don't mean ...?'

Asvattama was non-committal, but his eyes said much. 'Come,' he instructed with an air of finality. 'It's time we got you home.'

25

PARTHA WATCHED THE SUN AS IT DROPPED INTO THE SEA, silenced by the magnificence that lay before him. The mountains gently sloped into a fair stretch of grassland with alternating bogs of marsh and sand, leading ultimately to a gem-flecked stretch of blue promise. The untamed sea fell, relentless, against a harsh, rocky coast, each defying the other in playful battle. In the middle of the foaming waters, connected by a series of foam-covered shoals, rose a mighty rock edifice. Waves beat relentlessly against the stone, and were broken into white foam, churned into golden spray.

From the core of the rock, a city rose, floating between the sky and sea. Towering white spires made of crystal caught the sun, dispersing its rays in a medley of fire and colour that could be seen all the way to Gomanta, where Partha now stood. At night, the city would reflect the soft light of the moon, like a pearl that tossed on the waves of the ocean. Sometimes, he had heard, it would be lit by thousands of small lamps, creating a carpet of stars on the sea to rival the natural spectacle in the sky.

Dwaraka. This was where his tormented journey had brought him.

When Partha had left Hastina two months ago he had headed eastward, wandering as his fancy took him till he had reached the farthest nations of Aryavarta, the lands close to the city of Pragjya. Every day, though, even as he had urged his horse on, he had looked back with longing to the west. Finally, he had begun retracing his steps. But instead of passing through the lands of the Panchalas and returning to Hastina, he had ridden southwards through Dasarna and Vidharbha. Crossing the fertile regions fed by the River Charmanvati and its tributaries in the kingdom of Avanti, he had made good speed over the dry land that followed, to Anartta. Only as he began ascending the Raivata mountains, towards the peak known as Gomanta, had he admitted to himself where he was headed, where it was he had wanted to go since the day he had left home. Now here he was, and the dream that was Dwaraka was right before him.

Partha was amazed, as most people were, at the first glimpse of the citadel on the sea – its size, its prosperity and, most notably, its cheer. Colourful banners decorated the tallest towers and the gates were flung wide open in welcome. Two huge flares burned day and night, visible across many leagues both landward and towards the sea. The flames marked the gate to the port of Dwaraka and its adjoining harbour, which housed the Anartta and Yadu naval forces. Under the protection of this navy, many distant foreign countries sought to trade with Aryavarta. But, at all times, watchful eyes carefully judged whether an approaching fleet came to trade or to invade.

Despite its splendour the city was no compromise as a fort. The shoals connecting the island to the mainland had been identified and used to construct a great bridge and three other smaller ones. The main bridge comprised many guardrooms and turrets, all of which stored arms and flammables. Sharp, spiked gates were discreetly set into ornamented archways at different points along the bridge, and a complex mechanism of gears and chains operated the gates from within the fort. Before the bridge reached the main gate to the city it ran over a unique moat of weapons set into the seabed along the circumference of the island. Iron spears and lances lay covered by the sea, their pointed heads awaiting the unsuspecting invader.

The walls around the city were made of a combination of rock and crystal, for strategic as well as aesthetic purposes – they provided no hold for grappling hooks or ladders, particularly in case of an attack from the sea. The main gate, set into the wall, was a veritable tunnel and gave the impression that the wall ran over fifteen feet deep. In fact, the wall was more of a trench within which catapults and other armaments were concealed – though the elegant walkways and coloured shrubs set on top of the wall could well mislead enemies into thinking that the city was designed as an abode of pleasure, lacking completely in customary defences.

But few cities in Aryavarta were better prepared for war. Smaller walls of similar construction at the outer wall had been placed at various points within the city, splitting off the lower levels that housed the mercantile and trading activities from the higher residential and administrative zones. In case the fort was breached, it was always possible to retreat to another level of the city and continue to defend it from there. For all these measures, though, Partha had heard, Dwaraka, the many-gated, welcomed every living being into its fold. None was denied refuge, irrespective of his origin. In Dwaraka, every life was worthy of honour and respect.

Spellbound, he entered the crystal city on foot, leading his horse in by the reins. He had to see Govinda. He had to understand what sort of a man could build a nation like this one. He had to know what sort of a man could resist a woman like Panchali.

The guards at the gate watched the visitor with a practised eye, evaluating his fine horse and the mark on his shoulder left by his bow, which lay wrapped and concealed in a bundle of cloth. Partha tried to behave as any well-intentioned newcomer to the island city would. He did not have to try hard. Despite his weariness, he could not help but gape at the sparkling towers, gem-studded pillars and smooth marble terraces of Dwaraka's magnificent edifices, at its order, prosperity and splendour. His esteem for Govinda and Balabadra grew immensely.

Not wanting to make his presence widely know, Partha did not enquire the way to Govinda's residence, nor did he send any message. He made his way to the largest, most magnificent-looking building on the island, convinced that it must be the palace of the rulers of this great city. There were no guards to stop him here, nor attendants to guide him. He walked in through a gateless archway to find himself in a garden that housed the rarest and most spellbinding of trees and flowers. Some, he knew, had to have come from outside Aryavarta and were heard of only in legend or read about in travellers' accounts. He walked slowly, conscious of the gravel crunching underfoot with every step. Only when he paused to tether his horse to a beam set in the ground for that very purpose did he realize that the pathway was covered, not with gravel, but with an unbelievable assortment of gemstones.

Spurred on by his astonishment, Partha strode quickly to the massive marble doors of the building. Here, too, there were no guards or attendants. He sounded the small brass gong that hung from a low pillar nearby, but there was no answer, nor was any person to be seen. Realizing that the building had many entrances, he walked around it trying to open some of the doors. He also tried sounding the bells that were placed on the other three sides of the building. Still there was no reply. Finally, he saw a small wooden door, which appeared to be ajar, set almost at one corner of the edifice. Readying himself for the inevitable explanations he would have to give for his trespass, he let himself in.

The building was no palace, no residence even, but a single hall of mammoth proportions. Its interiors were a simple, crystalline white, and the starkness gave it a dignity that no opulence could have afforded.

'What place is this?' Partha whispered in wonder. 'Who lives here?'

'The people's dreams live here, my friend,' a voice answered. 'Freedom, dignity, hope – it is home to these noble beings. We call this place "Sudharma" – the hall of justice.'

Partha turned around to face the speaker. 'Govinda!'

'Yes, indeed! I was told that a rather handsome young archer had come into the city. I suspected it might be you and concluded as much the moment I heard a strange restlessness had fallen over all the young women of Dwaraka,' he said, coming up to grip Partha's arm in a gesture of greeting. 'This is a most unexpected but very pleasant surprise, Partha.'

'It's good to see you too, Govinda ...'

The two men stood looking at each other for a while, with all the awkwardness of acquaintances who knew little of each other. Govinda then laughed at his own omission and warmly invited Partha home.

It came as a yet another revelation to Partha that 'home' was hardly the gargantuan palace he had expected. Govinda's residence was immaculate and spacious, but hardly a contrast to other residences in Dwaraka. The concession granted to him, if any, was that he occupied one of the highest levels of the multi-tiered city, and every vista from the house commanded the most spectacular views of the ocean around them.

After he had seen to his horse, Partha was led to a comfortable room. Tired, he stumbled to the bed, and just about managed to remove his sword and put it safely aside. Lying back on the soft, comfortable sheets, he gradually grew aware of the soothing, rhythmic splash of the sea against rocks. Lulled by the sound, Partha fell into a dreamless, wholesome sleep. He slept through the night and most of the next day, and woke to a glorious sunset and the sounds of evening life around him. Stirring, he forced himself out of his bed and walked over to the large window on his left, which looked out over the city. Below, people went about their routine chores in the colourful medley that was common to large cities. Occasionally, laughter or song rose with the breeze, a tangy sea-wind.

Eventually, Partha turned away from the window to look at the room around him, wondering about a bath and clean clothes. As he stood, hesitant, there was a gentle knock at the door, which was then pushed open slightly. Two stunning women came in on seeing him awake. Partha silently waited, confused. The women wore fine jewellery and clothing, far too opulent for them to be slaves or even attendants. Courtesans, perhaps, he wondered, though they came in carrying what seemed to be silk robes. He immediately dismissed the notion. No courtesan he knew would lift even a feather with her own hands.

'Did you sleep well?' the first of the two asked conversationally, as they nodded in greeting.

Partha marked that they did not bow to him deferentially, as he was accustomed to, though they lacked nothing in politeness or courtesy. 'I did, thank you,' he replied, still a little curious.

The women smiled pleasantly in return and made their way about the room with simple efficiency. The first pushed open a smaller door that Partha had not noticed, to reveal a small, sparkling bathing chamber. A pool was set into the marble floor, and the clear water gave off steam from the hot rocks that had been dropped into it. Rose petals and fragrant oils floated invitingly on its surface.

The second woman gestured towards the room, also pointing out that clean robes of a fine silk had been placed on an ivory pedestal near the pool, ready for his use. Partha stepped into the chamber, wondering if the ladies meant to do more than just guide him there. *That settles that*, he thought to himself as they did not follow him in.

Well rested and refreshed, Partha meandered downstairs in search of Govinda. He stepped into a large dining hall to find that celebrations and jubilant merriment had already begun.

'Aah! There he is!' A red-eyed Balabadra cried, and rising from his seat at the head of a long wooden table came forward to greet him.

'Slept well, I trust?' a gentler voice said. 'I hope Sunanda did not wake you up too soon?'

'No, she didn't, Govinda,' Partha answered, as he was guided to a seat of honour at the table. Around them, busy in their revelry, were many young warriors, some whom he knew by face and others by reputation. All of them came up to him in ones and twos to welcome him or to introduce themselves. Yuyudhana and Kritavarman, both of whom Partha had met on many other occasions, promptly pulled up chairs next to his, jovially evicting the former occupants with feigned disdain.

The banquet was well underway, when Partha leaned over and asked Govinda in a low whisper, 'Err … Forgive me for being discourteous, but I fear that I may make a terrible mistake if I don't clarify …'

'Hmm?'

'Sunanda … is she … what … who is she?'

'Why do you ask?' Govinda queried, his expression inscrutable.

'I'm sorry if I offend you, but …' Partha hesitated, choosing his words carefully, 'it's usually not this difficult to understand whether such an attractive woman is sent just to wait on a guest, or …' Irked at being placed in such a position, he brusquely pointed out, 'To be honest, Govinda, I'm not used to asking this. I'd have already had my way with her but for the fact that this is your realm and that I have the greatest respect for you.'

Govinda laughed and genially slapped Partha on the back. 'My realm …' he softly repeated. 'This is Dwaraka, my friend,' he declared with pride. 'Here every life deserves respect. By our laws, if a man forces himself on a woman, whether she be his wife, a courtesan, a prostitute, anyone … the penalty may even be death.'

After that exchange, Partha did not find the banquet so pleasant anymore. He made his excuses after a decent interval, claiming that he was tired. As he strolled up to his allotted room, the pleasant sound of laughter came floating on the wind. He paused, looking around from the open corridor. He saw a woman in the courtyard below, exchanging some joke or casual banter with some others. It was not difficult to guess her identity, so clear was her resemblance to Balabadra.

So this was Subadra, Govinda's beloved younger sister.

Partha's first reaction was one of shock, even censure. No woman of Hastina's royal household would ever be seen this way, laughing openly, bantering with men, even if they be cousins or brothers. He continued to stare at her, enraged almost, when she suddenly looked up at him. Without hesitation, Subadra inclined her head in a polite greeting and went back to her conversation. Partha continued to stare for a while longer and then turned on his heel and headed into his room. Never had a woman been so unaffected by his presence. Most of them blushed, bashfully averted their gaze, or did something brazen, if not modest. Except, of course, Panchali – and now Subadra.

With a vigorous shake of his head, he forced both women out of his mind. He went over to the window and stood looking down at the wonder that was Dwaraka, trying to decipher the mystery of Govinda Shauri. A knock at the door intruded on his thoughts. To his surprise, Sunanda entered the room. This time, she was alone.

No doubt she comes to tuck me into bed, or to put out the wick lamp, Partha sardonically noted, waiting to see what she did.

Eyes lowered becomingly, the young woman walked over to where he stood and placed a knowing, expert hand on his chest. When he did not react, she gently guided his hands to the curves of her shapely body. Partha needed no further encouragement.

26

PANCHALI FOUND IT HARD TO PRETEND THAT HER MEETING WITH Asvattama had been of no consequence, though she managed to satisfy Dharma's curiosity with truthful, though incomplete reports of how much she had enjoyed seeing the pastoral side of life in Aryavarta.

Her own curiosity was far more difficult to settle, and she spent many sleepless nights trying to rationally order what she had now found out about the Firewrights and the Firstborn. Caught in a silent turmoil that she could share with no one, she settled for focussing on the more immediate mystery of how Wright-craft had played a role in bringing her to Hastina.

She took to poring over maps and reading through the few descriptions of the Kuru–Panchala region that she could lay her hands on. Most of all, she spent days listening to the bards, the keepers of history through the songs and ballads. It bred nothing but frustration but Panchali pushed on, trying to make sense of the lyrical metaphors that somewhere, deep inside their keeping, held a glimpse of fact. *One more good-for-nothing little saamanta described as a heavenly hero and I'll give up*, she promised herself almost every other day.

But she did not. And then, in some obscure lay about one of her great-grandfathers, she found a small reference to a gift from the gods to the kings of Panchala. A bow.

The bow. Panchali's mind instantly jumped to the archery contest where she had been the prize.

And that bow is here.

Making no effort to curb her excitement, she braved the stinging wind that swept the corridors in a prelude to some great storm and half ran towards the small armoury on the eastern end of their palace. The chamber was empty, given that it was almost midnight. A solitary guard was posted at the door. He looked at her with curiosity, but quickly snapped to attention and admitted her inside.

Panchali savoured the change from the chilling gale that screamed outside. Rows of torches burnt merrily in iron brackets set on the walls, their even arrangement throwing shadows in overlapping patterns on the roof of the armoury. Armouries were customarily built of the hardest stone and were naturally dark, but always kept well-lit in case of an exigency. The steady flame of oil-soaked linen was preferred to the more accident-causing wick lamps used in other rooms. Panchali smiled as she stood looking at the soot-stained walls, the familiar smell of oil-smoke bringing to mind the feel of strapping on battle armour, sliding a sword into its scabbard, the solemn yet joyful injunction to die well, the clear clanging sounds of heated battle and the flash of golden sparks as metal caressed metal. Thrilled at her surroundings, she ran a practised eye over the carefully stacked array of weapons.

At the far end a rack housed a number of wooden bows, all of them embellished with gold and small gemstones in tasteful patterns. Dharma's bow bore the insignia of a winged creature, Nakul's had the image of suns. Bhim's was marked with elephants and Sadev's with flowering creepers. Where the empty space for Partha's bow ought to have been was now *the* bow she had been looking for, the one he had brought back from Kampilya.

Panchali touched it reverently, marvelling at its strength and suppleness. Closing her eyes, she went over the events of the contest in her mind, trying to pick out the details that her eyes had seen but her mind had not quite marked. She tried to remember the way she had been won, as if she were a … a thing, a lifeless object. Her mind flitted despite herself to what had happened next, the way she had been passed on like an unwanted prize and married off to another, how she remained an object, a thing of use. Anger coursed through her as she remembered the touch of Partha's hands, his unabashed desire for her.

Maraka! Every curse in existence upon your head, Govinda Shauri!

As her fingers clenched the weapon she felt a slight unevenness on its surface, just at the grooved grip. Not quite sure if she had imagined it, she ran her fingers and then her palm over it a few more times and carefully examined the metal. She missed it the first few times and had to run her fingers over the shiny surface again to find it – an engraving. Panchali felt her heart speed up. It was not uncommon for weapons of such craftsmanship to be engraved with a mark or symbol identifying the maker or even the warrior meant to wield it. Squinting, she scrutinized the surface. To her surprise the engraving was not a symbol, but script. The lettering was tiny but unmistakeable. Her breath came heavy with excitement. Who else but the Wrights could have used writing so many generations ago, she supposed. Holding the metal up to the light, Panchali read the words.

Blessings on the Noble Lords of Panchala. May he who tames the elements bear this bow to great fortunes. Agni the Effulgent himself hath made this, and Varuna, Lord of the Waters, hath held it in his keeping.

Panchali smiled as, like the sun breaking out from behind storm clouds, she understood. *A bow made by Agni and kept safe by Varuna.* Agni, she knew, had to mean the Wrights. Varuna, she supposed, was a reference to water. And in all of Panchala 'water' meant just one thing. The Life-Giver, the River Ganga.

The next day, she demurely expressed her desire to visit her parents for a short while. Dharma was quick to oblige her.

Panchali was affectionately welcomed at Kampilya. She responded with mixed feelings to the news that Shikandin and Dhrstyadymn were both away on military duty and arranged for a message to be sent to them. Much as she longed to see her brothers, she was glad that they were not around to notice her movements and ask her questions. She had to act quickly, before they returned.

A couple of days after she arrived, once the excitement of her arrival had somewhat abated, Panchali asked for her horse to be saddled for her usual ride around the countryside. Her mother's matron and nurse protested, ineffectively, that she simply could not be as irresponsible as before now that she was married. Panchali silenced her with a glare and set off, her pace casual and unhurried. She rode towards the forestland near Utkochaka, but instead of entering the woods she turned eastwards. As the heat grew oppressive Panchali stopped to rest, settling herself in the shade of a tree while her horse grazed nearby. She pulled out from her saddlebag some leavened bread that she had requested her matron to have packed for her and a roughly drawn map she had brought from Hastina. She unfurled the map and studied it once again while she ate.

Panchali traced the course of the Ganga on the scroll. The map as well as the gradient of the land around her suggested that her path should have intersected with that of the river. But it had not. To her right the forest went on, unbroken. To her left she could see the bright flash of the river as it descended along the highlands in the distance and then merged indistinctly into the vast green-blue plains of the lowlands. It did not seem to enter the forest at all. There was nothing ahead but field upon field, simple, verdant and inviting.

Unlike Utkochaka.

Instinct drew her towards the ominous forest, the theme of many colourful, even frightening legends. Most of these tales were fantastical and implausible, but they served to keep out the villagers who tilled these lands. They had kept her out, Panchali noted. An involuntary shiver ran through her at the very notion of invading its depths. Rebuking herself for being silly, she swung back onto her horse, urging the animal on in a gallop before she could change her mind. She slowed down as the forest drew near but kept going and soon entered it. The woods – a thick mix of towering mahogany and sprawling banyan trees – clustered dark and heavy around her. Bramhi creepers fell in familiar curtains every now and then and Ashwagandha and other fruit-bearing shrubs grew clustered in places where sunlight came through the foliage. In these spots, Panchali could catch a glimpse of the sun but the view was never clear enough to check her direction. Eventually, she pulled out her direction-pointer, a light fish-shaped piece of iron hanging from the string that was passed through it, and used it as her guide. She was still going the right way, along the supposed course of the river that the map had indicated, though she now began to wonder if it would lead anywhere at all. Promising herself that she would turn back after a muhurrta or so, she headed deeper into the forest.

The landscape changed little as she moved forward and it seemed to Panchali that every clump of shrubs and cluster of trees she passed looked exactly the same. If it were not for her direction pointer, she would have thought that she was going around in circles. And then she heard the gurgle of running water. Panchali listened, trying to locate the direction from which the sound came. She urged her horse right into a thicket on her left, hissing slightly as a branch she pushed away whipped back and caught her on the shoulder. Just when she thought to draw her sword and hack away at the thick foliage in her way, she came upon the river.

The river ran crystal clear through the forest itself. The canopy of trees had given way here to let the sun illuminate the water in an almost incandescent green glow. Panchali dismounted. From the direction of the flow and the incline of the land she concluded that this was a hidden stream that had branched off from the river just before it hit the plains. *But the map shows no such thing ...* She pulled out the parchment and looked at it a second time, tracing the current path of the river, as it ought to have been drawn, with her finger. She gasped involuntarily as the explanation struck her. What if this had once been the main course of the river? As she considered the kind of effort it would take to divert the stream, she felt a renewed hope surge through her. Only the Firewrights would have had the knowledge, and the ability, to carry out such a diversion. Perhaps this was the right way after all. She washed her face and arms in the cool water, resisting the temptation to swim. As her horse drank thirstily from the stream, she settled on the grassy bank wondering what to do next.

'Upstream or downstream?' she said out loud, ostensibly asking her horse the question.

'That depends, Mahamatra, on whether you can keep a secret.'

Panchali jumped to her feet and whipped around to face the speaker, her hand instinctively moving to the hilt of her sword. A young man in rough ochre robes stood facing her, casually smoothing his short, dark beard. Panchali tried not to look too affected, but could not completely hide her surprise. There was no mistaking the familiar features, the undeniable resemblance to the scholar–priest Ayodha Dhaumya.

The man seemed to understand her confusion. 'You're wondering who I am, and the answer to your suspicion is, yes. But, beyond blood, my brother and I have nothing in common. My name is Devala Asita. As for who or what I am … Tell me, can you keep a secret?'

Recovering quickly, she said. 'Ah! That depends on what the secret is.'

The ochre-clad scholar did not reply, but stepped forward to take the reins of her horse. 'Come.'

Panchali followed him as he headed downstream, walking casually along the riverbank. He did not seem surprised to see her at all, and made light conversation, occasionally pointing out plants of medicinal value or identifying a bird by its call. Ahead, the river split into two, divided by a huge rock that was part of its bed. Panchali noticed that the smaller of the two streams had been diverted into a stone tank that was obviously of human make. At the other end of the tank, the water flowed over and fell back into the stream, pushing past a familiar-looking series of wooden wheels set on a single axle. It was, beyond question, Wright-work. The many-teethed cogs, the water wheel, the wooden beam pushing down into the ground, were almost identical to what she had seen in Northern Panchala, except she saw neither grain bin, nor mill. Also, a series of stone lattices were set into the ground a few feet away from the tank.

'The mill is underground?' she asked.

'Not a mill, a forge. The water-wheel powers the bellows for the furnace.'

Panchali gasped, delighted, as she understood the functions of the mechanisms before her and consequently the origins of the mighty bow. The wide water tank and the lattices were meant, obviously, to cool down the forge and make working there bearable. Her happiness soon faded as she tried to take stock of her recent discoveries and what they meant.

The scholar waited patiently.

'How many of these are there?' she eventually asked.

'Only this one. The one near Mathura lies broken to pieces. I've heard that Agniveshya Angirasa built another one during his days in hiding, but I don't know for sure.'

Panchali's voice was a whisper, a sad, hushed prayer almost, as she asked, 'How many more Wrights …?'

'I'm the last of the faithful among my order. Many traitors remain – those trained by us, who've turned against us, joining with the Firstborn.' He shook his head dolefully. 'I'm the last. I spent all these years in hiding. Few people know that I'm still alive. After Ghora died, I've tried to find those of us that may be left. So far there's been no one. Perhaps they're afraid to reveal themselves, or even think this is a trap set for them by the Firstborn,' he finished quietly. Then he drew himself up and fixed Panchali with an honest, compelling stare. 'It doesn't matter. *You* are here.'

'Do you know why I'm here?'

'I think I do. You have a good heart, Princess. Privileged you may be, but you haven't lost your sense of justice or empathy.'

Panchali was too startled at his response to say anything.

'We Wrights were inventors, discoverers, not just weapon-makers,' he went on. 'Through the centuries, we've found ways to till the land, irrigate it, work metal in different ways, mix herbs and essences to create medicines and poisons both … To be known as a Wright, even as the youngest of their students, was an honour across all of Aryavarta. But then, we were destroyed, from the oldest man down to the smallest infant …'

Panchali shifted uncomfortably, as she realized that her own little drama, the way she had been played as a political toy, now felt trivial in comparison. 'What do you want from me?' she finally managed to say.

'I ask for little, Panchali. In fact, I ask for nothing more than that you follow your heart, that you do what you know to be the right thing.'

Panchali tried to keep the quiver out of her voice. 'What ... what do you want me to do?' she asked.

'Govinda Shauri.'

'Govinda?'

'Yes. He'll listen to you. Perhaps only to you. You alone can turn him from the bloody path that he plans to take.'

'Govinda? Bloody path? I don't ...'

'Understand?' The Firewright smirked coldly. 'I'm not surprised. Few men hide their intentions as well as Govinda does. There's only one thing Govinda wants, my dear. He wants to be Emperor.'

'Emperor? Govinda?'

'Think about it. Think of how he slowly earns the gratitude of the Kurus and Panchalas, even as he undermines Jarasandha's power. He's not stupid. He's a consummate politician; in my opinion, a better diplomat than he is a warrior. Even the Vyasa fails to see where that cowherd is dragging them all.'

Panchali flinched at the Wright's derogatory tone. 'While you of all people seem to be able to see right through him?' she challenged.

'Yes. Because I know better than to trust him. Ever.'

Panchali was all set to retort, but hesitated as a mix of emotions struck her. Her first response was, strangely, happiness, even pride at the thought of Govinda as Emperor, ruler of all Aryavarta. It lasted only for a moment as the sad truth hit home. He had played her, toyed with her, spun half-truths to serve his ends. He had given her up for a greater cause – the cause of power, of empire. His empire.

The pain of the realization gradually filled her, turning into disgust, anger and, ultimately, the bitter heartbreak of betrayal. Tears stung her eyes, and she looked away into the distance, careful not to meet the eyes of the man in front of her. Yet, as she inhaled sharply to clear her head, Panchali could not imagine Govinda as Emperor without some sense of hope and even anticipation. She had no doubt that he would be a good ruler to his people. That was the most important thing.

'I can't help you stop him if that's what you want,' she snapped at the scholar.

He grimaced. 'I don't think we could stop him even if we tried.'

'What do you want then?'

'Help me save those that can be saved. Help me avoid bloodshed and battle.'

Panchali felt a shiver run down her spine. Not too long ago she would have thought Govinda incapable of wanton violence, just as she had once thought him incapable of betraying her trust. She suddenly felt afraid, but with each passing moment her fear gave way to a focussed confidence. *There are no coincidences in the Eternal Universe*, she reminded herself. Everything had a meaning, a purpose. She had found hers. Her own silent acceptance, her helpless acquiescence to the way she had been manipulated and used now felt like purposive patience, as though she had been waiting for fate to bring her to this juncture. It was her destiny.

She looked up at the Firewright, her eyes filled with a dull pain. 'How?'

Devala Asita smiled. 'When the time is right you will know what you must do. Till then we must be patient.'

27

LIFE HAD NEVER BEEN BETTER FOR PARTHA, NOR HAD HE EVER been happier than in the few months he had spent at Dwaraka.

Govinda was capable of companionship without speaking a single word, even for hours on end. They rode around the countryside together, sometimes hunting in the wild or else marvelling at the scenic beauty that surrounded them. At these times, Partha could just about believe that Govinda had once been a cowherd, but hardly a common one. The man loved nature and seemed to be a part of it, always. He could blissfully sleep on the grass, like he had never known the silk sheets and soft mattresses of his palace and he would drink water from a clear, gurgling stream as though it were ambrosia. Once, Partha had gone down to the stables adjoining Govinda's mansion, to find him stripped to a short waist-cloth, rubbing down Balahak and his other three Qamboja stallions – Shaibya, Sugriv and Megha – the way a stableman would. Yet, as the oil-stained, sweaty Govinda kept up an incessant conversation with his horses, Partha could have sworn that the animals not only understood him but also clearly answered in their own way.

At other times, Partha sat discreetly as an observer during Council meetings, marvelling at the way the Yadus ran their nation. He was most amazed by Govinda's ability to take control of any and every situation. Even after all these days, he still could not understand exactly what it was about the man that was so compelling, but there was no denying that behind that lop-sided grin and the light banter was an incisive mind and a keen sense of justice. Govinda was honest, undeniably honest, but not above innuendo, both in jest and as a tool of persuasion. His warm smile disarmed even the most hostile of opponents, and his equanimity was beyond belief. Nothing ever quite moved him, and the only extreme of emotion that he showed was to occasionally laugh out loud.

With a twinge of guilt Partha admitted to himself that he felt a lot more at ease with Govinda and without his brothers around. He loved the four of them, but with Dharma the Noble, Bhim the Mighty, Nakul the Handsome and Sadev the Wise around, Partha's only claim to fame had been his reputation as a womanizer. Of course, he had been the one to win Panchali ... With grim determination, he forced the thought out of his mind. It did not matter. Not here. The friendship and camaraderie he had found was far more precious, for Govinda neither judged nor indulged him. Partha made a firm resolution that in this matter he would remain unique; none of his brothers would ever be friends with Govinda the way he was.

Finally, reassured by his newfound friendship and the air of informality and camaraderie that was far removed from the staid routines of Hastina, Partha was ready. He found Govinda discussing the arrangements for the next day's mountain festival with Balabadra and Subadra. After a moment's hesitation, partly because he was reluctant to interrupt and partly because he felt his heart skip a beat when he glanced at Subadra, Partha asked Govinda if they could talk in private. Govinda looked surprised, but immediately obliged. Partha left the room without looking at the others. It was time for the conversation that had made him come all the way to Dwaraka.

The two men sat in Govinda's personal chamber, an airy room with large windows on every wall. By accident or by design, the soft mats on the floor and large seating cushions were all in shades of white and blue. At the far end, the room opened out on to a large terrace, set with the shining white fluted balustrades that were characteristic of Dwaraka. Partha felt like he was sitting on a piece of the evening sky or on the very ocean itself. Whether it was the pleasant dissipation of his anxieties, or mainly that Govinda was a patient listener, but he soon found himself recounting every incident, pouring out every feeling he had known, since the tournament at Kampilya.

Govinda showed no emotion throughout the narrative and stood staring out of the window, at the sea.

Then Partha tonelessly spoke of the events leading to his departure from Hastina.

Govinda said nothing still, but for just one moment, every line in his body, every muscle, every nerve, went rigid and taut. Partha did not dare justify his actions. 'Help me, Govinda,' he said, earnest and sincere. 'You have to help me.'

When he replied, Govinda's voice was even. 'What would you have me do, Partha?' he asked.

'Tell me, how can I make up for my actions? How can I go on with the rest of my life this way?' Partha met Govinda's gaze, as he admitted, 'We each wanted Panchali, there's no denying that. I won her, we all stood ready to defend her and Dharma married her. But to whom does she truly belong? How can we, all five of us, go on this way? What do we do?'

'Even if I told you what to do, you wouldn't be able to do it, Partha,' Govinda said. 'But I'll tell you anyway. Do nothing.'

'How can I do nothing? Don't you realize what a terrible position we've placed her in? Why did she react that way when I touched her? How can we set her free?'

Govinda chortled in disdain. 'Panchali isn't someone you set free. You can't tame her or cage her in the first place. She makes her own decisions, and she decided to submit to the circumstances and marry Dharma. You're not responsible for that.'

'What am I responsible for?' a disconsolate Partha asked.

'Yourself. Only yourself.'

'And you, Govinda? Do you hold responsibility only for yourself?'

Govinda paused. This was not something he wasn't ready to discuss with Partha. Not yet. He said, 'If you can't take responsibility for yourself, Partha, then there's no question of being responsible for more.'

They talked long into the night, but did not refer to Panchali again. Eventually, Partha bid his host goodnight and left. He retired to his room and lay on the bed in a daze. The sound of anklets sang softly on the wind. Partha quickly went to the window overlooking the courtyard. He remained standing at the window long after the pleasant tinkle had faded away.

Govinda sat on the cold stone floor of the terrace adjoining his room, leaning against the wall. Sleep eluded him. It was a few hours before dawn when, woken up and summoned by a pensive Govinda, Balabadra came to join him. To Govinda's surprise, so did Subadra. She sat next to him, her head on his shoulder, while Balabadra stood leaning against the low crystal railings that bound the terrace, looking at them both. Bit by bit, Govinda shared with his siblings what he had learnt from Partha that evening.

Subadra shivered, though it was not cold. 'What he tried to do ... to Panchali ...' she began, and then, with a meaningful glance at Balabadra, continued, 'I suppose this makes your case for my marriage to Syoddhan even stronger, doesn't it?'

'How did you know …?' Balabadra growled.

'I listen at doors,' she said snidely. The two brothers looked at her, astounded. She continued, calm, 'I'm not being vengeful, nor am I joking. I'm nearly nineteen, by Rudra! You should realize that I'm no longer a four-year-old with a runny nose, who tends to get lost in the woods if she lets go of your hand.'

'No, you're not,' Govinda admitted.

Balabadra continued, speaking for them both, 'You're a beautiful, intelligent woman, whom we both dearly love …'

'You failed to mention my excellent sense of humour and my immaculate grace,' Subadra responded in jest. She then fixed her brother with a cool gaze. 'There's no need to pretend you haven't considered this. Haven't you been planning it for a while now? Did you expect that I'd wait for you both to use me as a silent political pawn? I agree with you and so I act in consort with you.'

'And if you hadn't agreed with our objectives?' Balabadra asked.

Subadra laughed and ran her fingers through her soft, wavy hair. She did not answer his question directly, saying instead, 'I once thought of eloping, you know.'

'Who with?' Balabadra demanded.

She grinned mischievously, revealing a stark resemblance to Govinda, and said, 'It makes no difference, not anymore. If you want me to marry Partha or any of the other Kurus, I shall. Except for Dharma. I won't marry Dharma.'

Govinda laughed softly, but was interrupted.

'Govinda,' Subadra cajoled, 'why won't you let me have my share in your duty, my share of the honour? Do you believe that I lack courage? If you truly considered me your sister, and not the child of your father's other wife …'

'Subadra, please.'

She fell silent in response to the admonition.

At length, Govinda prompted, 'How did you learn to twist emotions with words so skilfully?'

Subadra gleefully replied, 'I'm sister to the best, to the master of puppets.'

'No one's a pawn. No one's a puppet. And I'm no puppeteer,' Govinda stated flatly.

Before Subadra could respond, Balabadra intervened to prevent what he knew would become a habitual sibling squabble rather than an argument on merits. He placed his hand on Subadra's head in a loving, paternal gesture. 'All right. We'll talk more about this. Seriously, we shall,' he assured her. 'Now go,' he said, sending her on her way.

Balabadra and Govinda stretched themselves out under the open sky, as they often used to when they were children, and gazed silently at the lightening expanse above. Gradually, lulled by the waves lapping against the city's walls, the two men drifted off to sleep.

Govinda dreamt of a sunny village by a river. A tree, its emerald-green leaves flecked with gold from the sun, caressed the crystal blue waters as they gurgled by. Hanging from the hard bough, now arcing over the water, and now over the land, was a swing, a simple plank of wood held up by ropes of hemp. Her long, black hair streamed out behind her, painting a dark blur. Asleep under the mild winter sky, Govinda smiled.

The next morning, during the mountain festival of the Yadus, Partha thundered through the merry crowd on a chariot, two of Govinda's white stallions yoked to it. Pulling Subadra on to the vehicle, he sped away before anyone could react.

The Council met right away, and the angry representatives proposed to chase Partha and give fight. Govinda and Balabadra looked uncertainly at each other, not sure whether Subadra had willingly eloped, even orchestrated the mock abduction, or, in fact, had been taken against her consent.

Keeping his jumbled thoughts to himself, Govinda addressed the gathered leaders. 'Perhaps it's for the best, my friends. An alliance with the Kurus is to our advantage, and in a way we might consider this an act of valour on Partha's part, that he dares take our sister from our midst. Besides,' he observed, 'he's yoked two of my four stallions to his chariot. Even if we give chase, we may not be able to stop him before he reaches his own kingdom. Imagine then, the disgrace to us all …'

His words effectively dampened the fiery spirits of the assembled warriors. After further debate it was agreed that a message would be sent to Hastina, informing the Kurus of Balabadra's willingness to give Subadra in marriage to Partha. This done, the Council dispersed.

Govinda and Balabadra sat quiet and still in the empty Sudharma Hall, not sure whether to consider the turn of events as providential or unfortunate.

'They took your horses,' Balabadra pointed out. 'It suggests that she was in on the plan,' he surmised, hopeful.

Govinda sneered. 'Do you dare ask her, Agraja? What if he's taken her by force and we've let her down because we didn't even try to help her? Even now, don't we already know …? It's just easier to pretend we don't.'

'We have no choice. Even if we are sure, we have no choice,' Balabadra said. 'Subadra knows that. She knows that a conflict between the Yadus and the Kurus could destroy us.'

Govinda nodded in acknowledgement. 'Yes. Conflict would destroy us. An alliance on the other hand …'

The two brothers sighed, neither willing to admit that Partha's visit could not have gone better.

28

IT WAS SAID, REVERENTIALLY, THOUGH NOT VERY OPENLY, THAT Dwaipayana knew what transpired in every nook of Aryavarta even before the gods watching over the land did. His hermitage was nestled in the distant Himalayan foothills, though for all practical purposes the little hamlet was the heart of the Empire. It was here that the Vyasa spent much of his time with his group of highly intelligent and dedicated disciples and the grey messenger pigeons he lovingly reared; here that he devoted himself to rearranging and dividing the scriptures, the treasure trove of Aryavarta's knowledge; and here that all news of Aryavarta reached Dwaipayana's ears. It was here, too, that Ghora Angirasa had died.

And, it was where one of Dwaipayana's trusty messengers brought news of the events at Dwaraka, which had culminated in Partha and Subadra's much-celebrated arrival at Hastina.

The Elder pronounced his blessings on the couple straight away, looking delighted at the turn of events. He said as much to Sanjaya, who sat sullen, without reply. Laughing, the scholar prompted, 'You don't agree with me, do you, Sanjaya?'

'This jeopardizes all our plans, Acharya! It was difficult enough to press Dhrupad to marry the girl to Dharma despite his enmity with Dron and the Kurus. Just when it seemed all was in place and the time was right for us to make the next move, Govinda Shauri rears his head and becomes brother-in-law to the Kurus. I should have known, I should have foreseen it,' Sanjaya ranted. 'Govinda gave up far too easily on the girl.'

'My son, you're a good statesman. But you still have a few things to learn before you become a great statesman.'

Sanjaya looked up eagerly. He knew better than to be disappointed when the Vyasa made such statements, for they were usually a prelude to the most valuable insights.

'It's like a game, of say ... tiger and lambs,' Dwaipayana continued. 'A good statesman, someone like Bhisma, for example, will cleverly aim to move the pieces one at a time, always keeping in mind what his opponent's response could be. Mind you, it is a difficult challenge and takes immaculate planning. But a truly great statesman is a philosopher of sorts. He recognizes that it is not just one move that matters; he sees the game in its entirety. Sometimes a single move changes your position from strength to weakness, or the other way around – not because the move itself is special but because of its effect on the other positions and on the game as a whole. The great statesman knows that the game can, and most probably will, be upset, and he accepts it. And he'll be prepared.'

Sanjaya laughed softly. 'So,' he said, 'it's important to keep in mind what the pieces were meant to achieve, rather than the moves that were planned.'

'Precisely! Balabadra had planned to marry Subadra to Syoddhan. An alliance was inevitable. I didn't expect Partha to go to Dwaraka, but when he did I didn't try to stop him. My anticipation was that Partha, being the womanizer that he is, would certainly court Subadra. Don't you see how this works to our benefit? We've used Govinda Shauri before ... Perhaps it is his destiny and ours that he serves us again.'

'Dharma can use Govinda's help to establish his own realm ...'

'Yes. What's important is that Dharma sees the opportunity that lies before him. We need to bring it to his attention, Sanjaya. Plant the idea in his head that *he* can rule Western Kuru. Get him to send for Govinda.'

'Who, of course, will come running to Hastina.'

With a laugh, Dwaipayana asked, 'Really, the curiosity is killing! Why does Govinda Shauri bother you so much, my son?'

Sanjaya did not deny the allegation. He squared his shoulders, glad that he did not have to politely conceal his contempt for the man. 'His ideas are ungodly, and worse still they are contagious. If they should spread ... or endure ... they can cause more damage than the man himself could in his lifetime. It would be easy for us to discredit Govinda and get rid of him. In any case, he has no legitimacy as a ruler and little earned as honour. He is, after all, the coward who ran from Jarasandha's armies.'

Dwaipayana replied, 'He has proven himself, on many occasions, to be a formidable warrior. How do you explain that?'

'Even demons and devils may be formidable. That does not make them different from what they are,' Sanjaya pointed out. 'What bothers me is that we give Govinda too much power, assuming that what he does is to our benefit. When we're done with him, when we're finished, how do we push this animal back into its cage?'

The Elder nodded his agreement. 'This is what I like about you, Sanjaya. You see things that even I don't. "Far-sighted" should be your title! Indeed, it isn't just I who think so, but Suka said something similar about you the other day ...'

Sanjaya inclined his head, gracefully accepting the compliment. However, he was not done. 'Acharya, it's never too early to lay the foundations of doubt in people's minds, a tiny suspicion that we can later use to control Govinda. As you've often said, a beautiful woman can be a dangerous weapon … There could always be rumour of … improprieties. Govinda clearly holds some affection for the girl, innocent or otherwise …'

'On the contrary. I want you to avoid any such rumours, whether baseless or not, at all costs,' Dwaipayana instructed. 'It would spoil our plans completely.'

Sanjaya was not convinced. 'If you say so, Acharya,' he grudgingly admitted. 'But coming back to the original point, I'm afraid Dharma is still unprepared to claim a realm for his own, with or without Govinda Shauri. Kandava is a very dangerous place indeed.'

'Which is why, Sanjaya, your king and his son, Dhritarastra and Syoddhan, didn't hesitate for a moment to cede Western Kuru to Dharma. Besides, when have my son and grandson ever refused me anything? The idea of giving Dharma a kingdom of his own should please the Grandsire Bhisma, too. As for Kandava, there's nothing to be afraid of. The blessings of Indra himself shall be on Dharma. Go and tell my grandson to do his duty and rightfully claim his own.'

Sanjaya hesitated for a moment, wondering if this was the best time to share his true suspicions about Govinda with the Vyasa. He immediately thought better of it. Bidding his farewell, he left the hermitage, riding straight for Hastina.

As soon as he arrived, Sanjaya quickly washed up and changed his clothes, doing away with all evidence of his recent travel and the urgency with which he had returned. Then, picking up one of many minor administrative scrolls he had kept by just for such an occasion, he called on Dharma. As was common between men of learning, the two spent a long time in pleasant conversation on many topics. Only when the palace guard changed for the night, did the two become aware of the late hour. Sanjaya immediately took his leave, remembering at the last moment to deliver the scroll that had brought him there in the first place.

Alone, Dharma cast a quick glance at the parchment and threw it aside, wondering distractedly why Sanjaya had considered the meaningless document so important. Brushing the question away, he sat down and turned his attention to the niggling idea that had arisen quite suddenly at the back of his mind. He lay wide-eyed and sleepless through the remaining hours of the night.

The next evening, when Dharma joined Panchali for a walk on the pristine lawns, as was their routine, he told her about Sanjaya's visit and the chain of thought that it had set off in his head.

Panchali cursed silently, as she puzzled over what it could all mean. She felt a chill run through her, though she was fairly snug and warm in a woollen tunic and the matching shawl of thick yarn that she had worn over her usual antariya. Some years ago, she had borrowed one of Shikandin's woollen tunics and found it to be most comfortable. Laughing at the sight of her in his oversized garment, her brother had immediately sent riders to Gandhara, where the women wore such clothing through their harsh winters. The feminine woollen tunics of that region had become Panchali's winter staple ever since. The rich, brocade-embellished garment she now wore was, however, a gift from Queen Gandhari. When she had heard of Panchali's fondness for clothing from her homeland, Gandhari had arranged for her best seamstresses to create a tasteful wardrobe of matching tunics and shawls for her. The queen had commented on the occasion that Hastina, after all, was both colder and windier than Kampilya. Panchali had not missed the innuendo in her words.

'What do you think, Panchali?' Dharma intruded on her reverie.

Panchali dithered a moment, but not for reasons of discretion. Unlike the palace, with its many hidden corridors and keyholes, the garden afforded a rare privacy. This once, however, she was unsure of what to say. 'I'm honoured that you ask me, Dharma,' she eventually said, 'but shouldn't you consult with your mother and brothers?'

'I'd be most grateful for your opinion,' he told her.

'We don't have a choice, do we?' Panchali ventured, a little hesitantly. 'The only alternative is to let things remain as they are …'

'True,' Dharma agreed. 'But are we, in fact, better off as dependants? I assure you, it is not possible to win Kandava from Takshaka in battle. It may well be a way to see us to our deaths. I don't fear conflict, Panchali, but I do fear dishonour. This wouldn't be an even fight by any token. But, as you said, do we have a choice? We've been here, at Hastina, for two years, come the next rains.'

'And you believe that Govinda can find a way to conquer Kandava?'

'Perhaps,' Dharma began, 'there are such things as destiny and coincidence, as Dwaipayana often tells me. Govinda Shauri is my maternal uncle's son, but that relationship has been long neglected. Now he is kinsman anew and, so, my ally. I hear he's dealt with the Nagas before. Perhaps it's a good time to invite him to Hastina.'

Panchali laughed softly. In a wistful tone she said, 'Brahman, the eternal universe, knows no coincidences. What we humans call coincidence is just our failure to see deeper meaning and purpose.'

'Panchali, your words are worth their weight in gold.'

'These aren't my words, Dharma. Call it coincidence, but it was Govinda Shauri who once said this to me.'

The two walked in companionable silence till they reached Panchali's rooms.

'There is one more thing …' Dharma slowly began, sitting down on a couch. 'I shall take courage from what you said a while ago and share something that's been on my mind for some time. I'm sure you know that Subadra is with child …'

Panchali nodded. She brought him a glass of wine and sat down beside him as he continued, 'I am of the opinion that her child, as the eldest of the next generation, ought to be heir to whatever domain we rule …'

'Dharma, that's wonderful,' she exclaimed. 'It's … I mean … I'm at a loss for words!'

'Thank you, my dear. But there's something more I need from you, if this is to be done.'

'Of course!'

Dharma reached out to take Panchali's hand in his. 'Legally, you and I will be the parents of all children born to us five brothers. I want them all to be brought up as one and never know any differences among them. You've seen how our cousins and we have been torn apart by such issues. I don't want that to happen to the next generation, at all costs, and so ...'

'Hmm?' she gently encouraged.

'We'll have no children of our own, Panchali. That way, there will be no difference, no basis on which the heir's title can be contested.'

Panchali repressed the surge of anger that she felt, forcing herself to look at the outcome rather than consider Dharma's true intentions. Despite his claims that his idea was rooted in a sense of fairness and in the interests of peace, she knew what his real motivation was. He needed Govinda on his side if Kandava was ever to be reclaimed, and this was to be Govinda's inducement, his bait: The thought of his line, his blood, on the throne of the Kurus in generations to come.

Or, she wondered, as she remembered her strange encounter with the Firewright scholar, was this entire plan of Govinda Shauri's devising after all. *Who manipulates whom? Who holds the strings that makes us all puppets?*

She realized that Dharma was anxiously awaiting her response to his proposal. One that was for the greater good, no matter what other private motives it served. *An individual for the sake of the family ...*

Panchali nodded her assent. 'But of course,' she affirmed. 'I agree that it would be best ...' She faltered, gasping as, without warning, Dharma pulled her close and into his arms.

To Panchali's surprise, there was no trace of the man she had known on her wedding night, the guilt-ridden, morally tormented man. Instead, Dharma was far from restrained as he romanced and seduced her. As he led her to the bed, she thought to resist him, out of sheer spite. She felt as though she were outside of her body, watching herself in Dharma's arms, amused and abstractedly pondering her own dilemma because the problem was far more interesting than the solution. Laughing softly, she gave in.

Later that night, as she lay in Dharma's arms, sated and tired, Panchali smiled softly into the dark. She would see Govinda again, very soon.

29

ALL OF HASTINA TOOK ON A FESTIVE AIR TO GREET GOVINDA Shauri. Dhritarastra gave explicit orders that no cost or effort should be spared on the occasion. If the order arose from the king's genuine affection for Govinda, that appeared to have been overlooked entirely as everyone, from the attendants to Dhritarastra's sons, laboured to show off Hastina's might and glory. Even the stones of the fortress and the marble walls of the palace seemed to shine brighter, almost dazzling the eye.

A few days before Govinda was due to arrive, every vassal and saamanta, every friend and ally of the Kurus rode to Hastina, accompanied by impressive guards of honour and some with even a full battalion of soldiers. At Dhrupad's insistence, Dhrstyadymn led in a full division of the Panchala army. Shikandin, however, came into the city as a discreet, lone traveller. He used one of the minor entrances to the palace grounds, a small portcullis manned by just two guards. Bhim met him at the gate and escorted him directly to Dharma's palace.

The moment Shikandin stepped into the hallway, Panchali threw herself into his arms and burst into tears. A thoroughly perplexed Shikandin tried to console her and she finally got a hold of herself.

'I'm sorry. It's just that I've missed you so much ...' Panchali smiled through her tears and added, 'Who'd have reckoned me for a sentimental woman?'

'Woman?' Shikandin exclaimed in mock astonishment. 'Panchali, only adults are considered women, not blubbering children ...'

'So say you, you overgrown infant!' Panchali retorted, and the two siblings laughed heartily.

The next few days, Panchali felt almost as happy as she used to back in Kampilya. Dhrstyadymn bore the brunt of the inevitable diplomatic meetings and exchanges with good grace, leaving Panchali and Shikandin with all the time they needed with each other. Despite his happiness at seeing his sister, though, Shikandin was clearly not comfortable being at Hastina. At first Panchali thought it the result of their father's usual distrust and malice, which indeed was reflected in how the Kurus dealt with him as compared to Dhrstyadymn. But she understood the real cause of Shikandin's unease when she saw his reaction to the small figure who sat alone on a stone bench under one of the many broad arches that artistically dotted the gardens of Hastina's palace.

Subadra saw Panchali look in her direction, but pretended that she had not noticed. She tried to ignore the pang of jealousy she felt for the slightest of moments, but gave up, feeling tired of the simple purposelessness of her own life. If it had not been for Panchali, Subadra knew, she would have gone mad at Hastina.

It had been easy for Subadra to be a rebel in the comfort and safety of her brothers' indulgent care. She had spoken freely, thrown caution to the winds and lived a carefree life. But Hastina was not Dwaraka, and to her own surprise she had found that she did not have Panchali's courage. She submitted to the expectations of Kurus and pretended to be the shy, passive woman they wanted her to be. A part of her wondered if she did so just to be anything but the person Partha had seen at Dwaraka. Perhaps, she concluded, this was her way of seeking a convoluted revenge for what he had done.

Panchali's support and affection had been unconditional. Not once did she judge or question Subadra's submissive behaviour, but in her own, silent way she signalled that she would not hesitate to stand up for her younger companion. In turn, Subadra had been what Panchali had needed to resume a cordial relationship with Partha. Still, his attraction for Panchali was not something he managed to hide successfully. Subadra, for her part, pretended not to notice, more for Panchali's sake than Partha's.

The young woman looked unseeing into the distance, fighting back the tears that welled up in her eyes. This was not what she had thought she would become. Worse still, this was not what Govinda had wanted for her. She dreaded her brother's arrival, as much as she longed for it; she dreaded to let him see her this way.

A painfully familiar voice intruded on her reverie. 'You look worried, whether you'll admit it or not ...' Shikandin was alone. Panchali, now a distant image, was headed back indoors.

Subadra looked at him with mild disapproval. 'I'm just bored,' she responded lightly.

'Bored?' Shikandin teased, 'Mahamatra, you break my heart. Barely moments of my company and you're already bored!' He clucked sadly. 'I really must learn to be more interesting.'

'But you don't need to be more interesting! In fact, your wretched situation is to your advantage. Women would lavish their affections on you out of pity, if nothing else. Then, of course, you'd have little time for me, but I suppose I must make this sacrifice for you,' Subadra finished with feigned resignation.

Shikandin stared into her eyes, marvelling at the innocence, the openness they held. She was trying to be playful, he knew, but every emotion, every move of hers was so obvious and clear to him. *How could anyone be so trusting*, he asked himself.

'I'm the father of a ten-year-old boy, Subadra. I don't think there is room in my life for a woman's affections anymore,' he casually said.

She did not reply. Shikandin took a seat next to her on the bench and looked at her. She was every bit as gorgeous as he remembered her to be. Subadra had Balabadra's light skin, and oval, cherubic face, but Govinda's cheeky grin. She wore a long antariya, wrapped around her hips to fall till her ankles, with a few pleats thrown in to allow for easy movement. A short, fitting, tunic covered her bust, and her upper robe discreetly hid the tell-tale bulge of her abdomen.

'I'm glad to see you, Shikandin,' she told him. 'It's been long, far too long.'

'I didn't think I'd ever see you here of all places, Subadra,' he replied.

'Or perhaps you didn't want to see me at all? I've been here so long, and Kampilya is but a day's ride … It would have meant so much to me to hear a kind word from you …'

'Hmm, let's see, a kind word. Do you remember when I told you that even if I were the dumbest stone, I'd come to life at the sight of you? That I'd gladly become a brick in the walls of Dwaraka just to have a glimpse of your enchanting face every day?'

Subadra laughed. 'You were drunk that day!' she reminded him. 'And you still haven't told me which poor poet you stole that line from,' she teased. 'Or will you now admit that you were driven to your wits' end by my incomparable beauty?'

'Beauty? What beauty? It was the shock of nearly being run down by you and your horses!' Shikandin roared with mirth as Subadra feigned offence. Finally, their laughter softened and stopped. The two enjoyed the brief quiet that followed.

'I'm glad to see you, too,' Shikandin suddenly declared, his voice hoarse. 'I just wish the circumstances had been otherwise.'

Subadra gasped and looked at him in amazement. His eyes said more than he had. 'What … what do you mean?' she whispered.

Shikandin looked down at his large, calloused hands. 'When I heard that two of Govinda's stallions had been yoked to the chariot it was easy to guess what had happened. If you'd eloped of your own accord, you'd have driven all four horses. I doubt Partha can manage that, skilled as he may be. The fact that only two horses were taken …' He shrugged.

Subadra said nothing, but turned away to stare into the distance once again.

'I hope you're happy here … with Partha.' With that, Shikandin stood and bowed regally before he walked away.

Inside the palace, Bhisma watched from a window as Shikandin strode across the green lawns.

'He would have made a great monarch,' Asvattama pointed out in his slow, sardonic manner, relishing the way Bhisma's smug smile disappeared. 'He's the kind of man who deserves First Honour at every ceremony he graces. But, alas, neither distinction will ever be his, will it?'

Bhisma glared at the younger man. 'I've done whatever it takes to preserve the honour of the Kurus. The son must pay for the sins of the father. Shikandin must pay for Dhrupad's errors, just as you must pay for Dron's. For my part, I've wished no one ill, but I won't hesitate to destroy anyone who threatens the glory of this great dynasty. Is that clear?'

Asvattama nodded. It was not without cause that Bhisma had mentioned his father.

'You wished to speak to me about something, Grandsire?' he asked, emphasizing on Bhisma's epithet. He wanted there to be no doubt that his deference to the older man was based on age alone and not on title. Bhisma was just a regent, where Asvattama was a king.

'You know that Dharma has been given the western half of Kuru as his to rule?'

'I do.'

'And? What do you think?'

'It's not for me to comment on the internal policies of the Kurus,' Asvattama said. 'After all, yours is a sovereign state, *just like mine.*'

The older man did not rise to the bait. He said, 'And the Nagas, what are they?'

Asvattama said nothing, but waited in silence, as if Bhisma had not finished speaking.

'You are a Firewright ...' Bhisma said at length.

'No. I'm merely a descendant of Agni Angiras.'

'It is more than birth, Asvattama. I've seen you since you were an infant, my boy; you have the Firewright talent, something that your father and your uncle Kripa both lack completely.'

Asvattama frowned, not sure if the old Regent meant to condemn or compliment him. His father Dron, he knew, would not be pleased at either possibility.

Bhisma went on, 'I just thought you might be in a good position to assess the chances that Dharma has of getting rid of Takshaka.

It seems to me that the Nagas have always had a surprising affinity, friendship even, with the Firewrights. I only wonder how deep that affinity goes. Is it possible that they have weapons more powerful than ours? I can't help but worry sometimes … What if there is some astra, weapon, far more powerful than every other force on earth? Do you believe in it, Asvattama? Do you think someone has it?'

Asvattama now understood what Bhisma wanted. It amused him a lot more than he let show. 'You must have considered all possibilities before you advised the King to give Western Kuru to Dharma. Ghora Angirasa's death, Agniveshya Angirasa's death – you must have considered the fact that no Firewrights remain to fight for your enemies, and against you and your kinsmen. What makes you doubt your own conclusions?'

Bhisma fixed Asvattama with a penetrating look. He found the man just a little too perceptive for his comfort. He turned away to look out the window, again. Shikandin was nearly at Dharma's palace, at the far end of the grounds, and would soon disappear from view.

'What about Govinda Shauri?' Bhisma asked, disdain ringing in his voice.

'What about him?'

'Is he … dangerous?'

'He remains undefeated in battle,' Asvattama replied.

'Which is no great feat if one surrenders or runs away from a fight,' Bhisma snorted. 'Besides, I can't think of any notable wars he's fought. Dwaraka was built on uninhabited land and there was no conquest there. His only claim to valour is the killing of Kans and, of course, the so-called downfall of the Firewrights. Frankly, that's far too much credit to a man who did nothing but stand aside and watch while others finished them off.'

'Itself a great achievement, I'd venture. Others would have gladly scavenged on the remains.'

Bhisma glowered with restrained rage. He was not as tall as Asvattama, but had the burly physique that was quite common among Kuru men. As a matter of habit, he hovered over Asvattama menacingly as he said, 'I am the Regent of Kuru, born of the blood of Pururavas himself. I've earned my arms and my reputation both by defeating the great Firewright warrior Barghava Rama in battle. Don't try my patience, young man!'

Asvattama, however, was not a man to be intimidated. 'I wouldn't dream of it, *Grandsire*,' he lightly replied, adding, 'it's unfortunate that you should think I would.'

Bhisma paused, then leaned closer still. Dropping his voice to a whisper, he hissed, 'Tell me, plainly, do you think Govinda is capable of treachery? Do you think he was a traitor?'

'A traitor to whom?'

A strained, palpable silence followed as Bhisma stepped back, carefully avoiding his companion's eyes. Eventually he said, 'Thank you for coming to see me. It's kind of you to indulge an old man.'

Asvattama nodded and turned to go. He was almost at the door when he turned around to ask, softly, 'Is there anything else I can do for you?'

A look of relief flooded Bhisma's face, as though he had been waiting for the offer. He nodded. 'Kandava is not an easy conquest, even for the best of men. Dwaipayana is a scholar and may have overestimated his grandchildren. Dharma and his brothers will need help if they really are to have a chance at conquering the Nagas …'

'And what is it you want me to do?'

'My teachers – the Barghava warrior–scholars – had some of the most excellent weapons ever crafted in the history of Aryavarta. I've heard that the last of the Jamadagni line passed many on to your father, and to you …'

Asvattama nodded. 'I understand. I'll make the arrangements.'

'It'll have to be done very discreetly. I don't know if Dwaipayana …' Bhisma hesitated, and then continued, 'it's best that these arrangements are known only to those who understand – not all scholars are warriors and many warriors are not politicians.'

'Yes, Grandsire,' Asvattama nodded reassuringly and left the room.

Bhisma turned back to the window. All was quiet and still, almost as if the palace was uninhabited. There was neither bird nor cloud in the sky, and nothing moved. Nothing at all. He found the scene oppressive. It made him feel helpless, as he had most of his life. A life filled with virtue, painstakingly earned by fulfilling every duty destiny had laid at his door. But it gave such little satisfaction.

30

BRAZIERS FLICKERED, ALIVE IN A SLOW, REASSURING PATTERN OF menial efficiency, as dusk fell over Hastina's palace. Partha cast a blurred shadow on the well-polished floor as he paced up and down. Dharma looked up at his brother, as the man fitfully strode around the room, sometimes eager, sometimes with a frown.

'He'll be here soon, you know,' Dharma said, laughing softly. 'And it's not as if he's bringing you his sister, you already have her here …'

The younger man stopped, and threw himself into a chair at his brother's desk. Dharma instinctively reached out to steady a container of ink as Partha knocked against the table with some force.

'You've got to see it, Agraja,' Partha said. 'You must see it to believe it – Dwaraka … It's nothing short of magical. I can't imagine us building something even close to it here in central Aryavarta. And the fort, the armies, the Narayaniyas. What commitment, what discipline! The wealth, the opulence, the very air seems to be full of joy and laughter, like Indra's heaven on earth.'

'He really has impressed you, hasn't he?' Dharma laughed.

'He didn't have to try,' Partha pointed out. 'You know I've always had some respect for the Yadu lot … I knew Yuyudhana and Kritavarman from before. Imagine, armies upon armies, the ranks teeming with soldiers of that calibre …'

'It may be as you say. But then, why did Govinda run from Jarasandha? Why surrender Mathura? You do realize he's no longer ruler of anything … he ceded his own kingdom.'

Partha emphatically stated, 'He gave up a crumbling, good-for-nothing nation and, instead, built this mighty power called Dwaraka. You may think he's lost his crown, but you have no idea what he's gained. You should see the way he's treated in Dwaraka. He's no king; he's a god to his people.'

Dharma shrugged. 'Well, I won't get into this argument with you, Partha, but I do realize this much – Govinda Shauri is a useful ally to have, and not just you, but Shikandin and Dhrstyadymn both insist as much. At the very least Govinda is popular with the Panchalas. And his personal forces, as well as the armies of Dwaraka, are indeed a fair strength. It serves no purpose to offend him, I think, and it wouldn't hurt to please him. In any case,' he concluded, 'he is our cousin and he's now maternal uncle to the legal heir ... so there is some natural affinity, I hope.'

Partha now broached the issue on his mind. 'Dharma, I'm sorry ... I know you plan to take another wife, maybe I should've waited ...'

Dharma understood, and reassured his brother. 'It's all right, Partha. All our children, all children of us five brothers, are legally the children of Dharma and Panchali. Your child is the eldest of the next generation. He will be the heir to our kingdom, if Kandava is ever reclaimed ...'

Partha tried to protest, but Dharma would have none of it.

'This is how it must be,' he said, with an air of finality. 'This is justice. But don't move your pieces before the dice stop rolling, Partha. Kandava is known as a pit of snakes for good reason. Few places in Aryavarta have such a dark reputation. Unless Govinda ...'

'Hmm?' Partha eagerly prompted.

'Never mind. Let him get here first. Let's see what he has to say.' Despite his dismissal, Dharma smiled. For all his efforts to remain unaffected, he found Partha's optimism contagious after all.

By midnight, Hastina settled into a restless repose, as if eagerly awaiting morning. Unable to sleep, Syoddhan prowled the corridors of the palace, looking out at the moonlit lawns. He stopped as he heard footsteps. The stride was purposeful and not the uneven ambling of the sleepless. To his surprise, it was his cousin Dharma. Syoddhan wondered what the man was up to, but only for a moment. It did not take much effort to realize that Dharma had, in all probability, been to see Panchali.

The very name flashed images across Syoddhan's mind. The mysterious woman, who, his spies reported, was no less brave than any man and was certainly more than she appeared to be at first glance. She seemed to have a better head for politics and the affairs of state than most princes and counsellors, and though she lacked nothing in feminine grace her devotion to forthrightness was notorious. What bothered him was that he did not know in whose interests she acted, for Dharma seemed clueless about her. And, of course, the question remained why Dwaipayana let her be. The Elder's spies, Syoddhan knew, were as good as his own. *Perhaps*, he wondered, *Dwaipayana uses her as bait, to tempt bigger game. Firewright game.*

Syoddhan chuckled in the dark, and tried to check his vivid imagination. *Think of something else, not these sordid conspiracies.*

And he did. Panchali, dark and beautiful, by his side, in his arms, his bed … With a sigh, he tried to shake these new images out of his head. It was not at all difficult, since all he had to do was think of his wife, the mother of his infant son, of her soft, loving touch. Syoddhan resolutely headed back to his own room, to the arms of the woman he loved beyond question. As he lay in bed, savouring the simple but priceless joys that filled his life, he vaguely remembered that Govinda Shauri would be arriving soon. That was one man he thought he might come to like, given a chance. But the fact still remained that Syoddhan had never really understood him. He had no doubts that Govinda's visit was not motivated by fraternal affection alone, but also held another purpose. Govinda's enmity with the Nagas, it was rumoured, went back many years to his brief reign as the prince of Mathura. Syoddhan knew better than to trust every rumour that floated around the palace, but he also knew not to dismiss outright even the most far-fetched allegations. It was, he thought, as the old saying went: Every rumour had a root. Somehow he had the feeling that if anyone could win back Kandava it would be Govinda.

Syoddhan had no complaints there. The last thing he wanted was Dharma clamouring for *his* throne. As for Kandava, it did not matter. Hastina was the heart of the Kurus.

And it would be his. Some day.

With that, Syoddhan closed his eyes, welcoming the tranquil sleep that only the truly content are blessed with.

31

GOVINDA ARRIVED WITHOUT FANFARE. HIS ESCORT WAS SMALL, but they bore numerous gifts. As always, he smiled congenially, made friends with everyone, was gentle in speech and never showed any extreme of emotion. He radiated tranquillity, a sublime feeling of happiness without any flurry or excitement. It was the kind of mirth that made one smile, but not laugh out loud.

The many cousins competed to spend time with him, show him favour and entertain him in special ways. They plied him with hunting trips and minstrel shows, and arranged for the most attractive of courtesans to attend on him. Govinda disappointed no one, playing both the decadent noble and the detached muse. He would drink with Partha and Bhim, play dice with Dharma, sit and gaze at the night sky with Sadev. To everyone's surprise, he even went hunting with Asvattama and Syoddhan.

Most of the time, though, he was content to be a spectator rather than a participant. He would sit back and watch things play out. Shikandin was always at his side.

Panchali too was often to be found in Govinda's company, though always with others around them, particularly Subadra. They did not spend a moment alone together and, strangely enough, she felt grateful for that. She wondered what she would say to him or do, realizing that perhaps there would be nothing to say at all. The thought frightened her more than anything else she could have imagined between them.

A few days into Govinda's visit, the friends came together for a special lunch – game from Dhritarastra's private forests, hunted personally by Nakul and Sadev and cooked to perfection by Bhim. The rather exotic meal was served informally in an airy pavilion on the lush green lawns of Dharma's palace. The company was unrestrained and merry, with even the usually subdued Subadra joining in on the banter. After a while, the group was driven indoors by the late afternoon sun and, as one, they ambled into the palace, enjoying the cool of the marble floor and walls.

It was meant to look impulsive, but Panchali could tell that Dharma had mentally rehearsed it many times. He casually paused at the door to his study and invited her and Govinda to join him for a discussion, bidding the others goodbye. The two stepped inside. Dharma then placed a filial arm around Partha's shoulders and walked him into the room, as though it were normal that he call in one brother and not the others.

Govinda did not miss the quick glance exchanged between the twins, the sudden narrowing of Partha's eyes and the fiery confusion in Bhim's. Dharma's behaviour seemed to have astonished them all, but none of them said a word. In that instant, the crux of the tie between the brothers became apparent. Obedience. The five were but one creature, and Dharma served as its mind. The others were its limbs, their strength at the direction and service of their elder brother. None would disobey the mind and one limb would willingly hack off the other if the mind so ordered.

And Panchali is in the keeping of this creature, Govinda noted, not without a dash of discomfort. On a sudden impulse, he gently ran a finger down her cheek, not caring that Dharma and Partha stood watching them. Willing himself to tear his gaze away from her beaming face, he looked around the room.

The space was immense and overlooked the gardens. The many doors that opened out on to the well-kept lawns were all thrown open, letting light stream into the room. Colourful drapes complemented the tasteful furniture – a wide throne-like seat on which Dharma and

Panchali sat side by side, and other smaller, matching chairs. Partha settled himself in one of these without a word. Govinda waved off the offer of a chair and walked around instead, looking at the various curiosities that had been set as decorations. That done, he gazed out of the window, taking in the lovely view of the gardens, as he half-listened to what Dharma was saying.

'... Kandava?'

The word was enough to snap Govinda out of his reverie. He turned away from the scenery and concentrated entirely on Dharma, as the latter explained the situation.

Govinda waited till Dharma had finished, and then said, 'Believe it or not, Kandava was once a flourishing region. The forest is actually a huge mountain tract that runs from north to south and connects through the Rohita and Madhu forests to the land of the Nishadas. The hill range is rich in iron ore, perhaps other metals, too. For generations, the Nagas have been smiths, mining and working iron. Mostly, they make weapons of black iron – a lot like the arrows and lances used by foot soldiers, except lighter and better. As you can imagine, nations the world over are eager to acquire these, in hundreds of thousands. Arrow-heads, particularly, are a speciality with Takshaka's people.'

Dharma pointed out, 'Iron is the least dangerous of Kandava's terrible treasures. The truth is, their craft is something they learnt from the Firewrights, along with many other terrible things. The trees that grow there, the many poisonous creepers and shrubs in its dark recesses, their sap and juices are the ingredients of the feared toxins that the Firewrights used as weapons. To just walk through the forest can be death! This is why even the largest of armies has failed to capture Kandava till date. It's impregnable. To add to it, the Nagas are hardy and exceptionally skilled at forest warfare, demonically so. Indeed, humans can't defend Kandava the way Takshaka and his people have. If old legends are to be believed, the grace of Indra himself is with them,' he concluded.

Govinda's voice was tinged with sarcasm as he said. 'Yes, and demons that the Nagas are, the nations of Aryavarta – that is, those who worship Indra and Varuna – are forbidden from any dealings with them, including trade. The Nagas have managed to survive by trading with Danavas and other foreigners, smuggling weapons across the western desert and out through Salwa. But, by law, smuggled goods can be rightfully confiscated by the ruler of the realm – in this case, the King of Salwa. He then sells the confiscated goods off to the Danavas, and also to other kingdoms in Aryavarta, at ridiculous prices …'

'What!' Partha exclaimed. 'But Salwa is faithful to the Emperor and to Magadha. How could Jarasandha allow such trade?'

'Where do you think Jarasandha gets the money to maintain his massive armies? My dear fellow, the reason why the Emperor has hunted down Firewrights with a vengeance has more to do with economics and less to do with any supposed loyalty to the Firstborn, or his metaphorical responsibility to Divine order on this earth. Truth be told, the Emperor was not the only one. Many kingdoms have considered political and economic expediency in taking a stand for or against the Firewrights – our own nations included. But that's neither here nor there. Kandava, though not an easy target, is also not such a big mystery as you might think.'

Dharma looked at him. 'Govinda, please understand … There's no one I trust more than you. My mother is your father's sister. She was born a Shauri, though later adopted as a daughter by the King Kuntibhoja. We are cousins by birth, brothers-in-law by marriage, and I hope we can also be friends. I'm willing to follow your lead in this matter. But I'll also confess that I have little hope it will come to anything beyond this conversation. I can't allow you to wage a bloody battle at a cost of many lives on our side. Even if I were to do so, I too doubt that Takshaka can be defeated. Perhaps it's best to let this matter go, and if that is your advice, I'll heed it without question.'

Govinda clucked his tongue softly. 'I wouldn't give up the idea so easily if I were you, Cousin. Let me sleep on it.'

In the early hours of the next morning, the eight-month-pregnant Subadra went prematurely into labour.

Panchali burst into Subadra's room moments after the attendant woke her up with the news.

'Where's Partha?' she asked the nurse, who shook her head to say she did not know and then discreetly nodded towards Subadra.

Panchali understood. Partha was with some courtesan or the other, and could not be found or disturbed.

Subadra did not seem to care in the least as she writhed silently in an agony that she refused to share. Panchali could do little but hold her hand and whisper comforting words.

'What happened?' she tearfully asked the midwife.

The other woman's expression held much dread as she said, 'This isn't natural, Mahamatra. It's far too sudden ... I can only guess that some herb or potion was used to ...'

The door flew open.

'Rudra be praised!' Panchali gratefully whispered as Govinda strode in.

He went straight to Subadra. He spoke a few soft words of comfort and love to his sister and then, placing his hand on her stomach, said a quick prayer. Tired, but finally unafraid, she managed a wan smile. Just as her contractions began again, Dhaumya arrived and tersely signalled for them to leave, even as he began barking instructions to the midwife to mix some potion.

Govinda came to Panchali and gave her a quick, grateful, hug. 'She'll be all right,' he said, and led her out of the room.

'But ...'

Govinda firmly guided her out and did not let her speak till the door was shut behind them. 'The midwife told me ...' she began.

'I know,' Govinda was grim. 'I realized the moment I heard. I've been such a fool!' He seemed to be speaking to himself rather than to her. 'I just didn't think he'd stoop so low as to do something like this.'

'Who?' Panchali queried anxiously, but Govinda did not reply.

'Go back to sleep,' he carelessly dismissed her after a while.

Before Panchali could react, he walked over to a corner of the room, and stood looking out the small window, into the darkness outside. Slowly, quietly, she sat herself down on a small cushioned bench just outside the door to the inner chambers. She did not take her eyes off Govinda for even a moment.

With the first rays of the sun, Subadra's son was born. She insisted that her brother be the first to hold the boy. Govinda willingly complied, cradling the infant in his arms with unexpected tenderness, his eyes showing a curious mix of sadness and need. Subadra laughed at his display and said, 'Go on. Tell us what you've decided to name him.'

Govinda's voice was uncharacteristically hoarse with emotion as he announced, 'Abhimanyu.'

32

PANCHALI HAD LEARNED FROM SHIKANDIN THE SKILL, OR HABIT even, of knowing when something was not quite all right. It was not a question of instinct or some such enhanced sense, but more a methodical and rigorous exercise whereby the eyes missed nothing and the mind meticulously registered every detail, and went over it all to identify the tiniest aberration. He had also taught her that the most crucial aberration could be that everything looked normal. On this particular day – the morning after a grand celebration of the hundredth day since Abhimanyu's birth – it was the sight of Partha riding out of the fort in his everyday clothes, his horse setting a slow, purposeless pace, a large, innocuously shapeless white bundle tied to the animal's side. In the plain light of morning the banality of the scene was excessive, contrived almost.

Without a second thought Panchali headed for the stables. She left the palace through one of the smaller exits, planning to catch up with Partha somewhere in the city. The two guards at the small trellis saluted her. She greeted them and asked after their children by name before casually riding on. Once past the exit she glanced around before quickly wrapping a simple linen robe around her head like a man's turban, except that she let the end fall in folds over her face, leaving only her eyes uncovered. She also threw a light cloak made of fur around her shoulders. It made her look bulky, almost burly. Urging her horse on at a gentle canter, in order to not attract attention, she set off in the same direction as Partha, towards the city gates.

Partha was easy to keep in sight, especially since the teeming crowds moved to clear the path in front of him. As Panchali neared the city gates, she discreetly manoeuvred herself into a convoy of traders. At first glance she might just pass for a guard hired by merchants to protect their merchandise from bandits and such. She indulged in a snide smirk under her veil. For all the trouble she was taking to be surreptitious, she had no idea whether tailing Partha was going to be of any use at all.

The ride was uneventful until they neared the city limits. Panchali broke away from the stream of travellers on the Great Road and moved towards the drinking well. From this point on the Great Road bent to the south-west, taking the mass of travellers along with it. Partha, however, continued to ride due west along a narrow trail. If she followed him, he was sure to notice her. Under her veil, Panchali bit her lip. She would have to let Partha get a lead on her and try to track his path on the dusty trail. Ignoring the rumble of hunger from her stomach, she pretended to check her horse's shoes and hooves for stones as Partha moved further away. The smell of leavened bread from a vendor's basket beckoned but she did not dare risk discovery by trying to buy some. Her stomach growled again, louder this time. With a silent groan she swung back on to her steed, hoping that Partha had gone far enough ahead.

The narrow trail was cluttered with many tracks from various animals. Panchali kept her eyes on the sides of the pathway to see if any tracks led away from it. As long as there were none, she reasoned, it meant Partha had gone straight.

The land was slightly undulating in places, but by and large it was even. On either side of the trail the dark loamy soil was streaked with the light brown of dry husk and dead leaves, turned into the earth and left to decompose. The spring harvest was over and farmers were preparing to sow their crops in time for the summer rains. Panchali saw a lone gwala, a young cowherd forced to brave the mid-morning sun while the others rested and ate under the shade of some trees. The boy effortlessly managed a herd of nearly forty cattle. She tried to imagine Govinda as he might have been years ago. Somehow the image that came to her mind was of an indolent youth lazing in some lush orchard, while the herd milled lovingly around him, the order and obedience among the animals nothing short of uncanny. Laughing softly, Panchali removed her veil, revelling in the fresh, cool wind blowing on her face. As her attention returned to the path before her, she noted with some consternation the wall of green that lay ahead. The trail she was on either went into a forest or stopped dead at its edge.

Panchali's thoughts rushed at her in a confused jumble. It would be impossible to track Partha once he was inside the forest. In fact, his trail was as good as lost already. At the same time, she was beginning to have some idea of where Partha was headed, which only made her all the more reluctant to go on. Swallowing hard, she reminded herself that she had been just as afraid to enter the forests near Utkochaka, only to later find the woods to be harmless. With a few words of encouragement to her horse, she urged him forward.

Not very far from where Panchali was making her way into the forest, Partha slowed his horse down to a trot and took in the pleasant coolness of the woods around him. He had continued from the trail directly into the forest, moving along a straight path until he reached the River Yamuna. He had then turned north. Fording the river at its shallows he continued northward, but started moving away ever so slightly from the water's course. Soon the land to his left began sloping gently upwards in the form of a small, grassy hill with just a few trees in a clump at the top. Ahead of him, the river curved steeply around the hill and was lost from view. Partha made for the crest. It was an easy climb and he was soon at the top of the hillock. The lands that lay before him simply took his breath away.

'By Yama's black bull!' he exclaimed. In contrast to the gentle slope that he had climbed, the other side of the hill fell away in a sheer, steep cliff. The small hill was the beginning of a series of crests and ridges, many of which were twice as high. Dark peaks jutted out above towering green-blue mountains, the dense forest that covered the slopes and ridges beginning at the lower foothills and rising almost two-thirds of the way to blend into a thick carpet of moss and creepers that grew in the many clefts and crevices. Only the peaks were bare, as though nature had intended them purposively ominous. The densely forested mountain range ran northward for many leagues, eventually blurring into the horizon.

Partha swung off his horse, and focused his attention on the nearer stretch of undulating land. He saw the occasional flash of blue as the Yamuna meandered on along the edges of the forest, but for the most part it was an impenetrable canopy of green. Huge trees rose to towering heights, their leaves thick and dark, their wood hard as iron. Thick branches, each the girth of a well-built man, intertwined with an unnatural grace to seal darkness in and keep light out. An eerie stillness hovered over the place, no shrubs rustled or creepers moved; no birds perched atop the trees or hovered, chirping, around the branches. It almost made Partha believe the stories of the weird and terrible animals that roamed the deeper parts of this forest, where even the sun and wind could not enter. He was a brave man, but the heavy stillness of this place was enough to send a chill down the spines of stalwarts. This was Kandava, the dreaded realm of King Takshaka.

Drawing himself out of his initial awe, Partha raised his eyes to consider the rest of the landscape. Further away, to the north, the river curved in to come closer to the forest. It then ran around it on two of its three sides, forming a border on the eastern and north-eastern flanks. The hill that he stood on was part of a range that similarly enclosed the woods on its southern and western flanks.

Impregnable Kandava. Hah! Partha laughed out loud at the forest stretched out before him. From his elevation it almost felt like the expanse of green lay at his feet. Dharma had certainly outdone himself this time.

When his brother had sent for him late the previous night, Partha had hardly expected it to be for this. It had been a day of unrestrained

210

celebrations in Abhimanyu's honour, but the celebrations and festivities were long over and even the palace guards had been slumped over in a drunken stupor.

'Why the secrecy, Brother?' Partha had asked.

Dharma had looked grim, uncharacteristically determined. 'Like it or not, Partha,' he had said, 'we are merely guests at Hastina. There are many here who would be happy to see us all dead and even the walls of the palace have ears … I could not take any chances. What I shall ask of you today, Brother, is to attempt the near-impossible. It's not a task without danger. I would not assign it to the father of a newborn child without good cause. For years Kandava has been unconquered, defended by the skills of the Wrights. The time has come to take from Takshaka what is rightfully ours. This is our chance. *Your* chance. I'd wager anything on this. If anyone can do it, it's you. Burn the forest down, Partha.'

Partha had been shocked. But there was more to follow. 'Don't worry,' Dharma had added, 'you won't be alone. You see, Govinda has a plan … But this is *your* duty to fulfil, Partha. In the name of all that is sacred, good and moral, burn down that pit of snakes.'

That simple encouragement had been enough and he, Partha, son of Indra and heir to Pandu Kauravya, had only been happy to comply.

Trembling with anticipation, he carefully undid the bundle that Dharma had given him. His mouth fell open. It was a bow unlike any he had ever seen before. The light, supple metal blazed in the sunlight as if it were molten fire. Not even the most burnished of mirrors showed such a keen reflection as the silver-white metal did. It was strong and light enough to lift up high, if required, and yet large and firm enough to prop up on the ground to avoid recoil. Partha ran his hand over the weapon, admiring its impeccable craft. His eyes then fell on the inscription. Partha read it out loud, his voice solemn with respect: 'I am Gandiva, whose call fills terror in the hearts of enemies.' With the softest of touches, as if caressing his lover, he plucked and then released the bowstring. It twanged a low, rich note, booming deep and long. Extremely flexible, it would let him vary the thrust and distance on his arrows without having to adjust its length every time.

The clatter of hooves drew his attention. 'What ...?' he whipped around in alarm.

Panchali pulled on the reins to bring her horse came to a stop in front of Partha. She had hardly dismounted when he came forward to meet her.

'What are you doing here?' he asked, angry at her sudden appearance.

'I could ask you the same thing,' she retorted. 'What in the name of the gods is going on? We shouldn't be here.'

'It's destiny, Panchali. Kandava will be destroyed today.'

'And you're going to be the one to do it? You're going to take on the Nagas all by yourself?'

'It's my duty, what my brother has commanded me to do, and I won't fail. Indeed, today the world will wonder if the two ancient powers Nara and Narayana themselves have descended to earth in my form,' Partha proudly declared.

'Surely,' a deep, familiar voice drawled from behind Panchali, 'to be one ancient power is achievement enough? To comprise both Nara and Narayana in one human form seems extravagant. I don't suppose you'd care to spare me one of your two alter egos?'

Govinda walked out from a small copse of trees, leading Balahak by the reins. He nodded casually at Panchali and told Partha, 'I didn't expect you here till much later, Partha. I was having a rather restful nap, an exceptionally fragrant nap, I must say, under that jasmine tree – the one with its flowers in full bloom. But now that I'm awake, we might as well get to work.'

Partha slapped Govinda on the back, laughing. It was almost like being back at Dwaraka, he thought, those wonderful months of friendship, selfless and without expectations. *A true friendship between equals.* Momentarily he revelled in the notion.

Panchali was unimpressed. She drew in a sharp breath and demanded, 'Now? You mean you're going to do this now? But ... how?'

As if in answer, Partha pulled an arrow out of the quiver on his back.

Panchali noticed that these were not the usual arrows archers used – these were flint-tipped. The shaft of the arrow, too, was longer than usual, no doubt to give it greater thrust to reach its target. Her eyes narrowed as she realized that the metal itself looked different; it was a lot lighter and shinier than the dull iron that was mostly used.

In growing alarm she cast her eyes upward at the sky. There was not a single cloud overhead and the sun shone down with unrelenting fury despite winter being hardly a month past. Even if the weather turned, it would take nothing less than a storm to extinguish a blazing forest.

'By the gods, you are going to do this! You're going to burn it down, you're going to burn them all!' she frantically said. 'Partha … have pity, those are people in there, human beings … children even …'

'How else can we fight this battle, Panchali? This isn't just about reclaiming what is ours. There is a greater purpose here: to destroy that which is evil. The forest is a labyrinth. Its complex, twisted paths are designed to drive any unfortunate wanderer insane. Neither sunlight nor moonlight can find their way in and deeper in the forest the trees grow close enough to form an impassable wall. Within that infernal darkness, the flowers and trees themselves bear poisons and hallucination-causing saps. Fire is the only answer.'

He laughed coldly at Panchali's furious stare, and added, 'Ask Govinda here, if you don't believe me, Panchali.'

'He's right,' Govinda affirmed.

'And so,' Partha declared, 'the demons of Kandava will burn in the very flames of the netherworld! This is war!' Then, closing his eyes, he whispered a prayer as he thrust the tip of an arrow into the hard ground. The impact set the arrowhead alight. Panchali watched, at first with fascination and then with increasing horror, as the flame, an iridescent blue streak rather than the yellow-orange of a normal fire, burnt strong. Setting the flaming arrow to his bow, Partha drew back the string and let fly the shaft. The arrow took a long, looping path to disappear into the canopy of treetops. Many more arrows quickly followed, all landing to form a perfectly straight line from where the first shaft had pierced the canopy to where they now stood.

Partha's reputation as one of the best archers in all of Aryavarta was undoubtedly merited.

As the three of them watched from the hilltop, the faint flash that had begun on the tree-canopy grew quickly into a steady blaze, the crackle and sizzle of burning wood and leaves gradually becoming louder. The arrows had done their work. Looking satisfied, Partha released the next line of arrows, building what soon would be an unstoppable forest fire.

'No! Stop! Stop it right now!' Panchali cried out. She looked around ineffectively for some way to deter the archer. Her panic seemed only to increase Partha's amusement, and he responded by lifting Gandiva up high to release the shafts almost straight up. The arrows flew high and covered an even greater distance before sinking into the trees somewhere well past the middle of the forest.

Panchali bit her lower lip in exasperation. Her anger against Partha, against Dharma and his ambitions, paled in comparison to what she felt when she turned to Govinda. The expression of calm on his face infuriated her. Spurred on by rage she ran to her horse and climbed on.

'Panchali, no! Wait!' Govinda shouted after her.

She swung around to face him. 'I won't watch helplessly. There may still be time if only they're warned!' With that she urged her horse into a gallop down the hill.

'Maraka! This woman ...' Govinda ran to Balahak, and set off behind her.

Partha watched the two until they were out of his view and then turned back to the task at hand. This was *his* duty, Dharma had said so. Clearing his mind, he sent another blazing arrow into sky and watched it till it disappeared into the sea of green below.

33

'FASTER! FASTER!' PANCHALI URGED HER HORSE ALONG THE riverbank. In blind fury she had desperately coaxed all the speed she could out of her steed to get here, but now she slowed down as she reached the fringes of the forest. She had hoped to find some guards or soldiers to whom she could convey the danger the Nagas were in, but not a single living creature, human or animal, stirred. Despite the fire-arrows there did not seem to be any movement or activity inside the forest. Instead, a dank smell reached out from its dark depths, as though warning her that it was death itself. She grimly realized it might already be too late for her to warn the Nagas. The thought was enough to spur her on, and with a whispered prayer she turned left, crashing through the leaves and undergrowth into the thick forest. She headed straight in until the edge of the woods was a tiny sliver of light behind her. And then that too was gone.

Panchali slowed her horse down to a walk as she tried to get her bearings, reminding herself that she had entered the woods facing west. Further inward the land would rise sharply, she knew, but here it was still level. The dank stink that now furiously invaded her nostrils came from the slimy lichen that carpeted the ground. The trees grew close and thick, just as Partha had said, forming a wall of wood as hard as one of any rock or stone. She tried looking up, but all she saw was darkness. This was different from the darkness that night brought – thicker, its uniformity somehow oppressive. Closing her eyes, she tried to rein in her other senses, focus them. But there was the silence, a horrifying blanket of emptiness that was more than the mere absence of sound. The horse's breathing, the slight jingling of bridle and rein, even the susurrus of her own movement, nothing could be heard.

A nameless fear crept up on her. Suddenly she felt dizzy and short of breath. Gasping, choking, she fell off her horse. The faithful steed whinnied and moved towards her to nuzzle her gently.

'No, no, no ...! Hai!' she tried to stop the animal from turning to her, but in vain. She clambered to her feet, clutching its reins for support. 'Oh Rudra and Hara!' Now she would no longer know which way was west. She was lost in the darkness of Kandava.

With a loud gasp, Panchali let go of the breath she had been holding. She became aware that this was not some horrid dream.

Somehow, the realization made her feel braver than she had expected. *Better to move, than to just stand here,* she reasoned. Squaring her shoulders, she began walking, not knowing whether her steps led her deeper inside or back toward the light.

Panchali knew it was hardly some time since she had begun walking, but it felt like a really long time in the strange darkness. She stopped, hoping that something had changed in the seamless black and that she could see something, anything at all. When she heard the soft steps, she first thought she was imagining things, or had perhaps been driven insane by terror.

She very nearly screamed as someone called out, 'Panchali! Over here!'

She heard it again, and relief broke out on her face as she recognized the voice.

'Devala! Oh, thank ...' she began, but he silenced her with a finger on her lip. Grabbing her wrist, he began walking into the darkness with familiarity. She had no choice but to follow. Completely unaware of where she was being led, and bursting with questions, Panchali matched the scholar's long strides. In her other hand she held the reins of her horse, who faithfully trotted alongside. After a while it felt as though the darkness around her was lightening up a bit and she peered ahead hopefully, looking forward to getting out of the damned forest. Her heart fell as the light took on a reddish hue and the smell of smoke began teasing her nostrils.

Devala was leading her towards the blaze.

Panchali stopped in her tracks. Unbidden memories of another fire made her stomach churn and she dug her nails deep into her palm to keep from screaming. Devala pulled at her, but she did not move. The light was enough now for her to see him clearly. She looked at him, letting him see the terror and panic she felt. Slowly, almost pleading, she shook her head.

The man considered her, frowning, and let go of her wrist.

'Are you satisfied?' he asked her, his voice cold. 'Do you see what your precious Govinda Shauri has done? As long as Kandava existed, as long as the Nagas held some scraps of our old skills, there

216

was hope. Now it's all gone.' His voice dropped to a sad whisper. 'I'd believed you could stop him. I thought you *would* stop him! I thought that where every human emotion had failed, you could perhaps get Govinda to show compassion. But he feels nothing, does he?'

Panchali failed to hold back her tears, though she only half understood Devala's words. 'I didn't know,' she screamed. 'Trust me, I had no idea it would come to this. I thought ... How could I have known that ...?'

'How could you not have known? Govinda lives to destroy us! All you stupid fools ever see are his petty squabbles with Jarasandha, you see him defy the Emperor and assume he's just another idiot of a ruler. His true feud lies with us, with the Firewrights! If only you knew what a son of a whore he really is ...' Words of contempt finally failed the scholar and he spat on the ground in disgust.

'No,' Panchali protested. '*You* don't know him ... He's not like that, he's not like that at all!'

Even as she said the words, it came to her that this horrific fire had been *Govinda's* plan. *He* had led Partha and Dharma to burn the forest. *He* was responsible for this horror! Devala was right, she should have known, right that very day when Dharma had first spoken to Govinda of this; she should have said something right then. But she had not. She failed in the very task Devala had entrusted to her. A part of her longed to run, to hide from the reality of her mistake by drowning in the sea of fire ahead, but even as confusion and fear dimmed her senses she was reminded of the events that had led to this moment, of why she had ridden into the forest. She turned to Devala, frantic. 'We must get the Nagas out of here,' she declared.

'Muhira!' the Firewright snorted in contempt. 'It's too late. No one defies the gods and the gods show no mercy to those who try. I shall pay for trusting you.'

With a last look at her, he walked on, right towards the raging fire.

Panchali watched, aghast, as he stepped through a wall of flame and disappeared from view. Devala's parting words rang in her mind. She had failed. She had been nothing but a child, indulging in her pretended revenge against the system; she had lived in the make-believe worlds of those around her. How stupid, how careless of her. She should have confided in her brothers, in Shikandin if no one else. He would have done something to stop Govinda, to prevent this destruction.

Screams and shouts echoed around her all of a sudden – the voices of men and women, the agonized cries of children. Panchali vaguely recognized her own wails of despair, adding to the din. Falling to her knees, she sobbed out loud, helpless and defeated. *How had it come to this?*

Her mind rifled through scattered memories, of the day she had first met Govinda, the day he had kissed her hand in an innocent gesture of friendship, the days spent laughing and talking, with him, with her brothers … The happiest days of her life, when she had felt neither like an orphan nor like the princess of Panchala, but just a person, just who she was. A person with dreams of a better world, a better life. How naive, stupid, childish she had been!

No one defies the gods and they show no mercy to those who try.

Panchali closed her eyes but she could still clearly see the burning forms, the faces of the dying. She felt a fleeting moment of clarity, of being able to understand many things. It turned into numb acceptance as she came to terms with her failure to stop the horror around her.

Govinda the gwala dared defy a king to become Govinda Shauri, just as I, a nameless, kinless orphan dared to become Princess Panchali. We are the two halves of a whole. I shall burn alive for his wrongs.

A sudden calm settled on her. Wiping away her tears, Panchali waited.

The fire drew closer.

34

GOVINDA PUSHED BALAHAK ON AT HIS FASTEST, BUT PANCHALI'S fury seemed to have given her horse wings. Nevertheless, he had managed to keep her within view and was swiftly gaining on her. If only she had stopped to listen … But he knew her well enough to realize that no quick explanation would have sufficed. It was best that she took a closer look for herself. He could always get her out of the forest before she put herself in harm's way.

A quick movement in the forest just beyond the first rows of trees caught his eye. He turned in his saddle to get a better look, even as he began wondering if Panchali was doing the right thing after all. Yes, he decided, there was no question. It was clearly a human figure, and it certainly was not Panchali. Govinda hesitated, wondering whether to continue his chase, or to find and warn whoever might still be inside the forest. *She'll never forgive me if I don't ...*

With a groan of resignation, he wheeled Balahak around and made for the gap between the trees where he had last seen the form. He stopped at the edge of the forest, letting his eyes, and Balahak's, get used to the dark before they went forward. He looked around intently, but saw no trace of any living creature. And now he had lost Panchali's trail. Cursing, Govinda promised himself that when this was over he would really let her hear it. Anger gave way to hope as he heard a soft sound behind him, but before he could move a sharp pain pierced the flesh on his left side, just below his ribs. An arrow, he recognized. But he could think no further as on the wings of the weapon came a terrible horde.

Through the umbra rushed creatures of darkness and shadow. Govinda did not know how he was able to see them in that empty blackness, but see them he did – in immaculate detail. The shadows were alive, distinct and varying in texture, in light and colour. Except that here, in this forsaken place, even light was black. Birds, beasts and other creatures of hideous form let out screeching wails that he felt rather than heard. The nameless creatures sank their teeth and claws into his flesh. Stirred by the pain, he tried to fight. With great effort, he pulled his sword out of its scabbard and swung at the enemy. The silver-gold flash of the blade pierced the darkness as though it were soft flesh.

Suddenly, the shadow-creatures were gone. Breathing hard, Govinda tried to regain his bearings. As the darkness thinned a little, he thought he could see the vague outlines of trees and huts in the distance, silhouetted against a dull light. He could also clearly hear sounds he had not heard before – the buzz of insects, the rustle of leaves. As if to prove it, someone called out his name. Children ran around laughing and playing. A boy ran up to him. Laughing, the child held out his hand. In response, Govinda swung his blade, hacking off the boy's head. And then he could not stop. Children, their companions, the mothers who ran to protect them, all lay dead. His sword cut clean through each one of them, hacking at their bodies, their limbs until they collapsed in heaps of flesh. Their eyes remained alive and accusing.

'No!' Govinda gasped in vain.

Laughing, the shadow creatures returned to peck at the bodies of those he had brutally murdered. He ran among the dead as a madman, till the creatures turned their attentions back to him. This time, Govinda decided, he would welcome the pain as they ripped off his flesh. Gritting his teeth, he bore the searing touch of the shadow creatures, but he could only take it for so long. A terrible scream rent the air, followed by more such ringing screams of agony. He realized that it was a familiar voice, a very familiar voice. Pain shot through him anew, as many more screams came through the darkness. An abyss opened at his feet, its depths beckoning. His last thought before he fell headlong into the chasm was of Panchali.

If only she were safe …

Her long, dark hair streamed behind her, gleaming like a black sun. She turned, saw him and ran to him, laughing. But before he could reach her, she burst into flames. He wrapped his arms around her and tried to put out the flames. Surprisingly, they did not burn him. But he could hear her scream in pain, the sound shrill and piercing. Her face, her lovely, innocent face contorted in unimaginable horror. Then she was gone and Govinda was alone in the woods – dark woods that now took the shape of indistinct memories.

The shadowy form of Shikandin was next to him, looking at him but not quite. At his signal, other shadows stepped forward, drawing their swords, and they all jumped out into a clearing, taking the Emperor's soldiers by surprise. Govinda hacked down two men, but his mind was not on the battle. There was something else he had to do, but he did not know what. Through a haze that clouded his vision, he saw the wooden trapdoor set in the ground. Grabbing the iron ring set into the wood, he raised the trapdoor and peered in. She reached out to him from within, arms thrown out, beckoning him to her. He wanted to jump inside, but could not. Shikandin pulled him away and shouted out orders to his shadow companions to withdraw. The door slammed shut, sealing her inside.

Govinda yelled out. Writhing free of Shikandin he tried to scramble back to the trapdoor. She was inside; he had to save her. A withered figure, his face and body covered with burn scars blocked his way. The words he spoke came in an insane cackle. 'She's dead … She's dead. We killed her, you and I!' the man said.

Govinda got to his feet and grabbed the man by his shoulders. 'Where is she?' he roughly asked. 'Where is she, Agniveshya?'

In reply, there was only laughter.

Abruptly, the maddening cackle gave way to soundlessness. Govinda was now in a dark pit-like cavern, watched by a tall, thin man who was both familiar and threatening. Pain coursed through him as he tried to move, to push himself off the ground and onto his knees. The chains around his wrists clanked. He looked down at his almost-bare body, bloodied and gashed. He tried to stand up but slipped, falling flat on his face on the slime-covered floor. His outstretched hand touched something … something he did not want to see. Something he had seen before. Bile rose up in his throat, flooding his mouth with a sick taste.

This, Govinda knew, was the most terrifying apparition of them all. Worse still, this was neither just imagination nor memory. He was living it, every excruciating moment of it, but with the added torment of knowing what lay ahead. If he turned, he would see …

He tried to scramble away with a feverish energy, but the darkness with its terrible creatures rushed towards him. Slowly, bit by bit, it pushed him closer, close enough to touch … He tried to push the darkness back, but it slipped through his fingers and came at him again. No light could enter this forsaken hell.

Unless ...

Some deep instinct brought to mind words, lost words of long ago, learned and forgotten, the forgetting but a means of keeping them safe for this moment.

It shines radiant
Like light, but is not.
Alive and incessant
Always moving, it is.

Govinda did not know what the words meant, nor did he immediately understand their purpose. But he knew he was meant to remember them.

The creatures of the darkness laughed at him. *How can it be that something is alive and yet you don't know it; alight, but you remain surrounded by the dark?*

In a voice that was his but not quite his, Govinda raised his head and silently replied, *Because I am that light ... I am Brahman, the Eternal Universe, self-perfecting, alive, incessantly in action.* He laughed out loud. In a stronger voice, more powerful than he had ever known his could be, he declared, *I am the darkness.*

The gloom vanished, along with its shadow creatures. In its place, at his feet, lay the headless body of the boy who had run up to him. Govinda did not flinch. A figure emerged from the darkness. Arms outstretched, blue-black hair flowing behind her, she ran towards him as if to throw herself into his embrace.

I am an illusion, as are the things I have done.

Unperturbed, unruffled, he ran his sword clear through the one he had loved for as long as he could remember.

Govinda opened his eyes to find himself on the damp ground. Balahak stood nearby, whinnying anxiously. With a groan he pulled himself to his feet. His head throbbed, and he felt sick. As he pressed his temples, he felt a sharp sting on his side, just below his ribs. The arrow was light and sleek. Govinda pulled it out easily; it had not gone deep into the flesh. The tip was sharp and engraved with a tiny crescent-shaped groove, which served to hold the dark poison the needle had been dipped in – not unlike the shafts that were used to deploy the Bramha-weapon, the terrible and powerful poison that could kill by causing the most grotesque and fearsome visions, hallucinations. His stomach gave a lurch, and for an instant Govinda wondered just how much longer he could have lasted against the illusions.

Blood dripped from the sword in his hand. Looking around, Govinda found the body of his attacker, almost cleaved in two. His assailant's identity did not surprise him in the least: Aswasena, son of the Naga king. Where Takshaka lived for his people, Aswasena, reckless and ambitious, cared for no one but himself. The man had been in the forest for a reason.

The scattered contents of the bag at Aswasena's waist confirmed Govinda's suspicions. He disregarded what he knew were trifles – highly precious gemstones and heavy gold ingots – and reached for one of the many fallen scrolls. They were letters of credit from various foreign personages, including kings and merchants. A quick look through a few of the notes had him clucking his tongue in astonishment. The sum Aswasena could collect on these would surely exceed what the Nagas had in their treasuries. Govinda stuffed the scrolls into his own leather pouch. He would deliver them to Takshaka himself and leave the monarch to form his own conclusions on how his son came upon such personal riches.

Bending down, Govinda quickly examined the arrows in the Naga's quiver and the bow that had fallen from his hand. It was light and made of a silver-coloured metal, not unlike the Gandiva, though the workmanship of the Naga's weapon left much to be desired. But there was no doubt. Aswasena's bow had been made by a Firewright, or someone who had been taught by one. Which meant …

Smoke stung sharply at Govinda's eyes, bringing him back to the moment and reminding him where he was, and why. Immediately, he pulled himself on to Balahak and urged him deeper into the forest. Soon he saw a massive wall of orange and red crackling in the distance. It rapidly drew closer, a host of shapes framed against its brightness. Among them, a silhouette that was clearly Panchali's.

She stood like a statue, still and unmoving. Her horse was free of its bridle and reins and trotted around her, nearly insane with terror but still faithful to his rider. Panchali finally moved, gently patting the animal and then pushing him away hard as though in the hope that the animal's instincts would lead him to safety.

Govinda could feel the heat on his face as he dismounted and ran towards her. Grabbing her hand he pulled her back, not bothering with questions or explanations. He helped her climb on to Balahak and then swung himself up behind her. A sharp whistle, and her grey stallion responded with a neigh and trotted alongside. The flames were still a fair distance away, but the heat and the smoke were enough to kill them well before the fire came close. Govinda tried to work out directions based on the fire and the wind driving it. As long as they were headed the right way – to the river beyond the edge of the forest – they had a chance, but the thick undergrowth slowed their progress. Looking around, he cursed. The forest was on fire, in many places, from many sides. It could only mean that the entire area had become so hot that fires were starting spontaneously. Anything could begin to burn at any moment.

'Why do you think I'd given up, Govinda?' Panchali said softly, reading his thoughts. 'I suppose it's only fair. I've failed. You've won. So many living creatures, so many innocent people, so many children, so many animals and birds will die such horrible deaths. I deserve to burn with them.'

Govinda looked down at her, shocked at her words. She leant back against him, visibly weary. Her tears had mingled with the soot from the fire, staining her cheeks. He gently wiped away the smears as best he could and held her close. 'There are no people or children in Kandava, Panchali, and the few animals and birds that may have been left would have escaped by now.'

'How do you know?' Panchali countered, unconvinced. 'You don't have to make me feel better, Govinda. I'm ready to die.'

'You're not going to die. At least not today. And I promise you, Kandava is uninhabited. I'd hoped to share the news with you and Dharma this evening – Takshaka has left the forest and taken his people north, to Kuru's Fields. The last of the Nagas left during the night. I'd love to discuss the niggling details of the treaty that Takshaka and I have spent days thrashing out, but this is not the time. Trust me, they are all safe,' he urged.

'All right,' Panchali said, her tone indulgent but still disbelieving. She closed her eyes and let out a sigh, as if she were about to take a restful afternoon nap.

Govinda wrapped one arm around her and held Balahak's reins in his other hand. The smoke was slowing him down, making him weak and sluggish.

Think, you foolish gwala, he goaded himself. A bolt of panic shot through him as Panchali's breathing turned shallow, even as she lay in his arms.

'Wake up, Panchali!' he tapped her roughly.

She responded with a soft chuckle. 'You do care … Don't you?' she whispered, managing a weak smile. Then, with a contented look on her face, she went completely limp in his arms. Govinda cursed, and tried to shake her back to consciousness, but to no avail. He realized they had very little time left. He had no choice. There was only one way out of this. He took one look at the senseless woman in his arms and resolutely moved on.

Soon, a new line of fire blazed up. Driven by the wind, it began sweeping forward as a wave of flame that headed away from them. As the huge inferno chased them from behind, the fire Govinda had created cleared the way in front at the same speed. At last, a glimpse of daylight and the bright sky. They were at the edge of the forest. As they burst into the bright sunlight and out of the clutches of Kandava, Govinda allowed himself a small smile at the irony of their escape. *After all that has happened, Agni the refulgent finally serves my need.*

35

'PANCHALI?' GOVINDA ASKED THE MOMENT HE WOKE.

'She's fine,' Dhaumya said. 'She was up briefly but has gone back to sleep.'

Govinda sat up in bed, groaning slightly at the stab of pain in his side.

On a couch nearby Shikandin woke with a start but relaxed when he saw Govinda sitting up.

'I should have known you'd be here, Shikandin,' Govinda said. 'You've been waiting for the chance to get me naked in bed forever ...'

Shikandin pointedly ignored Govinda, and looked at Dhaumya.

'He'll be fine. I'll sit with him,' Dhaumya reassured him. Turning to Govinda, the scholar said, 'I'm sure you won't be surprised to hear that this fellow hasn't budged from your side. In fact, he fell asleep late last night only after I slipped him a draught in his wine.'

'I knew it!' Shikandin exclaimed. 'Govinda, Panchali, me ... You make your sleeping draughts by the bucketfuls, don't you?'

'All right, all right! I'll apologize, if it'll make you go get some sleep.'

'Sleep?' Shikandin exclaimed. 'And let you two do all the talking? No way! If he's fine, then he'd better answer a few questions. You can save your apology.'

He sat up, swinging his long legs down to the floor and leaning forward, elbows on his knees. 'Before you ask, Govinda ... You got back to Hastina the day before yesterday, in the evening. Partha arrived some time before you and Panchali did, so we were able to sneak you both in and keep things quiet. Barring Dharma and his brothers, and Subadra, pretty much no one else knows she was involved. You've both slept straight through yesterday and most of today. Panchali was up a few hours ago, but has gone back to sleep. I think she must have inhaled some hallucinogenic vapours, along with the smoke. Her memories are garbled. In fact, she hardly remembers anything at all.'

'Kandava?'

226

'Razed to the ground,' Shikandin confirmed, 'except for the small tract bordering Kuru's Fields, north of the river. That canal you ordered to be dug worked. But, I must say, that was one huge fire …'

Govinda sniggered, 'It wasn't for nothing that Bhisma sent for the Gandiva and arranged for Partha to have it. The Grandsire would've loved to get his hands on it years ago, but has had to settle for letting Partha have the weapon and the fame that goes with it. The old man won't forgive him, or Dwaipayana, too easily for that!'

Dhaumya pensively added, 'Dwaipayana goes on and on about how Partha, son of Indra himself, was able to defy the gods and destroy impregnable Kandava.'

'And Syoddhan?' Govinda asked, with narrowed eyes. He knew that Syoddhan's reaction was crucial to how many others in Aryavarta, including Emperor Jarasandha, would react to the whole matter.

'He seems to be all right,' Shikandin replied. 'My spies tell me that his spies tell him that they – that is, his spies, not mine … What?' he asked, feigning great seriousness as Govinda began to laugh.

Govinda addressed Dhaumya, 'Are you sure it was just a sleeping draught you slipped into his wine?'

'Oh yes,' the scholar confirmed. 'His stupidity is merely congenital.'

'If you weren't a learned man, and you, if you weren't injured – I'd have done you both some damage, I swear,' Shikandin said. 'But as it stands, I'll live with the satisfaction of having irked you, which is what I was hoping for. Getting to the point …'

'Finally …'

'I said, getting to the point, Syoddhan knows Takshaka and his people are all right, that they left Kandava in time. I hear he's conveyed as much to his dear friend, the Emperor. Beyond that, even Jarasandha concedes that this remains an internal matter of the Kurus.'

Govinda said, 'Frankly, the whole affair should make Syoddhan happy. After all he'll now have Hastina for himself to rule. I'm certain that both Bhisma and Jarasandha would have found that an argument persuasive enough to turn a blind eye to my … erm … activities.'

'True, but I'm not sure it's enough to make you Syoddhan's best friend, though …'

'If you're trying to break my heart, Shikandin, I'm afraid it's not working,' Govinda quipped.

The three men shared a round of laughter, cut short as Govinda winced.

With a meaningful glance at Shikandin, Dhaumya pulled back the covers to take a look at the bandaged spot on Govinda's side. 'We haven't told anyone about this,' he said.

Govinda responded with a noncommittal nod and lay back in the bed, revelling in the fresh, crisp scent of the silk covers. After all the soot and smoke, it was a relief to feel clean again.

'Well?' Shikandin prompted, not in the least distracted.

'Would you two believe it was a common spear?'

Neither of the men bothered to respond and Govinda had little choice but to continue, 'The Bramha-weapon …' he was terse. 'Except that …'

'Hmm?'

Govinda searched for the right words to explain. 'The poison in the Bramha-weapon is supposed to work by pulling images out of your subconscious mind, causing hallucinations, a confused view of reality. It works best on a crowd or group, usually because it leads to chaos – soldiers killing their armies, people burning down their homes … But this … what I felt, it was more than chaos …' He shivered slightly at the memory.

Dhaumya said, 'Do you realize that it's unheard of to survive a direct attack using the Bramha-weapon? It's renowned for never failing, even against those trained to resist it, if the arrow or blade with the poison pierces the skin.'

'It seems to have failed this time …' Shikandin pointed out.

'Then it wasn't the Bramha-weapon,' Govinda declared. He wondered whether he ought to mention how he had managed to fight off the hallucinations, but then decided against it. Instead, he turned to Dhaumya, 'Did you have a chance to examine the poison? There must have been some left in me …'

'Yes, I had to bleed you a little to get it out. The contents were similar to the Bramha-weapon, but not the same. In any case, this wasn't some simple Ganjika herb. Surviving this weapon, Bramha-astra or not, was no small feat. You're either a tough man or a fortunate one. Maybe both.'

Govinda ignored the compliment, and the implied question. 'A new weapon made from a new poison,' he said solemnly.

'Agniveshya?'

'Yes. This was Agniveshya's work, all right. I can only suppose he was trying to recreate the Bramha-weapon with new ingredients, ones that were more readily available. He must have ended up with this instead – a poison that draws on your deepest fears. It magnifies them, exaggerates them, it makes you relive them. Except it is worse than reality. It's the most horrible way to die that I can think of. Yabha!'

A strained silence met his statement, and despite the warm orange-red beams cast by the setting sun on the white marble floor, a gloom seemed to descend over the three friends.

At length, Shikandin ventured, 'At least we know how his killer found it so easy to get to him. It'd be dangerous and pointless, too, to keep Agniveshya alive if there was nothing more to be gained from him.'

Govinda looked from one downcast face to the other and said. 'Unfortunately, all we have is our guesswork … But I'll make do with that for the moment.' He indulged in a prolonged stretch and an ostentatious yawn, making his two friends laugh and bringing back cheer to the conversation.

At last, when they had settled down, Shikandin said, 'Conspiracies, and more conspiracies. I wonder, Govinda – you and Dwaipayana – who's the master and who's the puppet?'

'These are tangled skeins, Shikandin. I believe that I'm master of my own self and Dwaipayana believes the contrary. Is one of us wrong? Perhaps we're both wrong and someone else holds the strings …'

Shikandin groaned his protest and mumbled something about waking up when Govinda was done philosophizing.

Govinda laughed. 'Let me see, how can I put it in a way that might interest … what was it … one with congenital stupidity, such as you? Ah! Got it!' He inclined his head to one side, and said in a cheeky tone, 'It's like the difference between a courtesan's seductions and those of a mistress.'

Dhaumya stood up with a smile, saying, 'This is not a conversation for my innocent ears. I am, after all, a man of renunciation. I ought to leave before you two debauched men corrupt a pious soul.'

Shikandin raised a disbelieving eyebrow, first at Govinda and then at Dhaumya, who was now at the door. 'You're joking right …?'

The scholar waved it off, saying he had other things to attend to anyway, and left.

'Where were we?' Govinda said, the moment he was gone. 'Ah, yes! When a clever courtesan comes across a debauched and foolish possibility, like Prince Shikandin of the Panchalas, she knows that to keep his interest she'll have to constantly surprise him, entertain him, vary the prize she offers. But the really ambitious courtesan, whose aim is to become Prince Shikandin's official mistress, will play the game differently. There is just one prize, an immensely desirable prize. That does not vary. But she keeps you on edge by never letting you know how close you are to winning it. Just when you think you're almost there, she'll pull away … not completely, mind you. Just enough to make you go all silly and chase her again.'

Shikandin forced a serious expression on to his face, though he longed to laugh. 'I'm sorry, Govinda, I don't understand,' he said solemn. 'Are you seducing Dwaipayana, or is he seducing you? I didn't realize you found him attractive, by the way …' He tried to maintain his stolid seriousness, but soon burst out in a loud guffaw.

Govinda joined in heartily, saying, 'Good thing our dear friend left …'

'But you've made your point,' a slightly breathless Shikandin conceded at length.

Govinda shrugged as he added, 'Of course, it is possible that Dwaipayana uses me in ways I don't even see … I'm no puppeteer, and I don't think I'm a puppet. Well, I hope I'm not.'

Shikandin stretched himself on the couch, hands behind his head.

He stared at the vaulted ceiling for a while and then said, 'What if, Govinda … what if everyone is a toy?'

'You mean in the hands of fate? Hu! I didn't realize you of all people were Dwaipayana's faithful, all these years!'

'You know I don't believe in fate. I believe in the Eternal Universe and its perfection, but not in fate.'

'Then?'

'I mean, ultimately, who holds the strings? You act based on what *you* think Dwaipayana seeks to achieve … What if Dwaipayana has let you think as you do so that you act as you do? And then, of course, what if you've let him think that if he lets you think as you do, you'd act thus, when actually … you see what I mean, don't you?' Shikandin finished.

'True …' Govinda admitted. He sat up in bed, cross-legged, pulling the silken sheet in place around his bare hips. 'I've been bathed,' he suddenly noted.

'Indeed you have, and by a rather attractive handmaiden too. But that's beside the point.'

'I was going to say,' Govinda continued, 'that there is no point.'

Shikandin nodded, but said nothing, leading to a short, comfortable lull in the conversation. Eventually, Govinda began, sounding grim now, 'Shikandin, what can you remember about the time when we were in Kandava … I mean, when you and I …?'

Shikandin regarded his friend with concern and hesitation. 'The poison … it stoked things hidden deep in your subconscious mind, didn't it, Govinda? It's been, what, almost seventeen years? You've never asked me about what happened, until today.'

'I'm asking now.'

With a soft grunt Shikandin sat up again. He gazed out of the window at something in the distance. And then, without looking at Govinda, he began in a matter-of-fact tone, reciting his recollection of events. 'There were twelve of us, including you and me. We picked up the trail from the ruins of Ghora's village, near Mathura. It took us four days to make it to the heart of Kandava and another day to locate exactly where they were keeping Agniveshya …'

'He was there, wasn't he?' Govinda interrupted.

'Yes, he was. He was working underground in what looked like a forge, but lived in a nearby hutment. We saw him being taken down by the guards and resolved to attack the next time they brought him out to the surface.'

'And then ... we attacked, didn't we? I remember we attacked ...'

Shikandin nodded. 'Something was wrong. The Nagas standing guard over the trapdoor hurriedly pulled Agniveshya out. He was screaming. That's when we attacked, the twelve of us.'

Govinda nodded, trying to piece things together in his mind. 'I went for the trapdoor, didn't I?'

'Yes.'

'Why did you pull me back, Shikandin?' Govinda asked. 'You pulled me back and gave the order to retreat. Why?'

'The forge was on fire, Govinda. You would've jumped in at any moment.'

Govinda simply stared at Shikandin. For the tiniest moment his eyes were blank, holding no emotion. He shut them in an effort to remember and forget, both. And then, his usual composure, his cool, unflappable, commanding presence was back. After a while, he asked, 'Why didn't we take Agniveshya with us? We could have ended it all that day, if we had taken him with us ...'

Shikandin cleared his throat and stated as plainly as he could, 'He asked to be left behind. He was ... badly burnt and in great pain. He asked me to leave him my dagger, and I did. Perhaps he had no intention of killing himself or, perhaps, he was recaptured before he could take his own life.' He waited, knowing that Govinda had every right to berate him for the slip. Especially since it had now come back to haunt them.

Govinda sighed. 'You're not the only one who's made such mistakes, Shikandin. Yesterday ... no, the day before, I saw him – Devala Asita. I suppose I should be happy that I've flushed the snake out of its hole. Or I could regret that I didn't kill it in the first place.'

Shikandin was grim. 'Does Dhaumya know?'

'No. And I'd rather not mention it. Dhaumya won't ever acknowledge him as a brother ... Not after what he's become.'

'A Firewright ...'

'One could say that, yes.'

Shikandin studied Govinda for a while and then said, 'All right, so what other stupid confessions am I yet to hear?'

Govinda let out a breath he did not know he had been holding. He lay back against the pillows and said, 'The woods, they always mean madness. Speaking of which, what ... what was I doing, you know, back then, after we left Agniveshya? I can't remember that part at all ... how did we get out?' he asked.

Shikandin smirked mischievously, the gleam on his face dispelling the sombre mood that had fallen over them both.

'What?' Govinda urged, smiling in anticipation, without really knowing why.

'For all the trouble you've given me, it was worth it ...' Shikandin replied, relishing the moment. Grinning widely, he said, 'Just after I pulled you back, I punched you so hard that you didn't come to until we were halfway to Kampilya ...'

A few weeks later, a great host convened at the place that had once had been known as Kandava. Amid much fanfare and splendour, Dharma laid the foundation stone for a new city, the capital of his kingdom. Panchali stood on his left, holding a handful of the freshly dug, fragrant earth mixed with auspicious unguents and incense. Govinda stood at Dharma's right, in the place of honour. He had found it curious that Panchali had not spoken to him even once of what had happened and, in fact, she carefully avoided the topic. It puzzled him still, much to Partha's amusement.

Partha's theory had been that Panchali felt too embarrassed at her own actions to revisit the matter. Govinda knew better than to assume so. Her silence told him many things, but he decided to let the matter go. The important thing was that it was done, and Takshaka and his people were safe. As was Panchali. Dharma, of course, deemed the entire event a wonder of divine providence, the vastness of which was beyond individual comprehension. He went on about how the benevolent gods had not only made it his duty to destroy Kandava, but also, acting through Govinda, had ensured that innocent Nagas would be safe, as was their destiny.

Destiny ...

Govinda glanced at Dwaipayana, who joyfully observed events from his place of honour on an elevated dais, next to the Grandsire Bhisma and King Dhritarastra. It was, Govinda knew, for the same reasons of destiny that the Vyasa and Dharma both preferred to overlook Panchali's actions as well as the events that had followed. They had made sure that no one came to know that she had been a part of the episode at Kandava. It would not do to reduce the dramatic version of events by introducing prosaic explanations for what had happened.

The Vyasa frowned ever so slightly as his eyes met Govinda's. Govinda, however, immediately bowed with every bit of respect due to an elder and scholar. His humility was nothing less than endearing. Dwaipayana was moved to smile. Despite himself he mouthed a blessing, 'Varuna protect you, my son.'

Govinda's eyes twinkled with a hint of mischief. Dharma had to call to him twice before he turned to listen. At Dhaumya's instructions, Dharma and Govinda together lifted the consecrated foundation stone and set it gently into the ground, while Panchali sprinkled the sanctified soil around it. Straightening up, the two men embraced each other spontaneously.

'Swasti!' Govinda said, wishing all prosperity on the kingdom. 'May every harvest be plentiful and every sowing peaceful.'

Dharma was visibly stirred. 'What shall we call this city, Govinda? What shall we name it?'

Govinda looked up as the first drops of rain fell on his forehead. In moments, the strong, sudden downpour had soaked him to the skin. Around him, many ran to seek cover under the makeshift shelters of bamboo and woven leaves that had been set up for the day. Dharma and Panchali did not move, letting the torrent drench them within and without.

Laughing, Govinda placed his hands on Dharma's shoulders. 'Indr-prastha,' he said. 'Call it Indr-prastha, the city of Indra on earth … My King.'

Dharma found himself unable to speak, overcome as he was by emotion. Finally, he managed to rasp, 'Stay, Govinda, please?' His voice took on a note of urgency. 'Stay here with us … Help me build Indr-prastha.'

Govinda glanced at Panchali. She showed not the slightest trace of any emotion. With a sad smile he replied, 'This is your home, Dharma. It's time I went back to mine.'

Part 2

1

DAWN BROKE OVER KAUNDINYAPURA, THE CAPITAL OF THE
Vidharbha kingdom, as Govinda rode up to the city gates. The entire
city was brightly festooned and decorated in preparation for a royal
wedding. In contrast, Govinda was dressed in simple, well-worn
clothes. His weapons were concealed. He observed his surroundings
carefully, as he weaved through the celebrating masses. In time, he
spotted the temple dedicated to Goddess Parvati. He swung off
Balahak and led the horse to the shade of a nearby tree, pretending
to tend to him as he waited.

A sudden flurry of activity on the street announced the arrival of
Vidharbha's princess. Rukmavati stepped out of her royal carriage and
walked into the temple. An amazed Govinda studied her discreetly.
Despite her bridal finery, she looked younger than he had expected,
hardly eighteen or so. Her skin was even and creamy, touched with
shades of pink from the warmth of the sun. Her long brown hair had
been done up in a large, complex knot on the crown of her head,
highlighting her slender neck and graceful gait. Large doe-eyes were
set in a rounded face, conveying the innocence of a child. Only her
lips, full but unsmiling, showed the state of her mind.

A crowd began gathering as a grand procession made its way
towards the temple. At its head rode the bridegroom – Shisupala,
heir to the Chedi throne. To his right was Syoddhan, his friend and
ally, and on the left rode Rukmi, the Crown Prince of Vidharbha and
father of the bride. The three men also had the distinction of being
Emperor Jarasandha's most trusted vassals, and Shisupala was as dear
to the Emperor as a son.

Son or not, Govinda noted, Jarasandha's hand was clearly behind the wedding. The nations of Vidharbha and Chedi had consistently refused to join the Confederation of Yadu Nations, preferring to align themselves with Magadha. Now that the Panchalas were kin to the Kurus or, more precisely, to the fast-rising power that was Western Kuru, Vidharbha was the next political prize. The kingdom was strategically located to control the southern route across the span of Aryavarta. As a result, if Rukmavati married Shisupala, it would seal the Emperor's influence over the southern roads, and leave Dwaraka in an extremely precarious position.

The chain of events was far from unexpected. Govinda had known well that something like this was inevitable ever since Kandava had gone into Kuru hands. And so, despite Dharma's invitation to stay and help build the new city of Indr-prastha, he had returned to Dwaraka. He had waited and watched patiently for nearly three years, almost certain that it would be Vidharbha that came up as a political issue. But, he admitted to himself, he had not expected it would also become a personal one.

I'm here because it's essential to the security of my people, to the future of Dwaraka – even Aryavarta.

Or was it? He ignored that doubt, along with the other question that nagged him: *Wouldn't I be here even if this weren't Vidharbha?*

Govinda had been compelled to act when he had seen Rukmavati's message, smuggled out of Vidharbha in the hands of a travelling monk. It had been simple and direct: 'Come, save me from marrying that ogre Shisupala, or I shall die.'

Rukmavati's description of Shisupala, while excessive, had also been dramatically effective. Indeed, it had brought a smile to Govinda's face, though admittedly Shisupala had his strengths as he did his faults. The man was old-fashioned in many ways, notably in the belief that some men were meant to rule, while other men – and all women – were meant to serve. When it came to his preferences on how women might best serve him, though, Shisupala's views were as innovative as they were vile. Having now seen the young, innocent Rukmavati, Govinda could not bear the thought of her in Shisupala's bed of horrors. Taking a deep breath, he concentrated on the scene before him. If he had any plans of getting past Shisupala, Rukmi and their armies, not to mention Syoddhan and the battalions of men sent by Jarasandha as guard of honour, he had to stay focussed.

Her prayers over, Rukmavati was about to exit the temple. She glanced at the assembled crowd of onlookers as she gracefully came down the steps. For an instant, her gaze rested on Govinda before moving on. Then, oblivious to the furious shouts from her brother and the others of her escort, she walked away from her waiting carriage. There was no turning back now. What the girl had just done could not be ignored. Govinda swung on to Balahak in one fluid move, ready for what was to come.

Rukmavati beamed, radiant with delight, as she realized her daring had not been in vain. She clung tight to the strong arm that went around her waist, lifting her on to the silver-white steed. 'Hold on,' a voice whispered in her ear, and she complied.

Before anyone could make sense of what had just happened, Govinda was weaving expertly through the crowd, making for the city's main gates. The guards made to draw shut the huge metal-spiked doors, but he let loose a slew of arrows, jamming the hinges. Rukmi shouted out orders, but they were lost in the general confusion. It took the soldiers a while to respond to the commands, but they finally dropped their weapons and began heaving at the doors, sheer brute force straining the precisely wedged arrows. With a great, cracking sound, the arrows broke, allowing the hinges to swing the gates shut. But it was too late. Rukmavati was gone.

They rode at breakneck speed, as fast the horse could go. Rukmavati clung on, oblivious to the world, looking up at the young face of her rescuer. Heading west and south, they reached a river. Just across the waters, on the opposite bank, the first hills marked the beginning of the Western Mountains that ran down into Dakshinavarta. The stallion slowed down and made for a small copse of trees, stopping on command.

Rukmavati let go of the man, feeling suddenly self-conscious at all that had happened. He nimbly got off the horse and began leading the animal towards the water. She could wait no more. She dismounted, and threw her arms around him in a passionate embrace. He gently pushed her away, smiling to put her at ease.

'Mahamatra, I consider it an honour that you called on me to help you,' he chivalrously began, 'though I'm sure you would have found a way out of that … erm … situation even without my assistance Now, if you'll tell me where you wish to go, I'll see you there without further delay.'

Rukmavati hesitated, surprised. She then asked, 'When you came to rescue me didn't you know what it would mean? Won't you take me with you to Dwaraka?'

'I came because you asked for my help in getting away from Shisupala. I can't offer you more. I can't take my country, my people, to war over you.'

She hung her head in despair. Despite her best efforts, her body heaved with silent sobs.

'Princess,' he began, but she snapped her head up to interrupt him.

'Please allow me to speak before you say anything further,' Rukmavati stated, wiping her tears away with determination. She took a step back and looked up at the tall man. 'I know I put you in a difficult position when I sent you that message. Whatever I may feel for you, I can't demand that you find affection in your heart for me,' she gracefully admitted. 'I've heard of how the women of Dwaraka throng around you, driven to madness by your looks and your manner. That may be a ridiculous exaggeration, an astounding fact that defies all reason, or maybe even the truth. But I don't care. All I know is how I feel.'

Rukmavati paused as she noticed the man's sudden tautness. She gently rested her cheek against his unyielding chest and said, 'If you choose not to take me with you, I'll wait right here for my father and Shisupala to find me.' She laughed as he looked at her sharply. 'What,' she taunted, 'did you think that I'd want to kill myself? No, I won't die. What use is that when it'll still lead to war between our nations? If you leave me here, I shall marry Shisupala. And every time he touches me

I'll think of you and call out your name. No matter what he does to me, whether I feel ecstasy or pain, it's *your* name that I will call out.' With a charming look, she added, 'There. I've finished.'

A warm, pleasantly deep voice cut in and said, 'Indeed you've finished, my dear. I doubt the vagrant will ever dare cross you for the rest of your lives together.'

Rukmavati turned, startled, even as she heard the surprised whisper from the man next to her. 'Father!'

Govinda Shauri stepped into view, leading Balahak and a brown charger from Vidharbha behind him. 'I had a feeling you'd try something like this, Pradymna,' he said.

'Father!' the younger man repeated and ran forward to embrace him.

Govinda wrapped one arm around his son's shoulder, and extended his other arm out and nodded to Rukmavati. She made to kneel, but he pre-empted her.

'You're now a daughter of mine,' he said, 'so behave like one. Never be afraid to speak your mind or stand up for what you think is just and good. Honour and virtue lie in your heart, not in the judgement of others. Freedom and self-respect are yours to assume and keep, and not another's to give. Not even,' he said, with a pointed look at Pradymna, 'your husband's.'

Rukmavati regarded Govinda doubtfully. She had not expected a man so young, or so cheerful. His frank words and honest face won her over. 'Yes … *Father*?' she said.

'That's right.' Govinda nodded. 'Come, we have to decide on our next step. Let's get you on to a horse each, it'll be faster that way …' He moved away to check the saddle on the brown horse.

Rukmavati turned to Pradymna and whispered, 'Maybe I should have written to your father instead … he's a wonderful man …'

Pradymna looked deflated at the comment.

'Wait for a while, and I'll show you exactly how wonderful I think *you* are …' she teased, restoring cheer on the young man's face.

Govinda pretended to be busy with the horses, and did not show that he had overheard what was clearly a private exchange. *Life and time move on, Govinda Shauri,* he told himself with a quiet smile. *Your son is already his own man.*

2

SYODDHAN RODE SILENTLY NEXT TO A PENSIVE SHISUPALA, AS AN array of soldiers from the armies of Vidharbha, Magadha and Kuru marched out of Kaundinyapura. A furious Rukmi led the pursuit of his daughter's kidnappers. Each of the three men had about a division of hundred soldiers under their command. The rest of the armies were being mustered in sections and would follow in due course if they were needed. But, as Rukmi had pointed out, it was better to make the initial move quickly and with fewer men, since Govinda and his scoundrel son were on their own. His spies had assured them that there had been no notable army movement towards Vidharbha in the preceding weeks and Govinda Shauri himself had no escort.

Govinda Shauri, Syoddhan said the name in his mind. Despite the incessant tirade of expletives that Rukmi kept spewing, his respect for Govinda remained, though a little grudgingly. What Govinda had done that morning had perhaps lacked something in nobility but not in courage. No matter what anyone said, he was not a coward. Pradymna and Rukmavati were probably unaware of the peril he had faced in order to give them the chance to escape.

Even as the couple had raced out the gates, Govinda had single-handedly barred Rukmi and Shisupala's way. Of course, he would have known that Rukmi could not order the archers to fire at will in the middle of a crowded city street. But there still had been the marksmen on the fort's turrets to contend with and the barrage of soldiers who had closed in from all sides. Nevertheless, he had calmly released arrow after arrow at the advancing soldiers, holding them off for as long as he could. His chance at escape had come only when the city gates had been opened again to let the mustered forces give chase to Pradymna and Rukmavati. Govinda had then sped off at the first chance he got, with Rukmi's men right on his tail.

Syoddhan looked up as a rider came towards them at great speed. The man's uniform showed him to be one of the elite soldiers of Rukmi's guard who had gone after Govinda. Jumping off his horse, the soldier knelt low on the ground. Syoddhan immediately knew it could not be good news. Indeed, the soldier's voice was strained as he said, 'My lords, Govinda Shauri is nearly at the river. All three of them – our princess too – are making their way down the bank to the water's edge.'

'Paayu!' Rukmi shouted, enraged. 'How could you let him escape? Why didn't you follow him, you good-for-nothing son of a bitch?'

'The others are dead, my prince. I retreated to inform you where the three are heading.'

'Dead?' Rukmi was aghast. 'Eight of you against one fleeing man and you tell me seven are dead? Are you men or squealing whores?'

The soldier crouched down low and silently faced his master's wrath as Rukmi continued to rant.

'Perhaps we should let it go,' Shisupala suddenly said. 'After all, it isn't Govinda who'll marry your daughter, but Pradymna – and Pradymna's heritage can't be denied. Unlike Govinda, he was born honourable, an Arya beyond doubt …'

Syoddhan was taken aback, though pleasantly so, by his friend's declaration.

Rukmi turned to them, just as astonished but far less pleased. 'Except,' he pointed out, 'the boy is Govinda's adopted son and legal heir. Whatever he may once have been, he is now the son of a bastard cowherd.'

Shisupala argued. 'Pradymna is true blood. If this had been the good old days, I would have arranged his wedding with your daughter myself! Look, I've bedded enough women – whores and otherwise – and in all probability fathered enough bastards to respect the blood of our forefathers when I see it. Pradymna is Arya. He's one of us. Let it go.'

Syoddhan flinched silently at Shisupala's casual admission, but kept his thoughts to himself with the ease of a man who had many brothers, some of them far worse than the man before him. If he had Dussasana and a few more of that lot flogged as often as Kuru law deemed they deserved, Syoddhan knew he would either be less some siblings or, perhaps, his own head. 'Princes will be princes,' his father would often say as he ordered Syoddhan to set right what had gone wrong – from the farmers who had ended up in the prisons of Hastina for failing to bow fast enough when one of his brothers had ridden past to the dead virgin handmaidens unfortunate enough to have caught a lustful eye. At that moment it was difficult not to think of Shisupala as one of his errant younger brothers, perhaps even the best of the lot.

With an indulgent shake of his head, Syoddhan said, 'I'm with Shisupala on this one, Rukmi, though for less colourful reasons. I know you have a long list of complaints against Govinda, but I see no cause to blame Pradymna. If your daughter likes him, then perhaps you should indulge her wishes.'

Rukmi was adamant. 'No!'

'My friend …'

'No! I said no!'

Syoddhan sighed and turned to the still-kneeling soldier. 'How much further?'

The soldier turned slightly to point to a grove of trees that lay a stone's throw ahead. 'Beyond that grove is an open plain. Beyond the plain lie the western hills that run southward for many leagues. The river is about midway across the plain. It's in spate, and the currents are strong. Perhaps they think that by crossing it they may dissuade you, my lords.'

'And beyond the mountains?' Syoddhan questioned.

'The coastlands south of Dwaraka and Anartta,' the soldier replied. 'If they get over the mountains, they might try to board a ship. But I doubt they'll try to climb across – the horses would never make it. The only thing they can do is head north along the mountains till they are past the range and then cut through Anartta on horseback. It's a long ride …'

Shisupala opened his mouth as though to say something, but decided against it. He looked questioningly at Rukmi instead.

'It doesn't make sense,' Syoddhan voiced his doubt. 'The hills block their way and they'll be cornered. What does he plan to do? Do you think he's waiting for reinforcements?'

'Only armies wait for reinforcements,' Rukmi was contemptuous. 'Lone men wait, and pray, for help.'

'Call it what we may, the more time we give him, the more likely he'll get something or the other. We need to move quickly, if we decide to move.'

'What do you mean, *if*?' Rukmi snapped.

'You still have a choice, Rukmi,' Syoddhan pointed out. 'Shisupala himself believes Pradymna to be a suitable match for your daughter, and I agree. You know that your father, King Bhismaka, will also concur. There's talk that Pradymna may soon be made Commander of the Yadu armies even at this young age and then, in effect, he will rule Dwaraka. Your daughter will be his first and principal, if not only, wife. It *is* an attractive alliance, in all fairness.'

'I ....' Rukmi faltered, and then said with an air of finality. 'It's not about my daughter, anymore, Syoddhan. It's about the impunity with which Govinda Shauri and his ilk act. Let me tell you that my daughter's life is already forfeit for the shame she has brought upon our family.' With a snarl he added, 'The boy shall die first as my daughter watches, then she shall die while Govinda Shauri watches, painfully aware that he has brought this upon those children. Then, when he begs for death, I shall kill him ... *slowly!*'

Syoddhan pursed his lips and quietly considered the declaration.

Shisupala appeared visibly shaken at Rukmi's words. Clearing his throat, he declared in a formal manner, 'Then you must forgive me, for I shall have no part of this.'

Rukmi looked at him, astounded, as Shisupala continued. 'I really liked your daughter,' he said. 'Enough, that I would have treated her with nothing but respect. I had hoped to share my life with her, give her every joy she could wish for, and like the fool I am I thought she could somehow make me a better man. I can't just forget all that and take part in her killing.'

'But ...'

'Please! We're allies, so I'll leave you my forces. You also have the Emperor's battalions with you, and I'm sure Syoddhan will gladly place his companies at your service. But please, let me ... let us, leave. Syoddhan and I shall wait for you at Kaundinyapura.'

'In that case, tell my executioners to have three stakes waiting for the heads I'll bring back,' Rukmi rasped.

Before either of the other men could say anything further, he whipped his horse into a gallop and set off down the road. At a signal from Rukmi's captain, the armies followed. Shisupala and Syoddhan watched them ride off. Then they turned around to head back the way they had come.

3

RUKMAVATI KEPT LOOKING BACK AS THEY FORDED THE STRONG currents of the river. She could have sworn she had heard her father calling out to her. Perhaps it was a dream, or even wishful thinking.

Pradymna reached out to take her hand. 'This is my fault,' he confessed. 'When you sent me that letter, I was sure my father would find out about it. I was glad because I didn't have to tell him what I planned to do and he'd still know where I'd gone and why. But not once did I think he'd come to Vidharbha, and in this way. If I had known he would risk his own life ...' He faltered, as his eyes fell on the man riding in front of them.

Govinda seemed to be admiring the scenic vista as though they were on a picnic. 'Don't believe a word, my dear,' he suddenly cut in, turning in his saddle to look at them. 'He's just pretending to be a good son and all that.'

'Oi!' Pradymna exclaimed, looking very much his usual cheeky self. He then went on, 'You're right, Father. Being serious doesn't suit me at all!'

Their cheerful expressions changed quickly as the faint thunder of hooves came on the wind.

'They're on the plains,' Govinda urgently noted. 'Change horses with me,' he instructed Rukmavati, quickly sliding off Balahak and into the water.

The river was moderately deep, the water swirling almost level with their saddles. Govinda treaded water as he brought Balahak close to Rukmavati's horse. She tried to slip off, but he restrained her and gestured to Pradymna, who helped her clamber directly onto Balahak. Wet, and cursing from the effort, Govinda finally pulled himself on to Rukmavati's brown steed. 'Keep heading in a straight line towards the hills,' he told the young couple.

'What are you doing?' Pradymna cried out, trying to make himself heard above the roar of the river.

'I'm going back. I want to speak to her father.'

'Father! Don't do this please, let's just go …' Pradymna insisted, even as Rukmavati dejectedly looked away.

Govinda was firm. 'She's a child, Pradymna. Just because she loves you, you can't expect her to turn her back on her family. Let me talk to Rukmi, and we can settle this quietly and quickly.'

'With all due respect, Father, Shisupala's out there. That man has spilt more blood over lust than he has over honour.'

'With greater respect, Pradymna, Shisupala would never, ever, kill one of his own. In his own way he's always been fond of you. That could be to our advantage.'

'Please,' Rukmavati added. 'It's not my father's armies alone that you must face. The Emperor has sent us a lot of his soldiers in a show of friendship. Those men are a bloodthirsty lot.'

'Like most imperial soldiers,' Govinda said, then added cheekily, 'and for future reference, my dear, that kind of observation is more likely to send me scurrying towards trouble, not keep me from it.'

'But …'

'No buts. You two do as I tell you.' With that, Govinda turned the horse around and headed back across the river.

Rukmavati and Pradymna stood where they were, watching the disappearing figure for a while.

'Come,' Pradymna eventually said. They continued across the river and clambered on to the other side. 'Go straight,' he mumbled.

'But it's just the hills ahead,' Rukmavati said.

'Govinda Shauri doesn't speak in vain,' he told her. His voice filled with pride and renewed energy he declared, 'My father knows what he's doing. Go. Ride straight. Use that line of shadows to keep direction.'

'What about you?'

'I can't leave my father behind to fight alone. You know that.'

'Then let me stay too.'

'Rukmavati, please,' Pradymna urged her. 'You have to trust my father. He has a plan, of that I'm sure. Go now, hurry. And whatever happens, keep going.'

Rukmavati nodded, feeling more afraid than ever. On an impulse, she leaned across and gently kissed Pradymna. He looked at her with surprise, then displayed his usual cheeky grin. Without waiting for her to leave he wheeled his horse around and headed back to join Govinda.

Rukmavati urged Balahak on. The undulating land rose in a small peak, before it began to gently slope downwards to meet the mountains. At the crest, Rukmavati turned back for one last look. Pradymna had caught up with Govinda and the two men were cantering towards Rukmi and his massive army, as though father and son had no cares in the world. With a sob, she turned away and continued forward. Within moments, she was out of view.

Time stopped for Rukmavati. She let Balahak amble on towards the mountains. The tears she had held back now flowed freely. There was no way Govinda and Pradymna could escape. She had led them to their deaths with her stupid notions of romance and adventure. It was all her fault. As Balahak came to a stop, she hung her head and sobbed her heart out. Then, still sniffling and weeping, she looked around her.

It seemed like a normal day – pleasant and serene. The sky was shot with purple and gold as the sun had began to set, falling behind the mountains with unexpected speed. The huge shimmering red orb was unnaturally large as it disappeared from view. In the dimming light the dark outline of the mountains looked inviting, like sleep after a long day. Across the river, she suspected, Govinda and Pradymna were probably already dead.

Rukmavati resolved to ride to the foothills as she had been told to, even if it was only to stand in front of the impassable rock and wait for her father to find her. Despondent, she nudged Balahak on.

Suddenly she saw a flash of light – like a spark, only much larger. Taken by surprise, she gasped. In that moment, it was gone.

She flicked the reins but found it was unnecessary. Balahak reared up of his own accord and set off at a gallop. As the stallion gathered speed she saw the flash for a second time – golden and red fire in the colour of the setting sun. It took a moment, but Rukmavati realized with a shock that it *was* the setting sun. There was a gap between the mountains, a pass of some sort, which just barely let the beams through. Her heart thudding wildly, she rode on, making straight for the flash. She had no idea how Govinda had known, but this had to have been a part of his plan. She rode faster still, but darkness swiftly descended around her.

Rukmavati cried out softly in despair. She knew she was not very far from the mountains but she could no longer make out their detail, for they appeared as one dark shadow despite the light of the moon. Ignoring her anguish, Balahak kept going. She screamed unwittingly, thinking the horse was about to smash into the rock, but to her surprise they went clean through a narrow pass.

Balahak came to a stop in that darkness with a precision that came from his familiarity with the surroundings and memory of his absent master's previous commands. Rukmavati, however, was more lost than ever. Her breath resounded softly in the space, telling her that she was in a cavern of some sort. Even as a new wave of panic settled on her, a voice gently reassured her that she was safe. She cried out in fear, feeling far from reassured, but gradually noticed that Balahak was calm and seemed to recognize the speaker. Rukmavati took courage from that fact and tried to calm down. Her eyes gradually got used to the dimness and could begin to make out the outlines of things around her. She heard the rasp as a flint was struck and by its yellow light saw a kind, rounded face she recognized as Balabadra, Govinda's brother. The light then fell on a man holding up a banner and she could distinctly make out the emblem of a soaring eagle – Govinda Shauri's emblem. She realized these men had come to his aid.

'Hurry!' she burst out. 'Across the river, they're on the plain there. My father has over three, four hundred men, many of them imperial soldiers.'

Balabadra called out to his commanders and ordered all the torches to be lit. He turned back to Rukmavati, 'You'd better stay here. We'll come back for you.'

She shook her head and in a tremulous voice said, 'Pradymna ...'

He sighed and then gestured to a young man, who came forward. 'Samva here will take care of you. He's Pradymna's brother and his best friend ...'

Rukmavati nodded and stood aside as the men filed out of the narrow pass.

Once they were past the entrance, they fell into formation as two wings and made to cross the river. The light of their flares as they swooped down the slope towards the water was enough to create a panic amidst Rukmi's forces. Astonished, even terrified, cries rose into the night.

Rukmavati rode at the rear, along with Samva, who alternated between looking at her and at the men riding ahead.

'He told me, you know ...' Samva began without preamble. 'Pradymna ... He told me you had to be the most beautiful woman he'd ever seen. I thought he'd gone mad, the way he went on and on about you ...'

'He'd seen me before?' Rukmavati asked, surprised.

Samva nodded. 'At Indr-prastha, when the foundation stone was laid. You were sitting with your father and grandfather.'

She began to feel less bashful now. 'How did you all know? And how did you get here just in time?'

'We sailed down the coast from Dwaraka and took the pass through the mountains. Your father's spies had no clue ...' he chuckled.

'Amazing!'

'Mahamatra,' Samva said, with a mock air of formality, 'if Dwaraka

252

is to be your home and Pradymna your irredeemable slave in matrimony, then there's one thing that you should never forget …'

'Which is …?'

Samva said, with discernible pride, 'Govinda Shauri always has a plan.'

He slowed down as they reached the elevation just before the river and then came to a stop. 'Look,' he pointed.

The moon shone down as bright as the sun, and the clanging of metal against metal and the cries of men carried well across the water. Despite the distance at which the battle was taking place, Rukmavati could see that the last of the Yadu soldiers had now forded the river and had thrown themselves into the fray. Though outnumbered, the men of Dwaraka fought bravely, tactically using cluster formations that allowed them to fight back-to-back. Her eyes searched out and found the figures of Govinda and Pradymna as they fought together at the frontlines. She clenched her fists tight as she saw Pradymna raise his sword to land a fatal stroke on her father. But the blade did not fall as another gleam of metal intervened. Govinda had barred the blow, and he was furious with Pradymna.

Rukmi and Govinda then briefly spoke, after which Rukmi turned away and shouted out orders to his men to withdraw. Jarasandha's soldiers, led by a surly captain, were the last to comply, but Govinda and his men had already lowered their weapons and let the Emperor's forces retreat, unharmed.

It was over. What should have been a massacre of two men had turned, in moments, into an even battle, which had ended as quickly as it had started.

Pradymna was greeted with loud cheers from the men as he rode swiftly towards the river.

Winking at Rukmavati, Samva said, 'Well, goodnight then. I'll see you in the morning. Don't let that rogue bother you too much …' Before she could reply, Samva was already making his way across the river.

The two brothers met on the opposite bank to embrace and then Pradymna was splashing his way across to Rukmavati. Crying with relief, she dismounted and ran to him. He swung off his horse and took her in his arms. Neither of them cared that the entire army of Narayaniyas applauded them on with all gusto as they kissed passionately. With an inaudible shout at the jubilant soldiers, Pradymna took Rukmavati's hand and led her away from the river, out of view.

Dwaraka welcomed Pradymna and his bride with great fervour and unceasing festivity. Initially, Rukmavati was a little frightened by the splendour of the city and the open-hearted jubilation of its citizens. She had hardly spoken to men in all her life and here she found herself surrounded by Pradymna's cousins, who good-naturedly teased her and openly joked with her about her new husband's foibles.

Thankfully, Balabadra's wife Raivati, who was both perceptive and sympathetic, took Rukmavati under her wing. That, however, could hardly stop the customary bantering between the women.

'They're just a bunch of louts,' Raivati gleefully informed the younger woman. 'You just keep a sharp tongue ready, my dear, and you'll be fine!'

Rukmavati smiled shyly. She already felt much more at ease. Dwaraka's people were brave and honest and she did not see the slightest sign of either fear or sadness in anyone's eyes. But there were also many things she did not understand.

'When do I meet your father's wives?' she asked Pradymna a few days after she had arrived.

Pradymna laughed.

'Why ... what?' she said, perplexed.

'My father,' Pradymna bundled her close into his arms and replied, 'has thousands of wives ...'

'What!'

'Once, in the early years, when we had just founded Dwaraka,' Pradymna began, 'a great host of women came to our gates, seeking refuge. Some were concubines and prostitutes by profession, others were slave-born women. There were also women of royal lineage, abandoned because they had been taken away as plunder, or raped and left behind, when one kingdom warred with another. They'd heard about the many-gated city that welcomed everyone ... They came from all over Aryavarta, braving cold and heat and hunger. Some of them had walked leagues and leagues, barefoot through blistering deserts and over harsh stone mountains, just to reach Dwaraka. These women, hundreds of them, were thrown into dungeon-like caverns, while the newly formed Council of Representatives leisurely debated over what ought to be done with them. In the end, those willing to pursue their lives as courtesans, prostitutes or entertainers were offered jobs in the city itself.'

'And the rest?' Rukmavati prompted, wide-eyed.

'The rest were a damned inconvenience. The Council turned them away. Many of them were just girls. My father stood on the turrets over the city gates and declared that each and every one of those women was to be treated as his wife and accorded every respect. He said they were free to come and go as they pleased, answerable only to the laws of the land and to their own consciences. To dishonour them would be to dishonour him.'

'Where are they?'

'Why, Dwaraka is full of them. My father would gladly support them, but ... I don't think many of them would give up their newfound respect so easily. They earn their own keep as administrators, port officials, medics. A few are soldiers too. Even those who work as courtesans and attendants, some of them right here in our mansions – you can tell them by the way they carry themselves. There's a kind of pride, a simmering confidence they possess, if I can call at that. And you can always, always, tell them by the way they look at my father ... There's a certain something in their eyes. Love, adoration ... I don't know what to call it. I've seen the contentment, the power even, that they feel by trusting him completely – like they've solved one of life's greatest mysteries.

'Everything we do – our scriptures, our notions of duty, all our history and our common sense, all of it tells us that there is a greater truth that we aspire for, an understanding of some higher knowledge that will give us ultimate liberation. Somehow, these women find that in this complex relationship they have with my father. It's like they become one with the world, they look at every living creature with loving eyes and tender affection.'

Rukmavati felt tears well up in her eyes. She buried her face in Pradymna's chest and tried not to cry, but he gently raised her chin, forcing her to look up. Only then did she realize that he too was fighting back tears.

'I never really understood, all these years …' Pradymna said, his voice hoarse. 'You know, he'd always joke and claim he had no time for matters like falling in love, or marriage, because Dwaraka was everything to him. And that's what I used to think, too. I used to think that it's the land of hope and freedom, that it was the only thing in life worth anything … Then I found you, my love. Now, I understand the empty life my father has chosen for himself. Nothing is more precious to my father than the people of these lands. Govinda Shauri cannot belong to any one person. He never could …'

4

'YOUR COUSIN DOESN'T LIKE GOVINDA, DOES HE?' PANCHALI ventured as she pulled irately at the gauzy veil she had worn to King Dhritarastra's royal assembly at Hastina that morning, forgetting the jewelled hair-pin that held it in place. Hissing at the slight pain she inflicted on herself, she walked over to the burnished mirror to carefully remove both pin and veil. Turning around, she threw them onto the bed in exasperation. Dharma came over to help her undo the heavy necklace that Dhristarastra had gifted her long ago. It was not an ornament she liked too much, but to not wear it to the assembly would have bordered on an insult to the king. Panchali nodded her thanks for the assistance as Dharma took off the necklace and placed it on the table.

'Perhaps Govinda *was* being hasty – turning up with his men the way he did,' Dharma said casually, in reply to her earlier question. 'The girl was, after all, spoken for by Shisupala. Having said that,' he added quickly as he caught Panchali glaring at him, 'if the girl sought to marry Pradymna, the young man was duty-bound to oblige her. As a father, Govinda has every right to be involved in the affair.'

'This is about more than romance and hurt egos, Dharma. If the alliance between Chedi and Vidharbha had gone as planned then Dwaraka would effectively have been cut off from central Aryavarta. Sooner or later, Shisupala and Jarasandha would have attacked them and we wouldn't have been able to go to their aid. Govinda has achieved what many considered impossible, and that too without a war. Here, in the centre, the Kuru–Panchala alliance holds strong, while the Chedi–Vidharbha alliance has been foiled. Shisupala and Syoddhan did not actually fight Govinda – don't you realize what that means? Already, Jarasandha's power has been undermined. His most faithful followers have begun to think for themselves instead of blindly supporting him. Vasusena will follow Syoddhan, and half the vassals to the Kashi kings are kinsmen to the Angas. It's like a stack of clay pots – pull one out from the bottom and they all come tumbling down.'

'Then the Yadus are asking for war …'

'War? Hardly,' Panchali scoffed. 'War was averted the moment we were married and the alliance between Panchala and Kuru was cast in stone. Since then, Subadra's marriage to Partha, the burning of Kandava, and your investiture as king have all served to deflect war further, that too in a way the Emperor probably did not foresee at all. Why, Jarasandha has already drawn back most of his troops and waits uneasily for Govinda's next move. He seems to be on the defensive. If you think about it, it also explains why Govinda was willing to give up the secret of the passage through the mountains – which is what, I suspect, really irked Syoddhan.'

'As it probably does many others,' Dharma pointed out. He lay down on the bed with a tired sigh, and said, 'Rukmi's scouts had no idea of its existence, even though one end of the passageway opens out on to their lands. It raises many questions, including how the Yadus came to know of it or even whether they built it. The latter seems unlikely, though. Something like that would take years, decades to carve out and it certainly couldn't be done surreptitiously. The only likely explanation I can think of is that the passage must be a natural feature. The Yadus must have found it when they were exploring the area around Anarrta during the building of Dwaraka. No one's ever really bothered much with that region. In fact, the marshland and mountains were largely uninhabited till Dwaraka was established.'

Panchali considered the argument as she walked around the room putting out all the lamps, save one. She drew a latticed iron shutter over the last lit lamp before slipping into bed next to Dharma. 'In that case,' she said at length, continuing the conversation, 'Govinda is in an even more powerful position than I had thought. True, he had other motivations, like gaining an alliance with Vidharbha and, of course, one supposes he loves his son. But he wouldn't have given up what essentially seems to be a strategic secret unless he was sure that his position was strong.'

'In *that* case,' Dharma pointedly said, 'he's made a tactical mistake. He is not strong. He still faces the risk of war, and this time with all of Aryavarta. At the end of the day Jarasandha is the Emperor of Aryavarta and we owe him our allegiance. Even if that means war against Dwaraka, against our friends ...'

For an instant Panchali seemed lost in her thoughts. 'The Emperor of Aryavarta ... Hah! The power to create and destroy, to turn kin against kin and friend against friend, in the hands of one man ...' she softly muttered. She yawned and stretched, exhausted from her long day and their rather fast ride home from Hastina. And then she was asleep. She did not notice the peculiar expression that flickered across Dharma's face, nor that he lay awake for a long time afterwards.

The next morning, Dharma sent for Dwaipayana. The Vyasa arrived as soon as he could.

In these times, it took just a few days to travel through the Kuru kingdom. When Kandava was burnt, Takshaka Naga and his people had migrated north to Kuru's fields at the border of the kingdom. There they had used their skill in working rock and stone to build a passage that connected directly to the five rivers that patterned their way through the Sindhu and Gandhara kingdoms. Trade with the Danavas and other nations to the west had boomed beyond expectation and it had soon become necessary to extend a section of the Great Road from Hastina to Indr-prastha. Meanwhile work had begun on a wide, well-cobbled caravan trail from the northern pass, running right through Western Kuru. It met the Great Road at Indr-prastha, making it much easier for foreign travellers to enter central Aryavarta from the northern borders.

Despite such glory Dharma had one regret. He could never forget that his triumph rested on the achievements of others.

It had been Partha who burnt down Kandava, and Govinda who had returned with a treaty with the Naga king Takshaka, negotiated and sealed. Govinda had also helped build the newly appointed army of Western Kuru, sending his war-hardy captain Daruka to help train the forces. Even Panchali had played a part in the rising prosperity of the kingdom. She had suggested floating barges on the River Yamuna to transport heavy goods and livestock south and east, to the other nations of Aryavarta. This had prompted many a citizen of Aryavarta, even people from Eastern Kuru, to move and settle down in and around Indr-prastha to ply their trade there. A large number of migrants had followed to offer the many services that a booming population required, from entertainment to physical labour.

Indeed, Dharma was now monarch of a bustling, prosperous nation, one he ruled from his ethereal capital, which many said was the most beautiful city in all of Aryavarta. Yet nothing here was of his making. Now he had an idea, a way to ensure that he could indelibly etch his own mark on history.

He shared it with Dwaipayana the moment the two of them were alone.

Dharma then sat back, waiting anxiously for the scholar's reaction. He was relieved when Dwaipayana smiled.

'I'd hoped that you'd see the duty that lies before you soon enough, Dharma,' Dwaipayana began, 'and so you have. It gladdens my heart to think that a worthy, truly noble man will reign over Aryavarta after all these years, and I wish with all my heart that it will be a long, peaceful reign that lasts not only my lifetime as the Vyasa but also my son Suka's. But, there is more to becoming Emperor than just being crowned, my son. First, the kings of Aryavarta must accept you as their liege-lord. Second, the noble scholar–priests must sanctify your ritual sacrifice and willingly perform your coronation. Above all, the gods must accept your offering and consecrate you as Emperor. Perhaps the third is the easiest of all. In your heart, in the depths of your conscience, do you believe that you deserve to rule? For then the gods can't deny you the opportunity and, for that matter, neither can we of the priesthood.'

'Then it's up to the kings of Aryavarta.'

'Yes. You must get them to accept your dominion. You'll have no problem with the Panchalas, thanks to your wife, and as for the Kurus, I assure you that the Grandsire Bhisma and I will be happy to advise your uncle to support you. Your cousin Syoddhan has many allies and they too can be made to accept you as Emperor. But there remains a fundamental problem. To solve it you'll need some help. You'll need Govinda Shauri.'

Dharma regarded the Elder with open disappointment. 'Govinda?'

'Surely you know the old adage, that your greatest enemy's enemy is your best friend …'

'Jarasandha …'

'Yes, Jarasandha. Dharma, make no mistake. Jarasandha is Emperor and as king of Western Kuru you owe him your allegiance. For you to dethrone him and then declare yourself Emperor would be … unwise. The legitimacy of your actions should never be compromised.'

Dharma frowned. 'But ought I not to first establish myself as a conqueror? What better way to do that than to …?'

The Vyasa interrupted him with an impatient shake of his head. 'Dharma, listen to me. Aryavarta doesn't need civil war. Everyone knows that. Even Jarasandha. As I said, I can get many of the kings – your uncle Dhritarastra and your cousin Syoddhan included – to accept you as their Emperor, provided we don't upset their reign, or their consciences. For both of these you need to let Govinda bring down the Emperor for you. Let it play out as a personal affair between the two men, with you doing nothing more than you would as a friend and cousin. I, too, won't interfere, except perhaps to ensure discretion and smooth a few ruffled egos once the deed is done. Then, when Aryavarta lies bereft of leadership due to Govinda Shauri's actions, you will step forward to bear this burden. Trust me, my son, on no account should you be the one to dethrone Jarasandha; at least, not directly.'

'But what's to stop Govinda from making a bid for the empire? If he kills Jarasandha …'

'Emperor? That cowherd? Hah!' the Vyasa sneered. 'Don't worry, Govinda knows better than to lose the legitimacy he's gained over the years by risking the wrath of the Firstborn. Besides, he knows that if *he* wants to be Emperor it *will* take civil war. No one wants to avoid that more than he does. Get him to come here at once. He'll be useful, you'll see.'

Dharma flinched inwardly at Dwaipayana's casual dismissal of Govinda, but forced himself to ignore it. Taking a deep breath, he nodded his agreement. He felt uneasy, yet strangely relieved as he remembered what Panchali had said to him earlier about the way Govinda had slowly, almost surreptitiously, deflected Jarasandha from conflict and placed him on the defensive. On balance, though, Dharma had no doubt that Govinda was the right man for the task. This time he did not wait till the next morning to send a message.

The messenger from Indr-prastha arrived at Dwaraka well past midnight and handed over his scroll to the captain on duty. Sealed as it was with Dharma's insignia, the scroll found its way to Balabadra's hands without delay. The burly man cursed at being woken up at the late hour; nevertheless, he opened the scroll. He perused it quickly and went to look for Govinda. He found his brother out of his bed, standing on one of the many terraces of their mansion, looking out pensively at the foamy night sea.

Govinda's curly hair was dishevelled and he wore his robe as a makeshift wrap around his bare hips. 'Don't ask,' he said as Balabadra gave him a questioning look, wondering mischievously which woman had kept his brother up so late.

'All right. I won't.' Balabadra held out the scroll. 'Dharma's invited you to Hastina. Any guesses?'

'Only that we have some eventful and busy days ahead. It's only a matter of time before the imperial conquest begins.'

'*Conquest*? Govinda, do you realize what you're saying? The first thing any would-be Emperor has to do is ...'

'Defeat Jarasandha, I know,' Govinda replied. 'That's why Dharma wants me. Rather, that's why Dwaipayana has advised him to call for me. And the amusing thing about it is that the Vyasa will help me get rid of Jarasandha. He will help me every step of the way.'

'Are you sure? How do you ...?'

'Yes, I am. I'm pretty sure that Dwaipayana intends to see Dharma as Emperor of Aryavarta. What better way to rid himself of Jarasandha without really seeming a traitor than to enlist me, Jarasandha's lifelong enemy? Who can fault Dharma for my deeds? Neither of us can really justify dethroning the Emperor of our own accord, but if we act together we just might succeed. As they say, all is fairly done that's done for duty and the empire. It's not a bad plan, if you ask me.'

'And I'll wager it is exactly as you'd expected?'

'More or less ...' Govinda cheekily admitted.

The two brothers exchanged glances and shared a robust laugh.

'So,' Balabadra said, 'I see now where you've been leading us all this while. Here I've been wondering how to defend our people against the inevitable, especially since everything that happened at Vidharbha. I should have known that you'd go one step further and make plans to pounce straight at the enemy's throat.'

'You know we can never live peacefully as long Jarasandha remains

Emperor. Sooner or later, Agraja, he will strike us. He *will* attack Dwaraka. Can we really afford to wait and watch?'

'But why such a complex plan?'

'Because it isn't just about killing Jarasandha. It's about doing it with honour. You and I can't get away with it; we'd only be called selfish murderers. And it's not us but Dwaraka that'll be forced to pay the price,' Govinda said. 'Like it or not, Jarasandha is Emperor. We need a very good reason to go against the man so many kings consider their liege-lord. This way, complex though it is, we move against our enemy with Dwaipayana's blessings. He'll ensure that everyone's conscience is mollified.'

'Nevertheless, we'll pay a price. We'll end up bowing to one more would-be conqueror, and barter and trade our pride to hang on to what we've built on our own, with *our* sweat and blood,' Balabadra testily observed.

'So be it,' Govinda said, casually crossing his arms across his chest. 'Things have been heading to this pass since ...' He paused and then said, 'There's something you need to know, Agraja. I was the one who brought Ghora Angirasa out of hiding. It took me the better part of many years, but I found him at last and made him come back to Aryavarta.'

'What?' Balabadra was astounded. 'But ... why?'

Govinda met his brother's shocked gaze without flinching. 'It was the only way to bring things to this pass. To finish what I had begun two decades ago. Ghora's death was inevitable, and essential.'

Balabadra said nothing for a while, and stood looking out at the dark sea around them. He had suspected Govinda of much and had been patient solely out of trust in his younger brother. But this – this kind of cold, methodical scheming – was beyond his wildest imagination. Before he could stop himself, he found the words spilling out, along with his brewing anger. 'I was hardly a few years old, when our father brought you to the vraja, to Gokul village. My mother, Rohini, and I were already there.' His voice took on a hint of surprise at his own words, for he could not remember ever having alluded to the fact that he and Govinda were, in fact, only half-brothers, sons of the same father.

Trying to find solace in the memories he treasured, Balabadra quickly continued, 'They used to call you Krishna because of your dark skin. It was I who gave you the name Govinda. Did you think it was just another name for a gwala boy? The name contained all that you meant to me. The cows that we used to tend are just metaphors for the senses with which every human chases the light of truth, the quest that defines us in every waking moment. You were a herdsman of those senses, my brother. You made me believe in the goodness of human beings, you made me dream of a better world, of something to live for, and that is why I named you Govinda. But now…' He shook his head and a hard edge crept into his voice, 'You're playing with darkness, Govinda. With darkness and fire. It's a dangerous game, one that may destroy us all.'

Govinda shrugged, a gesture of grim acceptance.

Balabadra could not help but yield as he felt the emotion slowly extend to cover him. With effort, he pushed all traces of anger and disappointment out of his mind and said, 'So Dwaipayana will form a Kuru empire after all.'

Govinda nodded. 'Dwaipayana shall form an empire, yes … a peaceful empire. As to whose empire it'll truly be …'

He smiled, content at the thought.

5

THE TWO MEN WERE ALONE IN THE WELL-APPOINTED ROOM, IF a room it could be called. Heavy green creepers languorously wound their way up crystalline pillars, and tiles of marble and grass alternated in precise patterns on the floor. Huge windows, almost indistinct when open, led out onto a lawn that rolled on and on in unbroken verdure save for the carefully placed stone fountains and carved statues, each one distinct in design. The weather was pleasant and sunny, and the gentle sound of the wind in the trees and the occasional chirp of some bird or the other gave the scene an idyllic air.

Govinda sat at ease, his body still and his expression tranquil, neither impressed by the surroundings nor indifferent to them. He had arrived well before dawn and gone directly from the stables to Dharma's private palace. There he had bathed and dressed, but refused all food and drink till he had spoken to Dharma. He also refused to allow the attendants to wake his host or interrupt his routine, preferring instead to wait, as would a common audience seeker.

When he was finally told of Govinda's arrival, Dharma was pleasantly surprised at this formal display of friendship and loyalty. Govinda was notorious for his dislike of social ritual, as much as Dharma found them comforting. Such routines, Dharma believed, clearly established the hierarchy and order of things without causing discomfort or loss of face for those involved. It was the civilized, noble way of doing things.

The wind suddenly fell, and all was quiet. Unbearably quiet.

Dharma broke the silence. He said, 'Tell me ... What do you think of me, Govinda?'

'What I think isn't important,' Govinda replied. 'What's important is why you choose to ask this question.'

Dharma paused. He shifted in his seat to directly face Govinda and said, 'When my uncle gave me Kandava, I almost refused. I had little desire to be king and was content to lead a simple, honourable life.'

'And have you now changed your mind?'

Dharma was taken aback a little by the incisive question. He carefully replied, 'Many generations ago our ancestors whom we revere on par with the gods – Pururavas and Yayati – ruled over a huge dominion from this very place. This was the heart of Aryavarta, of a mighty empire, before it fell into ruin. Now that we've rebuilt this city, it would be a shame if it were not the capital of the empire once more. I ... I long for a simple life, Govinda, but that doesn't make me a simpleton. I'd be a fool if I ignored the various interests that are tied in with mine.'

'Indeed,' Govinda politely affirmed.

'And for that reason I am forced to confront my own duty as a warrior, a duty to conquer and craft.'

'Oh? But why should that bother you?'

'Because much of what has transpired these past months has been providential, even serendipitous. I have no explanation for all that has happened except that it was divinely ordained. Nothing can stem the tide of destiny whether it leads to joy or sorrow. But the fact remains that I have been greatly blessed and it is my solemn duty to give thanks to the gods that have been kind to me by spreading their glory. I can't ignore the purpose for which the gods have placed me in this prosperous and powerful situation. Their will must be done.'

Govinda remained silent.

Leaning forward eagerly, Dharma continued, 'Yet, I remain confused. I don't know if it is the right thing to do ... Is glory all there is to life? Is there no value for piety? Please, tell me what you *really* think of me ...'

Govinda smiled and said, 'I've heard it said that you earn by your very word and deed the name that was given to you at birth, Dharma. Isn't it impossible for you to think an unrighteous thought or to speak an untruth? That you've contemplated this implies that it must be virtuous.'

Dharma mulled over the well-chosen words. Almost warily he began, 'There remains, of course, the matter of Emperor Jarasandha. Most of the kings around the region either fear him or owe their allegiance to him. Rukmi of Vidharbha, Shisupala of Chedi, Saubha the king of Salwa, the Nishada chief Ekalavya, Vasusena and, of course, our cousin Syoddhan of Hastina ...' he counted off despondently. 'They are all formidable. And then we have the vassals within Magadha. Above all, there is the Imperial Army.'

'Before we even get to that, by law and right, Jarasandha *is* Emperor. For another man to declare himself such, he must overthrow Jarasandha. That, and the fact that once Magadha is yours so are all its vassals, especially those in the eastern kingdoms.'

Dharma shifted again in his seat, uncertain and tense. 'But how do we get rid of him? Govinda, forgive me, but even you retreated before the Emperor's might …'

Govinda good-humouredly waved the comment aside. 'Even if you won a war against him the aftermath wouldn't be worth it. The kind of taxes and tributes that you'd have to impose on your vassals just to set right the devastation and rebuild your armies would make you very unpopular. You'd be asking for a reign filled with rebellion and conflict.'

'Then there's no hope,' Dharma said, sitting back in a sulk.

'Jarasandha's not a stupid man,' Govinda continued. He stood up and looked down at Dharma with a smile. 'He knows you can't afford a war and will try to escalate hostilities and declare war the moment he can show just cause. The slightest whiff of an attack or any offensive against him, and he'll march out with his army. We need to meet the lion in his den, get him on the defensive. We have to fight him without giving him time to consider alternatives.'

'That's impossible,' Dharma declared, rising to his feet.

'Nothing's impossible. Leave it to me … But don't speak of things beyond the immediate to anyone just yet, Dharma. Don't speak of an empire to anyone. Not even to Panchali.'

Dharma looked at the man, trying hard to not appear overly effusive. Nevertheless, he could not help but show some excitement, and joyfully embraced Govinda. As he returned the gesture, Govinda wondered what Panchali would have to say about all of this.

'You … you piece of … You!' Panchali hissed at Govinda the moment she saw him.

'I'm well, thank you, and how are you?' he sarcastically responded.

She ignored him, and went on, scathing now, 'Again the great Govinda Shauri walks in and out of Aryavarta, in and out of our lives, as though we were … nothing. I haven't heard from you in all these days, and now you just saunter into my room and expect me to say that I'm happy to see you?'

'Panchali …' he tried to speak but she cut in, swatting off the calming hand that he placed on her shoulder.

'You come running at Dharma's beck and call ... You do enjoy your newfound role as hero to the Kurus, and enjoy it enough to support this ... this abominable war against the Emperor, don't you?'

'Panchali, please ...'

'... this ... this *thing* will ruin our people with useless bloodshed and unfair taxes ...'

'Panchali ...'

'... not to mention that we can't hope to win. And if we do leave Aryavarta without the firm leadership it needs, it'll spawn an entirely new breed of corrupt vassals who will do nothing but backstab and bicker among themselves! You and Dharma ... you ... you *men*! You arrogant animals, all! Hah!' She flopped into a chair, in a dark and determined sulk.

Govinda bent down, resting a hand on each arm of Panchali's chair. 'You should have considered all that before you began meddling around, as you have,' he told her.

'What do you mean?'

'Where did you think it would lead? You trade, you build new roads, and maybe someday you'll even farm the barren, lifeless desert ... Did you think the rest of Aryavarta was going to watch you with glee and shower their blessings on you? Did you even consider what the next step was, after Dharma sat on the throne of Indr-prastha? You don't have a choice; none of us do. This goes way beyond anything you could imagine.'

'So you admit, then, that you foresaw this? You foresaw that we would go up against the Emperor?'

'Foresaw? I've tried my best to bring things to this ...'

'Then you also admit that you've used me in this game of yours?'

'Do you object?' he asked, looking a little amused.

Panchali said nothing, but evenly met his gaze. She felt a certain calm knowing that things were going as predicted after all. First Govinda would use the Kurus to destroy Jarasandha. And then ...

'Trust me,' Govinda urged, cutting in on her thoughts.

'Trust you?' she said, incredulous. 'Hah! Govinda, the world is divided into those who admire you and those who fear you. Neither lot questions you, and you mistake that for trust. But trust is something that only an equal can give, it's something that each one of us must earn by his or her word and deed. You can't go around being secretive like you are and expect people to trust you.'

Govinda straightened up and stood with his arms crossed across his chest. Panchali looked up at him for a few moments.

Letting go of her anger, she tried to reason with him, 'I know Govinda Shauri always has a plan, but why doesn't anyone ever know what it is? Why won't you ever share what's on your mind, truly and completely?'

'Then it becomes rather boring, doesn't it? No more mystery, no more excitement left in anything.'

'But it's so unfair of you to hoard all the fun and excitement. What will become of petulant princesses like me if you don't entertain us?'

'Fair point,' Govinda jestingly conceded. Softly, he added, 'But, surely, there are other activities both of us would find more entertaining to share?'

'Stop flirting with me, Govinda,' Panchali commanded lightly. 'Rudra knows you've said and done enough to break my heart already.'

Govinda ignored the veiled truth in her words and said instead, 'So, does that mean I have to beg some more, for forgiveness?'

'Just a little bit more.'

'What if I said you look lovelier than ever?' Govinda teased.

'Oh, shut up! As if I don't know you … Don't bother trying to mollify me with such ridiculously old-fashioned lines.'

'Should I try some new lines then? How about if I said that you look more intelligent than ever, that a new wisdom sparkles in your eyes?'

'How about if you said you'll spare me all this indulgent banter that obviously assumes I have the intellect of a six-year-old?'

Govinda threw his arm around her shoulder. 'Go on then, tell me what I should know about what I've just done. Rather, agreed to do.'

'And you'll listen?'

'Why not? Haven't I, before? And shouldn't I all the more, now? After all, from what I hear, the finances and most other affairs of Dharma's establishment are in your care. And now I find he and I cannot even have a private discussion without you coming to know of it …'

Panchali considered Govinda for a while, becoming aware by the moment that this was her chance. Choosing her words carefully, she began to explain, 'Aryavarta is in great danger – you know that better than anyone else. The threat of civil war and the threat of foreign invasion both lie heavy over us, though many would want to deny it. But a new empire, a different emperor – these aren't the solutions to the problem.'

'Then what is?'

'Listen to me, Govinda. The vastness of Aryavarta has cajoled us into being nurturers and lulled us into a false sense of security, making us easy targets. It's also tied us to the land. We not only lack skill as seafarers, but we also lack what I can only call a sailor's heart, the sense that the vast oceans and what lies beyond them are relevant to us, part of our view of the world. I know someone from a smaller nation, or an island kingdom, would be more at ease with these ideas …

'Unfortunately,' Panchali continued, with a slow, sad shake of her head, 'it's not in me and not in most Aryas to see the oceans the same way. It's not in us to seek out distant, new lands to conquer and colonize. Which is why we have civil war, one cycle of upheaval after another. Emperors overthrown by their own vassal kings, and kings by their saamantas. We make war either against our own kin or against our friends and neighbours. But you? You have the heart of an explorer, Govinda. You have the seas and the lands beyond to conquer. You don't need war, not with Jarasandha. Not with anyone in Aryavarta. Don't do this!'

She looked at him in earnest as she finished, hoping that this time she could achieve using reason what she had failed to using emotion, back at Kandava. She fought back the bile that rose in her throat at the thought of a war with the Emperor, the inevitable bloodshed that would come upon them if she failed to convince Govinda.

She could not fail. She would not fail.

Govinda, however, seemed less than persuaded. He studied her for a few moments, a slight frown creasing his forehead. His eyes remained hard and impenetrable, as they often were of late. 'And Dharma?' he finally queried.

Panchali did not know what to say, except for what she honestly believed. 'An Arya's sense of honour is driven by the belief that conquest and glory are part of our divinely ordained duty. Such passionate principles have been instilled in most of us over generations and they can't be expected to subside overnight. In Dharma's case, these strong foundations have been significantly repressed, all in the name of peace and nobility. He longs to emulate someone like Grandsire Bhisma, where he can lay claim to virtue through personal sacrifice but not give up on that which defines him as a warrior and an Arya. But ...'

'But?'

'Whatever the reasons, he's been forced to do the opposite. His reputation for nobility has been earned in a public role, as a lover of virtue and justice. He has been left to gratify his need to feel like a warrior through personal trifles, like gambling. To make him play the part of conqueror would be to place unfettered power in the hands of one who believes in morality but lacks the self-restraint to live with it.'

Govinda chuckled. 'I'm really impressed with your analysis. And, for what it's worth, I quite agree with you. War against Jarasandha is a bad idea for many reasons, including the very persuasive ones you've just pointed out.'

Panchali rose from her seat in a sudden move, forcing Govinda to take a step back. She set her hands on her hips in a gesture of defiance, tilted her head back to stare straight into the tall man's eyes. 'But you won't change your mind, will you?'

'No, I won't,' he admitted.

'In that case, let me speak frankly. You can't go to war. You shouldn't go to war. You'd never win.'

'What should I do then, Princess?' Govinda asked, a gleam in his eyes. 'Ask Jarasandha nicely? Maybe tell him it's someone else's turn to play on the imperial throne?'

Panchali squared her shoulders and declared, 'Assassinate him. It's the only way.'

6

GOVINDA PACED THE SMALL ROOM BHIM AND HE WERE SHARING in a nondescript inn a day's ride from Jarasandha's capital. Pensive and grim, he scratched at his three-week-old beard. He desperately longed for a shave, but that minor inconvenience aside, their plan or, rather, Panchali's plan was working perfectly.

'Jarasandha will soon realize what we're up to,' she had pointed out to Dharma after convincing a visibly impressed Govinda of her scheme. 'Maybe we can get him to believe that driven by our own arrogance we mean to challenge him in open war. If we move Kuru forces eastward and get Yuyudhana to lead the Narayaniya troops through the south towards Magadha ... And ask my father to move the Panchala Eastern Guard through the Kosala kingdom. It would surely distract Jarasandha for long enough before he realizes that the armies are a feint.'

'Distract him from what?' Dharma had asked.

'Our assassin,' Govinda replied.

Dharma had winced visibly at that. He had said no words of approval or encouragement, but he had done nothing to stop them either. That had been enough.

The chosen assassin was one of Shikandin's most trusted soldiers. He was a pleasant-looking man of Govinda's years, half of which he had been spent serving in the notorious Panchala Eastern Guard and the other half as Shikandin's spy. He had neither family nor friends other than his brothers-in-arms and his eyes held a fearless honesty. Above all, he was willing to do the deed, not for money or honour but simply because Shikandin had ordered him to. Govinda had liked him instantly, more so when the soldier had received the name of his quarry without as much as a murmur. The man also took with the same equanimity the news that he had, as Shikandin had phrased it, less than a trasarenu molecule's worth of a chance of returning alive.

About a week after the man had set out, his identity and the exact details of his assignment a secret from all but Shikandin and Govinda, the armies were mobilized. It was then that Govinda had announced his intentions to ride to Magadha.

'But why?' Dharma had protested. 'Yuyudhana leads your men and Partha leads the Kuru armies.'

'I want to be there, just in case,' Govinda had insisted.

'In case of what …?'

Panchali had coldly finished, 'In case the assassin fails.'

This had only perturbed Dharma more. 'And if he fails …?'

'We deny all responsibility, of course. Though I doubt anyone will believe us.'

'It's too dangerous, Govinda. If your man fails, we'll have no choice but to meet Jarasandha in battle. He'll attack even if we don't. We can't risk open war with the Emperor. It's suicide.'

'We'll see,' Govinda had flippantly dismissed.

Despite Dharma's anxious protests, Govinda had left the very next day with Bhim. The two had marched with a single battalion of soldiers along the mountain roads almost till the borders of Vidharbha. There, in full view of imperial spies, they waited and met up with Yuyudhana and the soldiers from Dwaraka. The trio, along with their armies, then ostensibly continued towards Magadha, their progress slow and confusing to anyone who kept watch.

In fact, Govinda and Bhim disappeared, leaving Yuyudhana to lead the men. Playing the role of wandering mercenaries – two more in that teeming breed of battle-trained Sutas who would never have the honour or title of being true warriors – they had quickly travelled north until they were close to the borders of Magadha. This was a perfect disguise, for they rode their horses and carried their weapons without drawing attention to themselves. But they were also forced to choose rather simple inns and rest-houses for their lodgings. The two men cared little for such inconveniences and, in fact, found the variety of fellow-lodgers and the colourful tales they told rather entertaining. The one story, the news they waited for, however, never came.

Much was whispered about the omens of war – both man-made and supernatural – and in all those tales Jarasandha was spoken of as being alive and well. Either their assassin had yet to make his move, or had perhaps died even before getting close to his target. There remained, of course, the possibility that he had tried and failed, but both men tried not to think too much about that.

Bhim cursed out loud, bringing Govinda's attention back to the moment. He too, was rubbing his jaw and seemed equally peeved by his rough stubble. Like Govinda, and unlike many of his brothers and cousins, Bhim preferred to stay clean-shaven. 'All this, to overthrow a tyrant,' he complained, turning onto his side on the hard plank that passed for a bed.

Govinda drew up a chair with his leg and sat facing the other man. 'Is that what we're doing? Think carefully before you answer, Bhim. Do you claim that this is a revolution against a tyrant? If not, what just cause do you have to overthrow him? Your own uncle Dhritarastra owes him allegiance. You can't just brush away Jarasandha's legitimacy and pretend he is unfit to rule.'

'Oh? Then how does one judge when a monarch must be overthrown?'

'Ah! I seem to remember asking myself the same question many, many years ago. You'd be surprised how many different answers there are to that one.'

'How so?'

'Consider this,' Govinda began. 'One fine day, a royal emissary comes to a Yadu village and claims that a seventeen-year-old boy is the son of the Surasena princess Devaki and the Vrishni chief Shura. He claims that the child and his half-brother had been sent away as infants to live in hiding for fear of their maternal uncle Kans, who ruled over the kingdom with an iron fist. Tell me, Bhim, if I were that seventeen-year-old boy, would I be justified in killing Kans?'

'But of course! Your right to do so stems from the fact that Kans

274

was a usurper but the people were far too terrified to say anything about it. That isn't true assent.'

'In that case, how can we be sure that the people of Mathura weren't afraid of me and Balabadra? What gave *us* legitimacy but not Kans? After all, he took the throne from my grandfather because he felt the existing policies were far too conciliatory and not in the interest of the kingdom. Either he was a justified revolutionary and so were we, or both parties are equally guilty of tyranny. Don't you agree?'

Bhim said nothing, but frowned in an effort to think things through.

'Consider also,' Govinda continued, 'that the same policies that made Kans take the throne led him, in the longer run, to put the whole of Surasena to sword and fire. He imposed unbearable taxes to fund the Emperor's campaigns and his soldiers often seized grains and livestock, leaving many to starve. When our turn came, out of sheer desperation and anger, the cowherds of my village stood up to Kans's vassal lord with what little weapons we had. Everything that followed was social inevitability. In the end, the people rose against their hated ruler. That's what truly happened, no matter how unromantic the tale is.'

'The people placed you on the Surasena throne,' Bhim argued. 'The people deposed Kans. Choosing their new ruler was their lawful right.'

'And that brings us back to where we started. Are we really overthrowing a tyrant? Jarasandha has been a good ruler to his people, and what we're doing hardly qualifies as a revolution. But then how many does it take to dissent? Has he truly been a good Emperor in everyone's eyes? Is it in Aryavarta's interest to align with outsiders such as the Yavanas to wage war against our own people?'

'No king can hope to please everyone. All that matters is the greatest good.'

'And how do you decide what is the greatest good? Who decides?'

'The kings, the rulers of Aryavarta! That is what they're here for. How difficult can that be?' Bhim exclaimed.

Govinda inclined his head slightly, thinking. 'When I was a young boy,' he said at last, 'we had a particularly bad monsoon and our cows were starving for lack of pasture. All over Surasena vassal lords sent orders to each village, instructing them to slaughter half their herds as an offering to Indra. I was livid, not only because I'd loved each and every one of those animals as a brother or sister but also because I saw that it was only the beginning. Depleting our herds would simply increase our dependence on the seasons and the fickle yield of the land.'

He grimaced, and added in a low growl, 'Of course, our noble saamanta and his priests argued that I was committing sacrilege, and that by giving up half the herd we could save the other half. But for that you wouldn't need the blessings of the gods – if you killed half your herd you'd have only half left to maintain over the same stretch of pastureland. The problem is that with fewer cattle the land you can till is less and you need to use human labour, which is not as effective. We'd also have less milk and so would need more grain, but without cattle to help till the land there'd be no more grain, do you see?'

'Not really,' Bhim pointed out. 'Those cows might've perished anyway.'

'Except,' Govinda countered, 'a random loss of livestock is very different from planned slaughter. One cow means the world to the common peasant, but what's it to a vassal lord who owns many herds? Also, those with larger herds would stand to gain more because pasturelands are common resources, but cattle are not. The fewer cows others have means more pasture for my herd, even if I have to lose an animal or two myself.'

'Yes …'

Govinda continued, 'So, what is the greater good? Who decides what is just? A few years after I'd become prince, I refused to order another culling. Then, the very same lords who'd once agreed with me began to find my policies unjust. Mathura was in an uproar, and the vassals and chieftains were appealing to Jarasandha for help, asking him to get rid of the crazy prince with his new-fangled notions. And so the Emperor marched against us in the interests of the greater good – the greater good of the powerful.' His voice remained even throughout, but his eyes burned with fervour.

Bhim regarded him with a slight touch of awe. At length, he said, 'It's not my place to ask, Govinda, but why … ?' He hesitated.

'Why did I surrender Mathura?' Govinda coldly prompted.

Bhim chose his next words with care. 'You're not a coward, my friend,' he began. 'You didn't leave because you were afraid. I can only assume that having been brought up a gwala you failed to see that your duty, your honour as an Arya, lay in fighting Jarasandha. Don't get me wrong …' he hastily added. 'You might've thought that bricks and mortar were not worth human lives, which I completely agree with. But perhaps you didn't see that you gave up the very identity, the sovereignty of your people. Their honour was lost, along with yours …'

'My honour?' Govinda raised an eyebrow.

'I'm sorry, I …'

Govinda waved him into silence. 'I'm not offended, if that's what you're apologizing for. I just find it rather amusing. Most of us, including you, Bhim, talk of honour and nobility as the things that define us. How then can something so essential, so fundamental, be given or taken away? And that's why I neither explain nor apologize for what happened.'

'Fine. I ask for neither explanation nor defence, but I do want to test my conjecture. Won't you tell me the true reason why … ?'

Govinda sounded detached. 'My people were on the verge of civil war, Bhim. The Surasena kingdom was the last bastion of Yadu unity and it had held together only because of a shared terror of Kans. Giving up Mathura was the only way to avoid a bloodbath.'

Bhim merely nodded in response. They sat silently for a while and then, as a matter of discipline, went to bed. It took Bhim a long time to sleep that night.

7

IT WAS NEARLY EVENING BY THE TIME GOVINDA AND BHIM looked down from the peak they stood on at Jarasandha's capital city, Girivraja – so named because it was nestled in a valley between five hills.

'Truly impregnable,' Govinda noted. 'No wonder Jarasandha can afford to be such a conqueror – these hills protect his own people from assault and the verdant abundance makes food and water available in plenty. But I think I understand why he wanted Mathura so badly ...'

'Oh?' Bhim was curious.

'In a way, Jarasandha is not unlike me, a cowherd at heart,' he indicated to the huge flocks that grazed on the hillsides. 'How could he not be tempted by another pastoral heaven like his own home? It explains why he wanted Mathura, and why, even now, he nurtures hopes of conquering Dwaraka.'

'Ah, but the difference is, Govinda, you wouldn't covet his kingdom for your own.'

'I wouldn't be too sure, Bhim. If I knew I could have it, I might just want it.'

The two men gazed down at the city for a while longer, until Bhim said, 'What now?'

'We wait for morning and make our way in with the throngs. It's full moon tomorrow night ...'

'Ah! Market Day!'

Govinda laughed at that. 'My dear Bhim! We'll make a gwala out of this Kuru prince yet! Yes, Market Day. Should make for a fair crowd in the city.'

'And once we're in?'

'I just want some news, Bhim. We can scout around a bit and hopefully get out by evening. We can head back to one of the outpost inns and wait there. What else can we do?'

'And I thought this would be quick and dirty!'

'It's politics. Dirty yes, but hardly quick. But enough of all that. Be a good man and light a fire, will you. I'll see to our horses.'

As the sun went down, the light of many small campfires could be seen on the hills around the city. A little after dawn, all the campers began making their way down the hillsides to join the already teeming masses on the road to Girivraja. Govinda and Bhim fell into that crowd, mingling unnoticed into it.

It was not long before Govinda frowned, clearly not at ease. Bhim nudged him and threw him a questioning glance.

'It's too crowded,' Govinda replied.

'You don't like crowds?'

'No, that's not what I meant. It's too crowded for just another Market Day. Something's happening.'

'The city seems to be on high alert. There are guards posted everywhere.'

'Hmm. Look over there.'

Bhim glared at the convoy that marched in a slow, steady rhythm, coming at them from within the city. At a shout from the guards, the crowds shuffled off the road and to the sides, making way for the troops. He cursed under his breath. 'He's sending out the troops. He's marching to war!'

Govinda stopped in his tracks for a moment, considering something. He then turned to a group of men walking next to him and struck up what appeared to be a completely frivolous conversation. Bhim walked patiently alongside, watching him joke and laugh with the men, who looked like they were farmers from the Magadhan countryside. When Govinda ended his banter and turned back to Bhim, his face was grim.

'It's no simple Market Day, Bhim. There's to be an execution ... Careful now, they're watching. Look excited. Laugh!'

Bhim forced out a loud guffaw, as though delighted at the prospect of watching some criminal die a gory death. He quickly quietened down into a morose silence. 'It could be someone else,' he said. 'Some thief or rapist or ...'

Govinda did not reply.

The two men did not have to wait long to find out. The crowd took them directly to the central square of the city, where a makeshift platform had been set up. People filled the square on three sides while the fourth, which opened on to the path that led to the royal enclosure, had been sealed off with a light wooden barricade. Soldiers stood guard in front of the platform, vigilant and watchful. Two elephants also waited there, swaying restlessly from side to side. Occasionally one of them would let out a loud trumpet, the noise ringing over the square and sending the gathered throng into a renewed bout of frenzy. Horror, excitement and the strange relief of being a safe spectator hung in the air.

Govinda found the moment disconcertingly familiar. It reminded him of another crowd, another would-have-been execution. At the end of that day there had been another king, a dead one who had set him on the path that had brought him here today. Taking a deep breath, he shut out the noise and all thoughts of the past.

'Look!' Bhim exclaimed.

The crowd began jeering as a group of guards made their way on to the platform dragging a bloody, mangled figure along by his chains.

'Mih!' Both Bhim and Govinda swore under their breaths as they got a good look at the prisoner. The sockets of his eyes were bloodied and empty. Strips of skin hung from his naked frame like tattered cloth. The flesh was gone in some places, probably burnt away, and the white of his bones showed clearly for all to see. The jubilant crowd had suddenly fallen silent, shocked at the sight of the living remains of what had once been a man. A stink rose as someone retched nearby. Some spectators looked away, even as many others stared, transfixed. A young man sobbed quietly and whispered what sounded like a prayer.

'Is that … ?' Bhim asked in a low whisper.

Govinda nodded. Despite the state of the prisoner, he had no doubt that it was indeed the man they had sent.

'He's been tortured badly,' Bhim went on. 'Do you think he's talked?'

'No, but he doesn't need to. Our armies are less than a fortnight's march away. It's kind of obvious, isn't it?'

The two men watched in uncomfortable silence as the prisoner was brought forward, his legs twisted and useless, the result of broken knees and ankles. The guards threw him unceremoniously on the floor of the platform and stood in a loose formation around him, laughing as they kicked him and prodded him with their lances to make him squirm some more for the crowd's entertainment.

Shouted conversation soon picked up.

'So it's true,' an old man said. 'I'd heard that the Emperor had been attacked.'

An equally wizened figure next to him added, 'The medics feared for his life. It was a blow to the neck, almost. A lesser man would've died.'

A young man argued, in a rough whisper, 'Liars! I heard nothing of the sort.'

'Of course you didn't, you rascal! You think they'd announce that the Emperor is fighting for his life?'

'So how do *you* know, old man?'

'My son is a palace cook. Even so, he swore me to secrecy, till today ... He saw it all, you know! Happened to be waiting on the king when that son of a whore attacked.'

'And what did your son do? Hide?' the young one taunted.

'I'll have you know he nearly died for his Emperor,' the old man retorted. 'He would've throttled the assassin with his bare hands, but Lord Jarasandha ordered the guards to take the man alive.'

'A relief for your son, I'm sure!'

'Why, you fly-ridden dungpile ...'

'Now, now,' the first man gently intervened. 'It all ends well, that's what matters. Our Emperor is invincible. The old blood of the Solar Line runs true in him. These wretched Kuru kings and their hired killers can't do a thing to him, Hara be praised!'

'Puuya!' the young man swore. 'Who needs the elephants? If you ask me, we should tear that man apart ourselves for what he tried to do!'

The words seemed to ring through the mob, infecting it. Two men broke through the light barricade and vaulted themselves on to the platform. The guards gave them an indulgent look and made no move to stop them. Urged on by the crowd, the men ran up to where the prisoner lay. One of them bent down, and spat with accuracy into the empty eye sockets. The other pulled aside his waist cloth and began urinating on the near-dead man, to wild applause from the mob.

Govinda watched without flinching, his hand in a strong grip around Bhim's wrist. 'Keep calm,' he said. 'We can't do anything, Bhim.'

'Can't, or won't?' Bhim growled.

Govinda gave him a piercing look, and turned his attention back to the bloodied prisoner. The brave man had been a steadfast soldier and done what he had set out to. Govinda would have liked to tell him so, to assure him that despite what was happening to him he had kept his honour and died well. But he knew better than to waste time or emotion wishing for it.

A trumpet trilled from the roof of a nearby building. Immediately, the soldiers threw the commoners off the platform and stood to attention in two straight lines that flanked the prisoner.

'The Emperor! The Emperor!' The excited whisper built up into a shout and then into a resounding chant. 'Hail the Emperor of Aryavarta! Hail Jarasandha the Mighty!'

The thunder of hooves drew close and loud as Jarasandha's ceremonial chariot trundled towards the square and drew to a halt behind the platform. More soldiers ran forward, forming a guard of honour leading from the foot of the vehicle to the platform. A courtier, whom Govinda supposed was Jarasandha's minister, led the Emperor on to the stage.

As one, the crowd bowed, many going down on one knee or both.

'Get down!' Govinda hissed and pulled on Bhim's arm.

'For what?'

'This is *his* realm. He is its ruler till our task is done. It won't kill you to bow to him.'

Grudgingly, Bhim went down on one knee, but both men raised their heads to look up at the Emperor.

Jarasandha was a huge man, one who deserved his reputation for strength. His hair was more grey than black, but the muscles of his arms were taut and his girth was hardly soft. Even at the slight distance, the battle scars on the Emperor's right forearm and shoulder were clearly visible. There was, however, no obvious evidence of an injury from the assassin's attack. Bhim and Govinda exchanged glances.

'If only ...' Bhim whispered. 'If this isn't misfortune, what is? To get within striking distance, and fail ...'

'I think it's more than misfortune. Our man wasn't one to take chances or be careless. The Emperor knew. He was ready.'

'He knew? But ... that would mean ...'

'Yes. We're expected. Perhaps betrayed.'

'By whom?'

Govinda did not answer.

Jarasandha raised his right arm, calling for silence. A heavy stillness fell over the square. Govinda imagined he heard a soft whimper of pain, but could not tell whether it came from the prisoner.

'My citizens, fellow men and women, people of Aryavarta ...' Jarasandha's deep baritone boomed over them all. It was enough to make the mob snap. They rose to their feet, cheering and praising their Emperor, until Jarasandha held up his hand again.

His tone was honest and warm, though in no way lacking authority, as he gently conceded, 'Truly, it's your love for me, your prayers that keep me safe and alive. But wait. Hear me out completely before you give voice to your joy once again.'

The crowd murmured softly and soon settled down, urged by the occasional stern look from one of the soldiers posted to keep order.

Jarasandha continued, 'For nearly a week now, Kuru and Yadu armies have stood at our borders. But the attack they've made is not the one you might think. Snivelling cowards as they are, they've sent a mangy jackal to hunt down a lion – an assassin to murder their Emperor!'

Despite the Emperor's injunctions, the mob was in uproar. This time Jarasandha let them shout themselves hoarse, watching with an indulgent, paternal smile.

Govinda turned to the astonished Bhim. 'You didn't expect this, did you? You didn't expect that people would actually like him?'

Bhim shook his head, letting some of his horror show.

'It's we who make monsters of our enemies, Bhim. We call them evil demons and pretend we do the world a favour by killing them. It's the only way we can live with ourselves.'

'Speak for yourself,' Bhim snapped before he could restrain himself. 'I'm a prince. It's my sacred duty to conquer and rule.'

Govinda considered the statement and then shrugged. 'That delusion works, too, I suppose.'

Bhim made to retort, but realized that the crowd had fallen quiet and the Emperor was about to speak.

Jarasandha came straight to the point. 'I have ordered this public execution,' he announced, 'not only to show to our enemies that we will not take aggression lightly, but also as a sacred sacrifice. Even as I speak, as we stand here, the mighty armies of Magadha have begun marching towards central Aryavarta. In two weeks' time, our brave soldiers will meet the Kuru and Yadu armies at our borders in open battle, while forces from our garrison at Mathura will attack from the west. Unlike my enemies, I make no secret of my plans, but lay an open challenge for them to accept, if they dare. Or else ...' The Emperor laughed and let his words ring in a terrifying growl as he declared, 'We all know that this isn't the first time that men have fled before the might of Magadha. But let this be the last! Jayati! Victory!'

The crowd was jubilant. 'Jayati! Jayati!' they took up the victory chant. Even those who had flinched or turned from the tortured prisoner now looked on him with fearless pride. This was war and he was but a sacrifice, the first of the enemy to die.

Jarasandha folded his hands in prayer and with a charming smile stepped aside. He nodded his instruction to the executioner-mahouts and one of them led his elephant forward. The platform creaked with the weight of the animal as it made its way towards the prone prisoner in a drunken stupor that would allow it to kill on order. At the same time, soldiers came forward to carefully position the prisoner on his back. The tendons of the man's neck had already been severed and his head lolled back towards the crowd for them to see his face.

'Stand back!' the Emperor ordered the mahout and also waved off the soldiers around them. The men retreated to a respectful distance. Drunken elephants were not to be trusted. Jarasandha reached out to caress the royal elephant's trunk, whispering to it some words of affection, or possibly command. He led it forward, unafraid of its uncontrolled might, till both he and the animal stood over the condemned man. An expectant quiet fell over the crowd. At a gesture from the Emperor, the elephant raised a foreleg and brought it down precisely on the prisoner's stomach.

The man screamed. The dreadful sound tore through the forced calm, rising and ringing in an endless hell of agony. Then the screaming squelched to an abrupt stop. Where there had been a man, with a body, a head and a face, there was nothing now but bloody pulp.

Jarasandha cast one last look at his would-have-been killer before striding off the platform and towards his chariot. The mahout ran forward to take charge of his animal, even as prison attendants stepped up to see to the dead man's remains. The crowd came out of its stunned daze and began to disperse.

'Come on,' Govinda pulled at Bhim. Bhim turned, vaguely aware that he was trembling and that his hands were clenched into angry fists. Govinda remained impassive. 'Come on, we need to get out of here quickly!' he urged.

Bhim stared at him with a new loathing. 'By Hara, Govinda! What sort of a man are you?'

Govinda sighed, as though he had anticipated the question and was perhaps even tired of it. 'I'm a man who wants to stop a war we can't win,' he lightly said, adding, 'as, I assume, you are too. Can we please go?'

Gritting his teeth to stop himself from saying anything more, Bhim complied.

The two men quickly made their way to where they had stabled their horses. They left Girivraja well before noon, making their way out with the still-awed crowd that spoke of nothing but the morning's execution and the war the Emperor would soon win.

8

'BY VARUNA AND INDRA, I DON'T KNOW!' DHARMA SHOUTED. 'I need more time!'

Panchali watched him, unperturbed. If there was one thing she had learnt over the years it was that Dharma was incapable of true wrath. What he passed off as anger was nothing but anxiety. Whether she was glad that her husband was, on the whole, excessively inclined to towards harmony was something she had not quite decided.

Sadev looked a lot less comfortable than Panchali, especially since he was in the unenviable position of having to respond to his brother. 'We don't have more time, Agraja,' he urged. 'The rider has been spotted. It takes but a short while from the main gate to the palace and a little while more to dismount and present oneself here. Unless, the rider stops to refresh himself ...'

'Which isn't likely,' Dhaumya tersely pointed out. 'Syoddhan's going to want an explanation. He's sent one man and not a delegation, and that person is neither a fool nor a dandy courtier.'

'Who do you think he's sent?' Dharma stopped his anxious pacing, to ask.

'I'd have guessed Sanjaya, except ...'

'Hmm?'

'I don't know,' Dhaumya suddenly confessed. 'It's been nearly a month since Govinda and the armies left here. We have no news as yet from the east, but Shikandin sends word that the garrison at Mathura has been put on high alert. Jarasandha is upto something but whether that's just a result of our troop movements, or ... But I do know we need to be ready with our answers.'

'What answers, Dhaumya? What in Yama's bloody name am I supposed to tell Syoddhan and my uncle? That I decided to march my armies against my lawful Emperor? Or that I've sent an assassin? Or that Bhim and Govinda have disappeared, and that I have absolutely no clue what they're up to? What in Rudra's name can I possibly tell him?'

'The truth ...' Panchali stated.

'What?'

'She's right,' Sadev said, frowning as he thought the matter over. 'We have to tell the truth. Don't you see, we really don't know what's going on. That's all we can say.'

Dharma stared at him, at a loss for words, or perhaps at a surfeit of ones he deemed inappropriate for use in front of a lady. The inelegant silence continued, till at last an attendant appeared at the door. Dhaumya stepped up to hear what the man had to say and then turned to the others. 'Asvattama Bharadvaja.'

Panchali looked up in surprise. 'Syoddhan's sent Asvattama? That's good, isn't it?'

'It is,' Sadev affirmed. 'It means our cousin is asking for answers, not making threats.' He turned to Dharma, 'We should see him right away, Agraja. It wouldn't do to keep a man of Asvattama's position waiting.'

'And what position is that, Sadev?' Dharma snapped, before adding, in a resigned tone, 'Show him in, Dhaumya.'

Dhaumya stepped out. A short while later, the sounds of light conversation came floating back towards the room as Dhaumya led Asvattama in, asking in the meantime about his journey and whether he would like something to eat or drink.

'Welcome, Asvattama,' Dharma managed to greet their guest with the proper degree of enthusiasm.

'Thank you. Sadev, Panchali, hope you're both well?'

Panchali noticed he was wearing his customary jewel on his forehead, as he did on all formal occasions. 'As well as can be under the circumstances, Your Highness,' she replied, knowing full well how her use of the title amused the usually sombre Asvattama.

Indeed, he chuckled softly and said, 'And what circumstances might those be, I wonder.'

'The ones you're here to talk about. Won't you please sit? Some wine?'

'Thank you.' Asvattama settled himself into the comfortable seat and said, 'In that case, let me get straight to the point. Have you declared open war against Emperor Jarasandha?'

Dharma frowned at the question, while Panchali and Sadev

exchanged a brief but meaningful glance. It was all Panchali could do not to smile as she said, 'Is that a question for your friends or for the king of Western Kuru?'

Asvattama's chuckle changed to an uncharacteristic grin, one that surprised Sadev and Dhaumya, as much as it did Dharma. 'I ask, if you permit, as a friend.'

'In that case, the answer is: No.'

'And if I were to ask the king of Western Kuru?'

'Then you'd be making a serious mistake, questioning the lord of this land in his own audience chambers. And the answer would still be: No.'

'And the movement of your troops, as well as your brother's men and the Narayaniya forces towards Magadha? I suppose they're all coincidences?'

Panchali was categorical. 'We won't pretend it's mere coincidence. But this much I swear to you: when those troops left here, they had no intention whatsoever of attacking Magadha. In fact, they had no intention of even crossing the border. That is the solemn word of King Dharma Yudhisthir.'

Dharma allowed himself the slightest sigh of relief. Panchali was right. When the troops had set out from Indr-prastha there had been no talk of mounting an attack on Magadha. They had just been sent to be a decoy for the assassin. As for the man's whereabouts, Dharma truly had no idea. Govinda had, he remembered with mild chagrin, insisted that it be so.

Asvattama studied Dharma, then Panchali, before turning his attention back to the former. 'And if the Emperor were to consider this a hostile act on your part? You do realize that it would place your kinsmen and your friends, me included, in a difficult position?'

It was Sadev who replied, 'With all due respect, it's not for us to speculate what the Emperor might or might not think, is it? We must each do our sovereign duties, as we're sworn to.'

'And what does duty demand of King Dharma?'

'That he protect his realm from invasion. If Jarasandha were to attack us we might have no choice but to defend ourselves.'

'At which point, having your armies and that of your allies in place along Magadha's borders would prove to be an unexpected, but most welcome, happenstance.'

Dharma now intervened, 'You forget, Asvattama, that Jarasandha has a garrison at Mathura. What does it say about our intentions regarding open war that we've moved no troops towards the west? If the Emperor should decide to attack us we're completely unprotected.'

Asvattama smoothly countered, 'Yet another reason to avoid open war with the Emperor, isn't it? By the way, on another note, have you heard from Govinda Shauri? I believe he marches with the Narayaniyas, doesn't he?'

Panchali hesitated for a moment before saying, 'He left here with his men, yes. But no, we haven't heard from him since.'

'I hope he's well. If you should send word to him, please do convey my personal regards.'

The words struck cold fear into Panchali. For many days now she had been trying hard to dismiss the image of Devala Asita walking into the flames of Kandava from her mind. She had not seen him since that day, but something told her that the Firewright was far from dead and far from helpless. The possibility now frightened her more than it had all these days as she realized that Devala would surely try to stop Govinda and he would find unique means of doing so.

'What do you know that we don't, Asvattama?' she asked, her eyes adding words that she dared not say out loud.

'Many things,' he replied, though not unkindly. 'Some of which are best not spoken of at all and others you'd do well to find out about at once.'

The cryptic statement filled the stillness until, eventually, Panchali nodded.

Asvattama took it as a signal and stood up. He turned to Dharma and bowed politely. 'Thank you for seeing me. I should be getting back.'

'Won't you stay and eat with us?' Dharma offered.

Asvattama shook his head. 'Not today. But something tells me that I shall feast here at Indr-prastha before long.' With a cold smile he added, 'One way, or another.'

Panchali's lips rounded in a silent gasp, but before she could say anything Asvattama made his way out, escorted to the door by Sadev.

Dhaumya waited till their guest was out of earshot before saying, 'That went well, I think. Though, I must admit, it wasn't too difficult. Asvattama heard exactly what he wanted to hear. He knows as well as you and I do what's happening out there. All he wants is to go back and tell Syoddhan that we swore our men did not leave here with the intention to attack Jarasandha.'

'Which *is* the truth. Else I would never have accepted it,' Dharma vehemently declared.

Sadev let out a tired breath. 'It's politics, Agraja. Accept that. And on that note, Panchali, I dare say you'll make a fine diplomat. Your brothers have taught you well.'

Dharma said, 'I agree. I shall surely breathe easier for that conversation.'

Panchali, however, sounded highly unlike the consummate diplomat Sadev had just mentioned as she burst out, 'Damn my brothers and damn us all! We need to send messengers out to Partha and Yuyudhana right away. We need to know what's happened out there.'

'What's wrong, my dear?' Dharma gently asked, his earlier anxiety slowly returning.

'Asvattama isn't a man to throw words around lightly. He's telling us something's happened. He's warning us!'

'Warning us of what?'

'War.' Panchali spat out the word. 'He said that he'd feast at Indr-prastha one way or another. He's telling us that the Emperor's armies are marching against us. The assassin has failed.'

Sadev frowned, his disbelief turning into painful certainty as he ran the conversation over in his mind. 'But … Govinda …' He faltered as Dharma's unintentional admission rang loud in his mind: *If the Emperor should decide to attack us, we're completely unprotected.*

It was Dharma who forced out the words that no one else seemed willing to speak. 'Perhaps we've been outwitted after all. Perhaps Govinda Shauri has failed, too.'

9

PARTHA HAD SET OUT FROM INDR-PRASTHA WITH A SMALL battalion of men and marched through Panchala into Kosala. Behind him, along the borders of Panchala, Dhrupad's armies had been mustered. It gave the appearance of a well-considered battle strategy: Partha appeared to be set to attack Jarasandha from the north and west, while Bhim would attack from the south. The size of their forces may have suggested a hidden plan to a suspicious few, but it was dismissed by most observers as foolhardiness. The fact remained that no force was large enough to face the mighty Imperial Army.

When Govinda and Bhim presented themselves at Partha's camp, looking worn and disreputable, two days and a night after the assassin had been executed, the sentry treated them with all due suspicion. But the two gave the right passwords and so were brought to Partha's tent. Partha assured the escorting guards that the new arrivals were indeed known to him and waited solemnly until the soldiers left, still unconvinced and suspicious. Then he broke into uproarious laughter.

'You make an excellent bear, Bhim,' he quipped, trying in vain to catch his breath.

Govinda joined in the laughter, saying, 'Just you wait! Some more time on the road and you'll soon look like this, or worse still.'

'I think I'd be more of a lion, like you, Govinda. You look good.'

'You're just saying that out of fear of my sister.'

'Vathu!' Bhim snapped. 'Shut up, Govinda! It's your fault we're in this mess!'

Partha frowned, unsure of what was going on. 'What happened? Is something wrong?'

'Something is terribly wrong, Brother. Our man was caught and executed at Girivraja. Jarasandha has declared war on Indr-prastha and his armies are on the way here as we speak. We've both ridden with hardly a break for the past two days. Is that enough for you?'

Partha stopped mid-guffaw and stared at Bhim, aghast. Then he turned to Govinda, who nodded. 'Oh Rudra!' he cursed and sat down on the edge of the wooden camp-bed. 'This is bad. This is really bad. We need to hold them off, give Dharma time to put the defences in place. They'll have to round the Eastern Forests and follow the river, so if ...'

'What defences?' Bhim shouted. 'All the Emperor has to do is snap his fingers and the entire bloody garrison of Mathura will empty upon Indr-prastha. There's nothing we can do, Partha! Unless, like Govinda here, you'd rather surrender and run away to Hara knows which corner of this world and ...'

'Or,' Govinda interrupted, 'We could finish the job ourselves.'

'Govinda, please ...' Partha began before Bhim could erupt a second time.

'I mean it. We leave tomorrow morning, the three of us. We head back to Girivraja and find a way to do this.'

An uncertain silence followed the declaration. Both Partha and Bhim stared at Govinda, who looked unseeing into the distance, lost in thought. After what felt like a long time, he stirred, and wearily declared, 'I need a bath.'

Partha gestured to a small exit on the other side of the tent. 'There's lots of hot water in the large copper urns just behind there ...'

'For that, I shall owe you the pick of Dwaraka's courtesans!' Govinda said. Putting his weapons and other belongings aside, he left the large, room-like tent. Soon they heard the sound of splashing water and a merry voice rose in a bawdy army song.

'What the ...' Bhim swore. 'Is this man for real? I tell you, Partha ... he didn't flinch! You should've seen what they did to that poor man, but Govinda? He didn't even blink. And now ...? Listen to him! He's raving mad!'

'For suggesting that we kill Jarasandha ourselves? What choice do we have, Bhim?'

'I know we have no choice, but ...'

'It bothers you that he's so cold about it.'

'Yes!'

'Wouldn't you do something like this to protect that which you love?'

'What on earth could a man possibly love so much that it turns him into this? Power?'

'His people.'

Bhim looked unconvinced. 'He's using us. He's using us to destroy his enemy. And you, my brother, seem to have no problems with it!'

Partha placed a calming hand on his brother's shoulder. 'Look,' he said, 'I don't like this any more than you do. But war, honourable as it is, won't save Dharma's throne or his life. We've got to trust Govinda.'

'Trust! Hah!' Bhim gave a disparaging snort, which indicated the end of the conversation.

The company of three slipped out of the camp in the early hours of the morning. At Govinda's insistence they left behind their weapons and dressed in the ochre robes that a couple of soldiers had managed to procure for them during the night. Hair and beard long and unkempt, Govinda and Bhim bore the look of ascetics. Partha still looked a little too well-groomed for the part, but wrapped his thin upper robe around his head and part of his face.

Bhim complained to Govinda, 'He looks too neat. And we look too scruffy.'

'Ah, but that's the point, Bhim,' Partha replied. 'We leave behind our weapons, travel unsuspected as ascetics and find our way into the palace through the kitchen gates – the ones used to admit beggars and such. Once we're in, we knock down a few guards, take their swords and find Jarasandha.'

'It's dishonourable, that's what it is!'

'It's as honourable as it was when you lot did it at Kampilya,' Govinda snidely remarked. He then reined in his temper and added in a neutral tone, 'We'll give him a fair fight when it comes to that, if you like. For the moment, let's just focus on getting to him. Unless you have a better idea, in which case, say it now.'

Partha played mediator again. 'It's a good plan, Govinda. No one would expect us to turn up without our weapons, certainly not Jarasandha.'

'He's not the only one,' Bhim grudgingly muttered, feeling naked without his sword.

The trio reached Girivraja without incident. Bhim could not help but shudder as he entered the city gates for the second time in recent days, reminded of the horror of the execution. Partha and Govinda, however, were more interested in the security arrangements within the city, especially the palace. The three wandered around, carefully observing the routines and the movements of the palace guards.

Bhim whispered, 'The troops seem to have left. Seems kind of quiet, and not in a nice way.'

Govinda discreetly scrutinized the palace entrance. 'They're checking each person who enters the palace. That man there seems to be the usual milliner. The guards obviously know him, but aren't letting him off without inspection.'

The three men made their way around to the rear entrance to the palace kitchens, where, by tradition, alms were given to beggars, mendicants and others who asked for food. After all they had seen, it did not surprise them to find the gates closed and well-guarded.

'Great!' Partha remarked sarcastically. 'How are we supposed to get to the man?'

Bhim said, 'There might be tunnels alongside the underground waterways that drain into the river. Most palaces would have some sort of a sewerage system and we could get into the grounds that way ... But we don't even have our weapons to fight our way into the main building.'

Govinda did not reply and, instead, watched keenly as a bearded and cloaked man made his way out of the palace and swung on to a horse. Rider and steed weaved quickly away through the crowd in the general direction of the city gates.

'I'm not sure fighting would help, Cousin,' he said, at length. 'Something tells me that the palace is impregnable. But we need to act, and quick. Yuyudhana and the others are in for trouble. I have another idea. If we can't get into the palace on our own, we must get invited in.'

'There's no point getting ourselves arrested,' Partha said. 'Unlike Kampilya, the prisons here are separate. They're part of the garrison, not the palace.'

'Then we need to get in as guests.'

'If we try to seduce a sairandhari or some such attendant … ?'

Govinda did not hide his scorn. 'Why not try for a princess, while you're at it?'

Bhim was less dismissive. 'We certainly can't demand admittance as monks or sages,' he said. 'We can't lie outright! All of Aryavarta would spit on us if we defeated Jarasandha by cheating and lying.'

Govinda gave a derisive snort. 'True! It would be unspeakable! Trivial matters like winning the hand of a princess dressed as a scholar, or sending in assassins to kill an Emperor – such things are fine, but this – perish the thought!'

'Say what you want, but I won't lie.'

'Then keep your mouth shut. Don't speak.'

'What?' Partha exclaimed.

Govinda sighed, as if he were tired of arguing. 'Don't speak, Partha. Indeed, you might do me a favour and try to observe a vow of silence. It'll go well with your clothes and hair, in any case.'

'And I suppose, by standing around silently we'll be ushered into Jarasandha's presence?' Partha snapped.

Govinda's eyes narrowed as something suddenly occurred to him. To Partha's surprise he broke into a sudden smile and said, 'Something like that.'

10

THE THREE MEN MADE THEIR WAY TO THE OUTSKIRTS OF THE CITY.
Govinda found a calm spot by the river, a small but strong tributary that would join the mighty Ganga not too far away. There, seemingly

oblivious to Partha and Bhim's questions and recriminations, he laid aside the beads and ochre robes that were currently his only possessions, and waded into the water. He knew that time was a luxury they did not have, but he needed a few moments in the womb-like silence of the dark, deep currents, to think his plan through. By the time he stepped back ashore, his mind was clear and his eyes held a conviction that the glowering Bhim and Partha could not argue against for long.

'It won't be easy,' Bhim cautioned. 'We're asking to attract attention to ourselves. One slip, one inadvertent word or action out of place, and they'll arrest us for being spies. Of course, once they find out our real identities, that can only make it worse – not just for us but for Dharma and, of course, your people as well.'

'He's right,' Partha added. 'Passing oneself off as an ascetic for a short while is no matter; we've done it before. But to do as you say; to not speak or eat or drink … only the best of men, or those trained for such hardships can do that, Govinda. The mind starts to play tricks when faced with hunger and thirst. It's … it's a dangerous ploy.'

Govinda smiled and said, 'But an effective one if we succeed, yes?'

'Yes, but …'

'Then it's settled. Let me do this.'

Exchanging reluctant glances, Bhim and Partha finally agreed. Reminding them yet again of their newly assumed vows of silence, Govinda made for a banyan tree, next to the river, and sat down under its shade in a meditative posture. The two brothers exchanged sullen glances, but took their places alongside him.

At dusk, Bhim and Partha stirred, thinking of food and then sleep. To their surprise, Govinda did not as much as twitch. Whether he remained still out of incredible discipline, or he was truly lost inside himself in meditation, the two brothers could not tell. They waited for a while and then, rather than draw suspicion to themselves, decided to play the part of acolytes. Silently, they gathered some fruits and made as best a meal as they could. Bhim proposed that they sit up with Govinda and Partha agreed. They passed a quiet, restless night. The next morning, their routine induced less guilt. They kept themselves occupied by building a small thatched hut, in case it rained. In the evening they made do with a little food, and then slept a while, taking turns.

On the fourth day a few Magadhan citizens approached the trio, silently offering fruits and seeking blessings. Within a week, their audience had grown into a small crowd. Many people stood around looking on with curiosity, some with suspicion, at the never-moving ascetic. Most of them sat in prayer, waiting with patience that could only be inspired by devotion. The lack of water, rather than food, began to show on Govinda's appearance. His features took on frightening gauntness, his skin looked leathery, and his lips were cracked and bleeding. Still he did not stir.

Sunset on the eighth day drew the largest crowds of both onlookers and would-be devotees, as well as a huge thunderstorm. Partha and Bhim silently gestured to their audience to take shelter in the small hut as best as they could and stood in the doorway, watching. Through the storm and the rain, Govinda did not move. This was no longer just an act.

At some point during the stormy night Partha could not take it any more. Under the cover of thunder, he whispered quietly to his brother, 'Govinda has to be the craziest man I've ever seen.' Bhim simply had to agree. This madness was beyond what either of them could understand. Hunger, pain, weariness – these were things that every soldier was trained to fight against. But to suspend all action, perhaps even thought, to bear discomfort with serene surrender, was not the way of the warrior. For a moment, Bhim thought himself justified in the simmering anger he had been feeling against Govinda for the past some days. Perhaps, he wondered, Govinda was not quite Arya after all. His mind did not seem to abhor surrender – be it in the military sense or the philosophical – the way any true-blooded warrior's ought to. And yet, as Bhim continued to look upon the tranquil, rain-drenched figure, he felt his rage dissolve and a grudging respect take its place.

The next morning, as the rain abated, even the most sceptical of onlookers silently bowed to the ascetic and sat down in prayer. Many more came to join them, moved by the man's austerities. A rumour began running through the crowd that the Emperor himself was on his way to invite the holy one to the palace. By noon, the approaching contingent of royal guards confirmed that it was so.

Bhim expected that he would have to remind himself to keep from attacking Jarasandha as soon as he set eyes on him, but the Emperor's dignified behaviour surprised him into restraining himself. Jarasandha had come from the city on foot. He left his retinue, his crown and sandals at a distance and approached the ascetic, still meditating and immune to the world, barefoot. With folded hands and bowed head the Emperor respectfully invited him to grace the royal palace. To the surprise of all assembled, the ascetic stirred. He opened his eyes to look at the Emperor, and slowly nodded his assent. The three ochre-clad men joined the royal contingent, which made its way to the palace.

Jarasandha personally saw the three men to lavish rooms, and made every comfort available to them. He left them to rest in privacy, but made sure that the attendants reported back to him on what transpired next. The ascetics, he learnt, ignored both the courtesans and the fine silk beds placed at their disposal, and slept on the floor. They ate only fruits, and did not speak a word, even to each other. Caught between doubt and certainty, Jarasandha invited them to his court at midnight when, his royal priest advised, the scriptures allowed for vows of silence to be temporarily set aside.

Despite the late hour, all the nobles had assembled and taken their usual places. The ascetic and his companions, too, waited for the Emperor. Jarasandha entered the court and, making his way directly to the guests, welcomed them.

'And what may I offer you, wise acharyas?' he asked most formally. 'The Emperor's riches pale in comparison to the gods you seek, but whatever it is you wish of me will be yours.'

A strong voice replied, 'My only wish is to have a duel with you, Your Imperial Highness. I challenge you to single combat with me. Accept if you dare.'

A benumbed silence filled the space.

It was broken as Jarasandha laughed a loud, fearless laugh. Finally, turning to the trio, he demanded, 'And who are you to challenge me, you pretenders? Do you dare reveal your identity?'

'Our identity was never hidden. All you had to do was ask, but you didn't,' the man replied. Eyes blazing, he stepped forward. 'I am Govinda Shauri of the line of Yadu and Vrishni. With me are Bhim and Partha, mighty Kuru princes, sons of Pandu, brothers to Dharma Yudhisthir, king of Indr-prastha.'

The Emperor appeared taken aback, but only briefly. His astonishment was soon replaced by the most apparent disdain. 'You're challenging me to a fight? *You*? A man so obviously afraid of me that you've sneaked into my palace in disguise ... Why would I fight a coward like you, Govinda?' He sighed in mock exasperation and continued, 'Didn't you ever wonder why the Emperor of Aryavarta, the man whose armies are feared and respected through the entire world – didn't you ever ask yourself why I've let you be all these years? I could have killed you as you ran, tail between your legs, from Mathura. But I didn't. You're just the son of a slave, for all I care. Do you know how many of *you* fill my dungeons and clean the horse-shit from my stables? Why, some of *you* even wipe my backside! When I want one of *you* dead, *gwala*, I send him to the rat-catchers. For you, you coward, I think even that is a waste of good men. As for your challenge ... Mih! I refuse to fight you!' he thundered. 'I refuse your challenge, and I piss on it!'

With that, he spat on the ground at Govinda's feet. Not a sound came from the gathering of nobles, and then, as one, they burst into mocking, cackling laughter that rang, deafening, off the walls.

Govinda stood in the middle of it all, letting the barbs of ridicule, the shame and derision all wash over him as though he cared nothing for it. In fact, he smiled – his very own mysterious but undeniably sad smile that he alone knew the meaning of.

It was more than Bhim could take. Seething with anger, he stepped forward. 'Then I dare you to fight *me*!' he challenged Jarasandha. 'Fight me here and now, as we stand, and I'll prove by your blood that Govinda Shauri is no coward!'

A horrified Partha looked from Bhim to the impassive Govinda, and then at the delighted Jarasandha. The Emperor was known not only to be a hardy fighter but also a tough wrestler, on par with Balabadra himself. Bhim had been undoubtedly one of Balabadra's best students, but … Partha shuddered at the thought of what defeat would mean to them all. 'Bhim, are you …' he began in an urgent hiss, but fell quiet as he saw it was too late.

Jarasandha considered the exchange with an amused expression, as though waiting for Bhim to back out. He then chortled maliciously and said, 'Very well, son of Pandu. If the gods decree that Kuru blood be spilt for this son of a slave, then so be it. But for my part, once I've beaten you I'll avenge and honour your death by cutting Govinda's head off his neck.'

Without further ado, the Emperor cast aside his upper robe and stripped off the crown and other jewels he wore. He ordered his noblemen and soldiers to move back, creating a ring-like space in their midst.

Bhim could not help but notice that Jarasandha bore no signs of injury, no mark at all from their assassin's attack. It reminded him of what Govinda had said about the Emperor having been forewarned. With it came the chilling realization that perhaps their presence here, too, was expected and their efforts doomed to failure. Pushing the thought out of his mind, he tried to focus on the moment. Handing over his robe and ascetic's beads to an anxious-looking Partha, Bhim pulled his long hair into a tight knot and stepped up to face his opponent.

The two men regarded each other for a moment. Without warning, they threw themselves at each other, grappling furiously, moving fast and striking hard. Around them, the courtiers shrunk away in fear, astonished at the animal rage that coursed through both fighters. Jarasandha drew first blood, beginning with a series of hard punches to Bhim's face and then by lifting him up and throwing him over his shoulder.

Partha swore out loud, visibly astonished at the Emperor's strength. Few could match Bhim move for move, as Jarasandha was. He glanced over at Govinda. The man looked as unflappable as always, but his dark eyes smouldered with a new emotion that Partha did not recognize.

Bhim quickly got back on his feet, but Jarasandha had a psychological advantage and he pressed it. He threw scathing remarks at his opponent, which the many nobles around them also took up, adding a few insults of their own. Bhim responded by rushing at Jarasandha, but the monarch was ready. Grabbing Bhim's arm, Jarasandha used the force of the attack to twist it, slowly forcing him down on one knee. For a while it looked as though neither man was moving, though their muscles were taut with the effort. The audience fell silent, hardly daring to breathe. At last, after what seemed like ages, Bhim slipped out of Jarasandha's grip. With a cry that echoed through the air, he landed a hard backhanded punch to the side of his opponent's head and followed through with an elbow to the man's stomach. Then, as Jarasandha staggered back, Bhim butted him like a raging bull.

Unsteady on his feet, the Emperor still tried to grab hold of Bhim. The younger man deftly side-stepped the attack and wound his left arm around Jarasandha's neck in a stranglehold. He then locked his right hand around his left wrist and began pressing down on Jarasandha's windpipe. It was the toughest thing Bhim had ever tried to do. It took every bit of strength, will and courage in his body, mind and heart to execute the move. Jarasandha kicked and flailed, clawed at his opponent's arms, elbowed him in the stomach. He had gone red in the face, and his eyes were nearly bulging out of their sockets, but he still would not give up.

Bhim felt his arms burn from the effort. Teeth clenched, he tried hard to coax a little more strength out of his body, but it was all he could do just to hold on. Sweat poured from his forehead, trickling down into his eyes, making them smart. He had to do something, and quick. In a sudden move, he let go of Jarasandha, and in the same instant brought his knee up to hit the man hard on the small of his back. Before the Emperor knew it, he was face down, on the floor. His chest heaving from the exertion, Bhim stepped back and waited for Jarasandha to get to his feet.

Gone was Jarasandha's earlier arrogance. The Emperor was obviously in great pain, and though he tried to push himself up, he was unable to. He looked around him in a helpless daze, as though he could neither see nor think clearly. With a groan, he finally managed to get onto his hands and knees.

Bhim snarled at the spent Emperor, goading him to stand up and fight. As he waited, fists clenched, he felt a gentle touch on his arm.

In the middle of the tumult, of that noisy torrent of primal fury and hatred, Govinda's presence was as cool and soothing as a spring breeze. 'Enough,' he gently advised Bhim. 'This fight is over. You attack a man when he's tired and weak, you will kill him in ways you can't imagine. Enough, my friend.'

Jarasandha staggered to his feet, seething with hatred as his bloodshot, bulging eyes stared at Govinda. Govinda met the Emperor's stare, the silent odium and the implied accusations in them, without flinching.

Bhim felt rage flow through him, renewed. In that moment, he knew: As long as he lived, he would never forget the sadness he had seen in Govinda's eyes. One chance to kill Jarasandha in fair combat and thereby salvage his pride, one chance to avenge himself against the man who had driven him out from his own home, reduced him from the Crown Prince of a great nation to an object of ridicule – and Govinda had given it up.

For what, Bhim wondered as blood thundered in his head. Power? Friendship? Surely not for Dharma?

The people, Partha's words rang in his ears. A voice in Bhim's own mind added an answer of his own he dared not whisper aloud or even admit to himself. It coursed through his limbs like fire, giving him a strength he did not know he had left in him. With a terrible yell that stunned every onlooker, Bhim threw himself at Jarasandha, pinning him down to the floor once more. The weary Emperor had no strength left to resist.

A courtier screamed, guards began to move towards the duelling men and the room filled with the sounds of panic, anger and confusion. Partha threw himself at the nearest guards, laying a few punches of his own as he screamed out warnings, first to Bhim and then to Govinda. Both men ignored it, their attention on nothing but the man who lay spread wide on the floor, no longer an Emperor, nothing but mortal like them all. A man made of flesh, blood and fading hope.

Bhim glanced again at Govinda, at the silent, expressionless stance, which suddenly seemed to speak volumes that he had never noticed or understood before. Govinda's pained detachment was more than he could take. With determined precision, Bhim placed one knee against Jarasandha's spine, braced his other leg against the man's right ankle and wrapped his arms around his torso. With a loud yell, he drew on every scrap of strength that he had left and pulled.

The thundercrack of Jarasandha's backbone snapping in two could be heard above the tumult. It was followed by the softer, more gut-wrenching sound of muscle and flesh tearing apart.

11

PANCHALI HAD NEVER THOUGHT SHE WOULD BE THIS RELIEVED to see Govinda again. But she was. She had casually walked into Dharma's outer chambers, and stopped in her tracks when her eyes fell on Govinda.

'Ah, Panchali,' Dharma greeted her. 'I was just about to send for you …'

But she had already broken into tears as she faced Govinda. 'When did you arrive? How tired you look!' she said, in a gentle, chastising way, 'And you haven't combed your hair in ages.' She reached up to touch his curly hair, still short but thicker and more unruly than she had ever seen it. He was in his dirty, travel-stained robes, with some of his gear and weapons still strapped to his back.

'Panchali …' Govinda whispered, feeling content at the mere sight of her.

He hardly took his eyes off her for the rest of the evening, as he emotionlessly, tonelessly, reported every detail of the expedition to

Dharma and Panchali. He told them also about Jarasandha's son, who lacked his father's ambition but not his sense of honour and pride. After Jarasandha had been defeated, Govinda had installed the young man in his father's stead as the king of Magadha. The newly crowned king had been grateful, particularly since he had no advisors to suggest he feel otherwise. He took easily to Govinda's suggestions and not only pledged allegiance to Dharma of the Kurus but also sealed the alliance in the time-honoured fashion of Aryavarta – through matrimony. His sister, the princess Valandhara, was now Bhim's wife.

Panchali smiled softly to herself at that, but made no comment. She had seen far too many politically motivated marriages to feel anger, or even surprise, anymore. Dharma left soon after to speak with Partha and Bhim. Govinda and Panchali sat together well into the night without exchanging a single word.

The next morning, bathed and looking more like his old self, Govinda entered Dharma's study to find all five brothers assembled there.

Dharma stood up to embrace him. 'Brothers,' he announced, 'our wisest counsel and dearest friend. He shall lead us to great glory!'

Govinda accepted the compliment with a polite bow. 'As always, you give me far too much credit.'

'Then, perhaps, you'd consider earning some of it,' Panchali snidely remarked as she walked into the room. Dharma looked happy to see her, but she did not seem to notice him as she calmly took a seat. 'So ...' she continued, her voice soft but commanding, 'Jarasandha is no more ...'

'Ah!' Dharma exclaimed. 'And now, there are many contenders for the imperial throne. But few have what it takes to rule an empire and fewer still count among those whom the kings of Aryavarta might willingly accept as their sovereign. '

A strained hesitation filled the room. Panchali tried hard to keep her breathing neutral and her face expressionless as she waited for Govinda to guide them to the inevitable conclusion. Soon, she supposed, Dharma and his brothers would present the idea for the first time, as though it had never been contemplated in the first place – Govinda Shauri, Emperor of Aryavarta. Slowly, they would convince him to accept the role he had always wanted, and when he had grudgingly acquiesced, the five brothers would become his most loyal ambassadors and allies, paving the way for his accession as Emperor. The immaculate planning sickened her as much as it impressed her. Her lips fixed in what she hoped was a neutral smile, she looked up.

To her surprise, Govinda was beaming mysteriously at all of them. Slowly, deliberately, he declared, 'Then it's time that the esteemed kings of Aryavarta considered the best man for the role – Emperor Dharma Yudhisthir.'

Govinda paused, his eyes holding a muted fire as he studied each of them, patiently waiting for their reactions

Dharma remained still, trying hard not to show his enthusiasm and his utter lack of surprise at the suggestion. The others, however, were clearly grappling with various degrees of confusion and even shock. One by one they all met Govinda's gaze, Sadev and Bhim in silence, Partha with an admission of awe, and Nakul with an exclamation of disbelief. Panchali too was on the verge of saying something, but then appeared to decide against it. She turned away and gazed intently at some indistinct spot on the floor.

When Dharma eventually spoke, his voice was slightly hoarse. 'How?'

Govinda continued, as though he were stating the obvious, 'We need to put the idea of Dharma as Emperor irrefutably into everyone's minds before the issue of dominion begins to swing one way or another. But for that we must get their attention first. We have to do something impressive, some that few have ever managed. The mistake most emperors make is to suppose that the key to the empire lies in controlling the western frontier. Even Jarasandha had his heart set on that. But that's not the answer. Your goal should be to take the north and north-eastern frontiers, the mountain kingdoms. You can then have complete control over all the land routes into Aryavarta.'

Nakul gasped audibly, while Bhim and Partha exchanged meaningful glances. Sadev mumbled something under his breath. Panchali apparently heard what he said, for she nodded tersely.

Dharma was pleased at their consternation. It made him think that perhaps what Govinda suggested was impossible after all. The thought brought with it the soothing satisfaction that perhaps he would be forced to remain free of ambition and pride after all. In an indulgent but sceptical voice he said, 'Govinda, no emperor has truly conquered the north, and for good reason. By the time the Great White Mountains are crossed the centre is often lost. Perhaps it is an impossible dream.'

'Perhaps not. None of the emperors had brothers such as you do. Northern campaigns have always come at the cost of losing some other part of the empire because the emperors themselves have marched out to conquer. In your case ...'

'I'm not convinced. Assume the north can be taken and held, thanks to my brave brothers, but if we throw all our strength there how can we cover the rest of Aryavarta? And even then I don't see how the basic problem is solved. There is no pass through the mountains that can admit an entire army, and by the time soldiers carve a way through they will be in no position to do battle! And how does one build a pass through hostile lands without fighting to keep it open? It's a circular problem, one that has perplexed Aryavarta's kings for years!'

'Except,' Govinda declared, 'you don't have to build a pass, do you? Well, not all of it! You have a passage waiting for you: the Nagas' trading route at Bhogavati heads north through the mountains before it turns towards the north-west. I see no reason why we can't widen that road and follow it part of the way.'

This time the response was a unanimous silence.

Govinda chuckled at their reaction. 'You see,' he continued, 'imperial domination is difficult not just because the campaign is difficult, but because the slightest failure is nothing short of complete failure. You can conquer nine-tenths of Aryavarta and even beyond, but one successful challenger, one vassal undefeated, is enough to undo all that has been achieved.'

Dharma shook his head. 'I don't understand. You sound like you are for this, but then you point out why it's already doomed to fail ...'

'I point out what makes it difficult so that we can consider how to succeed. The factors that make a bid for imperial dominion so hard are also what make it possible if handled right. This isn't just war, it's also politics. One challenger can bring you down, yes, but no one wants to be the sole, defiant enemy to an emperor whom everyone else is pleased to accept. So every kingdom *will* look to every other kingdom before it responds, Dharma. What we need to do is time things perfectly. Extend the imperial domain simultaneously in all directions.'

'But how?'

'Remember, Magadha is already yours. All we have to do is bring the northern armies down through the pass at Deva-prastha, further east of Magadha, and you can rest and refit the troops there. This way you won't lose men to the terrain or to the weather. Creating a garrison at Magadha also gives it status as a diplomatic base. Use that to negotiate a strong alliance with the king of Kalinga, Srutayus.'

'Why Kalinga?'

'The Kalinga kingdom controls all sea routes on the eastern coast, just as Dwaraka does on the west. Most of the coastal kingdoms of Dakshinavarta have to pay some consideration to either or both in return for protection against pirates as well as for the use of their ports, trade routes, even sea vessels. If you can get the protectors to acknowledge your suzerainty, the protectorates naturally come along.'

Partha, Bhim and the twins looked admiringly at Govinda. Dharma alone was frowning.

Govinda continued, unaffected. 'Your progress in the northern regions puts you in a better position to negotiate strong treaties with the south. They know well that if you hold the north, you can do much for overland trade. You'd have the power to enhance their prosperities by getting the Kyrgs and Cinnas, for example, to use their ports to send goods out across the ocean. At the same time you reduce the dependence of the central lands on the coastal kingdoms, thereby giving you a strong base.' He flashed a mischievous glance at Panchali as he added, 'It's time Aryavarta looked to the seas ...'

Pausing, Govinda looked around at the five brothers, and waited till each one of them met his eyes and nodded their assent. 'With all this taking place,' he continued, 'central Aryavarta will fall into place of its own accord, as will the west. There are many kings who are either allied to Kuru or Magadha. If you can establish yourself over the periphery, these kings will accept you as their overlord. Consider the Sindhu–Sauvira region: the saamantas there, including the Trigarta kings, owe their allegiance to Jayadrath, Syoddhan's brother-in-law. In the east you have Vasusena of Anga, who is, again, Syoddhan's friend. I believe that the Vyasa will prevail on your cousin and your uncle to support you, but irrespective of that all the kings of Greater Aryavarta, in their own interest, will be happy to support an emperor who can control the periphery of the empire. You may still have to fight; a non-violent conquest is near impossible. And, don't forget, this isn't something that'll happen in a day. We're talking of a campaign that may take five or six years, maybe even longer. But at the end of those years you'll be in a position to maintain a military base on the other side of the White Mountains as well as a garrison at Magadha, and that will suffice. Once the Empire is formed, it serves everyone's interests to stay united. What brute strength can't achieve, we can do using the power of trade.'

Govinda fell silent, allowing the five brothers to consider and understand the implications of what he had just told them. At length, as the prospect of adventure and victory gradually sank in, they began to grin. All but Dharma, who continued to glower, apparently at the unviability of it all. Slowly, he realized the others awaited his reaction, his four brothers with undisguised excitement, Panchali in silence, and Govinda with what Dharma considered an indulgent smile.

His voice slightly strained for his reluctance, Dharma began to speak, issuing the orders he knew were ostensibly his to give. 'Bhim can go eastwards to his in-laws' house, such as it is now. Partha can take the northern campaign. He is, without doubt, the best among us, and if anyone has a chance to win the north, it'll be him.'

Bhim slapped Partha on the back, and made a jovial comment about him acquiring more in-laws, especially among the mountain people, at which Govinda laughed

Dharma waited for the three to settle down, which they did with the guilty charm of truant children, and continued, 'We will also need to be ready for some heavy diplomacy and negotiation with Kalinga and the southern and south-eastern kingdoms. I'd be grateful if you took that up, Govinda. After that Sadev can lead a diplomatic mission into central Dakshinavarta, where we should be able to present ourselves as Kalinga's allies.'

Sadev could not help but smile. 'Central Dakshinavarta? You mean the monkey-kings of Kishkinda?'

'Indeed,' Govinda said, chuckling softly. 'Though I think they would prefer to be known more kindly – and accurately, mind you – as the kings of the monkey-banner.'

Dharma ignored the banter yet again and turned to Nakul. 'Nakul, the west is yours,' he said.

Govinda added, 'Yes, Nakul. Fortunately for us, the king of Madra is your maternal uncle. With his help you can reclaim the northern frontier lands from foreign kings, especially the Hunas and the Pahlavas. It might also be possible to speak with the Danavas, negotiate something ... At least make sure the trading routes are uncontested. We have already discussed Sindhu–Sauvira. That leaves ...'

'Matsya?' Partha suggested.

'Ah, Matsya,' Dharma began. 'I'm not sure I want anything to do with that forsaken desert. Besides, its people are nothing but uncouth tribals, uncivilized nomads. I doubt they'd even understand much of our kind of politics. They basically survive by hiring out their armies as mercenaries to foreign kings.'

Govinda raised an eyebrow and his voice held just a tinge of amusement. 'They understand battle very well and their coffers run deep but, yes, Matsya is happy to leave the rest of Aryavarta alone if we afford them the same courtesy. They don't care who rules Aryavarta, or why, given their more pressing issues, like survival. In any case, we can't take armies through the desert so we won't need to deal with them.'

'Salwa needs dealing with, though. And that too carefully,' Panchali gently ventured, looking down at her hands as they lay on

309

her lap. It was the first time she had spoken since Govinda had begun describing his plans. 'They're too busy these days competing with Dwaraka over sea trade to want to battle with us, but they can't be happy about Kandava ... Ever since the Nagas moved to Bhogavati and began plying their masonry and metalcraft there, they have had no cause to make or deal in illegal weapons – which means Salwa can no longer trade in confiscated weapons, as they claimed they were. As for the other nations of the west ...' she trailed off.

The brothers regarded each other uncertainly and then glanced at Panchali. She stared into the distance, apparently oblivious to the tension amidst them. Govinda smiled. He knew what it was they were all waiting for. 'The Yadus are a free people, my friends,' he said, with pride. 'They are their own sovereign and they rule themselves. But I, Govinda Shauri of the Vrishnis, shall pledge allegiance to Emperor Dharma Yudhisthir.'

The words roused Panchali out of her stupor and her eyes flashed for an instant. Then she said in a whisper, 'Unfortunately, Govinda of the Vrishnis, melodrama won't hide the truth. This business will be bloody, like it or not. Many will die, and their curses shall lie heavy on all our heads.'

Her words hung in the air as she rose and left the room.

Panchali made hurriedly for the privacy of her rooms, worried that she would blurt out the long-suppressed, decidedly dangerous thoughts that flitted through her mind.

This, she realized, had been Govinda's plan all along. He had known there was a way to the north. He had made sure of it. He had moved the Nagas to their new city knowing that they would inevitably trade with other kingdoms, that they would use their skills to build a pass through the mountains. He had burned Kandava to make them leave. To achieve that he had brought Dharma back to Hastina, married to the Princess of Panchala. He had planned everything in meticulous detail. And now he would lead the Kuru princes on an imperial campaign, a campaign that was doomed even before it began. Panchali's head reeled as she came to see how long it must have taken for Govinda to move things into place. Then, in a singular moment, her confusion distilled into a sparkling gem of clarity and she understood – no, accepted – what it was that he wanted.

An empire. Strong but weak, his own yet another's. The Firewright had been right; he had warned her that this was what Govinda was after, all along, and had begged her to somehow stop him. But she had failed. Time and again, she had failed. She had tried to appeal to Govinda's compassion; to his ego; and, finally, to his intellect, but her efforts had gone in vain. Govinda felt nothing; cared for nothing.

Panchali slumped on the floor on her knees, uncaring that it was hard and cold, screaming silently in the recesses of her mind. *Damn you, Govinda Shauri! Damn you!* She beat her fists on the floor, desperately needing her violent anger to stop her from crying. Finally, tired and defeated, she stretched out on the cold marble, trying to control the sobs that shook her from the inside. She had no idea how long she had been lying there, but stirred as she heard footsteps and hurriedly composed herself as Dharma burst into the room.

'Did you know of this?' he harshly demanded. Gripping her hard by the wrist, he yanked her up from the floor. She winced in pain but he did not let go.

'Did you plan this with *him*? Is this why you agreed to marry me, even though Partha won you? Did *he* tell you to? Is that why you've spurred me on at each step, pretending to be interested in my glory? By Rudra, how the two of you must have laughed behind my back at the stupid, helpless puppet I've been!'

'Dharma, please!' Panchali burst out. 'I had no idea! I assumed he …' she stopped short, keenly aware of how her own words had just condemned her.

'Oh Varuna! You thought …' Dharma's face contorted as his shock turned into rage, the emotion genuine this once. 'All along you've been spurring *him* on. You thought *he'd* be Emperor, didn't you? You conniving bitch, you …'

Panchali drew herself as tall as she could, channelling every bit

311

of her anger against Govinda into pride. 'Dharma, I swear by my honour, I didn't know.'

Dharma glared at her, his breath coming deep and fast. Her fiery appearance eventually convinced him that she was indeed telling the truth. With a sigh, he relented, and pulled her into his arms. A bewildered Panchali resisted for a moment, and then, slowly, let her head rest against his chest, bound to him, this once, in her confusion and despair. For what it was worth, his pain was no less than hers.

'Be calm,' he said gently, trying to soothe her, though they both knew he meant to console only himself. 'With Varuna's blessings this will go peacefully. There's nothing to worry about or fear ...'

'What can you do, Dharma?' she snapped at him. 'And what do *you* need to fear? Govinda will see you Emperor of Aryavarta!'

Dharma shuddered as the words tore through the comforting illusions he had clung to for so long now. He felt wasted and weak, as if he were nothing, a trivial piece of existence so servile that he did not count at all. Everything he had in his life was actually a scrap thrown to him by Govinda Shauri.

Why? Why must it be this way, his mind screamed.

The answer rang out louder than his question. He gave a slow shake of his head, the gesture his private act of acceptance that shook the pieces into their destined places. His voice was unusually cold as he pointed out, 'No, Panchali. Govinda will see *you* on the throne. He will see *you* Empress of Aryavarta. It's the only thing that makes sense.'

With that, he pushed her aside, and stalked out.

It took a while for Panchali to understand what Dharma had meant. It took her longer still to accept the irony of the situation. Dharma thought Govinda was doing this because he cared for her, even desired her. And why not? Partha had obviously wanted her, and though no one spoke of it, for years now, Bhim had looked at her with a pained adoration that he'd never dared express. But Govinda ... *Hah!* All this while she had felt betrayed, she thought Govinda had given her up for an empire, she had felt enraged at that vile barter. Now she knew there had been no question of choosing an empire over her. There was nothing to give up. She meant nothing to him.

Panchali knew she had no right to feel hurt, but she did. Hurt, used and furious, too, that she had allowed Govinda to make her feel this way. She longed to despise him, tried to will that emotion into being, but she simply could not. All she could think of was that Govinda had set himself on a course that placed his very life in danger. There were those who would now seek to stop him in ways that were for more direct than hers. As cold fear pushed all the rage and silent rhetoric out of her mind, Panchali found herself praying for the man she wanted to hate but could not.

Oh Rudra, please, please keep him safe!

12

THE YOUNG, BEARDED SCHOLAR WALKED THROUGH THE PALACE with the deference expected of him. He effusively greeted every dignitary, and stood hesitantly at doorways till an attendant came to his aid. Even then, his manner was meek and apologetic. In all, he played to perfection the part of a young acolyte raised to the unexpected honour of an audience with the Grandsire of the Kuru line of kings. He very nearly blushed when Bhisma came into the room.

Bhisma, however, was not amused to see his visitor. He tersely got rid of the others present, even the attendants. 'We're alone,' he finally declared, 'you can stop your pretence.'

Devala Asita raised his head. There remained no trace of his former deference. As a matter of habit, his hand moved to his beard in a prelude to speech. 'You know why I'm here …'

'Yes. And I also know that your journey is wasted. There's nothing I can do.'

'But …'

'Nothing you say can make me change my mind. In any case, it's too late. The last of Dharma's troops marched out of Indr-prastha over a month ago. His campaign has now well and truly begun and it's for the people of Aryavarta to judge Dharma's worth as an Emperor-aspirant, not for you or me to decide.'

'Surely,' the scholar began, 'you wouldn't refuse assistance to one who begs it of you?'

'I have every right to refuse assistance to an immoral end. Don't argue with me!'

'And you owe us nothing? You, the epitome of morality, claim that you owe us nothing? Forgive me, but I always thought that the debt of a student to a teacher is the greatest duty of them all ...'

'There's no need to be sarcastic. In any case, *you* are not my teacher.'

'But those of my order are. It's on Barghava Rama's shoulders that your reputation as an unparalleled warrior was earned ... *Grandsire*. The Firewrights have been your teachers, we've been your friends, keeping your secrets and aiding your cause when you've needed us the most. Yet you've turned your back on us when *we* needed *you* the most. Our blood is on your hands. I'm here to claim on that debt, to hold you to it.'

'By whose authority?' the Grandsire asked. 'The Secret Keeper is dead. The order of Firewrights is broken. Go back to your hermitage, or wherever it is that you came from, and spend your days in prayer.'

'You of all people should know better. The order can never be broken.'

'Ah! One stupid myth to hold up another!'

'It's no myth. Ghora did his duty. He taught those who were the best of students, me included, and prepared us to take his place.'

'Except, of course,' Bhisma scathingly noted, 'he did not anoint you as his heir! Are you telling me that you've been so appointed? That you are, in fact, the Secret Keeper?'

'Alas, I'm not. But when a nation has no king, a regent must suffice, isn't it? My time will come. I will rebuild my order before I rightfully make my claim to lead it.'

A tense silence followed, broken at length by the younger man. 'I had hoped that Agniveshya – Ghora's grandson – was alive. But with the fall of Kandava and then with Jarasandha's death I've lost that hope. Now, as one of Ghora's chosen, I am in fact the head of our order till such time that a better Wright comes forward to relieve me of this burden. By this authority, I charge you to fulfil your obligations to us.'

Bhisma stared at him, disbelieving. Then, with some effort, he stirred. 'My *obligations*, such as they may have been, were discharged long ago, and many times over,' he tersely pointed out. 'In fact, it's only kindness, not gratitude, that keeps me from having you arrested and executed this very moment. You have shamelessly revealed yourself as a Wright in the presence of the Regent of Hastina, no less. It's a crime, one that is punishable with death. I can only put down such folly to your youth and inexperience … Go, Devala! Leave before I lose my temper. Or else even your brother's good name won't keep you alive in Hastina.'

Devala's eyes blazed with anger and his chest heaved as he tried to keep his temper. Finally, when he trusted himself to speak he softly said, 'Very well,' and made to leave. He had taken just a few steps towards the door when he glanced back at Bhisma. 'Don't you think I know? That neither you nor Dwaipayana imagined for even a moment that Govinda Shauri's blood will emerge as heir to the Kuru throne? Why do you still pretend then that you rule these lands? The truth is you are but puppets in the hands of that bloody cowherd! I don't know what promises the Vyasa has made to you, but he is an idiot, and you're an even greater one that you follow him blindly. I warn you, Grandsire, if the imperial campaign continues, your kin will die for your stupidity. You have no idea what I'm capable of.'

Bhisma looked at the young man askance, and a cold and mirthless laughter broke suddenly from his lips. The Firewright was dumbstruck.

'Bakaa! You fool!' Bhisma chortled, still laughing. 'You poor, pitiful fool! Do you really believe that there are terrible weapons hidden somewhere? That you'll find these and save the Wrights? Hah! You were at Magadha … Don't bother denying it – everyone knows you were there! You promised to help Jarasandha defend his empire and reaffirm his power over Aryavarta, in return for what? Did you find even a single Wright worth saving in his dungeons, or weapons worth oiling in his armoury? What did you get for all your trouble? And at the end of it all Jarasandha died at the bare hands of a better man. Certainly not an end you'd expect for a king with Firewrights at his beck and call. There's nothing left!'

'Do you really believe that? You know how desperate Govinda and Dharma both were to avoid open war with Jarasandha. Do you really think there's nothing left?'

'There was a time when I didn't,' Bhisma admitted. 'And, yes, perhaps a part of me still does believe that there are weapons out there, weapons worthy of an Arya warrior. But that they were made by your people counts for nothing, and they certainly won't bring you Wrights back to power.'

'Worse things could happen. If you won't let us control these powerful things we have created, you risk letting them fall into the wrong hands; hands that may now seem to grip yours in friendship but would just as soon squeeze your neck. Take it from one who knows the bitter pain of betrayal – Govinda cannot be trusted.'

Bhisma clucked his tongue in an indulgent way. 'This is Dwaipayana's realm,' he softly declared. 'What the Vyasa believes is what matters. After all that has happened, you still don't see who holds the reins of Aryavarta in his hands? You're the fool then!'

'But …'

Bhisma came up to the young man and placed a hand on his shoulder, as he would with one of his grandsons. His expression showed a mixture of emotions – pain, anger, even despair – as he said, 'There's a demon that haunts us all, my boy. Within us all, within every human being, even Aryas, there is a corner of darkness. With the blessings of the gods and the help of the scriptures, we fight this darkness, overcome it to become honourable men. He … he guides us through that darkness. Every human weakness, every foible, each despair and every hope – he knows it all, and he helps us fight it.'

'And what if he fails? Dwaipayana – what if he fails?'

'And what if he doesn't?'

'By Hara! What power does Dwaipayana hold over you that

you fear him so? You, the man who once defeated the best of the Firewrights in fair battle?'

Bhisma glared at Devala. His tone was again clear and commanding as he firmly said, 'I can't do what you ask of me. I can't stop Dharma.'

Devala's eyes held grim resolution. 'Then you leave me no choice.'

Syoddhan watched as the young ochre-clad scholar left Bhisma's chambers and quickly made his way out of the grounds of the palace. With a sigh, he turned back to where his son, Lakshmana, was training with Vasusena's son, Vrishasena.

'Higher there. Block him! Block him! And you, Lakshmana, go under his shield-arm,' he called out instructions to the boys with the instinct of experience, even as he turned back to watch the scholar till he disappeared out of view.

He tried not to bristle at the thought that followed, but was only partly successful. Hardly had the news of Dharma's imperial campaign made its way to Hastina, first as rumour and then as fact, than Dwaipayana had begun his persuasion – persuasion that Syoddhan found to be less than palatable. First the Vyasa himself and then his acolytes had consistently impressed on Bhisma and Dhritarastra how important the campaign was to the Firstborn, to the establishment of an empire of divine order and to sealing the fate and prosperity of the Kurus. It was, Dwaipayana had pointed out and Sanjaya had echoed, of great economical and political benefit to Eastern Kuru should its western namesake become the imperial capital of Aryavarta. Syoddhan, however, had been less taken in by the talk than his father or his grand-uncle. He had soon understood what Dwaipayana wanted of him: Silent support, not only his own but also that of his friends and allies – support that Dharma did not and could not hope to have on his own.

Syoddhan had found it rather amusing that he seemed to enjoy far greater popularity and support in Aryavarta than the Emperor-aspirant. In fact, the more he dwelt on it the more convinced he became that perhaps his own claim on the imperial throne would have been better justified and certainly more successful. But his patience had prevailed and he questioned neither Dharma's campaign nor the Vyasa's injunction that he support it. Slowly, as he watched the armies of Indr-prastha march out in different directions, many of them through Eastern Kuru, Syoddhan came to terms with the sad fact of the matter – if he made a bid for imperium, it was bound to fail.

The reasons were many – the foremost being that he certainly could not trust his brothers the way Dharma trusted his. If he sent Dussasana or some of the others out to conquer the periphery, he could surely expect them to declare themselves rulers of those lands with the intent to sooner or later annex Aryavarta. Those who remained with him at Hastina would constantly be on the lookout for the opportunity to capture the throne from within. Indeed, this was the very reason his father gave to justify his remaining king of Kuru – to keep his heirs from squabbling for the crown. Yet another reason, Syoddhan sullenly admitted, why he could never aspire to be Emperor. At the end of the day, he was not even a king. He was just a prince.

'Ah! Why you …' A shout went up from one of the two boys, drawing Syoddhan out of his ruminations. Vrishasena stood clutching at one shoulder, his training sword on the ground, even as Lakshmana stood apologetically by.

Syoddhan rushed to the injured boy, dispelling all thoughts of Dharma's imperial campaign from his mind. The only trace that lingered was a casual calculation of how imperial campaigns were few and far between and, even so, for every five campaigns that were well-begun four were doomed to failure. Dharma's had no cause to be an exception. Indeed, he noted with a trace of grim satisfaction, there was nothing exceptional about Dharma at all.

13

AS PLANNED, GOVINDA AND BHIM MADE THEIR BASE AT MAGADHA and set about the eastern leg of the imperial conquest. It took them half a year to move all their men eastwards to Magadha and another few months to set up a full garrison there – particularly since Govinda insisted on disbanding Jarasandha's Imperial Army and re-mustering the soldiers to form new troops.

'You should trust them,' Bhim said, protesting against the disbanding. 'They're all good, honest men.'

'Indeed, they're good and honest,' Govinda said, 'and that's why we cannot trust them. Not yet.'

Bhim remained unconvinced, but he soon forgot his concerns as the endless preparations were finally completed and the real conquest began. He set out from Magadha, leading his new troops much further east, beyond Pragjya.

Govinda stayed back, his task now one of diplomacy, a role that was also mirrored at Indr-prastha by Dhaumya and Panchali. It did not take long for Govinda to set in a place a treaty with the Kalinga's King Srutayus – one that gave them all much cause to celebrate since it proved to be a persuasive point during Sadev's negotiations with the ruler of Andhraka in Dakshinavarta. The possibility of access to trade with the peninsular regions of the south also paved the way for a subsequent treaty, a year later, with the foreign Danava kings. The agreement ensured that the Danavas would not interfere in what the treaty diplomatically deemed as the internal affairs of Aryavarta. In effect it meant that the Danavas would not interfere as Nakul forcibly reclaimed the north-western lands from the Hunas and Pahlavas and brought them under the control of his uncle Shalya, the king of Madra.

Around the same time, it became clear to Govinda and Bhim why Srutayus had been so eager to accept Dharma's overlordship. It was the only way Srutayus could survive or even keep his own throne safe from his vassals, the coastal chiefs of Kalinga as well as those of the neighbouring regions of Vanga. Though these coastal chiefs had accepted Srutayus's rule in name, it soon became apparent that they were little better than pirate lords. Their fortunes were made by capturing merchant ships that were sailing close to the coastline and leading them into the thick forests, murky swamps and humid mangroves that covered most of Vanga as well as the coastal stretch of Kalinga. Then the pirates would either sell off the stolen goods or else demand huge ransoms for the release of the merchandise and crew. Imperial presence, the pirate chiefs knew, would bring with it strict enforcement of law and little mercy for piracy. And so they did everything possible to disrupt Dharma's campaign in the region, often resorting to ambush and sabotage against Bhim's soldiers.

Bhim tried his best, but neither he nor his men were adept at fighting in this sort of terrain. Srutayus and his forces too were of no use, for the king and his nobles merely looked to their new overlord for protection, though not with much hope. After all, they pointed out, even Jarasandha had found it easier to ignore the pirates than engage in battle in the dark, murky swamplands of the region.

'It's hopeless, Govinda,' Bhim despaired after he had personally led a futile expedition into a thick swamp not too far from Kalinga's capital, Rajapura. 'Snakes, tigers, scorpions … and not to mention the pirate lords and their men, who are like animals themselves. Only a creature of the wild can survive in there!'

At those words Govinda burst out laughing, wondering how he had overlooked the obvious. He then suggested they send for Shikandin and Panchala's Eastern Guard.

Dharma received Govinda's small scroll bearing this suggestion within days, thanks to the messenger pigeons for which Panchali had petitioned DwaipayanaVyasa at the very beginning of the imperial campaign. The Vyasa had graciously acquiesced and his beloved messenger pigeons now seamlessly knit the web of information that held the campaign together while more permanent methods of communication were put in place.

If Dharma found the slightest joy in the ease of correspondence, he did not show it, reluctant as he was to follow the advice that this particular missive held. Over time he had come to notice both Govinda's fondness for Shikandin as well as Dhrupad's dislike of him. Both factors made him reluctant to trust the man.

'Perhaps you should lead the men there instead, Dhrystydymn,' Dharma suggested to the younger Panchala prince.

Dhrystydymn said, 'With all due respect, Dharma, do you have any intentions of putting an end to the piracy, or do you just want to look like you're trying to do something?'

'Why, certainly I plan to end this horror. I want those pirates brought to justice!' Dharma bristled.

'In that case,' Dhystydymn pointed out, 'send Shikandin.'

Panchali too prevailed on Dharma in her own, subtle way, sympathizing with his need to make the difficult moral decision to send his brother-in-law on such a hopeless mission. 'One can't even roll a pair of dice there to bet on his chances, I suppose,' she jested. 'I hear there's hardly any land – it's all one huge swamp.'

Her persuasion, coupled with the news of more casualties, finally led Dharma to agree. And so it was that four years and a month to the day since the first of the troops had left Indr-prastha, as Nakul marched to war to reclaim the frontier lands, Shikandin and fifty of his men from Panchala's Eastern Guard arrived at Magadha to begin their own smaller, but equally dangerous, war with the pirate chiefs of the east.

Shikandin and his soldiers were no strangers to ambushes and waylays or to jungle warfare. For generations the Eastern Forests of Panchala had been the veritable border between central Aryavarta and the lands beyond. The men of the Eastern Guard had been trained to defend their homeland against every kind of enemy. What made these soldiers unique, though, was that the Eastern Forests were dangerous in themselves, serving as home to many wild beasts as well as deadly forest tribes who chose to live in seclusion and fought hard to protect it.

Bhim expressed his relief at the arrival of the hardy fighters, but it was not without some concern.

'Just the fifty of you? You won't last two weeks in that place!'

'Your Highness, Shikandin alone could last years in there and wreak havoc while he's at it. Fifty of us is more than enough,' said Devajit, a tall, lanky man with a sharp, patrician nose. He was Shikandin's half-brother by a palace concubine, and proud of it. His easy familiarity with Shikandin, however, came not from this relationship but from hard-earned rank. Devajit was a captain of the Panchala Eastern Guard and a fellow fighter.

True to Devajit's words, though their numbers were small, Shikandin and his men moved about like ghosts, avoiding every trap the enemy had laid and setting up many of their own. For two years they disappeared, seemingly without a trace. The forest dwellers spoke of them only as a nameless force, a dreaded creature of the woods, who appeared out of nowhere and was gone before it could be seen. As for the pirate chiefs, they finally met their match in these men. Shikandin's tactics were unlike any they had encountered so far. In addition to the usual stake-lined pits and hidden creeper nets, Shikandin and Devajit devised an underwater trap – a simple rope loop, which they set into the shallow bed of the swamp. When one of the pirates stepped into the loop, it sprung a reed lever, which immediately pulled the rope tight around the man's leg and dragged him into the water. It was tough work laying the long ropes in the sticky clay bed of the canals that made up the swamplands, but once the traps were set they were difficult for any quarry to spot and once caught they were impossible to escape from. The legend began to take root that the forests themselves had come alive to destroy evil.

Shikandin was only too happy to give up due recognition and encourage such tales, something Bhim did not quite comprehend. 'A man can give up anything but this,' he argued with Govinda. 'Valour and honour are the only thing that truly defines us. How can Shikandin not care for these things?'

Govinda smiled affectionately at the thought of his friend. 'Shikandin,' he said, 'believes that valour lies in getting things done. He knows that these legends will last and serve to keep new pirates from coming up long after he has left the place. If he takes credit the piracy will start again the moment he leaves.'

'By that logic,' Bhim pointed out, 'even empires should fall once the men who built them are gone.'

'Indeed they will,' Govinda said. 'Unless you make legends of them too.'

Bhim's reservations were soon assuaged as news began to come in that the pirate lords who were still alive were surrendering, one by one, to the kings of Kalinga or Vanga, asking for mercy and reprieve. As the Kalinga coast regained its ancient reputation for safety, trade boomed and the region began to prosper. In the end, a newer, stronger treaty was set in place with the grateful King Srutayus and work began on extending the Great Road from Magadha to the key ports of Kalinga.

At this time Panchali proposed mirroring the new eastern stretch of the Great Road in the west. Linking Dwaraka to the Great Road, she observed, would connect it over land to Kalinga, resulting in a much shorter journey than sailing around the southern peninsula of Dakshinavarta. The proposed highway served to seal Sadev's negotiations with the powerful kings of Kishkinda and Pandya, as well as their allies. Soon after, work began on the web of roads that would connect the two great ports of the east and west, and link the northern mountain pass to the peninsular plains. Aryavarta was becoming one glorious empire. Dharma's empire.

14

WITH MATTERS SETTLING SOMEWHAT IN THE EAST, GOVINDA SPOKE to Bhim of returning to Dharma's side at Indr-prastha. But news reached them at Magadha that Partha had run into trouble on his northern mission. For the past six years, the northern conquests had gone better than planned and Partha had been able to raise a vast fortune through tributes from the newly acquired vassals there. The many victories had, however, cost him dearly in terms of his armies. More than two-thirds of his forces had been lost and what remained of it was simply not enough to defend the fortunes he had raised on their journey back through hostile territory.

Govinda left right away with more than half of Bhim's troops, as well as food and other supplies, to help Partha. He followed in reverse the same path Partha was to have taken on his return, trekking through

Deva-prastha, a gorge in the White Mountains that connected the northern-most hill ranges of the Kashi–Kosala kingdom – the largest and most loyal vassal of Magadha – with the mountain kingdoms of Nepa and Cinna. That particular year though, there were an exceptional number of landslides in the region; enough, in fact, to suggest that nature was not the only malevolent force at work.

It was, therefore, with grim relief that Partha welcomed the weary Govinda and his bedraggled soldiers. He threw his arms around the other man, letting go quickly as Govinda winced, ostensibly from the pain from some injury. 'What happened?' he asked, more as a matter of course than of conversation.

'Landslide,' Govinda replied. 'Or rather, I should say, landslides. At least six of them.'

Partha's eyes widened as the hidden implications of such events came to mind. In a hushed voice, he asked, 'How many men have you lost?'

'More than half,' Govinda replied. 'We saved most of the food and other supplies though. Hopefully, it should be enough for us all to get back.'

'It will take us at least three months to reach the borders of Kosala …' Partha pointed out.

Govinda shook his head. 'It will take us much longer. The trail through Deva-prastha is blocked. We'll have to find another way home.'

'Blocked? By Hara! But … how …?'

'Like I said, landslides.'

Partha's joy at seeing Govinda again all but disappeared. 'If we can't go back through Deva-prastha …'

'We'll have to go further east, find another pass. And the faster we move, the better. Winter is almost upon us. Many of these mountain paths will become inaccessible and I want to be out of the highlands before that. It's not going to be easy, Partha, and there's no point pretending that our position is anything but precarious. But if we get out of the higher regions before winter sets in …' Govinda shrugged lightly and left it at that.

Partha nodded. He had faced extremes of weather since he

had left Indr-prastha on his journey of conquest, to the point that he had almost forgotten the familiar, native climate of Kuru. In the first couple of years, the trek northwards from Bhogavati had been, in retrospect, comfortable enough. For the most part he only remembered the cold, and that too with some astonishment that there could be so many different degrees of chilly weather. There were the more subtle but deadly dangers of the icy winter along the Great Mountains and the misery of freezing winds that ripped all life from barren mountainscapes during the so-called summer months. The pleasantly warm sunlight had initially promised some reprieve from the wind, but Partha had soon learned that the thin air of the high altitudes turned the sun into a silent killer.

By his third summer in the mountains, Partha no longer noticed the irony of sweating under thick furs while a cold wind blew all around them. By the fourth winter – his sixth in total since he had left Indr-prastha – he had learned the most important lesson of them all. Men died in the ruthless winters of the White Mountains. The barren lands claimed their due victims every season, no matter what one did to try and stay alive. After all this while it had become a simple calculation for Partha, one that now told him that Govinda was right. They could not afford one more winter in these lands. None of them would survive.

His eyes dark, Partha asked. 'What power can do this, Govinda? What power could cause entire mountains to move, the earth to shake and explode this way? What demonic force conspires against us so?'

Govinda said nothing, though the nagging guilt that he should have killed Devala Asita even before the imperial campaign had begun tugged at him. But if he had, he would not have known how to explain it to Panchali. It would not do, Govinda reminded himself, for reasons of political expediency and personal preference both to have her hate him any sooner than she had to. But someday, he would have much to say to her, and no doubt, she likewise. His last thought as he fell asleep, lying with his back to Balahak's warm body, his second and third ribs bandaged tight by Partha's medic, was that he had not seen her in years.

'Your Highness?'

Govinda woke at the touch on his shoulder. He sat up, pushing aside the thick blanket that covered him, and wriggled his toes to restore the flow of blood to his feet. In these parts, anyone who wanted to keep their feet attached to their legs knew better than to sleep without the fur-lined boots that every soldier wore. He thought fondly, as he had every morning for the past some weeks, of a hot bath and the feel of crisp cotton robes, but settled instead for drinking in the white, pristine beauty around him.

On all sides, as far as the eye could see, ran tall mountains, most of them covered in snow. Their camp was located in the Highland Core, the sprawling plains between the different ranges of the White Mountains, an immeasurably vast tract of land that knew no comparison with any other place he had seen in all his travels. Its starkness and its sheer size were humbling, yet its silent expanse was comforting in its own way. Govinda breathed in deep of the thin air, enjoying the solitude that these harsh lands held in their keeping. His eyes then came to rest on a ridge of peaks that lay to the east. These, he knew, were the mountains they would have to cross to emerge from the flatlands on to the path that would lead them home.

'Your Highness?' The same soldier who had woken him up held out a bowl of boiling hot water for him to wash his face.

Govinda took it with a smile, and said, 'Henceforth, my friend, there are two things that I need you to never forget. The first is, wake me up before we break camp and not after.' He gestured to where most of the men stood, ready and mustered to march on. Even Balahak had been saddled, presumably by Partha.

'Understood, Your Highness. And the second thing?' the soldier asked, eager and obedient.

Govinda stared at him for a moment, taking in his youth, his unlined face. The man, more a boy, was hardly more than eighteen or twenty, he supposed. Brushing aside the host of thoughts that rushed at him, Govinda reached out to pat him on the back. 'The other is: Never call me Highness. My name is Govinda Shauri.'

Whether it resulted from the news of that friendly encounter, or the much more important arrival of food and reinforcements, Partha's men appeared to regain hope and energy. To his delight, they set out at a good pace. The entire company marched on foot, the thin air making it inadvisable to ride their horses unless they had to. What made the journey most frustrating was that while their destination lay clearly visible on the horizon, at the end of a day's march the mountains would seem no nearer than they had the previous day.

It took them nearly eight weeks to reach the foothills that marked the end of the Highland Core. Only then did the towering height of the cliffs truly strike them. The peaks that had looked ordinary from a distance now looked as though they pierced the sky. The weather, too, was daunting. Though winter had yet to grip the region, it had grown much colder and icy winds blew relentlessly. Partha, however, decided to continue onwards, citing the importance of getting across the mountains before the snow piled too deep. The crossing itself was a much slower affair. Most of their supplies and their many treasures were already loaded on to the yaks, animals native to the terrain that Partha had procured early on in his travels through the region. In some places, however, it became necessary to physically coerce the animals, especially the horses, to move. Govinda would grit his teeth whenever the men whipped one of the animals, but he also knew better than to intervene. Terrain such as this made for terrible tempers, and the threat of dissension and infighting was real.

By the time they reached the small settlement at the foothills of the mountains on the other side, they had lost a good fifty men and as many animals. In a clear sign of how nerve-wracking the journey had been, no one suggested stopping in order to make a pyre to burn their dead. Come the spring thaw, Govinda grimly noted, the wild creatures of these lands were in for a feast.

He did not, however, let the thought affect his appetite as he and Partha dined at the stone-cut house that belonged to the chieftain of the settlement. The two of them made good on the mead-like drink served to them, but refused to strain the resources of the chiefdom further, despite the chief's eagerness to display his allegiance to the

Emperor-to-be. After arranging to buy what could be spared of the settlement's winter supplies of oil, the two men returned to camp to discuss their next move.

'Due east,' Partha began as he stepped into the man-high tent he shared with Govinda. His voice was sombre. 'Four, no, nearly five years now in these accursed lands and I can tell you this much: There isn't anything left here that can defeat us now that we are out of the Core. We keep going east, the settlements get larger, and we can even reach areas that resemble civilization in about three months.'

'Or,' Govinda said, huffing slightly as he took advantage of the mead-fuelled warmth in his body to quickly change his anatariya, 'we could go south till we hit the gorge through which the Lauhitya river runs.' He wrinkled his nose at the dirt-stained garment, wondering whether he ought to indulge himself by throwing it in the fire outside, or put it away in case he needed it again.

Partha stared at him, disbelieving. 'You're mad,' he snapped. 'How in Varuna's name can we descend into the gorge? Don't forget that its upper reaches are almost as high as we now are, Govinda. We'd be dead within moments of even trying to climb down that sheer cliff! And what about the animals?'

'There's a pass, or so I've heard.'

'You've heard?'

'I've heard traders from Cinna speak of it. It's not frequently used and it's supposed to be quite narrow, but it's there. In fact,' Govinda chuckled, 'there are stories in Cinna that many decades ago Firewrights fled Aryavarta by that route ...'

'Stories! Hah! It will be the middle of winter by the time we reach the Lauhitya. Even if this path of yours really exists, we'd never make it down with all the frost and snow.'

'Winter is already on us,' Govinda softly pointed out. 'The next three months are the difference between life and death, Partha. Between your brother ruling an empire and his failure to acquire one. And death is near certain if we insist on staying in these lands. If we head south, we will reach the gorge in less than two weeks, but if we go east ...'

'Mih!' Partha swore, bristling visibly. 'First you say let's go east, and now when I say the same thing you say let's go south! Must you always object to everything? You're not the only warrior in these parts!'

Govinda's eyes narrowed slightly, but he did not retort. Nor did he object when, the next morning, Partha ordered the soldiers to break camp and begin marching east.

15

PARTHA STRODE FORWARD TO WHERE TWO OF HIS CAPTAINS waited, staring uncertainly at the way forward.

'What in the name of the gods is going on? What's the matter?' he roughly demanded. He had been giving instructions to the men in charge of the last sections of their convoy, reminding them yet again not to fan out too wide, when he realized that the cavalcade was slowing down. By the time he reached the head of the formation, they had come to a complete halt.

'Didn't you two hear me? I asked you what was going on.' Partha glared at them both. His rage was enough to make even the two war-hardy men hesitate.

'The Commander …'

'What commander? I am in command of this army!'

'Commander Govinda …'

Partha drew in an angry breath. For a moment, he looked like he was on the verge of losing his temper. When he spoke again, it was in a quiet, chilling tone. 'What did *Commander* Govinda say?'

'He … he said the ice is too thin.'

'Too thin?' Partha's voice rose to a shout. 'And how does he, a man with barely two months' experience in these lands, know ice from marble? Where is he?'

In response, one of the captains pointed. Some distance away, Govinda and Balahak were standing at the edge of what looked like a smooth expanse of ice, quite unlike the gravelled snow that crunched underfoot as Partha strode angrily towards them.

'Ah, Partha. The lake here ...' Govinda began as he heard the other man approaching him.

Partha wasted no time on pleasantries. 'Whose imperial campaign is this, Govinda?'

'What ... ?'

'I said, whose campaign is this? In whose name are we here?'

Govinda raised his eyebrows in surprise and then said softly, 'Dharma Yudhisthir.'

Partha nodded once. 'Dharma Yudhisthir. *My* brother. Now, I am ordering every soldier loyal to Dharma Yudhisthir to march across that frozen lake ... That ice goes a good two feet deep. If you really knew anything about this terrain, you'd also know that it doesn't get better than this in these parts.'

Govinda interrupted, his voice a low growl, 'Partha, please. Something is wrong here. Look at this, look at the number of fish that have been trapped in the ice, and that too so close to the surface. This lake froze over almost instantly and that is not natural. It won't take much for those who could bring down landslides on our heads to break the ice underfoot. Look, let's send scouts to find a way around it. In the meantime, we can camp here.'

Partha took a step closer. 'I said, every soldier loyal to Dharma Yudhisthir. The choice is yours.' He walked away to where his captains waited and ordered them to resume marching at once.

Govinda waited, letting the first few soldiers pass by him, till Partha stepped on to the ice. Then he silently fell in with the ranks.

When they were about fifty feet in on the ice, an eerie, high-pitched whinny rent the air, followed by what sounded like the crack of thunder. It was followed immediately by panicked shouts. Govinda and Partha, both of whom were in the middle of the convoy, reacted at once. 'Spread out! Spread out, and head back!' Partha shouted.

'Go!' Govinda told Balahak. Balahak snorted hard and turned to head back. By some unspoken communication, or perhaps by sheer herd instinct, many of the other horses made to follow.

In the meantime, Govinda ran forward to the spot where the ice had broken. He cursed out loud as he saw the perfectly formed circle of ice that had given way, as though some unseen hand had cut away at it. He had no time to waste on anger, he knew, and immediately threw himself on to the frozen surface in an attempt to pull out the men who had fallen into the icy water. But it wasn't just men who were in danger of drowning – seven horses had fallen into the water. Their heart-wrenching cries filled the air as they battled for life. Govinda forced himself to ignore their wide-eyed terror, their wheezing snorts of breath as they froze alive. He knew, no matter how much he wanted to save them there was nothing he could do. Indeed, it was a supreme effort to just pull the floundering soldiers out of the freezing cold water, weighed down as they were by their thick cloaks and now wet fur mantles. Govinda managed to drag two of the men out, and then grabbed wildly at a third. But it was too late. The man was dead. Govinda simply let his body go under. He frowned as he noticed that around him many other soldiers had come forward to save their fellow companions. Far too many.

'Get back!' he shouted. 'Get back now!'

He pushed himself up off the ice, hissing under his breath as he felt the frozen surface shift, ever so slightly. A small fissure was opening up, right where he had lain. The men he had pulled out were not yet out of danger. With a grunt Govinda picked up the lighter-looking of the two men and swung him over his shoulder. He tried to pull the other man along by his cloak but the wet leather slipped out of his grip.

'Maraka!' Govinda swore. He thought for an instant, and then, using his teeth, pulled the thick hide covering from off his right hand. Unmindful of the way the cold wetness shot through his fingers as he caught the soldier's wet cloak, Govinda began his harrowing trek back to solid ground.

The cracking sound grew louder. He heard a fresh round of screams and saw from the corner of his eye that to his right another piece of ice had given way. Grim and resolute, he kept moving forward, knowing that all he could do at that moment was get the two men with him back to safety. Around him, many others tried to help their fellow soldiers as best as they could, but for the most part they could only watch, horrified.

Govinda stumbled as he felt the ice give slightly underfoot, but it did not break. He breathed out hard, willing every bit of speed he could out of his limbs. Only then did he realize that he no longer had any feeling in his right arm; nor could he feel the weight of the prone soldier on his left shoulder. But there was no time to think as Partha shouted to him at the top of his voice and began to run forward.

'No!' Govinda tried to warn him, but his voice was lost in the loud, whip-like crack that rose and fell. He felt the sudden, painful, surge up his feet as the clear, chilled water of lake filled his boots. The man he was dragging along fell once again into the water. Govinda's mind told him to let go, that he could not pull him out again, that he still had a chance to help the other man. But he could neither feel nor move his fingers. His hand remained curled around the dead soldier's cloak and he felt himself being tugged into the water as the body began to sink.

Then Govinda felt Partha's arms around him. 'Keep moving, you fool!' Partha shouted. Together they stumbled the last few feet to safety, the two soldiers – one dead, one barely alive – still with them. Just as they touched solid ground, the ice behind them gave way completely. A sudden storm of cries rose into the air, some ineffective pleas for help but the others shouts of horror and despair. Slowly, the last of the screams faded and all was quiet.

In a low, tired voice, Partha ordered for fires to be built. He knew many more men would die before the day was over.

Night had fallen by the time Partha came up to join Govinda where he sat, warming himself up by a fire.

'Well?' Govinda asked pre-emptively.

Partha let out a sigh and threw himself on to the furs that had been laid out on top of a thick hide. 'We found a clump of dried-out shrubs not too far away, so firewood should not be a problem. As for the men – we've lost twice as many as we did in the morning. The medics are trying to save another twenty of them or so by amputating their limbs, but we can't say for sure if they'll survive. The soldier you carried out … he's going to lose a leg, probably both.'

Govinda sighed, but said nothing. His shoulder and chest still throbbed relentlessly, but he was almost glad of the pain for it told him that sensation had returned to his body. However, he still could not feel the fingers of his right hand and had to rely on his sight to keep the flesh from burning as he tried to thaw it. Around him, he knew, many soldiers had already made the mistake of letting their limbs get too close to the fire for the lack of sensation, and the unpleasant smell of charred skin and flesh that filled the air.

Partha cleared his throat, trying to find the words to say what he had to. 'The medic says that if you don't regain sensation in your fingers soon, we may have to …'

'Cut them off?' Govinda finished, apparently unperturbed at the prospect. 'Did you know that the Nishada prince Ekalavya is supposed to be a really good marksman, even though he's lost the thumb of his arrow-hand?' He considered his right hand for a moment, and then used the left to twist and turn his benumbed fingers a bit. 'I suppose, if the medics leave me a couple of fingers, I should be all right … I could get by using a sword with my left hand, but I don't think I'd be much good with arrows. Not that I'm half as good as you, anyway …'

Partha could not take it anymore. 'Govinda, I'm sorry,' he gasped out. 'I …'

'Enough, Partha,' Govinda gently chided. 'Your problem is that you take on far too much guilt. You really should learn to be a little more arrogant about your mistakes. There's nothing wrong in making them, as long as one does a good job of that …'

'But, I …'

'Please, let it go. Or else I'll have to get the medics to remove my ears, frozen or not.'

Partha drew in a deep breath and nodded. He watched the fire for a while and then stood up. 'I need to go check on our supplies,' he said. Pausing, he added, 'I hope to be able to leave here in two days. With so many men lost, we have enough horses for the injured to ride on, so I think it's best we move as soon as we can. I … we … we'll head south, Govinda. We'll head for the Lauhitya.'

Govinda nodded silently. He waited till Partha left before

stretching himself out next to the fire. He tried to remain awake and keep moving as much of his right arm as he could, but at some point a weary sleep took him. The next morning, he woke up to a sharp, stinging pain at the tips of his fingers, the beginnings of sensation returning to them. He also found out from one of the medics that Partha had sat up next to him all night, rubbing his numb hand.

As planned, they broke camp in two days and headed south. It took them a little less than three weeks to reach the gorge through which the Lauhitya flowed. The sound of the wild river thundered up the walls of the narrow gorge to reach them where they stood, looking down at its foam-flecked waters. A few murmurs of apprehension rose as the men considered the descent before them, but Partha remained resolute. He sent scouts to look for the path that Govinda had heard about, in the meantime quelling all discontent with an even mix of reassurances and punishments. It had been nearly a week by the time the scouts returned with news of a narrow but relatively clear path that had been cut into the face of the cliff.

The descent proved to be a test of endurance and courage rather than a danger in itself. The path was wide enough for no more than five men or two fully laden horses to walk abreast, which meant that the entire army had to spread out in a long procession. What also made it demanding was that, once on the path, it was difficult to stop for more than a short while, and absolutely impossible to set up camp of any sort. Fighting hunger and sleep, the men had to march on at a stretch.

It took nearly two days and a night of incessant trudging before the first group of soldiers reached the rocky ledges that served as the banks of the river. The air was palpably warmer and brought with it the first traces of verdure the men had seen in a long while. Despite his weariness, Govinda immediately stripped off his clothes and jumped into one of the pools formed by the spray from the raging river collecting in hollows along the ledge. It was far too dangerous to swim in the river here, or to even try and stand in the water along its banks. Partha laughed as Govinda finally emerged from his impulsive bath feeling a bit cold, but cleaner than he had in months.

'Almost there now,' he remarked. 'We are almost in Aryavarta.'

Govinda raised a surprised eyebrow. 'Almost? My friend, every person, every chief and king in the lands we have crossed owe their allegiance to Dharma Yudhisthir. This *is* Aryavarta.'

16

'SOMETIMES, PARTHA,' GOVINDA SAID, 'I CAN'T HELP BUT wonder ... Are we warriors, or politicians? The question has come to mind many times over these past years ...'

Partha adjusted the heavy armour he wore under his leather cloak, redistributing its weight on his frame. Underneath the metal, his clothes clung to his skin, wet and heavy. The two men stood on the turrets of Pragjya, the mighty city on the eastern border of Aryavarta. The city was nestled into the rocky terrain of a lesser mountain range that ran parallel to the White Mountains, taking advantage of what shelter the hills could provide against the rain. In all, it was a dreary, monotonous expanse of black rock and dark forests, ominous and foreboding.

It had taken Partha and Govinda another seven harrowing months to trek from where they had descended into the gorge of the wild Lauhitya in its upper reaches all the way down to where the river split, timid and harmless, on to the plains. From there, their journey had grown immensely more comfortable, for they had lacked neither hospitable vassals nor adequate supplies. When they had finally neared Pragjya, Partha had soaked, overjoyed, in the warm rains he encountered there. His joy had been short-lived. After all those years in the White Mountains, Partha had reckoned himself seasoned, both in terms of weather and in terms of terrain, but never in all his travels had he found the weather so enervating, depressing even. It never stopped raining in these lands.

Govinda, however, treated the elements with a mix of reverence and diffidence, which allowed him to find simple, though admittedly less-than-comfortable, solutions. In this instance, he had opted to discard his armour completely and let the heavy cloak rest directly on his thin tunic. The only obvious reaction he had shown so far to the rain was to express concern over the rust on the metal bits of his horse's saddle. Both men kept on their hide-covered boots, as did the rest of the soldiers. It would not do to underestimate the infestation of snakes and leeches in the verdant undergrowth that was the result of the unique weather.

And then there was the river.

The sparkling waters of the incredibly wide and mighty Lauhitya shimmered as far as the eye could see. Like a sea, the opposite shore lay out of sight, even on a clear day. Its sheer expanse was breathtaking, movingly so. And now it was also impassable. Humble and unaware of its own might the river meandered on, slow and inexorable. Incessant storms broke over it into a million insignificant drops of rain that were no match for the great sheet of water. The river simply consumed each droplet and moved on. The rain fell all the time. The river flowed on. Nothing, it seemed, could quench its thirst.

Once, many years ago, Govinda had been here. It had been one of the battles that had brought him his early fame. All of Aryavarta knew that he had fought and killed the former king of Pragjya. Few knew why that battle had been fought. Then, he had been here as an enemy and conqueror. This time he was the honoured guest of the young ruler, King Bhagadatta.

The son of the man I killed. Govinda had never thought he would return to this place, but now that he had, he knew better than to dwell too long on the fact. Bhagadatta had, so far, been nothing but genuinely friendly. He had welcomed them and their army without hesitation and he had also helped Govinda send a message to Magadha, advising Bhim of their arrival at Pragjya. As a result, Shikandin and his men joined them at Pragjya a few weeks later, bringing with them the news that Nakul and Sadev had successfully returned to Indr-prastha, their missions successful. Now, all that was left for Govinda, Partha and Shikandin to do was to make their way to

Magadha and then, along with Bhim, begin a victorious march home to Indr-prastha. The imperial campaign was nearly at its end.

Yet, Govinda found it hard to share in the general sense of victory and jubilation that was in the air. The conquest, he knew, was not over till it was truly over. Their intentions were no longer secret and Western Kuru itself was vulnerable and exposed. As for their armies – they still had to return to Indr-prastha. Now, it appeared, the hardest task would be getting them home.

Just that morning Bhagadatta had offered to have his best guides lead them south from Pragjya, following the course of the river to parts that were under his control. From there, Govinda, the others, and their men could cross the river and begin making their way westward, towards Indr-prastha. However, his proposal had not been without due warning.

'As a man of war,' Bhagadatta had pointed out, 'I must counsel you – the packed-mud bunds and the smaller bridges of the south won't take the weight of your marching armies. Death is not just a risk, it is a certainty. Given this weather, you're better off crossing at the ford into the kingdom of Kashi. It is the only one strong enough to get you across the river.'

Kashi was indeed the most direct and easy route back to central Aryavarta. To its south lay Magadha, the land stretching eastwards till it ended in a dark, dense forest along the banks of the Lauhitya – the effective boundary with Bhagadatta's kingdom. For all ostensible purposes Kashi and its king, Sudakshin, held no hostility towards the returning Kuru armies – after all, Govinda had passed through Kashi–Kosala to reach Deva-prastha. But the memory of the landslides at Deva-prastha still lurked in their minds and now Shikandin's scouts warned of a trap, of strange, inexplicable events that they did not quite know what to make of. Villages, it was said, had emptied overnight, farmlands left fallow, and strange men came and went from the forts around the eastern borders of Kashi. It was enough to make Govinda hesitate, particularly as Bhagadatta continued to dissuade them from crossing the river anywhere but at the ford into Kashi.

Partha, too, remained suspicious of their host. He wondered if this was part of Bhagadatta's plan to seek vengeance against Govinda. *Or perhaps I just blame him for the despair which already cloaks my reason,* he mused as he watched the rain cover the grey stone walls with a shiny veneer of green. The endless downpour, he noted, was enough to depress anyone, even someone as imperturbable as Govinda.

'You're a warrior in every sense of the word, my friend,' Partha finally replied to Govinda's questions. 'It's these endless conspiracies that have made a politician out of you. Does Bhagadatta lie, or does he tell the truth? Is the way through Kashi truly barred? Were the landslides at Deva-prastha really the act of an enemy, or a freak act of nature? How can we make any sense of all this?'

Govinda laughed. 'There's a phrase I once heard from a very wise man. He told me that there's a difference between the reason for something that has happened and the explanation for it. We often mistake one for the other. The landslides, Bhagadatta's warm welcome and his warnings ... We're left with only one way back home. Through Kashi.'

'Which doesn't sound too bad, really. After all, Sudakshin of Kashi, has only been too glad to accept Dharma's suzerainty in place of Jarasandha's. Not to mention that he has affirmed enough treaties to that effect and paid Bhim a generous tribute these past years.'

'And in return he has received a great degree of autonomy and independence – I can't help but wonder if it was a mistake. Rudra knows what he's been up to inside his old fortress. Don't forget, Kashi is an ancient kingdom and has historically been a powerful one till the past half-century or so. It won't do to dismiss it.'

'But Sudakshin's never shown any hostility towards us. Well, not yet ...'

'Neither did we, once, when Jarasandha was *our* Emperor. Never forget how we got here, Partha. Our would-be ousters will take exactly the same path. If this is a trap ...'

Partha looked despondent. 'Then, there is no way out, is there? The snare has been well set. Even if we win a battle against Sudakshin and his armies, the political repercussions are enough to doom the imperial campaign as a whole. And if we lose … If only we had more time!'

'We certainly can't wait any longer,' Shikandin said, coming up to join the two men. 'Bhim doesn't know why we are stuck here. He may even suspect Bhagadatta … I worry that Indr-prastha is already beset with rumours of our failure, even our death.'

'What I don't understand,' Partha said, exasperated, 'is why they can't get word to us! Surely, someone of Dwaipayana's wisdom and resources … Couldn't they get even a sage, or a spy dressed as one, out to us? And what about those pigeons? They worked even in the snow-tipped heights of the White Mountains, till we entered the Highland Core. Why then can't they get here? There's no way I can keep the men in line much longer. The weather here is enemy enough to kill them. It rains incessantly and the mist hardly rises. Sickness is inevitable despite Bhagadatta's hospitality, and so are discontent and rebellion.'

'Look,' Shikandin said, 'let me try getting across with a few of my men. Either we'll make it through and come back with reinforcements, or else I'll at least track down the messengers we've sent already. Give me a couple of weeks. I'll come back with news either way.'

'And if you don't?'

'If I don't, I don't. Frankly, I'm surprised that none of us is dead yet!'

'It's like the old stories the bards tell,' Govinda lightly remarked. 'The heroes never die.'

'That's because dead men don't make for good heroes,' Shikandin retorted. 'They are there in the stories all right – as the honourable friends and companions who fall by the wayside. And then the heroes go back and romance pretty princesses.'

'Ah, but the dead friends get the pick of Indra's nymphs in the celestial afterlife, or so we hear.'

Shikandin feigned a serious look, though the gleam in his eyes gave him away. 'Royal propaganda!' he declared. 'Nothing but utter rubbish designed to lure innocent fools like me into throwing their lives away for these entitled nobles. Dead men get nothing!'

Partha did not find the exchange amusing at all. 'Dead men don't win battles either. This whole plan is pointless, Shikandin. Worse, it may provoke our enemy in ways we can't foresee yet. It's sheer foolhardiness.'

'Is it?' Shikandin raised a contemptuous eyebrow. 'Think about it, Partha. If I don't come back, you'll know for sure that danger lies ahead. You can then decide what to do. It's better than sitting here, waiting and wondering if we ought to trust Sudakshin or Bhagadatta, not knowing whether to stay or leave. Let me do this ...'

'All right,' Govinda nodded.

'But ...' Partha began to object.

Govinda interjected, 'Do you trust me, Partha?'

'Yes, of course!' Partha regarded Govinda with affection. Either spurred by the feeling or for emphasis, he threw an arm around Govinda's shoulders and slapped him on the back.

Govinda nodded his thanks. 'In that case, prepare your armies. Spread the word that we'll cross over into Kashi territory at the earliest. In the meantime, Shikandin, go ahead with your plan.'

Partha stared, open-mouthed. 'But ...' he repeated.

'If our enemy's idea was only to dissuade us, they'll know that they've failed. Once we start mobilizing the men, our enemy, whoever they might be, will be forced to make their next move ... It may give us some clue as to what is really going on.'

'And then? What if it really is a trap ...?'

'Then we must walk into it,' Govinda said. 'We're running out of time and, sitting here, are far too isolated from Dharma and the others to change our strategy. We must get back quickly if the imperial campaign is to succeed. Failure means more than just dishonour, Partha. It means death. We and those we love wouldn't live for more than a week, with all the new enemies we've made ...'

Partha immediately longed to ask a question of his own, but restrained himself. The thought, however, did not disappear easily. A man like Govinda could have been Emperor if he had put his mind to it. Instead, he chose to remain a vassal to Dharma. For once, Partha could not help but wonder why.

17

THE WOMAN WAS ASTONISHINGLY GORGEOUS. HER ATTIRE WAS not sheer and revealing, like a courtesan's; instead, she was draped in the fine cotton robes worn by the highest class of attendants. Nevertheless, there was something seductive about her, and she knew it well. She walked into the main hallway of the palace without hesitation, inclining her head ever so slightly in greeting at the departing Shikandin. Shikandin's steps slowed down just that much and his eyes twinkled with appreciation, but he did not stop.

Just as well, the woman made a mental note. This was the Panchala prince she had been told about. While she knew better than to indulge her temptation and be rid of him, too, for a fleeting moment the thought did cross her mind. Not that he was safe from harm. If he was going into the forests on the other side of the river as his clothes suggested, death was certain anyway. As for her, she had another quarry to hunt. Govinda Shauri.

That evening, she came up to where Govinda sat in the banquet hall with Partha, bringing them some more wine. Govinda shot her an appreciative look. Her skin was smooth as velvet and her impossibly proportionate body was voluptuous, yet delicate. Her full red lips and her swaying gait were delightfully predictable, stereotypically feminine, yet he found her presence inexplicably pleasing. She met his gaze and colour flooded her pale cheeks. Lowering her eyes, she refilled their cups and moved away. A light, seductive fragrance lingered, stirring up the most primal instincts in the two men.

'She's new,' Partha noted, breathing out hard to regain his senses. Govinda merely furrowed his brows and nodded. 'You don't suppose this is Bhagadatta's doing? What monarch would allow new palace staff in times like these?'

'Times like these?' Govinda was disdainful. 'We're the ones at war, Partha, not he. But you're right. We'd better suggest to him that he double his guards and give them strict instructions not to let any new courtesans or handmaidens into his bedchambers.'

Partha was not assured, 'I doubt she's after him. Assassins are rather expensive, but worth every piece of gold when it comes to getting the task done.'

Govinda's tone was soft, but chilling. 'There are worse things to fear than a simple assassin ...'

'Oh?'

'She's a Kritya.'

'Kritya?' Partha was shocked. 'They're some kind of killers, right?'

'Indeed, Krityas are assassins like no other. They are brought up from childhood on a perfectly balanced diet of poison and antidote that makes their very bite and scratch lethal. They are also trained to use their body as a deadly weapon, not to mention the other tools they supposedly have – daggers that fold up into innocuous hair ornaments, jewels coated with poultices that can seduce a man or render him senseless.'

Partha glanced at the now-distant figure of the woman and let out a deep breath. 'I thought ... I thought only the ancient kings used Krityas and such. Do they really even exist anymore?'

'Apparently they do. You see, Partha, when the Firstborn sanctioned the scourge, the systematic hunting down of the Firewrights many decades ago, not everyone showed the same diligent obedience as the Kurus. Some kings, particularly those of the east, were happy to take young Firewright girls alive ...'

'To be trained as Krityas? Does that mean this woman is ...'

'I've no idea who she is. But of what she is, I have no doubt. Mmm! Bhagadatta's cook has outdone himself tonight.'

Partha grimaced at Govinda's sudden frivolity, but said nothing. He couldn't help but wonder if their host had been the one to engage the Kritya, after all.

The Kritya was waiting in Govinda's rooms when he returned from the banquet. She pretended not to notice him as he walked in, busy as she was with lighting the many lamps in the chamber. Out of the corner of her eye, she saw him throw off his upper robe and settle himself in a chair, with a scroll.

She turned around, feigning surprise at finding him there. Blushing slightly, she walked up to where he sat and, standing close, reached out to touch him. The tips of her fingers rested lightly on his inner wrist, exactly on the pulsing spot at a certain angle off the median nerve. No man she knew had ever resisted this gesture. Govinda looked into her eyes and smirked.

Embarrassed and enraged, she tried to turn away, brushing against him in the process. He ignored her, and went about his business as though she did not exist. He did not look up even when she ran out of his room, pretend tears sliding down her cheeks. It was, she admitted to herself as soon as she was outside, possibly a tactical mistake on her part. It would have taken just a moment to stab him if she hadn't felt the urge to kill him the way only she could. But then, she reasoned, this once she would allow herself the indulgence. After all, there was no way she could fail.

No man could resist her beauty, not even the famed Govinda Shauri. That was a lesson she had learnt early in life.

The Kritya paused for a moment in the open corridor, enjoying the clean breeze, the light spray from the omnipresent rain. She remembered little of the initial years of her training, except for the dark hall-like castle, which had been perpetually lit by braziers and fires. She had hardly seen the sun, and remembered no face and no name, not even her own. There had been no other children, just an endless bustle of adults, and though she lived in luxury and was waited on hand and foot, there had been something dismal and horrible about it all.

When she was sixteen, her guardians had deemed her ready to be presented to the king. She had walked into the room, dressed in bridal finery, expecting an old man. To her surprise, it was the young crown prince who was waiting for her.

'My little assassin!' he had greeted her. 'Father will soon leave me a splendid gift along with his throne, I see … Perhaps we can begin with a small demonstration of your skills …'

Rising, she had made towards the bed, only to stop as the prince began laughing uproariously, slapping his thigh in glee.

'Do you take me for an idiot? Or do you think that I'm as weak as other men? If I've resisted you despite your beauty, if I've let you train as a Kritya all these years, it was only because you'll be more useful in other men's beds than mine. The slightest nip of your teeth during a tender kiss, or a scratch from your nails in the heat of passion … I'd be a dead man!' he burst out laughing again. 'Go,' he waved her out of the room. 'You'll have your first quarry to hunt soon, I promise.'

That night she had cried for the first and last time in her adult life. It took a while for her to really understand the prince's words, for the last thing that she had thought to do was harm him. But, she realized, this was what she had become. No living being could ever trust her again, care for her. She was Death itself.

The prince soon became a king, and he kept his promise. She hunted many a man down, killing without a trace. She met the monarch often and he had soon warmed up to her. There had been times when the two of them had spent a pleasant evening in conversation. But he was always careful to maintain his distance. He would not as much as touch a glass of wine if she poured it for him, or take directly in his hands a scroll she held out. That apart, he treated her well. She had her own palace and staff, and occupied a place of honour at social occasions, even appearing sometimes at his court. Jewels, riches, land – anything she could want was hers. She was special, and he let her know it.

Years passed and there came a time when he summoned her only to perform the most critical of tasks – tasks that he undertook on behalf of Emperor Jarasandha. She had met the Emperor once. It was all the same – politeness, geniality and distance. As she left the room, she had overheard Jarasandha remark, 'It's a real pity! She's a fine woman. Almost makes you want to risk it …'

It had made her smirk with self-satisfaction. The only thing more powerful than her beauty was the fear of death.

Content for the present at that thought, she made her way through the dark corridors of the palace, towards the handmaidens' chambers. Just as she left the royal enclosure, one of the guards on duty accosted her. She neither wanted to submit to his attentions nor run the risk of drawing attention by calling out for help. She dealt with the leering man in the simple, effective way of driving one of her poisoned hairpins through his neck. Taking great care to draw the pin back out and making sure that she had left no tell-tale sign, she made her way to the room she shared with two other girls. In a place like Pragjya, drunken squabbles were common, and a dead soldier was not a matter for much comment.

As the Kritya had expected, Bhagadatta did indeed dismiss the death of the nightwatch as being of no worth. However, in a rare act that strained his authority somewhat, the commandant of Bhagadatta's personal guard sent for Govinda and Partha.

Govinda had to take just one look at the already-darkened skin around the dead man's puncture wound to know that the Kritya had done it. He mentioned nothing to Bhagadatta, and merely reminded the commandant to double the guards around the king's quarters. He waved off the offers for more sentries around his and Partha's chambers, and made his way back to the privacy of his room, a clearly irate Partha in tow.

'Why didn't you tell them? They could have hauled her out in moments and we'd be done with this.' Partha challenged Govinda, the moment they were alone.

Govinda didn't reply, instead posing a question of his own. 'What do you think it feels like, Partha? A life where you can't know simple human touch, the most meagre of affections, because people fear you? Or, worse still, because you're afraid of hurting them? How horrible it must be ...'

'Is that why you ...? Oh Rudra! Come on, Govinda. She's an assassin. She doesn't deserve such compassion.'

For a moment, Govinda thought to make some comment about Partha's rather obvious, and perhaps excessive, proclivity for female companionship, but then decided against it.

Oblivious, Partha went on, 'What are you going to do?'

'She'll be back tonight. I'm sure of it.'

'Right. Will you kill her, or shall I?'

Govinda's eyes were cold as he declared, 'I'll take care of her.'

18

IT WAS WELL PAST MIDNIGHT WHEN THE KRITYA RETURNED TO Govinda's room. The entire palace had settled into a deep stupor despite, or perhaps because of, the unexpected excitement the guard's death had caused earlier that evening. Govinda woke up as she lit the single lamp that hung overhead, just off his bed. Smiling all the while, she pulled off her robes languorously, letting him get a good look at her naked form. Then she slipped into bed next to him.

'Please,' she whispered, letting her tongue lightly graze his ear, 'please let me stay. Don't tell me to go.'

'Is that what you say to them all?' Govinda asked her, his tone amused but undeniably scathing. He lay on his side, one arm tucked under his head.

'Who am I to refuse orders …' she said, tracing her fingers across the tattoo-like mark on his bare chest, before slowly wrapping her arm around him and sliding closer.

Govinda did not stir. 'Indeed,' he said, 'especially if you've been ordered to take pleasure in your quarry's attentions.'

'Don't tease me,' she pouted, feeling confident of her skills once more. 'Which one of us is the hunter, and which one is the quarry? Women willingly become your prey at one look from you. What woman would turn down the attentions of Govinda Shauri, Commander of Dwaraka? Do you have any idea what's said about you, what's whispered among the courtesans and handmaidens? Every woman in the land longs to share your bed.'

'I just hope you have some new lines for me, young lady. I'd feel sorry to know that you repeat yourself to every man.'

'What do you take me for?'

'For what you are …' Govinda propped himself up on his elbows, still looking at her.

'And what's that? A prostitute, or a spy?' she asked, with a flash of anger.

He clucked his tongue in mild remonstration. 'A person. Perhaps a prostitute, perhaps a spy … but that doesn't make you more or less than what you are.'

She gave him a cold look. 'And is your sympathy, your false respect, supposed to warm my heart and make me melt? I don't need it!'

'No, you don't. You carry all the warmth and respect you need inside you – it's not something that I can give or take from you. And I must say, that's really why I find you so attractive …'

The woman sat up straight, not bothering to cover herself. Her voice was matter-of-fact, as she said, 'You needn't bother with the flattery. I don't expect it like your other lovers might.'

'What makes you think I flatter any of them? It would kill me to have to spout adjectives or endearments that I don't really mean.'

A peculiar look entered the woman's eye, like a cat studying the lone sparrow. 'You shouldn't speak so flippantly of death. You never know, Yama – the Lord of Death – might be listening. It could hasten your end.'

'The only way to speak of death is flippantly. Death is what makes life ironical – it eludes you when you want it the most, and seeks you out when you desire it the least. Perhaps, if we manage to perfect our longing for death, we may even become immortal …'

Her perfectly arched eyebrows rose in surprise. 'Why would someone like you long for death?'

'Why do you desire life?'

'Because, it's what is around us. It is reality.'

'So is death. Death is the only reality.'

She pouted and said, 'I hadn't taken you for such a dark, depressing person.'

'And I hadn't thought of you as a philosophical one.'

'I'm a quick learner.'

Govinda placed a gentle hand on her cheek and turned her face towards him. She gasped involuntarily as she looked into his eyes, losing herself in their darkness.

'Well then, aren't you going to finish what you came here for?' he asked her.

The Kritya's hand instinctively curved into a clawed weapon and her shoulder twitched ever so slightly as her mind went through the motions. She could reach for the poisoned brooch on her robes or strike with her bare hands, letting her nails rip right through his flesh to sink into his heart. Better still, she could let him take her, pleasure her, before she sunk her teeth into his skin, drawing blood and letting her poison seep in. A flush of some new emotion – a pleasant shyness mixed with brazen excitement – ran through her at that thought. She preferred to kill quickly, not wasting time on unnecessary intimacies, but perhaps this once, she mused, the exception might be worth the effort.

There was, of course, another choice.

As if he knew what was running through her mind, Govinda gently took her hand by the wrist and brought it close to his lips. He laid a gentle whisper of a kiss on her palm before placing her hand over his heart. She could feel the strong, fearless beat against her fingers. A shiver ran down her spine.

He knew. He knew exactly what she was, the excruciating death that lay ahead of him if she moved but one finger. But he neither feared nor loathed her.

She whipped her hand back and drew in a sharp breath before taking hold of her senses. 'No.' She turned and slid off the bed, her hand outstretched for the robes on the floor. Govinda sat up, and in the same move caught her by the wrist, this time his grip stronger, more urgent.

'Call it what you will,' she said, turning around to face him, 'but I've never killed a man who didn't fear death or hate me for bringing him to it. I can't kill you this way, not by sneaking into your bed and deceiving you. That's something I reserve for indolent cowards … But, before you ask, I'm not going to tell you who sent me. If you want to call the guards and have me arrested, go ahead. Although, something tells me you won't.'

'No, I won't,' he said, a smile slowly curving his lips, 'and that being the case I see no reason for you to leave. That is, unless you want to ...' He let go of her wrist.

The assassin considered him for a moment, before slowly reaching up for the sleek poisoned dagger that served as a hair ornament. She pulled it out in a determined move, letting her dark hair cascade down her bare back. She twirled the dagger between her fingers with practised ease, before throwing it aside. It landed on top of her already-discarded robes. Moving forward she placed a hand on Govinda's shoulder and gently pushed him back against the pillows. Slightly breathless, she then slid on to the bed and gracefully perched astride him, revelling in the feel of his strong body against hers. Slowly, she lowered herself into his embrace.

The first glimmer of dawn had just appeared in the cloud-laden eastern sky when the Kritya awoke. She lay as she was, pleasantly aware of Govinda's arm around her, of the way his chest rose and fell against her cheek, his breathing deep and even. A smile crossed her lips as she remembered the way Govinda had made love to her the previous night, how they had talked, how he had asked her real name and then held her close when she had cried because she did not know it. Her smile faded and she bit down lightly on her lip, letting the gentle pain remind her not to want what she could not have. With that, she reluctantly slid out of Govinda's light hold and began to get dressed.

'Leaving already?'

She gasped, startled, and then laughed with relief. 'By Hara! And here I was trying not to wake you. So much for my stealth and grace.'

'I think you're delightfully graceful where it counts,' Govinda teased. He got out of bed and removed the metal shade from the wick lamp in a nearby recess, letting a warm glow fill the room. Wrapping his robe around his hips, he moved across the space to pull her into his arms. She resisted for a moment and then gave in as his lips touched hers. 'Stay,' Govinda gently commanded. 'You'll be safe. Whoever it is that sent you, you'll be safe from them. And, I promise you, no one will ask you any questions or expect you to do anything that compromises your integrity.'

The Kritya studied Govinda for a few moments. It had seemed to her, after the events of the previous night, that there was little more he could do to surprise her. Clearly, she had been wrong. Affectionately she said, 'And then? Sooner or later, you'll leave Pragjya. I'll feel rather lonely then, don't you think?'

'Indeed. Which is why I'd have you come with me.'

'Where to?'

'Indr-prastha. And then home, to Dwaraka.'

The Kritya laughed again, reminding Govinda of someone he had once known. Placing her hand gently on his cheek, she declared, 'Your Queen must love you very much, Govinda Shauri, if she puts up with all your antics.'

'She's not *my* Queen. But, yes, she does put up with a lot.'

'She sounds like a good woman.'

Govinda nodded. 'She is. So much so that I'd gladly make her my Empress … Come with me, I'll take you to her. Something tells me you might become good friends. Of course, she'll probably kill you with her curiosity and incessant questions.'

The Kritya let her imagination paint a pleasant picture in her mind, but she shook her head. 'I have an ailing grandmother who needs me urgently …'

Govinda narrowed his eyes, unconvinced.

She shrugged. 'It's a fairly acceptable excuse, don't you think? That's what I plan to tell the chief of the palace staff.'

'In that case, I wish your grandmother well and hope she recovers soon.' Govinda pulled her close for another passionate kiss and then stepped back to let her finish dressing.

She was ready in a few moments. With one last look at herself in the burnished mirror, she made to leave the room. Govinda stood looking out the window, his mind already on other things.

The Kritya paused at the door. 'That man … there was a prince who left here just as I was arriving the other day …'

Govinda turned around. 'Shikandin.'

'Is he a friend of yours?'

'The best I have. Why do you ask?'

She hesitated, but only for a moment, before arriving at a decision. 'He'll need your help. Sudakshin's men watch every foot of the riverbank,' she said.

Govinda's eyes narrowed. 'We saw no troop movement. No soldiers at all ...'

'Yet, they're there. Cross the river at the small ford by the white rock and head north-west. You'll hit one of the smaller tributaries of the Lauhitya. Follow its course upstream to a waterfall. There's a cavern behind the sheet of water. That's where the men make camp. That's where they'll take your friend ...'

19

'THIS IS BAD, SHIKANDIN. THAT'S THREE TEAMS OF OUR MESSENGERS, as well as the four men Bhagadatta sent. There's one man unaccounted for, though. Perhaps he made it through?' said Devajit, bristling at the sight before him.

'I doubt it,' Shikandin replied, using the flat of his sword to turn over one of the corpses before him. Without flinching at the damp-decayed face, he continued, 'He's either still a prisoner, or we just haven't found his body.'

The two were all that remained of the scouting party of six that had left Pragjya nearly a week ago. Three of their companions had been lost in a skirmish with enemy soldiers in which none of the opposition had been left alive. The death of the fourth had been terrifying in its own way for the wilderness-trained men of the Eastern Guard. He had died in his sleep without a stir or a sound, of snake-bite. The dead messengers before them had clearly been less fortunate. Despite their already-rotting forms it was not difficult to see that they had endured great torture and much pain before their lives ended.

Devajit pointed out, 'The bodies ... they're untouched. No wild animal or scavenger has been near them. But they've decayed pretty fast.'

'That's because they've been poisoned. Their flesh has burnt from the inside and is deadly to anything that consumes it. Wild scavengers probably sense that.'

'Poisoned? But why? There are easier ways ...'

'And less painful. Maybe it was a hallucinogen, or some pain-inducing concoction – either as a threat to make them talk or as part of the torment ...'

Devajit spat on the ground in anger. 'Maraka! What sort of men do this?'

Shikandin merely shrugged. 'You think it doesn't happen back at Kampilya? Remind me to have you assigned on duty to our dungeons for a week. Our father takes great pride in the way we treat prisoners, you know.' He pointed to dead men in front of them. 'We sent them out by different routes. If the bodies all washed up at the same spot, it means that they were taken to the same place for interrogation. Maybe they even kept the first set of men captive and killed them all together ... There's probably a camp or base somewhere in these forests.'

'Somewhere upstream?'

'Yes. Upstream, and along this tributary. The Lauhitya is too slow to bring these bodies here. These men were washed ashore when this tributary, whatever it's called, joined the main river. That makes things easier for us. The stream is fairly narrow. It shouldn't be too difficult to find something on either of its banks.'

'In that case we'd better head back at once.'

'*You* need to head back as fast as you can and get word to Govinda. Tell him to send out eight, maybe ten, messengers in groups of two. They are to depart right away and head out at the same time. But they should try to make it through these forests using different routes.'

'But ...?'

Shikandin tersely explained. 'All these men, our men, are dead. It could mean that Sudakshin has his men watching the river and the forest, but not the plains beyond. There's a possibility that if we get messengers through this stretch, they can strike out for the southern regions and make it to Magadha that way. Or even if they get to Kalinga, our vassals there will help them …'

'*Our* vassals, Prince?' Devajit suffixed his contempt with the respectful form of address.

Shikandin drew in an impatient breath. 'They're my, *our*, sister's vassals. She'll be Empress once this is done. We serve her and her purposes. Are you clear about that?'

'I am,' Devajit snapped, this time tellingly omitting the honorific. He studied the dead men before him for a few moments and said, 'It's a good plan. Let's both go back and …'

'Like I said, you have to go back. The messengers are just part of the plan. If they're to have a chance of getting through this time around we need to find this camp or wherever it is that the enemy is. Unless that's destroyed, there's no point sending more men through.'

Devajit drew himself up with all the authority he wielded by virtue of being the older man. 'Shikandin, you can't do this alone. Let's go back and get reinforcements. We know where to begin. We just have to come back to the ford with the white rock and then keep going till we hit this fork in the river. It won't be tough to find, and …'

Shikandin shook his head, by way of reply. 'Go!' he commanded. And then, before Devajit could protest further, he slunk off into the undergrowth.

Shikandin headed upstream, moving confidently through the thick foliage as though he were a creature of the forest. He smiled to himself as it began raining again, and stopped every now and then to let the patterns of sound the raindrops made as they hit leaf and bark tell him what was around him and, more importantly, if he was being watched or followed. As the day wore on, the rain stopped and the forest around him grew denser still. Shikandin was glad for the thick leather cloak with its rather impenetrable hood. He was not a man to complain about a leech or ten, but he certainly did not enjoy them dropping off the branches overhead, right onto his face.

His earlier suspicions about the missing messenger were proven right when he found the body a little further upstream. Like the others, this one too bore the signs of torture and poisoning. His theory that the enemy's camp was situated somewhere along the banks of the tributary now reaffirmed, Shikandin began trekking through the marshy forestland with renewed vigour.

As evening drew close, he began to slow down. Stopping more frequently, he tried hard to catch wisps of smell that he hoped would guide him through the approaching dusk. It was tough, given that the air in the forest was, for the most part, still. At times, the fragrance of night jasmine hung heavy over him, otherwise there was nothing but the thick mossy odour that was native to heavy forests. Shikandin however, did not give up. Camps made for campfires and for hungry men, cooking and food – a smell that was alien to the freshness all around and therefore easily recognized and followed.

Shikandin's stomach appeared to be keener than his nose, for it let out a soft rumble. Moments later the smell of vegetable porridge – a soldier's staple – came floating on a reluctant breeze. Shikandin sniggered to himself. He was hungry, but it could wait – and wait a while if need be. Moving carefully from thicket to thicket, he followed the faint smell of food.

The roar of the river grew louder. Shikandin surmised he was nearing some rapids or perhaps a shallow waterfall. The foliage too had grown thinner around him. The dull glimmer of the evening sun some feet ahead told him he was approaching a clearing. He crouched at the edge of the thicket and peered out. It was a small, rocky space that ran from the patch of greenery where he was now, right up to a small cliff. The river was to his right, falling in a thundering waterfall down the face of the cliff into a natural pool before flowing on into the forest. The clearing looked empty but Shikandin decided to wait, thankful that there were a couple of muhurrtas of light left in the sky.

His patience paid off, for a man soon emerged from behind the curtain of water that was the fall, dressed in the uniform of the

Kashi army. He looked up, scanning the sky for a few moments, and then raised one arm up while holding a piece of meat in the other. Immediately, a mean-looking brown and white falcon-hawk, with yellow markings around its beak and eyes, wheeled down into the clearing and dropped something from its long talons at the man's feet before taking the piece of meat from his hand. It made quick work of the strip of raw flesh and took wing again, letting out a loud cry that tore through the silence of the forest.

The man picked up what the falcon-hawk had dropped. Shikandin could make out the grey-white colour and the feathery outline. He silently mouthed a curse as he realized that it was one of Dwaipayana's messenger pigeons.

The soldier pulled off the tiny scroll tied on the pigeon's leg, calling out to someone behind the curtain of water as he did. The man shouted to be heard behind the waterfall, and the sound echoed through the clearing to reach Shikandin where he remained hidden. He could clearly make out the words: 'Tell the magician we have another message ...'

The soldier then moved to a row of wicker baskets placed at the other end of the clearing, sloshing through the pool of swirling water as he went. It did not take much for Shikandin to guess what was within them. His conjecture was confirmed but moments later, as the soldier removed the lid from one of the baskets and dropped the dead pigeon inside. There was a whipcord flash of black and yellow before the cover came back down. As the man headed back to the waterfall another uniformed soldier stepped out and made his way to the cauldron over the small fire. Shikandin saw him stack up four bowls and allowed himself a small smile. Four men was not much to handle at all.

And then, he saw the bald man step out of the cavern. Shikandin felt no surprise, only mild resignation at recognizing the so-called magician. Devala Asita was missing his beard and his head had been shaved bald, but there was no doubting his identity. He now wore black robes, wrapped in the style of a fighting man. Shikandin thought for a moment of the man's brother, and of the close friendship they had shared as children. The memories pained him even more as he realized what Devala Asita had done. He slipped his bow off his back and set an arrow to the string.

'What does it say?' Devala asked conversationally as the first soldier handed him the scroll he had taken off the dead pigeon's leg.

'It reeks of desperation,' the soldier gleefully replied. 'It's coded, of course, but so obviously begging for some word that it doesn't take much to decipher it. It says if they don't hear from them soon, they will have no choice but to concede the campaign as failed, and surrender all their lands and men to their new vassals.'

'Well done, Shulya! This is good news. On that note, let me try some of your porridge there. This development has done much for my appetite …'

My arrow will do more, Shikandin silently affirmed, clenching his teeth as the memory of the maimed bodies of his men filled him with cold anger.

'But wait, pass me the meat,' Devala said. 'It's time to feed the rest our friends.' He held out strips of meat on his palm. This time three falcon-hawks came wheeling in.

Shikandin did a quick calculation. His decision made, he stepped out of the thicket and turned his aim to the sky. Three arrows left his bow in quick succession and flew unerringly towards their targets. Not waiting to see the inevitable, he whipped around, a fourth shaft on the string. An enraged Devala screamed out orders as he ran towards a small path that led up the cliff. Shikandin's arrow caught him on the shoulder as he turned on to the path. Devala stumbled, but kept going. He knew Shikandin would not shoot a man in the back.

Indeed, Shikandin cursed, and turned to face the three soldiers who were almost upon him by now. In one swift move he used his arrow to stab the nearest man in the neck, then dropped his bow to the ground, reached to his baldric and drew out his sword. The other two men came at him together. He stepped in close, slashing at the first, then pulling away to stab the one behind him, turning the sword about in a double-handed move, before coming back to finish off the first man with another thrust.

As Shikandin stood there panting lightly, he became aware of the man and his arrow. Devala Asita stood at the top of the cliff, his bow drawn and the shaft aimed directly at Shikandin. He fired. Shikandin did not move, except to bring his sword up at the very last minute as a narrow shield between the shaft and his heart. The arrow broke against the metal and clattered to the ground at his feet.

Devala smiled, a gesture of evil anticipation.

Shikandin frowned slightly as the first tendrils of uncertainty reached him. And then, he understood. Immediately, he kicked away the shards at his feet, trying at the same time to hold his breath so as not to inhale the invisible vapour that the hollow shaft of the arrow had contained. With a snarl of rage he dived for his own bow and, picking it up, tried to set an arrow to it. He could not. His vision blurred. An unbearable pain shot through him and he felt as though his heart would explode. His arms went limp and his knees buckled under him.

A hiss of pain escaped through Shikandin's clenched teeth as he hit the hard ground. Through burning eyes he saw Devala set another arrow to his bow. At least the agony would not last long.

It seemed the bald man had just been struck by the same thought. He let fall his arm and returned the arrow to a quiver on his back.

'Die well, *Prince*,' he called out, shouting to make himself heard over the thundering waterfall. With a final, leering smile, the man was gone.

Shikandin closed his eyes and prayed for the strength to endure a slow, painful death.

20

THE BLACKNESS FELT BLISSFUL. SHIKANDIN WAS NOT SURE IF this was unconsciousness or death, but he felt at peace. Just as he regained his senses enough to begin pondering the presence of sense, it hit him. Without so much as a warning, liquid flame pooled in his stomach, searing, swirling, painfully wrenching at him. Spasms rocked his body, his gut cramped and, in a burst of fire, the pain shot upwards through his chest. He felt himself flip over in a desperate effort to somehow stop the throbbing from reaching his head and making it explode. It appeared to work, as with a great churning, he felt the fire spill out through his mouth. Cramps shot through every part of him as the heat came up in waves, burning his throat, filling his mouth. At last, the heaving stopped. He lay back, his eyes closed, his body still shuddering at intervals.

'That's it. Get it all out. Don't hold back,' a kind voice was telling him.

Partha!

Shikandin opened his eyes and shut them again as sunlight pierced through them. He wanted to speak but his mouth felt dry and his throat seared with pain.

'Here, drink this,' another voice held a bowl of water to his lips.

Shikandin gulped down the water, flinching at the way it tasted in his mouth. With effort he forced himself up on one elbow, into a half-sitting position. His burning eyes slowly focussed on Govinda.

'The last time I saw someone get this sick and throw up with such violence,' Govinda calmly began, 'was Samva, when he was fifteen. Gulped down an entire jar of wine on a bet or some such. Made a mess all over his best silk robes, not to mention the entire courtyard of our house and part of the dining chamber too.'

Shikandin groaned and clutched at his head.

'Oh yes, Samva had the most horrible headache as well. He was miserable for three days and gave us the worst time of it. I hope you're not going to be as troublesome, Shikandin.'

'And it's good to see you alive too, Govinda,' Shikandin grunted in reply. He sat up straight and gestured for more water. Taking the bowl that Partha held out, he sipped cautiously from it before emptying the rest over his head. Wiping his eyes with the sleeve of his tunic, Shikandin took a deep breath, letting the fresh air clear his lungs.

Partha let out a sigh of relief at seeing him visibly recovered. 'What happened here?' he asked.

In as few words as he could, Shikandin told them the whole story.

Partha walked over to where the shards of Devala's poisoned arrow lay and gave them a disbelieving look. He said, 'You're a lucky man, you know. All we had was the antidote for snake-bite. Of course, we've pretty much filled you up on enough anti-venom for about twenty-five bites. I'm just glad it worked on whatever it is they used on you.'

'It *is* snake-venom. Concentrated and vapourized,' Shikandin said, nodding towards the wicket baskets at the edge of the clearing. 'In there. You want to be careful, now.'

'Speaking of careful, that really was a close call, my friend ...' Govinda said, his words finally betraying his concern.

'It was,' Shikandin admitted. His throat hurt less now, though his voice seemed to belong entirely to another creature. 'And all it took was a single, stupid, arrow! Moments like these make you reconsider your life, all your decisions. It's never the best times, of course, but the regrets that come to mind ... Or perhaps they go together ...' He apparently thought that he had said too much, for he fell quiet.

'Do you have any regrets, Shikandin?' Partha asked, a little amused.

Shikandin managed a wan smile. 'Don't we all? But never mind that,' he forced some cheer back into his voice. 'How did you two know where to find me?'

Before Govinda could reply, Partha interjected in a disapproving tone, 'There was a Kritya.'

'A Kritya? Wait, did this woman happen to appear just after I'd left?'

'Yes,' Govinda said. 'In fact, she said she'd seen you. She told me where you'd be ... Rather, where she thought you'd be taken. We followed her directions and ran into Devajit on the way. We left him and the rest of the men at the fork where this stream joins the Lauhitya and made our way here. Just as well, as it turns out. I didn't really believe her at first, but she was sure you'd get yourself into trouble ...'

'And you trusted her? You trusted her enough to go where she told you to? Yabha! Govinda, are you out of your mind?'

'She was right, wasn't she? Not to mention that she didn't kill me when she had the chance.'

359

Shikandin immediately turned to Partha. 'And you? How could you let him do such a silly thing, like romance around with a Kritya? Or were you too busy looking up your courtesans' robes to care?'

'You stinking Panchala dog, how dare you …!'

'Enough!' Govinda commanded.

To Partha's surprise, Shikandin was smiling roguishly at the exchange, and did not appear at all bothered by the insult. Nevertheless, he felt compelled to apologize.

'I'm sorry,' he perfunctorily declared. 'It's this miserable weather, not to mention that scheming bitch. What could I do if she seduced Govinda?' he directed the last statement towards Shikandin.

'That she did,' a sombre Govinda affirmed. 'She seduced me, all right. Completely and, I may add, effectively.'

The ostensibly weighty declaration forced Shikandin to chuckle. He shook his head in disapproval and muttered something about Govinda and trouble, but beyond that let the matter go.

Partha did not know whether to be irritated or amused. He settled for mild consternation, but nevertheless voiced his complaint about the affair. 'Of course, I still don't understand how you could let her go without finding out who had sent her …'

'She wouldn't have told me,' Govinda protested. 'She wouldn't have betrayed the one who hired her, even under duress and torture. It takes great discipline and the most rigorous of tests, before one is declared a Kritya. There was no more information to be got from her. Besides, I'm quite sure that Bhagadatta didn't send her, which is what you really wanted to know, isn't it?'

'Then who?

'Sudakshin.'

'Sudakshin? But that doesn't make sense. It isn't likely that he would dare do all this on his own. Someone must be behind him,' Partha argued, still looking surly.

Shikandin said, 'You're absolutely right about that. There is someone behind him …' he favoured Govinda with a meaningful look, to which the other man responded with an equally meaningful nod.

'You two need to see this,' Shikandin said as he picked up a grey and white feather he found on the ground. He set it on his palm and held it out for Govinda and Partha to examine. The woolly edges clearly showed that it came off a pigeon or dove of some sort.

'They had falcon-hawks,' Shikandin explained, 'which caught and brought in the pigeons. I saw one of the soldiers pull the scroll off from the pigeon, before he fed it to the snakes ... It's not just our messengers, our men, who couldn't get through. Dwaipayana's pigeons have failed too. Sudakshin has both land and sky covered.'

Govinda looked grim as he took the feather from Shikandin.

Partha mournfully observed, 'Then in Indr-prastha they probably think we're dead. They might even think it's all over. For all we know, Dharma might've conceded failure already ...'

Govinda shook his head. 'Panchali and Dhaumya would never let him do that, not to mention Dwaipayana.'

'Never is a long time, Govinda. I heard these soldiers talk about the last scroll that had been sent from Magadha and, like it or not, Dharma is considering admitting failure. We need to take this victory back to where it belongs, else it is just a matter of time before Dharma cedes his position – Panchali or no Panchali.'

Govinda said nothing, and appeared to be lost in thought as Shikandin stared pointedly at him. Partha looked from one man to the other, before realizing that Shikandin had something to say but would not do so in front of him. He felt a momentary pang of jealousy, one that he was slowly getting used to, but brushed it aside and said, 'I'll go find Devajit. We should gather the dead men and give them a proper cremation.' Then, with a final glance at the two men, he walked away.

Shikandin waited till Govinda looked up of his own accord. Without prelude he said, 'You could ask for help. You've had help in this terrain before ...'

'Do you think I haven't considered that? It's not worth it. Such help would come at a price. Not in terms of what I'd have to give to receive it, but in terms of the larger questions it would raise. It could compromise the entire campaign.'

'The campaign is already compromised. Nevertheless, it is up to you ... Just remember you weren't above such trade-offs the last time you were at Pragjya, a fledgling prince with nothing but a plain cloth for his banner ...'

'The stakes were different then, Shikandin. Or do you doubt my judgement? Perhaps it's my intentions you question, my loyalty?'

'Your loyalty to whom, Govinda?' Shikandin said. 'This is your empire as much as it is anyone else's. Why would I doubt your loyalty to yourself?'

Govinda did not reply, but met the man's cold gaze with a haughty glare of his own.

Shikandin knew better than to continue the argument. 'Like I said, it's your choice. As long as you're sure it's only the stakes that are different this time ...'

21

THE EAGLE PRESENTED A SLEEK, STYLIZED SILHOUETTE AGAINST the sharp crags of the mountain behind him. He sat impossibly still, balanced on the thin ledge. Below him, the sheer cliff fell away into a deep ravine that held nothing but emptiness and stone. With narrowed eyes, he followed the susurrus of movement in its depths. In these dark realms, everything that moved either died or brought death. It had always been so, but not this time.

Turning his head ever so slightly, he let out a cry that was distinctly his own but hardly out of place in the surroundings. It was answered by a young boy, barely nine or ten years of age. The child was lean, but strong. He bounded across the narrow ledge without hesitation. The Eagle nodded and the boy returned the way he had come, this time at a run.

Not very long after, sounds of conversation came floating gently on the wind. The Eagle turned, as the boy and his companion stepped out on to the ledge.

'It's good to see you, Govinda.'

'Likewise, my friend.'

The two men embraced heartily, and though neither spoke of it their minds flitted over their past adventures. If it had not been for the tribal chief, Govinda knew, he could not have defeated King Naraka, Bhagadatta's father. *If it weren't for him,* he silently mused, *I probably wouldn't be alive.*

The Eagle regarded Govinda with concern. 'You look tired. I suppose that is to be expected.'

'You know then ... ?'

The chief sighed. 'Sometimes I wish these mountains had remained undiscovered. Civilization, as people call it, hasn't turned out to be the blessing that it was promised to be. But then there's no point hanging on to the past.'

'Garud, my friend, my fears are for the future ...'

'I too used to worry for the future, once ... till I met you.'

'And then you gave up all hope?' Govinda jested.

Garud threw his head back and laughed, while the boy, his son, tried to politely stifle his mirth. Finally, the man drew a breath, steadying himself. 'How much time do you have?'

'A week at the most ... Partha's armies have been marching for the past ten days. We'll meet them by the river.'

'You plan to cross at the bend? That's good. It's the sturdiest bridge across the river and part of it is built on stone shoals, not wood. There's little risk of losing your men to the waters ... But still, I'm curious ...'

'Hmm?'

'What made you move the men all of a sudden? You're safe at Pragjya. Bhagadatta isn't the kind of man to hold malice.'

'I know. But there was a Kritya ... Whoever sent her will soon realize that she hasn't done the job ...'

Garud said, 'That narrows it down. I've heard that the former king of Kashi had revived the old traditions. Presumably, his son Sudakshin continues with them. I also hear talk of a magician, whatever that means.'

'No magician. That is Devala Asita. You remember him?'

'I do. Tall? Thin? Bearded man?

'Tall and thin, yes, but no longer bearded. Apparently, he's now bald and clean-shaven, following the traditions of the Old Magicians – the very kind the ancient Firewrights once fought against.'

Garud frowned. 'It doesn't make sense. Why become that which you abhor?'

'He thinks it might be a way to save that which he cherishes. It's a mistake many make at some time or the other. Look at Aryavarta, Garud. How easy it is now to trade loyalties and rewrite the very notions of good and bad.'

Garud gave his friend a questioning look. 'I thought you didn't believe in absolutes like good and bad.'

'I don't. I was just testing you.'

'Fine. I'll pretend I believe you …'

The two friends laughed softly and then settled into a companionable silence that had been their space of comfort ever since they had met.

Govinda grudgingly broke it. 'The Krityas – how many of them are there?'

'From what my men tell me, not many. I've heard of just the one – probably the girl you met. Sudakshin's trying to train more, though. Unfortunately, we hear it's not just orphaned girls he takes in. Any child who shows beauty or promise is abducted, the parents killed. But few have survived the rigorous training it takes. It's good news, I suppose, because it means that there's less of a danger. Having said that, it's disgusting too … these are just children, young girls … Much has been going on that's not right, Govinda. I'd expected you here some weeks ago. You're late.'

'Late? Perhaps. I grow old, Garud. Tell me, do you think I've changed?'

Garud looked grim and was silent for a while. At length he said, 'Did you kill her?'

'Who?'

'The Kritya.'

Govinda shook his head. 'No. I let her go.'

'You haven't changed much, Govinda.'

'Some would disagree.'

'Possibly with good cause. You *have* started thinking too much and that is unlike you. But where it counts, though, in your heart, you remain the same. The question is, do you still listen to your heart? As for what others say, I can guess who it is you have in mind and I'm convinced that he'll completely agree with me that you're as dramatic and silly as you always were.'

Govinda raised an eyebrow. 'Was that supposed to make me feel better or …?'

'Feel how you like. And I must add that you remain just as decent. It should be no surprise, then, that you're as foolhardy too. Your men are pretty much marching to your deaths once you cross the river …' He paused before saying, 'Why do I get the feeling this only makes you more determined to go on as planned?'

'You know what they say, Garud. To kill a snake you need an eagle. In this case, *the* Eagle.'

'This will take a whole tribe of Eagles,' Garud said. He turned to his son. 'Go, tell your uncles to have your brother ready to leave in the morning. And,' he added, a clear tinge of affection in his voice, 'tell your mother that I plan to spend tonight in drunken reminiscence with my friend, like the old man she accuses me of being.'

The boy nodded and set off down the sheer face with the nimbleness of a mountain-goat. He headed towards a narrow but voluminous waterfall. And then, suddenly, he was gone, lost in the foamy, bubbling stream at the foot of the falls. Govinda clucked his tongue softly. Behind the curtain of water, he knew, was most likely a hanging valley, a glen-like piece of land open to the sky but surrounded by the mountain on most sides. For the present it remained a pristine secret, one of the few untouched, sacred spaces that small tribes like Garud's could retreat to.

Simply stepping into such a virginal, unmolested tract of nature was to go back a millennium, for many of the more remote hill-tribes lived as they had in antiquity. Govinda had always come away from those poignant encounters confused and amazed. He longed to revere the purity and simplicity that these people preserved as a way of life, but he could not ignore that they were indeed disjointed from the world around them. Undeniably, there was something mysterious, almost mystical, about these lands, as though even the gods had deferred to nature's majesty and force. Legends of impossible waterfalls, hidden vales and glens, uncharted valleys and unconquered, sometimes invisible, peaks had been passed on dutifully and accurately over generations.

For centuries scholar–seers had claimed that somewhere within the bosom of these lands lay the eternal paradise on earth, Swyam-Bhala the self-sustaining or Sham-bala, as Garud's people called it. The many awe-inspiring myths of Aryavarta spoke of a land where the boundaries between earth and heaven were blurred and the Truth was revealed in its purest form. Some tales, even the Firstborn seers admitted, were older than their oldest records, for it was believed that the mystic nation had survived innumerable cycles of existence, the end of the world and the cataclysmic end of Time itself.

As a young man a partly disbelieving, partly sceptical Govinda had embarked on a youthful adventure to find this mythical land. He never spoke of what he had seen or found, but to those who had asked if he located Kalapa, the capital of this mystic realm, he cryptically replied that he had found what he had been searching for.

Water and rock, mountain and valley, joined together in symphonies of resistance and yielding. Obvious secrets and hidden truths, past and future, life and death – all existed together in a world as vast as the earth itself or as tiny as a dewdrop. It was where imperfection and symmetry, order and chaos, wilderness and civilization all came together. In this place, heaven and earth were one.

The touch of Garud's hand on his shoulder brought Govinda out of his reverie.

'The world as I've known it, as I've worshipped it, is almost gone,' the tribal chief observed. 'I sometimes think to grieve for what we have irrevocably destroyed. But I remember what you taught me: Destruction and creation are parts of the same whole, and that to see one and not the other is to be caught in an illusion. Don't tell me you've forgotten your own injunctions. Especially not after all that pontificating I had to endure!'

Govinda merrily laughed. He spread his arms out in a hearty stretch, soaking in the pine-scented, crisp air even as he instinctively made to return the quip but stopped himself. Garud understood. The stillness around them was far too precious, and powerful enough to remind the friends of the truth it had once brought them to.

The indestructible paradise lay hidden, within.

It was some time past midnight when Govinda returned to Pragjya. Uncaring of the late hour, he proceeded to wake Partha and Shikandin up. 'We move at first light. I've already sent a messenger ahead. Your men will be ready,' he told a bewildered Partha. Shikandin, however, responded to the untimely intrusion with a wide grin and the anticipation of adventure.

They rode out of the castle in the grey, wet dawn, having waited only to thank Bhagadatta and say their goodbyes. The small company made good speed, despite a torrential downpour. Using the hard bunds that ran road-like along the banks of the river, they were able to avoid the marshes and small landslides that were common to these parts. By the second evening they could see the faraway glitter of blue that was one of the Lauhitya's greater tributaries. The fork where the two joined was one of the widest stretches. Further downstream from the fork was the huge bridge where they planned to cross into Kashi–Magadha lands.

A little before dawn on the fourth day, the three men and their small contingent arrived where Partha's armies were camped. Despite the weather, the soldiers were visibly cheerful – the thought of sunny lands and of reaching home had rejuvenated their spirits in a way little else could have. Eager as the men were, the convoy set off quickly, Govinda and his friends riding at its head. Partha longed to ask Govinda what he had planned, but desisted.

The ride to the crossing took the whole day – the size of the river had made it seem nearer than it was – but by nightfall the entire army had assembled on its banks. The span of the river here was slightly smaller than it had been at Pragjya but it was still astonishing. What really took one's breath away here, however, was not the natural abundance of the surroundings but the work of men. A huge bridge, wide enough for ten men to march abreast, ran clear into the distance. It was, for the most part, a mix of woodwork and stone with some sections resting on large boulders or rock formations on the bed of the river. In other places, wooden platforms gently bobbed up and down, floating on barrel-like devices that had been sealed tight to capture air within.

'So, we camp?' Partha asked, almost rhetorically. To his surprise, Govinda shook his head.

'A short break,' he said. 'Let's eat, and keep moving.'

'In the dark … ?' Partha instinctively began before falling silent. Though there had been no indication of danger so far, prudence still required them to make the crossing in sections rather than at one go. Govinda, it was evident, had other ideas. He made no efforts at discretion or at caution and, in fact, led the armies in a few bawdy marching songs as the final preparations were being made. They were going home, plain and simple.

The crossing of the Lauhitya began in the early hours of the morning, by torchlight, and it continued well past daybreak. By the afternoon of the next day the entire force had forded the river without incident. Partha was nearly beside himself with happiness. *Perhaps*, he silently mused, *this is what Govinda has been up to in the past few days away from Pragjya. Perhaps there no longer is any danger*. He looked forward to a good night's sleep ahead of him.

He was disappointed, as dusk brought more surprises. It became apparent that Govinda had already readied the divisions for nighttime marching. The soldiers took turns at sleeping on the horse-led wagons, but the army as a whole kept moving forward. At this rate, they would reach Magadha in less than three weeks – if they reached at all.

At that thought, Partha lost patience. 'Mih! What in Rudra's name are we doing, Govinda?' he snapped.

Govinda's reply sent a chill down his spine. 'We're walking into the trap, Partha.'

The next ten days were the most unnerving of Partha's life. He was a hardy veteran, the man who had successfully led the campaign across the northern lands. Still, he did not have the stomach for this sort of warfare. The honourable fight, as he saw it, was the direct attack, open battle. This sort of waiting, this intrigue, was not to his taste and he openly expressed his disgust.

Govinda did not respond, but Shikandin made a sarcastic comment about Kandava. Partha said not a word more.

In what provided a pleasant reprieve, they left the incessant rain behind. While an occasional shower was impossible to avoid, the weather was mainly clear. It began getting warmer as they neared one of the large tributaries of the River Ganga. This time round, though, the crossing was not difficult. They forded the stream just as she cascaded out of the hills and onto the plains. Here, the waters were turbulent but narrow, and the many boulders and rocks deposited on the bed over time served as the foundation for a strong stone bridge.

Hardly had they crossed, when the three men noticed that something was very obviously wrong.

'I don't like this ...' Partha muttered softly.

'You're right. The tilling of these lands should have started a week or two ago, but it hasn't. It looks abandoned ... or evacuated ...' Shikandin added.

Govinda threw his head back and looked up at the clear blue sky. 'We keep moving.'

22

THE ATTACK WAS WELL-TIMED AND PERFECTLY EXECUTED. Sudakshin, the king of Kashi, had kept his armies hidden in the small woods for days. With no reports of troop movement coming in from the scouts, Partha's men were taken completely unawares. Unprepared though he was, Partha responded quickly the moment the first of the enemy poured out of the woods. He engaged them with a few of his men giving the others time to dig trenches and set up barricades of quickly built mud banks as well as overturned carts and spears planted into the ground. Very soon, they had established a position that was open only on two fronts, with barricades closing off the right and left flank from attack. This, they hoped, could not only be defended for a while, but it would also give them enough time to fall back to a place that afforded more safety. But it did not take them long to realize that Sudakshin's forces had them surrounded. There was no question of falling back anymore.

As darkness fell, the situation settled into an uneasy stalemate. Sudakshin's soldiers made the occasional attack on either front, but with some effort, they were repelled. Partha knew that these attacks were but minor skirmishes; far from the massacre he could expect if Sudakshin's army came at them in full force.

It was well past midnight by the time he called for a meeting of all his captains, along with Shikandin and Govinda. The group convened in the small command tent, which had been set up right at the centre of their position. To everyone's surprise, Partha retained little trace of his earlier irritation and looked completely at ease.

'I admit,' he told them, 'that I was worried. But I no longer am. To march into a trap such as this, to be caught in this position, is nothing less than folly. But of one thing I am certain – Govinda Shauri is no fool. The predicament we're in, unable to move forward or to retreat, is proof enough that an effective strategy is in place. Come, Govinda, it's time to reveal your plan. Tell us what is to be our next move.'

'We attack at dawn,' Govinda announced. 'We throw our entire might against the enemy behind us. That's where they'll least expect it.'

'And the other front? Won't they just rush in and corner us from the rear?' one of the men queried.

'No,' Govinda said. 'I'm … hopeful that we'll have help from Bhim. The trap the enemy has laid for us will turn into a trap for them.'

'By Varuna!' Partha exclaimed as the implications dawned on him. His earlier conviction seemed to leave him, and angry scepticism took its place.

Some of the others too looked doubtful. 'It's a huge risk you've run, Commander,' Partha's senior captain spoke up. 'I assume you've sent word to Magadha for reinforcements ... but how can we be sure that your messengers got through, where so many of ours and Bhagadatta's failed?'

'If you're asking me for certainty, my friend, I'm no oracle. I'm just a man ... There's nothing more I can offer you than the promise that I'll personally lead our rearguard and hold off an attack on the other flank.'

'Even so, that means splitting up our forces,' the captain countered. 'The men are tired enough from the relentless marching. If we attack with half or even three-fifth of our men, it may not be enough.'

'You won't need to split up the forces,' Shikandin added in a low growl. 'My men and I will fight to watch your backs well enough.'

'He's right. We'll begin the attack early, while it's still misty. We need to make them think that our rearguard is well-manned. They won't advance so quickly, then,' Govinda added.

Partha scowled, unconvinced. 'It's a dangerous idea ... When the enemy does attack, their force will be considerable. You'd have to fall back quickly, very quickly ...'

'Or, perhaps, not at all,' Shikandin dryly finished.

The comment roused the other men to defend their pride. 'In that case, we'll honour your death by fighting to the last man,' the captain added as his men heartily declared their assent. With a few more muttered exclamations and some indistinct grumbling, the soldiers settled down to plan their offensive.

The attack began a little before dawn. Govinda, Shikandin and the men of the Eastern Guard made full use of the darkness to take up strategic positions in the vacant trenches. Armed with an abundance of arrows, as well as flares to send signals to divisions that did not exist, they were all set to give the impression that there were more of them than actually were. The archers were arranged to shoot in alternating sequence so that a continuous volley of arrows could keep the enemy forces from advancing.

All preparations made, they waited. Partha came around for one last word before heading off to lead the attack on the other side. He found Govinda dozing. 'Where's Shikandin?' he asked.

'He's gone ahead to scout around a bit. We figured that if he can intercept the inevitable enemy messenger who brings back news of your attack on the other side, it may give us some more time. Also, we need to know exactly when they begin moving and get a sense of their pace.'

'He's alone?'

'Yes,' Govinda affirmed, shutting his eyes again and stretching his arms out before placing them under his head as a pillow. 'He likes to work alone, Partha. You should know that by now.'

'But ...'

'He'll be fine, don't worry,' Govinda added. 'I've known Shikandin a long time and the man still astonishes me with his skills.'

Partha felt a sudden pang of guilt. He remembered the time, all those years ago, when he had fought Dhrupad and Satrajit on Dron's behalf. As he had dragged a captive father and son to Dron's hermitage, Dhrupad had incessantly cursed the absent Shikandin. Partha felt a little sick, recalling how he had added insult to injury by calling Dhrupad the father of a coward. He swallowed hard and turned to Govinda, only to realize that the other man was watching him by the feeble glow of the small torch that flickered nearby.

'Yes, you should apologize. It might make you feel better,' Govinda said.

Partha gasped. 'How do you ... never mind!' He stood up to leave. Silently, he promised himself that if he lived through the day's battle he would indeed apologize to Shikandin. Whatever it was that had kept the man from fighting that day, Partha now knew that it certainly had not been cowardice. With a final nod at Govinda, he left.

Govinda settled down to resume his nap, but was roused again in a few moments as Shikandin slid into the trenches, right next to him.

'Ah, right when I was sinking into sleep. Partha just left ...'

'I know,' Shikandin replied. 'I was waiting for him to go. I didn't want to say this in front of him. Govinda, this isn't going to be easy. Sudakshin's got a full battalion on this side alone. If we're not getting any help … if Bhim thinks we're dead and hasn't sent men … Well, we soon will be. Dead, that is …'

If Shikandin was alarmed, he did not show it. Instead, he calmly pulled on the leather-finished cast metal armour that one of his men held out.

'Only one way to find out,' Govinda replied, sitting up to help his friend strap on the chest-plate. That done, the two men waited in battle gear, listening intently. The darkness had let up a little, but mist lay heavy over the land. They could hardly see their own hands in front of them. Soon, the distant sounds of battle came from behind them.

'If we can hear it …' Shikandin began.

'So can the enemy,' Govinda finished. He set an arrow to his bow, but did not take aim.

Shikandin whistled. His men were ready at once. He then crawled out of the trenches and moved a few feet ahead. Lying flat with his ear to the ground, he listened, judging the enemy's advance by the thudding of the earth. In a moment he was up on his feet. Quick as lightning, he drew his bow and released a shaft. The twang of his bowstring was signal enough and the men behind him released their first volley, quickly followed by the second. By the time Govinda had his third arrow on the string, Shikandin was back at his side. Wordlessly, the men worked in unison, the combined twangs of their bowstrings disguising their true numbers.

Around them, the sounds of battle grew more intense. The first of the enemy's spears rained down a short distance ahead of the trenches.

'Another ten feet, and we'll be within range …' Shikandin noted. Grimly, he continued to shoot arrow after arrow.

'Which means …' Govinda said, putting down his bow.

'Strike before they expect it?'

'Precisely. They'll expect us to fall back …'

'Instead, we go ahead. Nice thinking, Govinda,' Shikandin said. He whistled a long, shrill signal through the air. In response, his men readied themselves for a charge at the enemy. Drawing his sword, he said, 'Ready?'

'Always,' replied Govinda.

At Shikandin's signal, the men rushed out of the trenches with a fearsome yell. They crashed as one into the Kashi soldiers, breaking the head of the enemy's formation. But quickly, the Kashi soldiers, too, repositioned themselves and fought back with fierce vengeance.

Shikandin and Govinda stood back to back, facing the enemy soldiers with surprising glee.

'Down!' Shikandin shouted, slashing hard as he whipped around. His sword cut through the space where Govinda's head had been an instant ago and beheaded an oncoming attacker.

At the same time, Govinda spun under to thrust his sword through an enemy soldier. He pushed the blade deep and out the man's back to stab another of the Kashi soldiers. By the time he had pulled his flesh-encrusted sword back out, Shikandin had disposed of two more men by stabbing them, as Govinda had his adversaries, through the small gaps in their armour.

'So ...' Govinda shouted over the din of battle and the clash of metal on metal, 'We draw swords together, after all these years.'

'Yes, finally ...' Shikandin replied as he brought his weapon down fiercely on a Kashi soldier. 'By Hara, these men don't like us much.'

'I wonder why,' Govinda said. 'I don't suppose it has anything to do with being tricked?' The two laughed, enjoying their partnership.

Just then the sun broke through the horizon, setting their long blades afire in streaks of red and orange. As though of one mind, both men began to recite the same ancient verse. Around them the Panchala soldiers added their own war cries.

'We have drunk the soma nectar and become immortal!
We have attained the light, we have found the gods!

What can the malice of mortal man
Or his spite, O Immortal, do to us now?'

Despite their bold front, both Govinda and Shikandin knew that
their position was far from superior. They could barely see or hear
beyond the ring of vicious enemy soldiers hurtling at them, each
snarling face ready and eager to crush them brutally. Although the
element of surprise had initially given Shikandin's men the upper
hand, the enemy had rallied quickly. The other two opposition flanks
had also drawn near.

'Maraka!' Shikandin cursed out loud as he saw that more than half
his men were already down. 'Well, at least Partha can't complain,' he
commented dryly as he ran his blade through an enemy cavalryman, a
huge man with a leering tilt to his mouth. Wheeling around smoothly,
he slashed at another, letting out a growl of satisfaction as the man
fell. Following his lead, the Panchala soldiers fell on the enemy with
renewed vigour. Then they heard the sound. A solemn but uplifting
note; an almost impossible mix of deep booming and clear ringing.
The few men of the Eastern Guard still alive felt their hearts fill with
renewed strength and hope.

'What is that?' Shikandin exclaimed.

'Paundra,' Govinda said. 'The Great Horn of the East, the war
conch of the Magadhan kings ...'

Not much later, they heard the thundering of hooves behind
them. The Kashi soldiers began falling back into the woods, and
Shikandin and Govinda gradually lowered their bloodied swords,
panting heavily.

'I see that I'm just in time!' Partha's captain rode up, leading their
horses alongside. 'I hoped you'd ride with me,' he said bowing, 'but
you seem rather tired ... ?' Without a word Shikandin and Govinda
ran up to their horses and swung into the saddle. The three men
followed the rest of Partha's cavalry into battle.

Caught between the two fronts, the enemy soldiers struggled
to hold their ground. Those who tried to retreat were allowed to
do so through a small break in the formation. Those who engaged

were killed without hesitation. The flanks moved closer until at last Govinda could see Bhim's tall figure across the field. The two men greeted each other with loud cheers and fell back into the battle with increased determination. Soon it was over.

Partha greeted Bhim with furious delight. 'What took you so long!' he complained, even as he pulled his brother into a grateful embrace. Bhim returned the gesture with equal gusto, fighting back tears of happiness and relief. But more joyous than the reunion between the two brothers was the one between Partha and Shikandin. Indeed, Shikandin was pleasantly taken aback by the way Partha gripped him tight, even as Bhim looked on, slapping both men on the back.

'I'm sorry, Shikandin. I'm sorry for everything!' Partha said.

Shikandin did not quite understand, but knew better than to dig too deep. At last, Partha let go of him, and turned to Govinda.

'How …'? he asked, too perplexed for more words.

Govinda laughed and let out a shrill cry, the likes of which Partha had never heard before. The others looked around at Govinda, surprised. The call was answered with a faint but similar peal, as a huge brown and white eagle circled down from the sky. A cry of amazement rose from the men as the massive bird swooped down over their heads and came to rest on Govinda's gauntlet.

'My trusty messenger,' Govinda introduced the bird to them, 'courtesy of an ever-faithful old friend …' He whispered words of thanks and endearment to the majestic creature and clucked his tongue in a series of signals that the bird clearly understood, even enjoyed. The eagle then deftly stepped off his wrist to perch comfortably on his shoulder.

A whisper of admiration ran through the gathered men and many of them spontaneously saluted Govinda. He returned the gesture with a polite nod and turned to Partha.

'Now what, Cousin?' Partha asked, his voice filled with respect and affection.

'Now,' Govinda replied, 'you go home.'

'You mean we go home …'

'No.' Govinda was grave once more. 'Not me. I have some unfinished business to take care of.'

KASHI, LIKE MANY NATIONS OF ARYAVARTA, WAS A NAME SHARED by the kingdom and the capital city. In this case the nation's fame rested indeed on that of its capital city, home to one of the oldest and largest temples to Rudra, also known as Hara, the Destroyer. Of equal fame had been those who had worshipped there – the most beautiful of princesses, as also some of the first Firewrights.

But fame was fickle, Govinda mused, as he looked down at the city from a small hillock on its outskirts. The Firewrights were gone, though many self-declared magicians remained in the city claiming to possess knowledge of the most powerful spells. As for the princesses – ever since Ambalika and Ambika had been taken to Hastina as Vichitravirya's brides, no one spoke too loudly of the beauty of Kashi's women.

That distinction, though, is well-deserved, Govinda noted with a smile as he remembered his encounter with the attractive Kritya at Pragjya.

'Who knows … perhaps you'll see her again,' Shikandin teased, guessing what ran through his friend's mind.

'Perhaps …'

The moment passed and both men were grim as they considered the scene before them. They stood on a hillock overlooking Kashi city. The gates to the city had been shut, the roads around it wore a deserted look, and the boats and barges on the river were anchored upstream, well ahead of the small harbour. The Great Temple to Rudra dominated that scene of despondence, its stone spire rising as high as the columns of smoke that billowed out from the huge square courtyard that stretched from the main sanctum all the way to the riverbank. A little while ago a huge funeral pyre had come alight, blazing into sudden existence like some primordial beginning. Inside the Great Temple of Kashi, the killings had begun.

The Firewrights, Govinda pensively noted, had supposedly been the ones to perfect the arcane ritual known as the 'purusha-medha' – human sacrifice. But few knew what it involved, beyond what the name suggested, and when the Wrights were destroyed this was one of the many secrets they took with them. That in this day and age, an Arya would and could actually resort to this ritual was nothing less than a nightmare come true. But so it was. And it also explained something Govinda had found very puzzling.

Ever since they had survived being ambushed by Sudakshin's men a week ago, it had constantly bothered Govinda that an admittedly small vassal kingdom could so quickly grow to dominate enough vassals and build such a mighty army. It was, to him, a sign that the diplomatic strategies and the administrative processes of the imperial campaign – and the empire that would result at the end of it – were sorely lacking. What disturbed him even more was the fact that Sudakshin's rise had been fuelled by none other than Devala Asita. In any case, Govinda had decided, this was one enemy they could not leave standing.

And so, as Bhim, Partha and their armies had started for Indr-prastha, he had headed straight for Kashi city. To his surprise, Shikandin had insisted on joining him, despite Bhim and Partha's fervent urging that he would be needed on the trail back home.

'Why?' Govinda had asked him, when they had found a moment alone.

'I have to. I have to see Kashi,' Shikandin had admitted, a catch in his voice.

Govinda had said no more, and the two men had immediately ridden out, leading three hundred fit and fresh soldiers of Bhim's army and the four soldiers of the Panchala Eastern Guard who had survived the last battle. Devajit, one of the survivors, had gone ahead as a scout and spy.

Dressed as a less-than-prosperous merchant, Devajit was in the perfect guise to spend a few days in the city and visit the better, though still-inexpensive, taverns and brothels that were favoured by the palace attendants as well as soldiers of the Kashi garrison. In two days the Panchala captain had heard much and overheard even more. He silently noticed what he needed to and spoke just enough to appear commonplace. When he considered his task completed to satisfaction, he left, after haggling a little over what the innkeeper charged him, but not so much as to draw excessive attention.

He had met up with Govinda and Shikandin about a day's march from Kashi city. After a few polite but quick words of greeting, Devajit promptly began his report. 'Kashi is astir with just one topic, other than the usual and many merry tales of the king's debauchery ...'

Govinda chuckled and Shikandin laughed softly. 'Go on,' he urged.

'It ...' Devajit paused and chose his words carefully. 'I don't suppose this is true but what's important is that many ... most of Sudakshin's soldiers believe it completely! There's talk of Firewright magic. Some say a powerful magician now advises Sudakshin.'

Shikandin's response was a derisive grunt, but Govinda was curious. 'What sort of magic?'

Devajit looked uncomfortable, caught between scepticism and the clear possibility of danger if the impossible were indeed true. 'It seems that the erstwhile Emperor Jarasandha of Magadha had earlier captured fourteen men, Magadhan princes all. He had, it's being said, planned to offer them as human sacrifice. The talk goes that Sudakshin had them somehow smuggled out of Magadha after Jarasandha's fall and held them in his prison. Over eighty-six more were taken over these past two years – lords of the Kashi–Kosala region, and others of their families. Sudakshin is set to begin the sacrifice ...'

To his surprise Govinda broke into a grin. 'Ah, it's our privilege to see such great minds at work. You've seen what the Kashi soldiers are like – ruthless, tough and convinced of their own infallibility. If we let Sudakshin go through with his so-called sacrifice, his men will be convinced that they can't be defeated despite the battle they lost against us.'

'You mean you don't believe there really will be such a sacrifice?'

Govinda thought for a moment, staring into the distance. 'The original fourteen captives were nothing more than Jarasandha's political prisoners. I suspect that the others Sudakshin imprisoned are also troublesome vassals – probably those who were eager to join Dharma's empire. He means for them to die all right, but the talk of sacrifice is probably nothing but a trick to make the Kashi army believe it is invincible and to force the citizens to suffer wartime taxes without complaint. Or it may be that Sudakshin truly believes it will make him invincible. Unfortunately, if the rest of Aryavarta believes it too, it may even lead to him making a bid for the empire, eventually!'

'What if the sacrifices are real?' Devajit questioned, hesitant. 'I mean, if there really is some power in …'

'Then we have a much bigger problem than we imagined.'

Now, Govinda wondered if the worst had come to pass, after all. He found it ironic that the bedrock of civilization, of the rule of law and Divine order, had come to this. Though many dark histories had been lost, perhaps wilfully, in the mists of time, the truth remained that from the most ancient times people had fought each other just to survive. Sometimes they had fought over who had the greater share of a hunt, sometimes it had been tribes warring over hunting grounds. Even prosperity had not stopped war, leading only to greater fear and distrust. It only made tribes grow larger, stronger and more afraid for their future. Food was survival. The thought that someday it would run out was never too far from all minds.

Driven by enlightenment, or perhaps by a mixture of need and fear, the people welcomed what they now called civilization. The rule of might was replaced by the rule of law. The chief or king, sometimes a queen, was no longer just the strongest one who led the hunt, but the one who divided the kill. It was the beginning of an era of prosperity – life was less perilous and food more plentiful. Populations grew faster, and small migrant villages became huge, permanent cities. The fear of a return to the older, perilous times grew just as quickly.

Civilization responded yet again, this time by turning to the gods. Earth became a mirror of the Heavens. The ritual sacrifice of animals was born. Every morsel consumed was dedicated to the gods, all food divided only after it had been sanctified. There were no slaughters, only sacrifices. The whole city would gather to receive their rations of the sacrificial animals, and there was always plenty; but never excessively so. Implicit in every ritual prescription, in every detail of worship, was the notion of justice.

That rule of law, that noble way of life, had thrived here, at Kashi. The sacrificial courtyard of the Great Temple, Govinda knew, was stained brown with the blood of centuries; blood that was spilt for the sake of peace, never in excess, never in violence.

Till now.

'Hai!' Devajit sounded despondent. Shikandin squeezed his shoulder in encouragement, then turned to Govinda.

'That's the garrison,' he pointed out, 'that's the temple and, of course, the courtyard itself. To the left is the palace. Behind that, I think, is the royal boathouse ...'

Govinda said, 'Sudakshin knows we will attack him sooner or later. He may even expect us to try and stop the sacrifice.'

'In that case,' Shikandin continued, 'he'll have troops around the temple and near the river, but ...'

'... not many in the main city itself,' Govinda finished.

'Be that as it may, we're too late,' Devajit said, his voice full of regret. 'Too late to stop the travesty.'

'But not too late to avenge the dead,' Govinda declared as he urged Balahak to rear up and spring into a gallop. The men followed.

The sun shining bright off their armour, Govinda, Shikandin and their men crashed down on the main gates to Kashi city like a bolt of lightning across a cloudless sky. The few sentries on duty stood awestruck at the sight of the two men in the lead – one with long, matted hair and blazing eyes, the other bearing a huge, fierce-looking eagle on his shoulder as if it were a tame pigeon. They scrambled for cover as the riders broke through in an unstoppable tide.

Unchallenged, Govinda and Shikandin led their men through the crowded mix of marketplace and dwelling houses that formed the first section of the old city. Both men could have sworn that they were in Hastina or even in Kampilya. It was only when they entered the more affluent quarters reserved for the nobility that the city would take on its own, unique look.

Speed, and the element of surprise, gave them the upper hand as they thundered down the main street towards the Great Temple. However, as they entered the huge square that fronted the Great Temple it was their turn to be caught unawares.

'Pull back!' Shikandin ordered his men as the first rain of arrows showered down on them. He and Govinda managed to guide their horses under the wooden awning of a nearby structure, just in time.

'Go!' Govinda commanded the bird, still perched on his shoulder. Immediately, the eagle took wing. A few of the archers tried to shoot it down, but it wheeled deftly to avoid their shafts, and was gone.

Govinda turned to Shikandin. 'Now what?'

Before Shikandin could reply, a hail of stones rained down from the rooftops above them, cutting them off from the rest of their forces. Taking advantage of the moment, the soldiers guarding the temple set fire to a couple of hay-filled carts nearby and completely barred the way.

'I've no clue,' Shikandin said. He swore loudly and added, 'Where in Yama's name did so many men come from? And how did Sudakshin get them fitted and mustered so quickly?'

Govinda solemnly gave him the answer to that and many other unspoken questions. 'Devala Asita.'

'That miserable Firewright! If we get out of this alive I'll rip his head off his neck!'

As if to punctuate Shikandin's wrath, a powerful explosion ripped through the air. The ground shuddered with the impact and the awning above them came crashing down, throwing both him and Govinda off their horses. Coughing and cursing, they quickly got to their feet, shaking the collapsed awning off them. Shikandin spat out the blood pooled in his mouth from a cut lip, while Govinda pressed at his head, trying to rid it of the unbearable ringing in his ears. It took both men a few moments to realize that the explosion was not the work of the enemy army. Their own soldiers looked on, unharmed and astounded, as Sudakshin's men ran wild with terror. Many had thrown down their weapons and were screaming like madmen.

'Look!' Shikandin pointed.

Many of the buildings that adjoined the Great Temple were ablaze. Tongues of flame darted out from inside some of the buildings, and a dark layer of soot stained the crumbling walls. The streets around them were littered with debris and a heavy dust hung in the air.

'Come on!' Govinda nodded towards the temple and began moving towards it. Shouting out instructions to Devajit to take their horses, Shikandin followed.

Ahead, the huge iron doors leading to the temple complex were shut. As Govinda and Shikandin came closer, a small wicket-gate set in the door swung open and more soldiers poured out, making straight for the two men. Slashing and cleaving, the two friends forced their way through the attacking mob, each step taking them closer to the gate even as they left bodies strewn in their wake. Finally, they managed to squeeze in through the wicket-gate. Shikandin slammed it close behind them and Govinda quickly secured an iron rod through the latch to bar the way. Then the two men turned to face the hordes that they expected would rush at them.

But the temple courtyard was empty.

24

THE KRITYA WATCHED AS THE NEXT MAN WAS LED FORWARD. His face showed neither dread nor despair, unlike the many before him. Watching them fall, one by one, he appeared to have accepted the inevitable. The guard forced him to kneel and place his head on a stone block. He did so without protest, his passive submission sending a jolt of anger through the Kritya. Yet another dull thud of an axe, and the attendants dragged the man's headless body to the huge pyre and threw it, as though it were refuse, into the blazing depths. Another attendant reverently picked up the head and presented it to King Sudakshin.

Whispering the words as directed by a bald man dressed in robes of black, Sudakshin offered the head into a smaller ritual fire as his sacrifice to the gods. He felt the Kritya's eyes on him and favoured her with a smirk. She returned an elegant smile, before looking over at the bald magician–priest. The one who called himself a Firewright.

Whatever it was the true Wrights had meant by human sacrifice, she knew this was not it. Those Wrights had not been murderers, they had been creators. *If you truly believe it,* a voice inside her mind questioned, *why didn't you kill Govinda Shauri? Why didn't you kill the man who brought the Wrights down, and ruined so many lives?*

Much as she knew the answer, she could not admit it, not even to herself. With practised ease she restrained her inner anger, and allowed the slight hint of a smile to rest seductively on her lips.

A stifled sob broke through the quiet as the last of the men was led forward. He was young, little more than a boy, but he was Arya and the prince of a tiny territory in Kosala. The magician–priest had been clear. Nothing less than noble blood would suffice for this purpose. The Kritya had to grit her teeth to not speak, not move, not offer the boy some slight consolation. Disgust filled her being. This blood-fest was not Sudakshin's idea, nor Jarasandha's legacy as Sudakshin claimed it to be. The bald magician had set this in motion.

The magician, such as he was, had turned up a little over a year ago. He had not only called himself a Firewright, but claimed great prowess over the most difficult of their skills. Soon, he had Sudakshin completely ensnared, trapped by the promise of unimaginable power. He was denied nothing, no matter how abominable or difficult the request.

At first, the Kritya had found the whole affair rather amusing, so much so that she had asked the bald man in her charming, seductive way, 'Are you really a magician?'

He had been contemptuous. 'Hardly!' he said. 'When the real

Wrights were forced into hiding, they spent many years living among the forest-tribes, and even the nomadic desert-people. Over generations, people from these tribes have learnt some of our skills but haven't always imbibed the sacred meaning behind them. As a result, you get what seems miraculous and inexplicable. Still, it's certainly not sorcery! But don't tell Sudakshin that!' he finished, beaming widely.

She had almost liked him, then. For the first time, she had met someone who was not fearful of her proximity. It had given her a new kind of happiness, something she had not felt before.

Like all happiness she had ever known, it was fleeting.

All of the so-called magician's efforts had made the imperial campaign more difficult and bloody for the commanders leading the forces, but somehow it kept going on. He and Sudakshin were perpetually in a foul mood, and often squabbled like drunk madmen.

Eventually, her curiosity got the better of her. She asked him, 'This Dharma Yudhisthir. What does it matter if he's made Emperor?'

'What does it matter?' he had turned on her, enraged. 'Haven't you understood a thing of what I've told you? If Dharma becomes Emperor he will stamp what is left of us – my order – out. Dharma is nothing more than Govinda's toy!'

She was not one to be intimidated. 'What are you trying to protect by killing so many? What has this Govinda done that you hate him so?'

In response, the magician had grabbed her wrist roughly and almost dragged her across the palace courtyard to a deserted corner of the building. A guard had opened a padlocked door, which led to a narrow corridor. She had lost track of the twisting, winding path they then took but it had ultimately led to a dark, well-guarded stairway. Only as they descended its rank depths had she realized that the bald man was leading her to the palace dungeons. There, she met Agnivarna Angirasa, son, she was told, of no less a man than Ghora Angirasa. Like his father, she learnt, this man too was a Firewright. Unlike his father, though, he was a prisoner.

The man was naturally well-aged, but captivity had rendered him decrepit. Yet, he was far from insane or incompetent. He spoke with clarity, and told her many interesting things about his order, including how a man named Govinda Shauri had destroyed them. But, he also refused to answer the magician's questions, even accept him as one of them.

The magician had led her out in a huff. 'You won't believe what secrets, what great powers the Wrights of old held. I know much, yes, but there's so much more I don't know. If only I could get the old man to talk …' Imagine! I was once so close to learning their greatest skills, to being taught by this idiot's father, by Ghora Angirasa himself … But for that bastard, Govinda Shauri …'

Govinda Shauri. It was, the Kritya mentally noted, the only time she had ever failed. She had returned to Kashi and claimed that Govinda had suspected her to be a spy before she could even get close to him. She had waited for Sudakshin to cut off her head in a rage. Instead, he had merely given her a contemptuous look and said nothing.

Then, she saw the magician's dark glee. He threw her into the same dungeon with Agnivarna Angirasa, ostensibly as a punishment.

She had felt slightly afraid of the old man's recrimination for her failure, for passing by the chance for his vengeance.

'Govinda Shauri …?' he had repeated, when she told him of her failed mission.

'Yes, Acharya.' Her eyes then brimming with the memory of what she had shared with Govinda, she asked the old man, 'Is he really evil?'

'Evil is a dubious word, my dear,' Agnivarna had told her, with a sad smile. 'Those who live to rule become the good, and those who are defeated are consigned to the ranks of the evil. But yes, Govinda Shauri shattered our order in a way no one else could have; not the Firstborn, not these kings who took such great pleasure in hunting us down and killing us, one by one.'

'Then, should I have …?' She left the words hanging in the air, the very thought stirring up a pain that she could not explain.

Agnivarna briefly considered the question before finally saying, 'No.'

'Because Govinda is not evil?'

'Because *you* are not.'

She had hesitated, not knowing how to respond to that statement, when Agnivarna had asked her, 'Do you know anything at all about your parents? Your family?'

She shook her head. 'No. I know nothing. I remember nothing.'

A slight shudder passed through the old man, but he quickly pulled himself together and said, 'They took many of our children, the girls. Sudakshin's father believed that Wright blood was magical, that those girls would make the best Kritya. Many died or went mad from the terrible potions they forced down their throats. The others ... well, let's just say they were better off dead.'

She gasped, and said, 'You mean, I might be ...?'

'Perhaps. Or perhaps it's just the wishful thinking of an old man whose days are numbered. You see, I once had a granddaughter who looked a little like you. Her skin was darker than yours, but she had your smile ...'

They had spoken for a long time, of his family and many other things.

Three days later, the magician had stormed back into the dungeons, obviously enraged. She knew it had to be because Govinda had found his camp in the forests, and wondered if perhaps he suspected her. He appeared, however, to have other problems on his mind.

'Do it,' he told the old man. 'Make the poison, damn you, or *she* dies.' He had pointed at her.

'No,' Agnivarna had replied. 'Not even for her.'

'Then,' the magician said, 'we don't need you anymore.' Without any further ado, he pulled out a dagger and ran it through Agnivarna's heart.

The old Firewright met the blade without protest. His eyes sought out the Kritya one last time. Then he fell to the ground.

'Narayana,' he whispered and closed his eyes for the last time.

It was all the Kritya could do not to cry.

The magician had then taken her out of the dungeons and back to her palace. He had found another use for her; one more piece of magic she could help with. He had trained the falcon-hawks native to Kashi to hunt down the messenger pigeons Govinda and his friends had been using to communicate. Since he had lost his handlers in the attack on the camp, he now needed someone else to manage the birds – someone who could learn fast. She grudgingly obliged, riding out with him every day, helping him release the hawks, watching as they flew far and wide, searching out their prey and bringing it back to their master. It amazed her how faithfully they waited till he removed the tiny message-scrolls from the grey-white pigeons' legs before returning the dead bird to its hunter.

'They can catch anything and everything in the sky,' he proudly declared.

'Everything?'

'Almost,' he admitted. 'Everything except eagles.'

From that day on she began looking out for eagles. Somehow they gave her hope.

'Kritya!' Sudakshin called out. She saw him standing by the sacred fire, ready to receive the gods' blessings. Her feet felt sticky and wet on the splattered blood of a hundred men as she walked across the courtyard towards him. Sudakshin held a golden bowl in his hand and as she moved closer she saw its contents reflected in his insane, gleaming eyes: blood, the remains of the ritual.

Despite all her training, the Kritya could no longer hide her emotions. Her eyes filled with tears as she stared at the bowl. She looked up to see the magician staring at her. Her mind raged with hatred. How could he believe in this if he was a Wright? How could he have promised Sudakshin the power of the gods if the king offered a hundred men as sacrifice? *Perhaps, this is what they really were,* she wondered. *This is why Govinda destroyed the Firewrights. And now, I must do what I must do.*

'Hold this, Kritya,' Sudakshin held out the bowl.

Kritya. That was all he had ever called her. She wished she knew her name after all, just so that she could carve it on Sudakshin's chest with her sharp nails, the claws that terrified him so. But, she reminded herself, it was not all that important in the larger scheme of things. Smiling, she reached out with both hands, for the bowl. Before Sudakshin could realize how close she was, she struck.

Digging her talons into his chest, she wrenched his heart out of his body, the ultimate skill she had been taught, now perfected with years of practice.

Sudakshin stared, a stupid, uncomprehending look on his face, as he watched his heart beat defiantly in her hand before coming to a stop. Then he slumped to the floor, dead. Before the magician and his men could react, or even register what she had done, a loud, earth-shattering sound rocked the temple. It was followed by another blast, and then another. Agnivarna's explosives, which he had taught the Kritya to make and set off before he died, had done their work well. She laughed till she felt the sharp edge of a dagger at her neck.

'You bitch! You stupid, ungrateful bitch!' the magician shrieked, pressing the blade enough to hurt but not kill her.

She laughed again as she realized how afraid he was of her poisoned blood. For her part, she was not afraid to die, though she would have loved to see Govinda Shauri one last time.

At the thought, she raised her eyes to the sky.

An eagle circled overhead.

25

'LET HER GO, DEVALA.'

'Or what, Govinda? You'll never learn to stop with your heroics, will you? After all the wars and armies and scheming, it still comes down to you, me and a girl ...'

The area fronting the temple had been empty, but when Govinda and Shikandin had made their way through to the inner courtyard they had found that the place was well guarded, after all. The best of Sudakshin's soldiers now clustered around, weapons drawn and at the ready. Shikandin clucked his tongue and pulled a second sword out of his baldric. He twirled one blade in each hand and evaluated the opposition. 'I've got this, Govinda,' he casually said. 'You go ahead ...'

The magician nodded at the soldiers. Then, his blazing eyes fixed on Govinda, he plunged the dagger into the Kritya's flesh. At the same time, the guards rushed towards the two men, yelling loudly, but Shikandin barred their way, his blades flashing through the air in an impossibly quick blur. The first soldier was on the ground before the last had even stirred from his place.

Paying no heed to the skirmish around him, Govinda rushed to the Kritya's side. She looked up at him, tears rolling down her cheeks, her face suffused with an aura of contentment. 'I knew you'd come, Govinda.'

He said nothing, but lifted her up into a sitting position and rested her against his knee. Pulling her upper robe off from around her shoulders, he pressed it against her bleeding stomach.

'Careful ...' she warned him, but he did not seem to care.

Slowly, he took in her bloody hands and the dead king sprawled close by, his hollowed-out chest still bleeding, his mangled pulp of a heart by his feet. Govinda did not bother to ask her why – the gruesome remains of the sacrifice around them said it all.

'He ... It was him ...' she gasped in explanation, trying to point to the magician. He was already across the courtyard and at the river's edge. 'Agnivarna Angirasa ... old man ... dungeons ... he killed him,' she gasped.

Govinda thought for an instant, but decided not to leave the wounded woman's side. There would be time to deal with Devala.

'I'll take care of it ...' he reassured her. 'First we've got to get you to a medic ...'

With effort she raised her hand towards Govinda's face and touched his cheek, staining his skin with her blood. 'There's no point ...'

'Don't say that ...'

'Let it go, Govinda Shauri. Some things must come to an end. I am an aberration. Let me die.'

Govinda looked into her eyes, staring hard at her. For an instant, his usually inscrutable expression gave to a medley of emotions, all writ clear on his face. And then, he was as always, his dark eyes warm yet indecipherable. The Kritya met his gaze with mild surprise, felt her heart throb with newfound joy, even as the feeling faded into a hollow, hungry sense of loss.

Smiling weakly, she said, 'What if I'd killed you, Govinda Shauri? How could you have trusted me?'

'What's the point of living if I can't trust another human being?'

She smiled, finally at peace. 'Then, there's hope. There's hope for us all.' Linking her fingers tightly through his, she closed her eyes.

By the time Shikandin had finished off the last of his opponents and joined Govinda, her body was limp. He swore out loud and made to go after the fleeing magician, but Govinda stopped him. 'No,' he said, 'I need you here. There's much to be done. You can hunt him down another day ...'

Grudgingly, Shikandin stepped back and sheathed both his swords.

It was almost evening when Shikandin came to join Govinda, who stood watching the flames dance over the Kritya's pyre, the eagle perched solemnly on his shoulder.

'It's done, Govinda,' he said. 'Every building has been checked, down to the dungeons and cellars. The explosions brought down some parts of the old temple, the garrison and the royal palace, but most of the buildings are intact. The idea appears to have been to reduce the size of the army as much as possible. That she did,' he nodded towards the blazing pyre.

Clearing his throat lightly he continued, 'We've found Devala's workshops and armouries; he had every medic and healer in the city – some who claim to have learnt their skill from the Wrights themselves – at work, mixing his poisons and what not. Some of them claim they were kept prisoner, while the others ... Frankly, Govinda, half of them are nothing but raving lunatics. Anyway, I've had them all arrested and placed under guard.'

'Let them go,' Govinda said perfunctorily, without looking up.

Shikandin did not dispute the injunction. 'All right.'

'What about the people, the townsfolk?'

'They've all been shifted out and are already on the plains. Our soldiers as well as the townsmen are building huts and putting up tents as we speak. As for Sudakshin's family, his son and the queen are in Devajit's care. They will be treated with all respect. I've personally sent the queen a message assuring her that she has nothing to be afraid of.'

'The city is empty?'

'Yes.'

Govinda reached up to whisper something to the eagle before setting it into the air. It circled overhead a few times and then, with a single, haunting cry, rose higher and glided out of view.

'Burn Kashi down, Shikandin,' Govinda suddenly said. 'Burn everything down. Let nothing remain of this bloody past. Burn everything down, so that we can build anew.'

Shikandin studied his friend for a moment before nodding and moving away to carry out the orders.

Late that night Shikandin walked into his tent to find Sudakshin's widow, the queen of Kashi, waiting for him. To his surprise, the bereaved woman was dressed in bridal finery. She wore red robes of the best silk and had flowers in her hair. Her eyes were rimmed with kohl, her lips stained red with a fragrant paste of sandalwood and herbs, and the faintest trace of a musky, seductive perfume filled the space.

Shikandin stared, aghast, as she walked up to him with no trace of reluctance or sorrow and took him by the hand.

'Mahamatra …?'

She did not explain. Instead she led him to a seat and handed him a glass of wine before sitting down next to him.

'You must be tired from your day's battle,' she said. 'Perhaps you'd care for a bath? Or does Prince Shikandin prefer to take his prize still covered in the sweat and blood of his conquest?'

Despite her words, Shikandin did not miss the flash of anger. And then he understood. He stood up at once. 'You mistake me. I ... I've no ...'

'You are the conqueror of Kashi. I'm your newly won property. Don't you want me? Don't you want to see how my body glows in the light of Kashi's embers? Doesn't the thought stoke your desire?' she pouted seductively at him.

'I ...' Shikandin did not know whether to feel shocked, or ashamed, or even angry with her for presuming that he would expect her in his bed.

Mistaking his confusion for hesitation, the queen stood up and threw her arms around him.

Shikandin gruffly pushed her away as he stood up. 'I'm sorry,' he gasped, after a moment.

She looked at him beseechingly from where she lay sprawled on the ground. 'What do you want from me? Tell me, whatever you want, whatever pleases you, I'll do it. Do you think I'm some child, who doesn't know or understand? I swear I'll serve you as you wish, but please ...' Then her courage failed her and she broke down completely. 'I beg you, please ... spare my son's life ...'

'Hai!' Shikandin exclaimed. He longed to comfort her, but did not dare go near her or even touch a finger lest she misunderstand. He waited till the sounds of sobbing had quietened down to a terrified whimpering.

'Mahamatra ... ?'

Grudgingly, she looked up at him.

Shikandin was clear and reassuring. 'Your son is now the ruler of Kashi. He's a very young man, yes, but he will learn soon, especially with you at his side. I promise, no harm will come to you or your son while I'm here. Please, go back to your tent and tell your son whatever truth you may know about his father and the horrors he wreaked ...'

The queen was disdainful. 'Do you think your mercy is any better than your torment? I'd much rather that you'd have ravaged me, killed me even, in exchange for my son's life. That would have been honourable. Instead, you force us to choose between living off your charity and dying a despicable death ...' She stood up, pulling herself tall. 'I'll give you one last chance. I offer myself to you. If you don't care for me alive, then kill me. Why, I won't even ask for my son's life, but rather suggest you kill him too. If you leave us alive all we'll ever show you in return for your benevolence is malice.'

Shikandin's eyes twinkled as he asked, 'Will you restrain your malice till your city is rebuilt and your people are settled back in their homes?'

'I'll hold my malice even longer. I'll hold it till my son gathers his armies and marches to war against you. As the king of Kashi ought to!'

'Then I suggest we both get some sleep. We have a long day ahead of us tomorrow. Goodnight.'

The woman considered him with open confusion for a while. Shikandin met her troubled gaze with calm certitude. Then she nodded and said, 'Goodnight, Prince. And pleasant dreams ...' She gracefully left the tent.

Shikandin waited till he was sure she was gone. Muttering something about Kashi and women under his breath, he cast aside his armour and went to see about the hot bath the queen had suggested.

It took another two weeks for the rebuilding of Kashi city to begin. Meanwhile, Govinda and Shikandin called upon the vassals of the kingdom to reaffirm allegiance to the new monarch, Sudakshin the Second, and pledge their greater loyalties to the empire.

Govinda left the affairs of Kashi city to Shikandin's care, while he spent his time negotiating and dealing with the many saamantas, rallying the smaller chieftains to the cause of a united Aryavarta. Though he had lost none of his charm or fervour while playing the role of diplomat, Govinda was clearly more muted in private. At some point, Shikandin let his concern show.

'I'm tired,' Govinda countered. 'Frankly, I can't wait to get back to Indr-prastha and be done with this!'

'Is that all, Govinda?' Shikandin pointedly asked.

Govinda thought hard before he resolutely declared, 'Yes, that's all, Shikandin. I don't have the time or the energy to waste on irrational emotions. All that was done, every life and every death, was a calculated and well-merited sacrifice. There's no need to mourn for any of them. I'm just tired, that's all.'

Shikandin did not press his friend any further and kept his opinions to himself. After that conversation, Govinda was completely his usual self. The two men spent a few more days instructing the young Sudakshin and his mother in the many matters that were left to handle before finally setting out for Indr-prastha.

'Thank you,' the queen softly told Shikandin as he said his farewell. 'You've done so much for our people that we're all indebted to you. But, remember, this doesn't change anything between us.'

'I wouldn't have it any other way, Mahamatra,' Shikandin riposted. He swung on to his horse and with a graceful bow of goodbye rode away to join Govinda.

'That's one romance I never did expect from you, Shikandin,' Govinda teased him as they set out at the head of their forces.

'More like a non-romance, don't you think?'

'Passion is passion. Don't you think?'

Shikandin shrugged. 'Well, what can I say …? The women of this city find a way to claim my very soul! I suppose there's something to be said for them, after all.'

'Right. Will you tell Panchali that, or shall I?'

The two men broke into a loud, raucous, laugh that sent a wave of mirth through the army as a whole. Soon, marching songs ran up and down the ranks and the men set a brisk pace of their own accord. Hearts filled and content, the armies marched back home under the shade of blossoming spring trees, along verdant, harvest-laden fields. The imperial campaign was over. Aryavarta was one, a vast empire poised to reach the pinnacle of its power and prosperity.

For the moment, though, their pleasures were simpler. They were going home.

26

TEN YEARS AND A MONTH SINCE DHARMA AND GOVINDA HAD
sat together, the dream of an empire between them – and now, it
was time.

The day of the imperial coronation turned out to be inappropriately
overcast. An irritatingly soft, persistent drizzle had started sometime
during the night and continued past an unnoticed dawn. The weather,
however, did little to dampen the spirit of revelry that ran through
the entire city of Indr-prastha, culminating at the newly constructed
coronation hall – a mighty rectangular structure with high ceilings
and huge, intricately carved pillars of marble and stone that ran
around its vast periphery. Its walls were a translucent white, finished
with crystals. Just as it seemed that their starkness was tiring, one
saw the delicate gold trim that had been embossed into the surface.
Small fountains dotted the extent of the hall in what appeared to be
a purposively asymmetrical arrangement. Some of these were set
into the floor itself, spurting up suddenly to surprise and amuse the
unknowing guest. In the middle of that awe-inspiring grandeur, a
sacrificial fire crackled in jubilation. The rhythm of chanting rose and
fell, mingling with the hum of conversation among the thousands of
vassals, spectators and guests seated around the hall.

For months now, preparations had been on to ensure that the
guests had every comfort imaginable. Everyone who was attending
the ceremony, from king to commoner, was housed in luxury and
fed the finest feasts. Wine flowed freely at all times of night and
day. Musical performances and entertainment of various sorts had
been arranged for, and not a moment passed without the sounds of
laughter and merriment emanating from some or the other corner
of Indr-prastha.

Meanwhile, scholars and sages from the length and breadth of
Aryavarta had arrived to invoke the gods to bless the new empire.
Presided over by Dwaipayana Vyasa, his son Suka and the royal
priest Dhaumya at his assistance, the sages sat around the six massive
sacrificial fires that roared high in the huge coronation hall. The

sound of their chanting filled the air, drowning out the excited hum of conversation from the assembled guests.

This was the day they had all been waiting for, this was the pinnacle of all revelry and ritual. In a short while, Dharma Yudhisthir, aspirant Emperor of Aryavarta, would call on the kings of the land to offer him their allegiance and accept his reign. One by one, each of the Aryas would come forward to swear their allegiance by accepting Dharma's offering of the arghya – a fragrant paste of sandalwood, incense and gold.

Syoddhan smiled to himself as he recalled the pleasant smell of the paste, the way it felt cool and sent a pleasant tingle through his fingers. He knew he had been marked with the sacred arghya when he was born. But the last, no, the only time he had touched it had been at Dharma's investiture as crown prince of Kuru all those years ago. And now he would do so again at Dharma's coronation as Emperor of Aryavarta. To his surprise, the thought of bowing to Dharma irked him more now than it had back then. Perhaps, he mused, it was because he understood what the arghya meant to him, to them all. It was considered the mark of the gods themselves and was the ultimate symbol of overlordship that kings and preceptors, the best of the best, alone were permitted to sport.

There was something primal about the moment one bowed before the vessel containing the arghya, the way one filled one's hands with the sacred substance, relishing its smell and texture. Then followed the savage smear across one's forehead, the surrender to a symbol – not of man, but of the gods and of their noble way of life. The arghya was the very blood-and-marrow of being Arya. It was what gave meaning to the empire – life on earth as a mirror to the order of the heavens, to Indra's dominion. It was from this sanctity that every one of them derived his identity, such that Aryavarta became heaven on earth. And now, Syoddhan admitted with a frown, it would give legitimacy to Dharma's supremacy, his empire.

Syoddhan knew that at least a part of his muted anger was nothing but festered regret. When the imperial campaign had started, he had thought it but an exercise in Dharma's vanity, a futile endeavour that was better ignored than envied. Now he wished he had shown more ambition, after all. Instead, all he had done these past years was to watch, silent, when with the support he had rallied he could have risen to become …

No! Syoddhan stopped himself on the brink of what he knew was a very dark, angry path; one he had seen his father traverse. It held nothing but pain; worse, pain disguised as redemption, the promise of relief. It was not a road he wished to walk, no matter what lay at the end of it. Firmly, Syoddhan reminded himself of all the factors he had considered and weighed, nearly a decade ago, when he had watched Dharma's armies march through Hastina. The choice had been his, and he had made it. For better or worse, he had chosen to support Dharma. There was no point in hating anyone, including himself, for that choice.

Breathing hard, he returned his attention to his surroundings. He stood in the huge, airy corridor that lay between the coronation hall and the new assembly hall that had been built as its twin. The entire length of the corridor was set with huge vaulted windows – or were they doors – on one side. On the other ran an unbroken wall, decorated with the most intricate patterns of creepers, birds and flowers, which came together seamlessly in the centre to form part of a gold and silver inlaid depiction of the legendary battle of the celestial Indra against the demon Vrtra. Along the middle of the corridor, and running its entire length, water flowed through a sunken pool that was more than a few feet wide. Syoddhan sighed softly, enjoying the soothing cadence of the running water. Unlike the hall, the corridor was empty and for that he was thankful. He needed to be away from the noise and the crowd for a few moments.

Syoddhan sauntered along the edge of the pool, casually admiring the stonework on the walls till he reached the fountain at the centre of the hallway. Here the pool widened to occupy the complete width of the corridor, effectively bifurcating the passage in two. He considered the fountain with interest. Out of the base of the feature rose the sculpture of a tree made of marble and inlaid with gems. Emeralds were set as leaves, and rubies and yellow sapphires as fruits.

The fountain drenched the tree in a perpetual rain-like shower, the water trickling musically off the gems to fall back into the pond. This was a constant in the architecture of Indr-prastha, he noted – there were fountains everywhere and twice as many in the twin halls. This one, he found, surpassed them all.

Just the other day he had been standing in the same place wondering how to get across without getting his robes wet, when Panchali had happened to find him there. She had laughed softly at his predicament and explained, 'It's not all water. The water flows only along the edges of the pool and around the tree. The rest of it is crystal, cut to convey the effect of water. It *is* difficult to tell the difference.'

Syoddhan had been genuinely amazed at the craftsmanship and had spent a pleasant while discussing that and many other things of note about Indr-prastha with Panchali. Somehow, the thought of her as Empress irked him less than did the idea of Dharma as Emperor.

'They're assembling, Your Highness,' an attendant intruded on his thoughts.

Slowly, almost reluctantly, Syoddhan nodded at the man, who scurried off to find others to notify. With a last look at the fountain, he turned and made his way back to the coronation hall. Syoddhan looked around the congregation and walked over to a group of men who stood together, conversing.

'Ah! There you are, Syoddhan,' Vasusena greeted him. 'Come, I suppose it's time to go see the theatricals … It's a farce, this empire!'

'Well said!' Shisupala added. 'It surprises me that the coronation is such a grand one. Surely, Dharma knows that this is an empire in name and not in fact. Look around you. I, you, King Saubha here, Syoddhan … it's the likes of *us* who form the true might of Aryavarta and we've deferred to Dharma's reign as a matter of respect and goodwill. It's not as if he defeated any of us … he requested our assent, and we gave it. He can't presume that assent also includes allegiance!'

'My dear Shisupala, what difference does it make what you call it? Would anyone dare oppose Dharma even if the cause arose? In fact, it seems every cause under the sun has been abandoned – no one has questioned the shameful way in which Jarasandha was killed. Perhaps there was no affection lost for the former king of Magadha, but what bothers me is that tomorrow his fate may well be ours. I'd hate to think that such dishonourable conduct is beyond reproach,' Vasusena finished.

Syoddhan laid a gentle hand on his friend's shoulder. 'Dishonourable action is never beyond reproach, my friend. What does any Arya have at the end of his life but his honour? An honourable life and a valiant death! No, honour can't be forsaken, no matter who it is we must oppose to preserve it.'

The fifth man, who had stood for so long on the fringes of the group listening politely, now softly intervened, 'Ah, Prince, in you runs the true blood of the line of Pururavas. Your right equals that of the Emperor-designate. Indeed, one could argue that yours is the greater claim. Your father is the rightful king of the Kurus, the monarch who sits on Emperor Hastin's throne. Your grandfather Dwaipayana and your grand-uncle Bhisma love you no less than they do your cousin. But, sadly, they remain prisoners of politics. My station precludes me from calling it a shame, but I will nevertheless impose on our childhood familiarity to deem it exactly that ...' He looked resignedly in Dharma's direction.

'Sanjaya!' Syoddhan chided.

Sanjaya immediately bowed. 'My apologies. I'm clearly not myself today. Of course, the Grandsire and the Vyasa would do right by you. The First Honour at today's ceremony will surely be yours. You alone have the right to touch the sacred arghya before any other man here.'

'I should expect so!' Vasusena added. 'Is there another here who can stake claim to it?'

'There are many, my friend,' Syoddhan pointed out with a smile. 'The Vyasa himself, for one. For years now, across all of Aryavarta, wherever First Honour has been shown the recipient has been Dwaipayana or, with his blessings, the Grandsire Bhisma. Then there's Acharya Dron, who was teacher to us all. King Dhrupad – the eldest of the Panchalas. Don't forget that they're as old and respected a line as the Kurus.'

Sanjaya said, 'Age is just one part of it. The First Honour is a rare accolade, given only to those of exceptional valour, scholarship and nobility. Men defeated even once in battle, or those of low birth cannot aspire to it. I've heard,' he lowered his voice slightly, 'that even the former Emperor was refused the honour by the noble Firstborn seers.'

'That's rot!' Vasusena bristled. 'The First Honour always goes to the most influential man, irrespective of status, nobility, valour and that sort of thing. Military and financial might both lie in the hands of a few. And right now they lie dominantly in our hands, a fact Dharma would do well to keep in mind.'

'Surely, the Vyasa knows …'

'The Vyasa may or may not know, Sanjaya. Isn't what's happening around us proof of it all? Or have you forgotten what I said but moments ago, you two-faced muhira!'

'I do remember, and I beg your forgiveness for offending you. But I remain loyal to my liege and my teacher both, and I speak here of an offence against the one but not necessarily an offence by the other. There are others present at this coronation, those with great power and whom we have much cause to dislike … for more reasons than one.' With another bow and an inciting look that said much he walked away, blending quickly into the endless mass of royal glitter and finery that now filled the hall.

The others of the group too slowly dispersed, relieved at having expressed their displeasure but still burdened by their helplessness in the circumstances. One, however, stood lost in his thoughts.

'What is it?' Syoddhan asked, wrapping an arm around his friend's shoulder.

Shisupala pensively regarded Syoddhan. 'He's right you know … Sanjaya's right,' he began.

'Hmm?'

'This isn't just about you, your cousin, or the Vyasa. There is another here, one who has done much to bring this to pass.

Someone whom we have, as Sanjaya says, more than one reason to dislike.'

Syoddhan sighed, a little tired of the veiled statements, the underlying discontent and intrigue. A while ago, standing by the crystal fountain, he had felt light-hearted and joyful at the thought of the Empire, the unification of these lands. Now, it was back to the same, tired resignation that he tended to associate with the royal court of Hastina. 'What do you mean, Shisupala?' he asked, reluctant.

Shisupala said, 'There's an old legend back in the forests of Chedi–Surasena. It tells of how the Firewrights had the craft to cleave through rock and stone. Both the Danavas and the Nagas inherited their skills from the Wright scholars of old. The Danavas learnt how to fashion rock into brick and tower to build, and the Naga sacquired the skills to burrow through the very mountains. Strange, isn't it, that all it would take is such a tunnel through the Western Mountains for Dwaraka's armies to reach Vidharbha in less than a night?

'And who in this day and age could build such a tunnel? My dear friend, for all the talk of love and romance, the fact remains that Govinda Shauri could very well have planned the whole affair. There's nothing astounding about what happened at Vidharbha, if we're willing to admit we were outfoxed. Dwaraka's armies must have left some days earlier, sailed along the coast and somehow rounded the northern end of the Western Mountains. Or the yadus might have found the tunnel of old but kept it a secret. But to think that they could have carved a tunnel through sheer rock …? The Western Mountains are both broad and impregnable!'

Shisupala's voice was soft as he said, 'As were the mountains of Kandava, the rock and stone that once stood in this very place … Perhaps, my friend, a kernel of truth lies hidden in the most absurd of tales?'

'Shisupala …' Syoddhan looked at his friend askance.

'They also say the Danavas helped build Dwaraka. Even helped design Indr-prastha, if rumour is to be believed …'

Syoddhan gradually understood where this was leading and even the mere suspicion made him feel uneasy. He shook his head in an attempt at denial. 'Dwaipayana ... he would never allow it. You remember how he maligned Jarasandha's name by saying he harboured Firewright magicians? How then could he approve of Dharma's actions if ...?' He glanced at the largest of the six ritual fires, at which the Vyasa sat officiating as chief priest.

Shisupala appeared not to have heard. His eyes rested on a figure that stood laughing and bantering with a group of Yadu chiefs and nobles.

'Look at him,' he hissed, contemptuous. 'Look at that cowherd strutting around as if he were one of us! I first saw him when he was about seventeen. I was the same age. He looked every bit the lowly commoner he really is. And now? Does no one see what I see, Syoddhan? Or have we all become wilfully blind because all we care about is ourselves, our thrones and kingdoms, and our greed. Won't anyone ask how a man can come to this, how he can build a veritable empire, if the very demons of the earth haven't become his slaves? Hai! Even your Vyasa ... even *he* makes his peace with the evil Govinda is, just to see his grandson on the imperial throne. The blood of Varuna and Pururavas have indeed both failed!'

Syoddhan frowned. 'Are you saying this because of Vidharbha? Because of what happened there?'

'Vidharbha, Pragjya, Kashi, and who knows how many other places. Right from that whore Panchali's wedding ...'

'Shisupala!' Syoddhan instinctively railed at the insult. 'By Rudra, what's wrong with you all today? First Vasusena, then Sanjaya, and now you?'

A strained glance passed between the two friends.

'I'm sorry,' Shisupala eventually said. 'Look, just forget what I said. We'd better take our seats. It's time for the final ceremonies. We'll talk about this later. If you want to, that is ...'

Syoddhan nodded. Shisupala managed a wan smile and left to join his father and others of his family.

As he went to take his own place next to King Dhritarastra, Syoddhan tried hard to put the conversation out of his mind, to remove all suspicion and ignore all regret. The sight of Dharma

403

hurrying over to where the Vyasa sat in conference with Bhisma, Sanjaya standing meekly behind them, caught his attention. He reminded himself not to stare. Instead, he looked around the hall, at what Shisupala had called the true might of Aryavarta, trying to find pride in his beloved homeland.

Despite his efforts, Syoddhan did not entirely succeed.

27

DHARMA YUDHISTHIR WAS A HAPPY MAN, BUT NOT AS HAPPY AS he ought to have been. He strode the length of the hall, returning the many greetings and congratulations directed at him with the perfect balance of warm humility and pride that became a benevolent ruler, and meeting every smile with a nod that was neither overly respectful nor excessively condescending. The former, he found, was much easier than the latter. The occasion apart, the sheer splendour of Indr-prastha made modesty difficult. Dharma smiled to himself at the thought of the many monarchs who had stood astounded by the marvels of the coronation hall, and of course, the city itself.

Indr-prastha, he thought as he silently enunciated the word, was a fitting imperial capital. The capital of an empire that was his, yet not. Just as he was happy, yet not.

Dharma dismissed the notion and bowed lower than he had all day as he came up to where Dwaipayana Vyasa was seated. Next to the scholar, the Grandsire Bhisma shone resplendent in his finery.

'Acharya, you sent for me?' Dharma respectfully enquired.

Dwaipayana nodded. 'It's time, my son. The rituals are done. It's time to call things to order and begin the coronation,' he declared. He gestured towards the congregation at large. Dharma saw that the attendees were being ushered into their seats. At one end of the rectangular area at the centre of the hall was a slightly elevated dais on which the imperial throne now stood, awaiting its new master. Under Dhaumya's supervision, Sadev and Nakul carried a heavy, gem-studded cup of arghya to a pedestal placed in the large space that had been cleared at the base of the dais. Despite the anticipation, the arrival of the penultimate moment took the Emperor-designate by breathless surprise. He grinned, revealing an unusual nervousness that was charming in its own way.

Dwaipayana laughed softly at that before saying, 'There still remains a matter that must be discussed and decided upon – the First Honour.'

Dharma turned his attention to the two senior men, a hint of consternation on his face. 'Acharya, if there's room for discussion on that, it is perhaps on who ought to receive First Honour between the two of you. That delicate issue, too, I thought had been resolved by your kindness in acting as the hotr, the presiding priest, for the ceremony.'

'You think it ought to be your grand-uncle, then?'

'Certainly. Even Jarasandha offered him First Honour. As did Ugrayudha, Asvattama and countless others ... Really, I can't think of a coronation or investiture in the Grandsire's lifetime where he wasn't honoured as best among us all. Where you are first of the Firstborn, he stands as first among warriors. To honour a lesser man implies that I know nothing of honour, that my own rule is blemished! I ...' Dharma stopped short at the doubtful expression on Dwaipayana's face. He turned to the Grandsire. Bhisma sat silent and sombre.

'Acharya ...' Dharma uncertainly began.

Dwaipayana clucked his tongue in mild disapproval. 'What is the purpose of this public declaration of allegiance, Dharma?' he asked.

'To show beyond doubt the power and the legitimacy of the emperor. By swearing their allegiance, the kings of Aryavarta derive their authority to rule and command from the emperor and, in turn, they legitimize his reign as their sovereign.'

'And how do they then continue to show their allegiance?'

Dharma looked peeved at being quizzed, but nevertheless replied, 'Through the tributes and taxes they pay. The process of affirming allegiance also has an economic significance. That's as self-explanatory as it is basic governance.'

'Correct. And whom do we traditionally call upon first to so declare allegiance? To whom do we show First Honour?'

'To the one who most deserves it. The best of fighters, strongest of monarchs, the most learned of men. To the best of them all, the ...'

'Isn't that supposed to be the emperor?' Dwaipayana softly interrupted. 'The best of them all?'

Dharma frowned, uncertain. He glanced from the Vyasa, to Bhisma, to Sanjaya. Their expressions were inscrutable. He floundered for words, but could find nothing appropriate to say.

With a sigh, the Vyasa continued, 'In moments you will be Emperor. You need to accept that politics is as much a part of your coronation as it will be of your rule. My son, the First Honour is given to the best man there is – the man who is most powerful, economically and politically. It's given to him so that the emperor's rule is legitimized beyond a doubt and accepted by the one who is in a position to question it, shake it and even defy it. Recognize your greatest enemy and make him your friend; make him duty-bound by law and honour to defend your reign. Show First Honour to the one man who could have been Emperor, but isn't.'

Dharma's voice was hollow, as he said the name out loud. 'Govinda Shauri.'

'Yes. Govinda Shauri. Bind him to you, Dharma. Bind the man who helped build your empire to you, so that he can never bring you down.'

In the silence that followed, it seemed to Dharma that the tumult around them had grown louder than ever. He forced himself to think over the Vyasa's words, to see things with the cold, political acumen that was now expected of him. But he simply could not. Anger, regret and the ever-present sense of owing everything to Govinda cloaked him and left him with a heavy heart.

Dharma turned again to Bhisma, to the man he had longed to become, silently beseeching.

The Grandsire stood up and placed an encouraging hand on Dharma's back. 'He's right, Dharma. Your reign is more important than these trivial accolades. You will make a good emperor, a just and honourable ruler. Aryavarta needs you. It's important to accept that, and to do what it takes to support your reign. Let the First Honour go to Govinda Shauri.'

'No,' Dharma shook his head. 'It's not right. It's not fair,' he persisted. 'Sir, please ...' he looked back to Dwaipayana.

His pained reluctance made the Vyasa hesitate for a moment. The Elder exchanged glances, first with Sanjaya and then with the one person whom he trusted the most – his son, the silent, discreet Suka. Both men nodded.

In a firmer tone Dwaipayana said, 'Dharma, you must understand what I'm trying to tell you. Man's only goal is to imitate divinity, and to do so the cosmic order must be recreated on earth as a social order. The gods themselves have brought you to this juncture; they have brought everything to this juncture. Your empire will be the mirror of heaven, the golden reign of your forebears Pururavas and Hastin that the people still remember and long for. Don't disappoint them. Don't disappoint me!'

Dharma opened his mouth to protest, but the significance of Dwaipayana's words sunk in. He finally saw in his heart of hearts that he had been appointed by destiny, charged by the very gods to carry the burden to protect and preserve their ordained way of life. He hung his head for a few moments, trying to fight back the tumult of emotions within. At length he said, 'And if anyone were to ask how we overlooked the Grandsire ...?'

Bhisma squeezed Dharma's shoulder in reassurance. 'I will announce Govinda's name for the First Honour. No one will contest it then. It's as good as done, Dharma. Now, stand tall and take your place on the throne. It's time Aryavarta swore allegiance to you.'

28

'PANCHALI!' DHARMA WALKED INTO THE ANTE-CHAMBER where she sat with Subadra, sharing quiet memories of old times. 'Come. It's time,' he held out his hand. The action clearly contained less joy and anticipation than it ought to have, but Panchali said nothing. Instead, she stood up and smoothed out her dazzling red and green-brown silk robes.

'Wait, let me treat you with a little insolence while I still may,' Subadra teased as she helped settle Panchali's robes into place.

Panchali smiled her thanks and stepped out of the room, into the coronation hall. The mere thought of what was to follow took her breath away for an instant, and she bit her lip nervously. Needing reassurance, she looked around the space. Her heart brimmed with affection as her gaze fell on loved ones. Dharma's brothers waited nearby, each one's face reflecting the excitement she felt. Next to them was Dhrstyadymn, looking every bit the king he would soon be. Shikandin, quiet and confident as always, stood leaning casually against a pillar.

And then, the future – Subadra's son, *her* son, Abhimanyu – the heir to Dharma's throne. The boy stood at that precious threshold of youth where he had the bearing of the man he would soon be and yet possessed the innocence of the child he still was. Even now his attention was divided between the events around him and the game of tiger-and-lambs he was playing with his older cousin and best friend, Shikandin's son, Yudhamanyu. Pradymna watched them play with interest, his infant child in his arms. Aniruddha, Govinda had lovingly named his grandson. Sovereign of his own self.

Panchali felt a slight smile form on her lips as she saw Govinda. He had traded in his simple robes for a warm, blood-red silk cloth embellished with silver weaves. For once he wore a gemstone, a large ruby set in gold, which hung from a chain around his neck. It came to rest right on the symbol of Sri that was marked into his skin, drawing proud attention to the stories of his youth. She took in the slight smattering of silver-grey at Govinda's temples and the fine lines that showed at the corners of his eyes when he smiled.

While his friends and his sons found great mirth in dubbing him an old man, the truth was that Govinda's presence had only grown breathtakingly stronger as he came into the prime of his life. His eyes still sparkled with mischief, but he now exuded a quiet power and dignity. As always, there also remained that private darkness that no one, not even Panchali, could read. It made her wonder if she looked any different to him.

Ever since Govinda had returned from the imperial campaign, conversation between them had remained at a minimum. They had both been occupied with other things and he had also returned often to Dwaraka to see to the affairs of his nation. Panchali had not complained, nor had she asked about Kashi, or Devala, or the many other incidents that had come to pass during the campaign. Govinda, for his part, had offered no explanations;neither to her nor to anyone else. Nor had he spoken of what she had known or done, and for that Panchali was grateful. It had become instinct now to hide almost every honest thought and feeling from the one to whom she had once bared her soul.

The silent realization had a sobering effect, as her mind went to what lay ahead. Panchali fell in next to Dharma and the two of them walked towards the dais. The musicians struck up a buoyant tune and, around them, people began settling into their places.

As they neared the dais, Panchali could barely contain her excitement. She gently whispered to Dharma, 'Is everything all right? What did the Vyasa say?'

Dharma did not reply.

Panchali could sense his confusion, the horrible sense of wanting to hate the very dream that had come true, for it no longer remained a dream, but was now reality. A stark reality that reminded Dharma, relentelessly, of how little he had done to deserve it. She had neither words of congratulation nor consolation to offer him, though not for lack of kindness. Keenly aware that everyone was watching them, she forced herself to look up, taking in the moment, the brightness around her. She saw her father gazing at her with ostensible pride and perhaps the remnants of surprise that she had amounted to something after all. Vidur beamed at her happily, just a hint of concern in his eyes, and to her astonishment Asvattama flashed her a small smile.

Try as she might to avoid it, Panchali's attention, indeed her whole being, was drawn yet again to just one man. Govinda, now sitting flanked by Balabadra and Kritavarman. She knew it was just her imagination, but the quiet arrogance he emanated seemed to fill the hall. She could feel his gaze bore into her back as she turned and ascended the dais to reach the glittering throne. The music reached a dramatic high.

'Sit!' Dharma barked at her.

She silently complied, feeling none of the jubilation that the occasion demanded. Dharma's harsh tone made her stomach churn, even as it reminded her that indeed, she ought not to feel the least bit happy. This was wrong, terribly wrong. Dharma would be Emperor yes, but of nothing. Govinda would mark Dharma's reign indelibly as his own; this had been *his* empire since the day he had begun planning the campaign over ten years ago. This was what he had given up so much for. *Including those who've loved and trusted him. Including me.*

Panchali was tired of making her peace with that, over and over again. She was tired of being angry at Govinda, and longed to see him as she once had, an honest, fearless man with neither ambition nor guile. Her eyes filled with flustered tears, and she stared, unseeing, at the arghya vessel at the foot of the dais. She clenched her fists tight, willing herself to not give in to emotion, not now. This time, she could not, would not fail. This time, neither she nor Aryavarta would become Govinda's puppets.

At last, the musicians stopped playing.

Bhisma stood up and raised his hand, signalling for silence as the entire assembly respectfully turned their attention to him.

'In the name of Rudra and Varuna,' he began, 'the heavens have descended today, bringing with them the gods and celestials, for nowhere have we seen such a confluence of wisdom, valour, and virtue as have gathered here. Blessed are those who undertake the sacred ceremony of imperial dominion as are those who conduct it, and on those who attend the sacrifice, too, great honour is due. Now, my kings, it is time ... '

Bhisma raised his stentorian voice, 'Dharma Yudhisthir, of the line of Pururavas and Hastin, honours you as preceptors and overlords under his reign, beginning with the traditional First Honour to the best of us all. Accept Dharma's recognition and so declare him Emperor. Join me now in inviting the most worthy man here to lead us all in proclaiming our allegiance.'

A thundering applause greeted the Grandsire's words, along with the booming of horns and the sombre rolling of drums. Into that expectant crescendo, Bhisma dropped the words, 'Govinda Shauri.'

29

PANCHALI TURNED SHARPLY TO GOVINDA, BUT HE WAS NO LONGER looking at her. For an instant his eyes held a hint of surprise and then took on a distant glaze as he briefly considered Bhisma's words. Then, his face devoid of expression, he began making his way towards the dais.

A dreadful silence enveloped the hall. Many of those assembled looked on in confusion, others in irritation. As the assembled guests gradually began to understand what was going on, a murmur that could have been assent or discontent, perhaps even both, began to form.

For his part, Govinda cared not. As he strode up, his eyes came to rest on Panchali. He did not turn away from her when Dhaumya received him near the dais with an indulgent shake of his head, nor when a visibly happy Sadev escorted him the next few steps to where the Emperor and Empress designate sat towering over them all. Govinda did not speak, he made no promises of loyalty and swore no oaths of servitude. His vision, his senses, filled with his Empress, Panchali, and nothing else, he went down on one knee, not breaking his gaze even as he bowed.

Dharma fumbled to say the appropriate words of grateful acceptance and barely managed to nod his acknowledgement.

Govinda stood up, still solemn, his arrogance not diminished in the least. Slowly, almost sensuously, he dipped his fingers into the arghya. He filled his hands with the heavy paste and raised them to his face. His eyes closed for just a moment as he smeared it across his forehead and then ran his fingers back, through his hair, spreading the fragrance through the dark curls, as though revelling in the feel of the arghya and all that it meant.

Panchali watched, feeling as she had many years ago at Kampilya, reeling in the intimacy that she had locked deep into her memory when Govinda had run his fingers through her hair. The recollection was too much for her to bear. She wanted nothing more than to forget the intrigue, conspiracies and complexities around them, than for things to go back to the way they had once been, for life to be filled with the simple joys of Govinda's presence, his laughter and his equanimity. Her lips parted in the beginning of a serene smile, but before she could help herself a soft cry had escaped her throat.

The sound was lost in the loud thud that followed.

The next instant, the arghya vessel fell to the stone floor with a jarring clatter. An unpleasant grating echoed through the hall as it rolled round and round, caught in an excruciating eddy of motion till, at last, it hit the stone pedestal on which it had stood with a booming clang.

'How could you!' Shisupala's voice, strangely high-pitched, rent the air. 'How could you! How dare you even touch this!' he screamed again. He looked close to tears as he kicked at the fallen arghya vessel, letting his pain turn to rage. His huge frame quivered, and his chest rose and fell as he laboured hard to contain his temper. Whipping around, his eyes searched the hall till he found the man he was looking for. 'No, wait,' he said, his voice quivering from the effort to contain himself, 'I don't even want to talk to the cowherd. It's this fool of an emperor and his honourable advisors I ought to deal with. Bhisma! Bhisma Devavrata! How could you allow this? What have you fools done? Dhik! Shame on you! Shame on you all!'

Shisupala strode forward, to stand directly before Bhisma's seat. He continued, 'You call on monarchs and preceptors to legitimize the emperor, and a cowherd is the best you can find to lead us? And like a stray dog picking up scraps and leftovers, this slave-born bastard Govinda accepts ... He dares accept the First Honour; he dares to touch the sacred arghya? And you just sit there, smiling on it all! Yabha! Is there any honour left in the blood of Aryas? Answer me, Bhisma. Or have you turned senile once and for all?'

'Why, that son of a ...' Bhim began to move forward, but Bhisma grabbed his hand restraining him.

'Shisupala, my boy,' he began, 'I shall forgive your words as spoken in the impetuosity of youth. You ask why Govinda Shauri was given First Honour. The answer is simple: Because he deserves it. We considered ... why, I considered everyone here, young and old, and decided that no one merits this show of respect more than he does. Does that satisfy you?'

'Satisfy? It satisfies me that you're mad indeed! Don't you know the law? A man born into captivity, the son of prisoner parents, is nothing but a slave. What right does Govinda Shauri have to even be here? When fortune carried him to the brink of nobility, he pissed in its face. Can you deny it? Can anyone here deny that he surrendered Mathura? And you place this slave on par with the likes of us? How dare you treat him as our equal, our leader? This is an insult to us all. I will not be led by a cowherd, not in battle, and certainly not in proclaiming my allegiance to this muhira of an Emperor!'

The categorical declaration pulled the assembly out of its shock. The guests slowly began to comprehend Shisupala's argument. Many found his cause to be valid and said as much, while others tried to reason with them. As voices rose, harsh and angry, and the situation grew decidedly unpleasant, Syoddhan went up to Shisupala to try to calm him down. Shisupala simply pushed his friend away. Balabadra and Yuyudhana were already arguing with Kritavarman and some of the other Yadus who had taken Shisupala's side.

At a signal from Dwaipayana, Dron and Asvattama had discreetly placed themselves close to the unarmed cluster of priests and scholars as a precaution. Shikandin signalled to Pradymna to keep an eye on the young Abhimanyu and Yudhamanyu even as he and Dhrstyadymn silently moved close to Govinda. Partha and Nakul came to stand next to Sadev, their eyes on Dharma as they awaited his command. Bhim alone remained determinedly vocal. He let

413

out another menacing cry, punctuated with a few choice expletives and threats.

Bhisma restrained him yet again, this time loudly proclaiming, 'Let him be, Bhim. He's an imbecile. What does he know of honour, or law, or morality?'

Shisupala grit his teeth. He had neither patience nor respect left to waste on the Grandsire. 'You, Bhisma!' he called out rudely. 'Careful, old man! You can only condemn your kin with your blind folly for so long. Sooner or later, they *will* see you for the gutless woman that you are. You asked what I know of honour and morality. Where were *you*, noble and honourable one, when Govinda Shauri cheated and lied his way into Jarasandha's palace? Where were you when he killed his own uncle, Kans? Govinda is nothing but a murderer, but you allow him to be honoured as befits a king? You, who claim to worship law and morality – how did you ever allow all this to come to pass? Perhaps your great vow of chastity, too, should be suspect …'

'How dare you!' Bhisma bristled. In all these years not even the greatest or most revered of men had spoken to him the way this arrogant fool was. His hand flew to the hilt of his sword, but he did not draw it.

Shisupala noticed, and gleefully challenged him, 'Fight me, old man. For too long the great kings of Aryavarta have looked up to you, feared your reputation. It's time to show them that you are nothing but a sycophant, singing praises of Dharma and his cowherd lackey. You are but a spineless eunuch – possibly in more ways than one! Shandha! Impotent!'

Bhisma let out an angry cry, sounding every bit the warrior he was. 'Come then, you arrogant fool! Come and die!'

'Why would I fight you, shandha? You're a coward of the worst kind, for you justify your actions with no less a veil than righteousness! I used to hold much respect for you. You are, after all, Grandsire to Syoddhan – the man on whose silence Dharma's new empire stands. But it never occurred to you to even ask why Dharma is being crowned and not Syoddhan, did it? Rather, it did,

414

but you're just too damned afraid to speak! One word from you and none of this would've happened.'

At the mention of his name, Syoddhan tried yet again to intervene, this time by appealing to Bhisma. The Grandsire simply shook the younger man off, his eyes on Shisupala all the time. 'Enough boy! You're asking for a drubbing!' he cautioned.

'Boy? Yes, that's pretty much what we, the kings of Aryavarta, have been to you and your beloved grandchild Dharma, haven't we? Boys! Hah! We're great kings! We won't be treated with such impunity. We will not swear our allegiance to any fool emperor.'

'You question my decision? My fairness? Fight then, you bastard! And bring your great kings, as you call them, with you! I spit on them all! Not one of you has the bloody pluck to question me this way, leave alone speak of either being Emperor or receiving the First Honour!'

Shouts of anger, threats and conciliation all rose and drowned in one senseless drone of noise. Many more swords were drawn as the assembled kings erupted at Bhisma's words, their eager chants ringing off the walls.

'Burn the old man! What does he think we are, his slaves?'

'Kill the arrogant madman!'

'He's lived for far too long already. Syoddhan, Dussasan, rid yourself of this dotard and his stupidity.'

'If only it were stupidity … He's a coward and a hypocrite, too. Eunuch, rightly said!'

'Go on, Shisupala! Kill him. Do us all a favour and redeem the honour of kings.'

Vilified, Bhisma's anger rose and his face turned red. He tightly gripped the hilt of his sword. A confrontation was imminent. Yet, even as the gathering waited with bated breath, the imminent did not come to pass. Bhisma did nothing, nor did the Vyasa.

At that realization Dharma stirred. His reaction, still, was one of disbelief. 'But … how … why …?' Looking bewildered, he turned to Govinda.

Govinda stood still as stone, exactly where he had been when Shisupala had intervened. His head was bowed, not in shame but in silent acceptance, and he did not stir. Not even when Shisupala spat on the ground right in front of him.

'What ...' Dharma repeated.

Panchali watched silently, feeling her well-practised, quiet acceptance cloak her once more. She knew well what Govinda waited for and why: That one moment when Dharma, and all of Aryavarta, would turn to him to set things right. To resolve the situation as he always had and only he could. The moment of surrender that was far more powerful than receiving First Honour, or any declaration of allegiance, any crown or throne. Or, perhaps, he truly was crushed. For all that he had done, all that he had achieved, there were some things Govinda could never have. Perhaps, this once, he felt the pain of his loss after all. Panchali desperately wanted to believe it was so, and she knew a part of her did.

She sprang to her feet. The sudden action forced Dharma out of his daze, and he too stood up. The almost-Emperor looked around in helpless alarm, his gaze finally coming to rest on the woman next to him. Her calm countenance drove him to action. He ran down the stepped dais towards the centre of the altercation, Panchali right behind him.

Going directly to Shisupala, Dharma began, 'Your Highness, please ...'

This only made Shisupala break into raucous guffaws. He threw his arms up in dramatic despair, and said, 'Ah, now Dharma will beg, will he? At last, the *Emperor* will deign to speak to us! Why not? Honour, honour, honour – we all keep spouting this great word. But honour means no more to you than it does to your Grandsire there. He's spent his life licking Dwaipayana's feet and you continue the tradition. If only you'd chosen someone as worthy as the Vyasa instead of this bastard cowherd to serve with your grovelling ... But enough!'

His voice was sincere, even sympathetic, as he said, 'You've damned yourself, Dharma. Your coronation is now worthless, for no man here will swear allegiance to you. Your empire means nothing at all and your dominion is forfeit. Enough! Stop this travesty of a sacrifice at once!'

'But …'

'No, Dharma. It is done. You had your chance and you've lost it. You've lost all that you gained because you've lost your honour. You threw it at that slave-boy's feet and lost it all. You're a disgrace to every Arya.'

A speechless Dharma stepped back, his head hanging low in shame and agony. His surrender seemed to signal the end. Many of the assembled kings prepared to leave. A whisper of consensus ran through the hall, the words indistinct, but clearly mocking the farce the coronation had now become. In a slow, almost reconciled way, the crowd began to disperse.

30

'WAIT!' THE COMPELLING VOICE STOPPED THE DEPARTING KINGS in their tracks.

A tired, forced stillness fell over them all. Panchali sighed, feeling somewhat irritated by the predictability, the inescapable melodrama. It came almost as a relief to her when Shisupala refused to be taken in by it.

'Wait for what, cowherd?' he rasped. 'You're really nothing but a slave. Who are you to command us all?'

'I'm just a man like you, Shisupala …'

'You're nothing like me. You are *nothing*! The son of a slave mother, a liar and a cheat, that's what you are. And Dharma worships you? And that old eunuch over there happily consents to it all like a whore spreading her legs? Why, cowherd? Why, why, why?'

Snarling like an animal, Shisupala addressed the entire gathering, 'Come on, all of you, ask yourselves … Why, in Rudra's name, does Dharma give such importance to a man who's good for absolutely nothing? This man here, this Govinda, to whom Dharma shows First Honour – this spineless rat surrendered the city he was sworn to defend as its ruler, when the honourable thing, if he knew what that meant, would have been to hang from the palace tower or to slit his own throat. But no! Govinda Shauri pissed on us all, and lives to tell the tale. He then assassinates the same emperor he ran from and we all keep our silence and watch, the epitome of honour, Bhisma here, included.'

Shisupala walked up to Govinda, getting close enough for the other man to feel his breath, taste the venom and hatred in it. His voice was a hiss, a harsh whisper that curled its way through the entire assembly and sent a shiver down every spine. 'I'm not the best of men,' he declared. 'I know I stand here in the shadows of great kings. But I am Arya and I am a better man than this Govinda. We – every Yadu here – should have killed him the day he traded our kingdom and our homes for his ambition and safety. Yes, Govinda, we should have quartered you and left your head on a stake in front of the Varaha temple at Mathura for the crows to peck at and the common folk to piss on. And what do we do? We leave you alive, for you to stand here and claim First Honour today, to lead us all in bowing to your figurehead emperor. No! Worse,' Shisupala shook his head and added, 'we do so without question. We do it all without question, slaves to the slave!'

He glared at Govinda, who met his gaze without acrimony or amusement. Unperturbed, Shisupala turned his attention back to his rapt audience. He knew that the entire congregation hung on his every word and so chose them carefully. He now sounded more aggrieved than angry and to good effect. Anger was something that already simmered in their hearts. He needed them to use it, and use it well.

Shisupala's eyes sought out Syoddhan and rested lightly, meaningfully, on him for a moment before he looked over the assembled faces and asked, 'Answer me, great kings of Aryavarta. What could Govinda Shauri possibly offer Dharma that our would-be Emperor flouts the most sacred of laws and tramples on the very essence of being Arya with such impunity?'

The hushed stillness that greeted his challenge held many answers.

Soon, Shisupala knew, some of them – those who truly mattered – would hit upon the one answer to all his questions. When that happened …

He felt content at the thought. Squaring his shoulders, he resolutely turned back to Govinda. There still remained the final confrontation, the one thing left to be said.

Malice seeped from every pore of Shisupala's being. His eyes were red and bulging, the veins on his temples throbbed visibly and his voice was a low rumble as he began, 'I should have known, back then, in Vidharbha … Perhaps I did, but I refused to believe it. You can't fool me anymore, Govinda! You can cover Aryavarta with your tales and tricks, but you don't frighten me! I don't care if you're …'

For the shortest moment, emotion flickered across Govinda's face. 'Enough, Cousin!'

The reaction took Shisupala by surprise. He hesitated for a moment, smiling to himself as he thought of something, the gesture betraying his familial relationship to Govinda. He declared, 'True, Govinda. I've had enough. Come, *Cousin*. Let's finish this as we should have, three decades ago!'

With that, Shisupala drew his sword.

A chilling stillness took hold of the hall. It erupted in a roar as Govinda slid his blade out from its scabbard.

As he stepped back, Dharma instinctively pulled at Panchali's arm. She refused to move. For the briefest instant, her eyes met Syoddhan's, where he stood across the open space. Without words, the two of them turned back to the duel that was set to begin.

'He's mad,' Dharma whispered. 'Govinda's mad. Shisupala's one of the best …'

Panchali snapped under her breath, 'Best, strongest, greatest … Is there anyone we don't describe in superlative terms? Any Arya who's just a person and proud of it? By Rudra, can we get over ourselves, ever?'

Her irate words did little to hide her anxiety. Shisupala was clearly the larger and more powerful man, and the way he twirled his sword as he cautiously circled his opponent showed he was an expert at handling the weapon.

By contrast, Govinda stood where he was, the tip of his sword resting lightly on the ground, his eyes following Shisupala's every move. Without warning, Shisupala rushed at him, sweeping his blade down with all his might. Govinda raised his own just in time. The clang of metal on metal rang loud, followed by the scrape of burnished blade against blade as the two men drew apart.

For a man of his size, Shisupala was light on his feet. He sprang again at Govinda, jumping into the air to add more force to his blow. Govinda parried, and the two men moved around in a quick succession of strokes and counters that left them both breathless. Drawing back slightly, Shisupala resumed circling, looking for the right opening, while Govinda waited, his sword held up before him.

Once more, Shisupala came forward to attack, this time turning his downward stroke into a sideways thrust at the last moment. Govinda saw the feint, side-stepped it, and brought down the flat of his sword right where his opponent's blade met the hilt. It was a move that would have disarmed most men, at least painfully strained their wrist. The burly Shisupala merely grimaced and looked none the worse for it. 'Is that all you can do?' he jeered.Govinda did not rise to the bait. He stepped back and waited for the next attack.

A small group of Shisupala's friends and vassals joined Syoddhan where he stood. One of these men ran forward to throw Shisupala a shield, which the man happily accepted.

'Want one?' he cheerfully taunted Govinda. 'Don't complain later to Yama's minions that I killed you because you didn't have a shield, you coward!'

Immediately Dharma looked around to his own, wondering which one of his allies would do the same for Govinda. Nakul was about to step forward, when Shikandin firmly shook his head to tell him not to.

Govinda remained oblivious to these silent exchanges, his attention fixed on his opponent. Shisupala clanged sword against shield. The noise resounded through the hall, dispelling all traces of the festivities that had been on but a short while ago. This was battle.

Shisupala flew at Govinda again, grunting loudly as he threw all his strength into the stroke. Govinda brought his weapon up in a two-handed counter. Immediately, Shisupala used his shield to land a hard blow on Govinda's shoulder and chest from the side. Govinda took the blow, using the proximity to bring his left hand up to punch his opponent hard on his face. Shisupala staggered back slightly. He spit the blood from his mouth onto the marbled floor, supplementing the action with as much derision as he could muster. And then, he raised his sword and made ready for another attack.

This time, though, Govinda made the first move. He stepped in close before raising his sword, leaving Shisupala guessing. At the last possible moment he twisted inwards, driving his sword in a stabbing stroke. In response, Shisupala dropped his shield and used his now-empty hand to grab Govinda's sword-arm. He tried to twist it back, but quick as lightning Govinda spun around and mirrored the ploy. Both men were now caught back-to-back, each man's sword-arm in the grip of the other's fist. Sinews strained as the two tried to use brute force to twist the other man's wrist and get him to drop his sword.

Here, Shisupala had a clear advantage, in terms of his physical strength. With a loud yell, he willed every bit of his strength into his bulging arms and pulled. His plan, simply, was to pull Govinda's arms out of their sockets or get as painfully close to it as possible. Govinda knew it was futile to resist. He simply could not match Shisupala in terms of pure strength. He frowned against the pain, tried to shut out sound, smell, every sense of where he was and what was around him. Fighting the instinct to hit back or to struggle, he centred his entire being, his consciousness into the moment, a deeper oneness that didn't know Govinda, Shisupala nor even the battle between them. A particular lightness, an incorporeal relief against the pain, flooded him. He let his sword drop out of his hand.

A gasp somewhere nearby, a cry of triumph closer still and an amorphous cheer made of many voices filled the air. Govinda heard nothing. With calculated decisiveness, he twisted to his left, coming up from under Shisupala's outstretched sword-arm, to partly face the man. He then butted him in the head, hard. Shisupala reeled, as much from surprise as from the impact. It was just the opening Govinda needed. He pulled his now empty sword-hand out from Shisupala's grasp. At the same time he used his other hand, still wrapped around Shisupala's sword-arm, to jerk hard at the man's wrist. Shisupala's wrist-bone snapped with a soft crack. With a cry of pain, he dropped his sword.

Govinda spun down on one knee and reached out to catch the weapon before it hit the ground. In the same move, he stood up and turned around, whipping the blade through the air with smooth precision.

It was over. A terrible quiet descended on the hall, in which only the crisp crackling of the sacred fires could be heard. The sword hung loosely from Govinda's hand. The slight rise and fall of his chest was the only evidence of movement as he stood still, his eyes closed. His upper robe had fallen off and his bare chest was streaked with blood. It had splashed across his face and he could taste its metallic tang, feel it invade his every sense. Mixed with the fragrance of the arghya, it was sanctifying and sullying at the same time.

Slowly, he stirred. He opened his eyes, and in a matter-of-fact way, threw aside Shisupala's sword. He then picked up his own blade, returning it carefully to its scabbard. Finally, he bent down to grab Shisupala's waist sash and began dragging the man's huge bulk towards the doorway. In his other hand he held Shisupala's severed head.

At the threshold, Govinda turned, considering the scene he left behind. Bhisma, his chest still heaving, stared at the blood-stained floor and then at him. A wide-eyed Dwaipayana reached out to hold on to the tall, strong, Suka next to him as his well-masked fear finally gave way to obvious relief. Around them all, shock, awe, surprise and reverence played across the faces of those present as each one came to terms with what had just happened. Syoddhan alone showed no visible emotion, his face expressionless. His eyes nevertheless betrayed his pain; the excruciating torment of guilt and regret. The same pained regret flashed in Dharma's eyes as he finally looked up to meet Govinda's cold, piercing gaze.

'Finish it,' Govinda ordered and disappeared into the bright glare outside.

For a while there was only silence. Then, in a hoarse voice, Dharma gave instructions for the coronation to continue. A slow hum of activity rose once again but conversation remained muted. A sense of gravity, of newfound respect, infused the proceedings, as the sheer power of the new empire made itself felt.

Govinda did not return. He could not, for he was now tainted with death.

Panchali stood where she was, watching the empty space where Govinda had been just moments ago. He had not as much as glanced at her. She felt as though she was being melted, tempered and wrought in the blue heat of the sacrificial fire. The moment of blind joy that had filled her at the affirmation that power and ambition had meant little to Govinda after all, had not lasted long. She knew he had killed Shisupala for a reason and it had little to do with the First Honour. He had killed the prince to protect a secret, a dark, horrifying secret – one she had perhaps known for a while, suspected for a while longer, but admitted not at all.

There was no running away from it now, no turning back. She took her place for the second time on the huge, gem-studded throne, painfully aware that Syoddhan now stared at her with undisguised rage and hatred.

As one, Aryavarta's kings declared their allegiance. Then, to the resounding chant of the sacred invocation to Sri, the goddess and the very source of power in the imperial sceptre, consecrated water from many brass, silver and gold vessels was used to anoint the new rulers of the empire. With loud cheers, the entire gathering hailed Dharma and Panchali, while drums and trumpets rang loud.

The Empress of Aryavarta humbly accepted her new destiny, her hands folded in silent prayer.

31

DWAIPAYANA WATCHED FROM AN ORNATE WINDOW OF DHARMA'S palace as yet another royal convoy left Indr-prastha with due pomp and bustle, seen off by one or the other of Dharma's brothers, as was appropriate. He breathed in deep of the crisp evening breeze, feeling satisfied and content. The coronation was over. One by one the guests were leaving, returning to their homes as the loyal subjects of Emperor Dharma. It would not do to overstay their welcome, especially not after what had happened to Shisupala.

The old scholar smiled at the recollection of recent events. Although somewhat unexpected, the conclusion had been wholly gratifying. Sanjaya had been right to suggest that the First Honour go to Govinda. It had indeed placed the man, officially and functionally, in the highly useful position of protector of the Empire. Like the crack of a whip, Govinda's cold wrath and violence had revealed the might behind the benevolent face of Dharma's reign. It had made the coronation that much more effective and, to the Vyasa personally, infinitely more satisfying.

Dwaipayana continued to revel in the still-fresh memories, even as an attendant appeared at the door, announcing a visitor. A tad reluctantly, he turned. As he had expected, it was Dharma. Somehow, the new emperor brought him less joy in person than he did as a notion. 'My son, come on in,' he greeted him.

Dharma entered the room and went down on one knee in salutation.

'Come, sit comfortably, come …' the Vyasa prompted.

Dharma rose, and sat down on an ornate chair, saying, 'Your carriage is ready, Acharya. But must you leave already? Indr-prastha quickly empties of its guests. Just this morning I was crowned, and now …' he shook his head, looking doleful.

'Ah, the anti-climatic aftermath of a grand ending … Sadly, it's time to stop celebrating, and start ruling, Dharma. We all have our duties to get back to, you included.'

'Won't you stay a little longer?' Dharma urged.

'No, my son, I must go.' Dwaipayana began bustling about the room, collecting the many manuscripts strewn about the room. With genuine anticipation in his voice, he said, 'And this is one journey I look forward to very much. By divine providence, my retirement from politics in Aryavarta has come about sooner than expected, Praise be to Varuna! My students are an intelligent and impatient lot and Suka will work me hard to make up for their missed lessons. I'm an old man ... It's time for me to go back to my parchments and my quills. Besides, I leave Aryavarta in good hands.'

He paused, gazing contentedly at the younger man. With sombre satisfaction, he proclaimed, 'Dharma, Emperor of Aryavarta ... And the unhappiest Emperor I've seen, I must say!'

'Acharya ...' Dharma started.

With a merry laugh, Dwaipayana went on, 'I know you, my son. You're a man after my own heart, a man who believes in Divine order, in destiny, and the essence of being good. And your conscience, the one that gives you your name, now tells you that this empire, even your coronation, are tainted with things you find loathsome, isn't that so?'

'I ... Acharya ...' Dharma began to protest but the relief at being understood without having to explain himself shone on his face. He made to stand, as a prelude to pouring out his heart.

The Elder waved him back to his seat. 'It doesn't matter how you got here, Dharma. What matters is why. The mission of the Firstborn is fulfilled, thanks to you. You see, my forefathers believed that if they could concentrate all power and authority in the scriptures, some degree of accountability would be established. These scriptures set immutable notions of justice, duty and goodness. And that, my son, is what gives us stability. Birth, nobility, honour – these things did not matter to the Firewrights. They have fully paid the price. Their philosophy, their very system has failed. You now rule as emperor over a confederation that values virtue, and will remain united by their common duty. Life will go on according to the scriptures. But ...'

Dwaipayana put the scroll he was holding down on a table and purposefully went over to Dharma. In a soft but compelling voice

425

he said, 'It's your task to maintain stability and peace. I can't stress how important this is. You can't concern yourself with details, trivialities. All that has happened, loathsome or otherwise, is destiny. Destiny has brought you to rule over us all, because it's time for righteousness and good to prevail. This is how it was meant to be! Those who have served you, those who've built this empire for you – have done so in your name and by the will of the gods. Their fate, their future is their own to face. Don't think yourself beholden to them for honours you've showed them, or feel bound by their service to you. Do you understand me?' He paused, knowing that Dharma understood who it was he spoke of in such veiled terms.

The Emperor responded with a hesitant silence.

'I said this to you at your coronation,' Dwaipayana sharply continued, 'and I say this again. Listen! You may not have realized what a historically significant moment this is. Future generations will point to you and say that it was during your reign that the Firstborn taught the noble Aryas to walk along the path leading to the heavens and brought to earth the power of the gods. By your very life, you've earned your name, *Dharma*. Don't let me down, do you understand? Don't let me down!' he finished. His voice was strained and his cheeks glistened with tears of fervour.

The Vyasa's words stirred a host of emotions in the newly crowned Emperor. The happiness Dharma had denied himself for the past days, no, years, finally flooded through him, filling him with relief as it all made sense. This was how it was meant to be. Whatever means the gods had used, in the end, dharma, righteousness, would prevail. Just as he would now prevail, restoring order and honour to Aryavarta. Joy blossomed on his face, and he wished he could rip his soul from his body and lay it at the Vyasa's feet. Never had he felt so overcome with reverence and emotion.

'The gods have brought me to my destiny. It's my duty to see this done,' Dharma plainly stated.

Dwaipayana placed a hand on the younger man's head in blessing, and let out a sigh of satisfaction. Dharma, he knew, would now rule in peace.

'May your glory rival that of Indra himself!' he declared. 'Now go. Leave this old man to potter around with his memories for few moments. I'll see you and your brothers by the carriage in a short while.'

With a grateful bow, Dharma took his leave of the Vyasa.

Dwaipayana watched him walk away down the corridor and disappear from view.

'So, that's done,' he remarked, as Sanjaya stepped out of a small anteroom. 'You won't need me anymore, my son. Aryavarta's greatest days lie ahead. Make sure you deal with the loose ends that are left, won't you, Sanjaya. Dharma's rule must be absolute. Get Asvattama to hunt down that Firewright, Devala. Tell him to make sure that the bastard screams so loud that no one in Aryavarta ever dares utter the name of those heretics again!'

Sanjaya nodded, his face impassive.

The Vyasa continued, 'And then, of course, there's Govinda Shauri. He should be a happy man, I think. Recognized as first among Aryas, his sister's blood eventual heir to the imperial throne … and he and his people are now safe. Dwaraka will prosper under Dharma's rule, and Govinda will prosper with it. Yes, he's a content fellow indeed, I should expect. As far as we're concerned, the tiger having served its purpose has been tamed and caged, in no small part due to your foresight. Make sure, though, that it doesn't break free. Govinda must fade into obscurity, and if he is remembered it can't be as anything more than a womanizing charmer. He must stay out of Aryavarta's affairs.'

'And if the tiger should …'

'Then do what you have to, Sanjaya.' In a softer tone, the Vyasa added, 'The Firewrights are dead, Dharma is Emperor and the Firstborn guide his conscience, Aryavarta's conscience. Nothing else matters. I've waited very long for this day. There's nothing I want more than to spend my time in quiet meditation, in a place far removed from these mundane shackles and material quagmires.' His voice fell to a whisper, as if he spoke to himself, or perhaps to an absent one for whom he held great affection, 'My duty is done, my promise has been kept. It's time I seek the Truth, the Maker … or whatever lies beyond it all.'

Sanjaya went down on his knees as his emotions brimmed over. He made to speak, many times, but could not find the words. Eventually, he gave up, and bowed his head low.

Dwaipayana stirred and looked at him with affection. 'I've been fortunate indeed to have had you with me. You bear the burdens of my conscience and are the one who truly understands what I've done and why. But … have I done you wrong, Sanjaya? You came to me to learn of the gods and I have made a politician of you … You, whom I love as a son! But, it's not too late to let you go …' he remarked humorously. Then, with a sigh, he declared, 'I set you free of this old fool, of your binding to me as student. From today, you are your own man and your debt to your mentor is discharged.'

A moment of strained, almost painful speechlessness hung over them as both men came to terms with what had just happened. With that simple statement the Vyasa had relinquished his final hold not just over Sanjaya, but over all of Aryavarta.

Sanjaya bowed low again and remained silent for a while longer. In the end, when he spoke, it was in a measured tone. 'Acharya, I repeat the Emperor's question – must you really go?'

Dwaipayana let out a heavy breath. 'It's a relief not to be needed. One I intend to enjoy fully and in total seclusion. Come, the carriage is waiting. I wish to leave the city before nightfall. I shall travel till the foothills of the White Mountains as the Vyasa, this one last time. From there on I shall become Dwaipayana the ascetic once again.'

32

THE SUN HAD NOT YET RISEN ON THE FIRST NEW DAY OF HER imperial reign as Panchali rode towards the river. It was dark, but the distinct smell of morning was already in the air, a unique mix of midnight blooms and daybreak jasmine. A gentle, insistent wind tugged at her hair, pulling it out of its loose bun till it streamed out behind her. She smiled at nature's wild irreverence, thankful that some things remained beyond the control of any emperor or empress.

Empress, hah! The thought reminded her of why she was there, and she drew yet again on the anger and bitterness of many years that served always to give her strength.

Today, it would end.

Panchali swung off her horse and walked the remaining distance towards the river. She emerged out through a small grove of shrubs, right on to the riverbank. Tethering her horse to a nearby tree, she waited. Govinda's first act that morning would be to offer prayers for the man he had killed, Panchali knew that well.

Just as the blue night lightened to a purple dawn, Govinda waded out of the river, his hair sleek with the damp and his wet antariya clinging to his lean body. It was cold, but he seemed oblivious to it, despite his bare chest and feet. He picked up his sword from where he had left it and walked directly towards Panchali. She knew he was daring her to look away, to act modest and bashful as she ought to, but she did not take the bait. Instead, she brazenly met his gaze.

'Mahamatra,' he greeted her, his eyes sparkling with a strange light.

Panchali's expression was taunting. As he drew closer, she said, 'You remind me of Indra himself, Govinda, as Ahalya saw him, emerging from the water.'

'Do you find me that tempting, Panchali? Or do you fear that I will seduce you?' he asked, teasing and sensuous.

'Tempting, Govinda? Is that your opinion of Ahalya – an easy-to-seduce, desperate woman?'

'Ahalya,' he said, 'was a great woman and not just for her beauty. She was forced to marry a man other than the one she loved ... marry, bear him a son. And then, after many years, she met her beloved, Indra. What did temptation and seduction have to do with it ... they'd loved each other, always. Pity ...' he trailed off.

Panchali sighed. 'It always amazes me how such a wonderful tale was turned into such a frightening one. I've heard it said that

429

Indra deceived her and there was no fault on her part. If so, how did he remain the King of Heaven while she was cursed to turn into stone?'

Govinda's words were a whisper. 'She *was* turned to stone ... They'd both known others, but it didn't matter because Indra made love not to her body but to her soul. And once he was gone ...'

'Why did it have to end that way? Imagine, if things had been otherwise ... but it can't be, can it?'

'No, it can't. The world as we know it wouldn't make sense unless Ahalya were turned to stone. A world where love remains unrequited is an anomaly, an imperfection. Judgement and blame are the only way we can reason out the imbalance and continue to believe in a Perfect Universe.'

'Oh please!' Panchali was suddenly scathing. 'Spare me the philosophical explanations. I've had enough of you acting like the consummate model of reason and dispassion. I once used to think that you were just a masochist who believed that if he makes enough sacrifices, if he keeps giving himself up for the sake of some greater cause, he can fight the darkness. Then I realized you're something worse. Whether that makes you a god or a demon, I don't know ...'

Govinda looked amused. He clucked his tongue and said, 'What complicated threads are you getting in a tangle? I can sense your mind working into knots. You can't stop thinking, even if you try. But go on,' he urged, 'you know I find it absolutely wonderful.'

'Really? And I suppose you're equally amused by the way it has all fallen into place, aren't you? Aryavarta lies under your feet ... What will you do next, Govinda? What will you conquer now?'

For once, Govinda's eyes betrayed confusion.

Panchali stepped forward. She was much shorter than Govinda and had to look up at him, but the subtle pride with which she held her head up made her seem no less tall. 'Or are you done with your manipulation?' she taunted. 'I don't think you are, but you know what? It's too late. It's over. I'm done with being your figurehead, the so-called Empress of Aryavarta, through whom you will rule us all. It's all over and you've failed! You've lost, Govinda! Your condescension has been your folly. You never thought your puppet, your dear little Princess Panchali, would amount to anything on her own, did you?'

'Panchali ...'

'I won't be your toy empress. I will not give you that pleasure. This is the land of the noble and there's no room here for demons such as you. At every step of the way, I've fought you, don't you see ...?'

In a tearful whisper, Panchali added, 'Don't you see? I know everything, Govinda – right from Ghora's death to Shisupala's, it all makes sense ... You are nothing but a traitor of the worst sort, for you stand by no one. You're a man without allegiance or identity. All you want is supremacy, you want to lord over us all, and no, not even the First Honour can satisfy your appetite for power. I tried to stop you once. Yes. I'll confess that I did try to stop you. I was the one who kept Devala informed about all your plans. I tried so hard to save Kandava ...'

'I know,' Govinda interjected. 'I know that it was Asvattama who pointed you to the old bow and that's how you ended up meeting Devala. I also know that you tried to turn me away from war, from killing Jarasandha and, ultimately, from building you an empire. I won't deny that sometimes you made sense on the face of it, but for the most part you were just trying to stop me because you thought me ruthless and ambitious.'

Panchali looked away, biting her lower lip in frustration. She wished he would at least try to explain or defend his actions. She would willingly accept any excuse he gave, if only he would say that he really did care. That he had used her, yes, but had never meant to hurt her this way.

He remained silent.

Unable to bear it, she went on, wanting to hear herself say the words out loud. 'Kandava ... You know, that day in Kandava – oh yes, I remember every moment of that day. That day, Govinda, for the tiniest moment, I thought ... I thought I was more than just amusement to you. I thought you cared. And the truth is, you do!

431

It's been your only weakness. You care for me, and so you trust me ... I've longed to believe it and to deny it. I didn't want to betray you, but I can't bear the notion that you ...'

Fighting back her tears, Panchali made herself look at him. Govinda's face was cold and emotionless. It made her want to scream, but she willed herself not to. 'And so,' she continued, her voice even. 'I waited and I watched you as you built *your* empire, as you stripped Aryavarta of every shred of dignity, killing those who defied you. That's why you destroyed the Wrights, all those years ago, isn't it? And you went against those same Wrights in Kashi, not to weaken *them* but to destroy *us*! You're like the rest of them, Govinda. This has nothing to do with principle and everything to do with power. The good become heathens and the bad turn sacred. These are just words that the powerful ones use to justify their might. The victorious always became the noble, because they define nobility.'

'What's your point?'

'Do you really want me to make the accusation in plain words, Govinda? And what is it you want me to point out – who you really are or what you've done?'

'That's up to you. You know it doesn't bother me at all. I am, however, curious as to the reasoning behind the assertions you make – or don't make.'

'Careful, Govinda. You've made me *your Empress*. It's a little late for insubordination, don't you think?' Panchali paused, her eyes locked defiantly with Govinda's as she searched for the words she wanted. 'I hear,' she casually began, 'that for all their radical thinking, the Firewrights do hold themselves bound by law – their own laws, that is. Particularly in the matter of succession. One Secret Keeper must die for another to take his place, isn't it?'

'So I hear, too.'

'So you hear. I think you've done more than hear, Govinda. Of all people, you had the most to gain or lose when Ghora Angirasa died. His death set off the chain of events that has brought us to this moment.'

'The ancients call it karma, as you well know. The things we do, or don't do, have consequences. I fail to see how this implicates me.'

'Ghora took many secrets with him.'

'I suppose so. He was the Secret Keeper.'

'As did Shisupala. He wasn't the Secret Keeper, though, just a smart man who'd figured out the truth.'

'Battle doesn't turn into murder based on the acumen of the deceased, Panchali.'

'Irrespective of acumen, Ghora's death was murder.'

'Suppose it was. And my fault in that is … ?'

'You didn't look for his murderer, Govinda.'

'True, I didn't. Why should I?'

'Why not?

Govinda shrugged, a look of amused puzzlement on his face.

'Why not?' Panchali repeated. A hint of smugness crept into her voice, as she continued, 'You know who the murderer is. You know it, and you've done nothing. Is it too much to wonder why?'

'No, but the explanation could be a simple one. What if I just didn't care?'

'Oh, you do care, Govinda. You certainly do care about this. Your true enemies are those who see through you, who see the truth. And that's why you killed Shisupala, isn't it? But what are you going to do, now that I have seen through you? Will you kill me too, like you did Shisupala?'

Govinda laughed.

He threw his head back and roared with unrestrained mirth as a stunned Panchali watched, waiting for him to stop. He eventually did, with an acquiescent, grudging sigh. Then, clearing his throat and gathering his thoughts, Govinda said, 'Perhaps I should apologize, seeing as you're hurt. But I won't. You want to know what I really care about? Not the Firewrights nor the Firstborn, not kingdoms and titles. But I do care about Aryavarta, its people, and I care about *you*. I've done what was necessary, Panchali, and I won't apologize for it. This empire, *your* empire, is Aryavarta's greatest hope.'

'My empire!' Panchali sarcastically exclaimed. 'Hah! Don't you get it? I let you make me Empress because I was the only one I trusted to resist you, to stand up to you. For years, I've waited for this moment, waited to stop pretending that I'm just your puppet and tell you that it's all over. I won't let you use me to lord over Aryavarta. Neither is your plaything, Govinda. You've wanted us both, but you'll have neither.'

'I ...' Govinda hesitated, finding himself at an unusual loss for words. He then chuckled resignedly and said. 'Is that what you really think of me?'

'Then tell me what to think. Tell me the truth, at least now.'

Govinda drew in a long, wholesome breath, cherishing the moment of anticipation, the allure of freedom and the imminent relief of finally sharing his deepest secret, though both of them already knew the truth. At last, he said the words he had longed to say to her for years.

'Panchali, I am a Firewright.'

34

A FIREWRIGHT ...

Panchali did not know what hit her harder – the obviousness of his statement in retrospect, the fact that she had remained wilfully blind to it all these years, or the simple respite of having it out in the open, finally.

At last, she found her voice. 'How? Who? I mean ...' she stuttered.

Govinda understood. 'Many years ago, before I left Mathura. Ghora Angirasa. He was my teacher.'

Pancali was aghast. 'And you killed him?'

'His death shall lie heavy on my head, I admit. And yes, his blood shall forever stain my hands. But not so much my conscience. I brought Ghora Angirasa back to Aryavarta, hoping to upset the uneasy balance we had got ourselves into. I set off this mad chain of events that has led us to this. Did I kill him? No, but the distinction is perhaps irrelevant for I watched, wilfully helpless, as Ghora Angirasa stabbed himself with his own knife …'

'What … ?' Panchali felt the beginnings of a slightly terrified awe as she looked up at Govinda. The difference, she knew, between murder and sacrifice was simple legitimacy. *But what man can have the courage to make such a terrible decision, and yet sleep with a clear conscience?*

Govinda seemed to anticipate her silent question. He said, 'Of the many things Ghora taught me, the most important has perhaps been to look beyond myself, to be one with something larger. Perhaps it was the cowherd in me, but that idea came to define my life – to the extent that allegiance and affection both are nothing but illusions. What is real is that larger Oneness, the meaning of meaning …'

'Admirable sentiments. But they still don't justify your actions, no, your *heinous* actions. Ghora is but one victim of your trail of violence, Govinda. To use your own dramatic phrase, the Firewrights' blood has been on your hands, yes, but for a long time now. You destroyed them! You had them all hunted down like animals!'

Govinda remained unprovoked. His gaze fixed earnestly on Pancali, he continued in a calm tone, 'The Firewrights were failing, decaying, condemned by their obsession with secrecy, their own power and politics. The kings of the realm both feared and revered them, while the Firstborn despised them. Parashara – Dwaipayana's father – had sanctioned a scourge, something that would destroy every last one of the Wrights unless they made themselves useful and relevant once again, became willing to teach and share, and to be the inventors and scholars they were meant to be. I could see that, but none of them would agree with me. Except, of course, for Ghora. He saw what needed to be done and we both did it. The point was never to destroy the Wrights. We – Ghora and I – just wanted to weaken them enough, so that they had to reach out and rely on others.

'Which is precisely what has happened. Torn apart and thrown into disarray, the Wrights hid in the forests, passing their metal craft on to the Nagas. Some sought refuge at Dwaraka, bringing with them their art and architecture. The Bhargavas, who had already shared their knowledge of weapons and warfare with the likes of Bhisma, willingly, eagerly, began to train anyone who showed interest and merit – Arya or not. Men like Ghora, and even Devala Asita, travelled far from these lands, learning and teaching. The Wrights were destroyed, not as a scientific order, but as a fanatic group of secretive power-mongers. And because we did what we did the Wrights remain in spirit, their knowledge lives on surviving even the terrible war that the Firstborn, together with the kings of Aryavarta, have waged against them.'

With surprising vehemence, Govinda declared, 'I don't want to be Emperor, Pancali. I don't want First Honour, or any damned nonsense that goes with it. Power drives politics and I want so badly to remain free of it, to remain part of the objective larger Oneness. Always, always, I've tried to do what was right, what was in the interests of the greatest number, what was for the greater good of all. And that's what your empire is – it's a chance for us, the people of Aryavarta – not just its elite rulers – to find peace. It's a chance for reason to prevail. I …' he faltered, but only for an instant. Panchali clenched her jaws in a bid to remain silent.

'All that I have done in these past years is to continue the task Ghora and I began, together. Think about it,' he urged, 'Kandava, Kashi … Look at the pattern! What happened thirty years ago with the Wrights happened again, this time with those who'd learnt from them. By forcing the Nagas out of Kandava, their iron craft is now out in the open. They've truly become part of Aryavarta, part of the lives of the people, not just the kings! As have the medics of Kashi, who've been forced to wander Aryavarta ever since I burned down their city. Every time it looked like the Wrights were coming together to hoard their knowledge, form their secret order once more, I broke them apart.'

'So that you alone were powerful,' Panchali could finally take no more. 'You wanted to …'

Govinda interrupted, 'My intention was not to cast them down or to take their place. All I've ever dreamt of, ever longed for, is an empire of peace built on both the knowledge of the Wrights and the scriptures of the Firstborn. Built in a way that they're equal and inseparable. For that I needed you – and I needed you to understand who the Wrights truly were and what they were capable of ...'

'So you let Asvattama send me to Utkochaka?' Panchali demanded, incredulous. 'You sent me to Devala, even though you knew what he was, what he was capable of?'

'Yes and no. I wasn't quite sure Devala had crawled back out from whichever rock it was he had been hiding under. But you helped me bring him out ...'

'And Dwaipayana?'

'Dwaipayana's battle is with the Wrights, not with their knowledge. He has never had any problem letting those he trusts, or controls, use Firewright weaponry, as long as it is in what he considers the best interest of the Firstborn. And such is his attitude towards me. As far as he is concerned, I am a Wright-trained man, yes, but one who has served the purposes of the Firstborn well. The utility of my actions have far outweighed the burden of my identity. He has what he wants. His offspring rule all of Aryavarta. With the Wrights gone in name, at last the Firstborn can breathe a sigh of relief. But for that to happen, for the many, many things that have led us to this point to happen, the idea that the Firewright order no longer exists was an important one. Which is why, again, Ghora had to die and what better place to do so than the Vyasa's own hermitage? As for me – I've been rather useful to Dwaipayana, haven't I? I've pretty much destroyed the Wrights for him, not to mention built his grandson's empire! As long as I keep my nose out of Aryavarta's affairs henceforth, he probably won't care. Or he might just decide to finish me off, who knows? Doesn't matter really,' Govinda cheerfully concluded.

'And once you're gone?' Panchali challenged. 'What's to stop your precious empire from falling to pieces?'

'Trade, my dear!'

Govinda's eyes came alight with a hidden fire. 'As the Firstborn set up their hierarchies, their structured divisions of society based on duty and destiny, it will lead to specialization – those charged with the duty of farming become better farmers, those with the duty of trade become better traders. And knowledge grows – scientific knowledge. And then, as people start coming to terms with the huge distances, they'll learn to write and read, and keep accounts and records. You think power and might lies only in armies and brute force? Prosperity can be power too. If we truly achieve our potential, we become more valuable to foreign rulers as we are – they gain nothing from conquering us and by leaving us as an independent empire they can benefit from trading with us.'

'But …'

'Panchali, I've done what I had to. I know you think of me as an arrogant, ambitious, even bloodthirsty man. For that matter, most of Aryavarta has that opinion of me, and there are few who don't see me as honourless scum. But this isn't about just you and me, it's about Aryavarta. This is how it must be. It's for the greater good. Honour, nobility … being Arya has no meaning without Aryavarta, not just as a realm but as an ideal to stand up for.'

Panchali tried to make sense of what she had just been told, but facts, thoughts and emotions all collided into each other in a disgusting and surreal way, like maggots devouring a tree. She felt her anger dissolve and in its place a cold understanding took root. But she no longer understood whether she had been correct or not, only that she had to do the right thing.

'Who else knows?' she asked, suddenly feeling very small and tired.

Govinda replied, 'For a fact? Balabadra. Yuyudhana, Shikandin. Of course, Dwaipayana suspects as much. Devala, Dhaumya … I assume Bhisma also knows that I was once Ghora Angirasa's student. They also know I've worked hard to bring down the Wrights. Devala's all that's left of the old school and Shikandin will hunt him down, sooner than later. And then there's Asvattama – like me, he too struggles with his loyalties. That's all.' With a soft chuckle, he added, 'What does that make me, then, I wonder?'

'The last Firewright? Isn't that what you wanted?'

'Not really,' Govinda shook his head. 'Let me tell you this much, Panchali, though perhaps it's not a piece of information meant for the Empress of Aryavarta. The order of Firewrights lives on. There remains a Secret Keeper.'

Panchali's response oozed sarcasm, 'Indeed! No guessing who that is, I suppose? Or does another of your figureheads fill that role, while you yank at the strings? No, I think this particular title you do want for yourself. Otherwise, you'll remain a traitor won't you, an outcast from the order. But that's what you've always been, and still are ... A man without an identity, because he can remain true to nothing. Not to clan and kingdom, nor to order and allegiance.'

Govinda remained impassive. 'Now you'll accuse me of another ambition, will you? I suppose I should deny it, but it doesn't matter. Or perhaps, I will deny it and state categorically that I am not the Secret Keeper, if only to say that the one who is Secret Keeper is certainly a much better man than I. As for me ... What I am is and always was plain for all to see. I can't change that, just as I can't change what I know.'

'No, but you can choose what you do with it.'

'I already have.'

Panchali sighed. Govinda, she realized, found life in the tiny moment between two heartbeats, the potent silence between breathing in and breathing out. He hung on to that instant that was neither death nor life, and it fuelled his equanimity, his detachment and dispassion. He would know neither pleasure nor pain, neither desire nor satiation. In the very same moment, that instant between two heartbeats, Panchali lived many lifetimes, felt many passions. She saw Time as it was born, and as it died. She watched innumerable universes in infinite existences, in which the same story played itself out over and over again. Battles were fought, won and lost, between celestials and demons, and demons that became celestial and then fell from lofty heights, to begin the incessant, inevitable climb to divinity again.

I'm just a tiny speck against the vast universe, she told herself, but this speck is as complete and perfect as the universe itself, so why do I need to long for more? I'm just a drop in the ocean of existence, who can do little more than pray to the One who rests on its waves, in his dream – sleep that's neither life nor death.

'Narayana …' she suddenly whispered, giving in to the numbness that settled over her.

Panchali knew she had yielded, accepted what Govinda was capable of. She did not have the strength to pretend to herself that he made exceptions. He did not. Everyone, everything was an illusion to him, illusions that had no hold over him. But she had to make her choice, decide what she would believe in.

The words flowed out of her in an unstoppable stream. 'Are you truly so innocent, Govinda? Or have you deluded everyone for so long that you've starting believing that you do the right and honourable thing? Like the gods that rule us, you judge us all in your benevolence. But it isn't so. Do you really think that it's all over, that the world will merrily follow the path you've laid out? That your plan will work?'

Govinda shrugged. 'Why not?'

'Because you assume that men are guided by reason alone.'

'That's not correct. There's nothing rational about wanting power. I don't deny emotion.'

'Let me rephrase that. You believe that people are capable of seeing the most objective means to achieve their ends – ends which may be driven by emotion. Do you agree?'

'I do. And where's the problem with that?'

'You underestimate human nature and scorn the essence of humanity. There's a part of us that worships passion, not reason, no matter what pathetic mistakes it drives us to or how much pain it causes us. Whatever the end result you may have intended, your means destroy the core of what makes us special. If we followed you, we'd be forced to surrender every sense of compassion that we're capable of feeling. No matter what you say you believe in, you will only destroy us. I can't let that happen. I won't let it happen!'

Panchali forced herself to calm down and placed a hand on Govinda's cheek. Standing on tiptoe she whispered in his ear, a soft murmur of intimate but taunting secrets. 'You think I don't understand? The fact is, you don't understand! You can't understand, not as long as you remain devoid of the simplest human emotions. You can never belong to anyone, not even yourself. You'll forsake love rather than forsake dispassion or, perhaps, you already have …'

With a sad smile, she finished, 'You love, but you don't know what it is to love. You so desperately fight to save Aryavarta, but you don't know what it is you're trying to save, what you're really fighting for, do you? Emperor, but not; Secret Keeper, but not– You do all that you do and then claim to have done nothing at all, you hide behind explanations of reason and social evolution and all those words you throw around to deny your presence here and in this moment, so that you can continue to believe that you're some evolved, elevated being who is above us all. Truly, I pity you …'

Govinda said nothing. He pushed his wet hair back and watched as Panchali flicked off with her slender fingers the drop of water that had landed on her cheek, admiring her perfectly oval nails, which had been henna-reddened for the coronation.

Panchali studied him, no longer angry. 'Go away, Govinda,' she said at last, her voice flat and dull. 'Go away, or else we'll all become soulless monsters like you. I'll pray for you. I'll pray that someday you find something that moves you to the very core of your being. Then you'll understand what I've done and why. For now, go. And, on my honour, as long as I am Empress, don't ever, ever come back!'

Govinda smiled to himself. Much as he wanted to pretend that this was the angry rant of a heartbroken, scorned woman, he knew it was far too rational for that. It was far too accurate for that. In her heart, Panchali knew he was right. She also knew he had to leave, throwing her aside once again. This was her way of lashing out, of perhaps trying to salvage some last modicum of hope from her otherwise shattered soul.

Worst of all, Govinda had no regrets. He had dealt with Panchali exactly as he dealt with himself; he had been ruthless with her and treated her as little more than an idea, an instrument, and the means to a greater end. But her eyes, dark and innocent, haunted his dreams and pored deep into his soul. They had always seen the things he hid from the rest of the world. Well, almost always.

He watched Panchali intently, drinking in his fill of her, wanting to feel the warmth, the honest affection for one last time before he left her and his beloved Aryavarta behind. He yearned for one last smile to hold in memory along with the smell of lotuses, the sense of her that filled his very being. For a fleeting moment he wanted to stay, and for an even smaller instant he wished things could be just a little bit otherwise. Most of all, he longed to take her in his arms and whisper the words of affection he had held back for so many years,to make one last confession before bidding her farewell.

Smiling, Govinda told himself it did not matter anymore. It had all happened exactly as he had planned, and that was enough. To be understood was a luxury he ought not to desire. *Rudra, give me strength,* he prayed silently. Out loud he said, 'Goodbye, Panchali. Rule well.'

And then he was gone.

35

THE LONE RIDER MADE FOR A SAD, FORLORN FIGURE AS HE STOOD silhouetted against the sun, looking down at the city – except for the private, satisfied smirk that spread across his face.

Of course, he had much to smile about. He stood with Indrprastha, why, with all of Aryavarta at his feet, in more ways than one. Soon, the entire land would pay for what they had done to him, his family and his order. For what they had done to the Firewrights.

His plan, he mused, had been well thought out and immaculately executed. Dwaipayana would now relinquish control and truly distance himself from the affairs of the empire, ensconced in his illusion of righteousness and security. By the time the old, self-absorbed scholar could think to act it would be too late.

The man allowed himself an uncharacteristic chuckle. It still did not fail to amaze him how easily men were blinded by their beliefs and by their ambition. It had been unexpectedly simple to manipulate that impassioned muhira Devala to his purposes. In the aftermath of Ghora's death, the young Firewright had fancied himself the logical successor to the mantle of the Secret Keeper – in future if not in the present. Moreover, the ambitious idiot had assumed that he alone had any legitimate claim to the Firewrights' legacy. With his newfound sense of responsibility and power it had taken little to goad Devala and he had been only too eager to openly defy Govinda and his imperial ambitions. As for the fool – that cowherd – he too had surely aspired to the role of Secret Keeper, to the position, if not the title. But it had not been too difficult to make sure that Govinda had been left with no choice but to reveal his own secrets and who he truly was.

And then it had been just as easy to stir Shisupala into action at the coronation, to make him speak up and place seeds of doubt in the minds of all those kings. They would not forget his questions in a hurry. They would not forget that Shisupala had died for asking those questions. In any case, the rider noted with a sneer, he would make sure that they did not forget. The kings of Aryavarta would soon rise against this mockery of an empire, and their wrath would bring down not just Emperor Dharma but also the hypocritical Firstborn order.

What would they feel, he pleasantly mulled for a short while. Rage that the Vyasa had betrayed them? Shame that the Firstborn had failed? Or just sheer horror that this, a supposed empire of righteousness, had been built on the might of the Firewrights they had condemned? How would Dharma react?

The speculation brought the man much satisfaction. For all his self-recrimination and denial, Dharma would have no choice but to embrace those who were truly the fount of his power. As would all the other rulers of Aryavarta. Soon, it would be the Firstborn who were declared heathen outlaws and hunted down like animals throughout the kingdoms, while the Firewrights took the glory that was theirs by right.

The rider let the rays of the setting sun bathe him in their glow, drinking in their golden touch. He threw his head back, as a rare gasp of joy escaped him and he revelled in his hard-won contentment. A part of him humbly suggested that it was not smugness – no, this satisfaction had come at too high a price for that. For all that he had found easy, there had been many trials, much pain that he had endured. He had kept these terrible secrets buried deep inside for so many years, from the world, even from Dwaipayana Vyasa. Sometimes, he recalled, he had forced himself to forget the truth, lest he somehow say or do something to reveal what he knew. To reveal who he really was. The hardest part had been to watch and keep his silence as the last remaining dregs of the Firewrights had been systematically destroyed, one by one. So many times, he had reminded himself that it was necessary, that this was the only way. Sacrifice was inevitable.

In any case, it was done, and his selflessness would soon have its reward. Somewhere in the larger tide of events that would sweep across Aryavarta, was his own, personal revenge. The man who had brought the Firewrights to this, the traitor who had betrayed his own, would be destroyed. Before the end, Govinda would watch his beloved city fall, his people die, and his loved ones scream in agony. Or, perhaps, it would be immensely more pleasurable to keep him alive and make him suffer the same fate as those he had betrayed. Blinded and maimed like Agniveshya, or tortured for his secrets and knowledge like the old Agnivarna. The possibilities were endless.

Slowly, the man let out the breath he did not know he had been holding, forcing himself to relax and think calmly, to acknowledge the force of destiny that had brought him to this, to his rightful inheritance. It was time. The Firewrights would rise once again from the embers of their pyre, more potent, more powerful than ever. Soon, he would find the new Secret Keeper, the one Ghora Angirasa had left in his stead to rule not just the Firewrights but the entire empire. And then …

Sanjaya Gavalgani laughed softly at that thought. Aryavarta would never be the same again.

THE ARYAVARTA CHRONICLES
continue in

BOOK 2

FIREWRIGHT

Emperor Dharma Yudhisthir rules over the unified empire of Aryavarta – an empire that promises to surpass the glory and prosperity of his ancestors. An empire built for him by Govinda Shauri, with the blessings of the Firstborn and by the might of those whom everyone believes long gone – the Firewrights.

Now the Firewrights rise from the ashes of the past to find themselves divided – those faithful to the last Secret Keeper, who will sacrifice all to protect Govinda's dream, and those who will stop at nothing to cast down the Firstborn and all that is of their making.

As a cruel war looms ahead, threatening to tear Aryavarta apart once again, brothers rise against each other. And a revelation is more urgent than ever: Who is the last Secret Keeper of the Firewrights, on whom all hopes now rest?

COMING SOON!

For more on *The Aryavarta Chronicles* log on to
www.aryavartachronicles.com

Standing on the Shoulders of Giants
A NOTE ON SOURCES AND METHODS

The Aryavarta Chronicles is the product of research and analysis, with the latter drawing on the former. A slew of work is out there – critical, unconventional, even controversial – that revolves around the world of the Mahabharata. Many are in regional and vernacular tongues, existing as folklore and tales that have never made it into print as a cohesive tome. The *Chronicles* rely on a mix of these scholarly and popular sources, on histories that tend towards established fact, as well as those based on socially constructed beliefs of what constitutes fact.

THE EVOLUTION OF AN EPIC

The Bhandarkar Oriental Research Institute (BORI) version (also known as the Poona Critical Edition) of the Mahabharata, which remains the dominant source for most retellings and reinterpretations today, is estimated to have been prevalent around the fifth century AD, that is, the Gupta Age. That leaves a fair 3,000 odd years or so during which the story was told over and over, endlessly, forming a final 'layered' narrative filled with explanations and interpolations. The bard–narrator of the mainstream edition, Ugrashravas Sauti, states that he recites what he heard from the scholar Vaishampayana, who in turn is one of the five students who learns the epic from its original author, the Vyasa. Add to this the fact that the epic itself recorded its growth from 8,800 verses composed by Dwaipayana Vyasa to 24,000 verses, and then to the 100,000-verse version we have today. Somewhere along the line, the Harivamsa is added on, as an appendix. And there begins a journey – for history is not stagnant, nor is its narration.

UNRAVELLING THE EPIC

Bibliographically speaking, my study began with C. Rajagopalachari's *Mahabharata* (Mumbai: Bharatiya Vidya Bhavan, 2005). My main source, which forms the broad canvas of 'canon' Mahabharata, is the translated version by K.M. Ganguli (*The Mahabharata of Krishna-Dwaipayana Vyasa, Volumes 1–12*, Calcutta: P.C. Roy/ Oriental Publishing Co., 1884–96; Republished, Delhi: Munshiram Manoharlal, 1970) available online through www.sacred-texts.com. I read this in conjunction with J.A.B. Van Buiten's three-volume translation which goes up to the Udyoga Parvan (*Mahabharata, Volumes 1 to 3*, Chicago: University of Chicago Press, 1975–78); P. Lal's lyrical transcreation of the epic (*Mahabharata of Vyasa*, New Delhi: Vikas Publishing House, 1986); and Ramesh Menon's more contemporary retelling (*The Mahabharata: A Modern Rendering, Volumes 1 and 2*, Lincoln: iUniverse, 2006).

I have relied also on Pandit Ramachandrashastri Kinjawadekar's version of the *Harivamsa* (Poona: Chitrashala Press, 1936), as translated by Desiraju Hanumanta Rao, A. Purushothaman and A. Harindranath (http://mahabharata-resources.org/harivamsa), and on M.N. Dutt's version of the text (*The Harivamsa*, Calcutta: Elysium Press, 1897). H.H. Wilson's *Vishnu Purana* (Calcutta: Punthi Pustak, 1961; original copyright 1840) was invaluable especially when it came to cross-checking genealogies and timelines, as was the Bhaktivedanta Book Trust International's version of the Srimad Bhagavatam, available through the Bhaktivedanta Vedabase Network website (www.vedabase.net).

The subsequent analysis, such as it is, was not without method. D.D. Kosambi notes: 'Against the hypothesis of "pure invention", one must ask why the invention took these particular forms …'

('The Autochthonous Element in the Mahabharata', 1964, *Journal of the American Oriental Society*, 84–1, pp. 31–44). This has been the dominant principle I have chosen to hold on to, focussing on the *why*.

Two stalwarts have influenced my approach to this issue. First, I have borrowed liberally from Bankimchandra Chattopadhyay's deductive principles in his *Krishnacharitra* (trans. Alo Shome, New Delhi: Hindology Books, 2008). Chattopadhyay's analysis is based on a categorical rejection of supernatural events, interpolations and 'events that can be proved to be untrue in any other way' (p. 27). A similar perspective is evident in K.M. Munshi's series *Krishnavatara* (Volumes 1–7, Mumbai: Bharatiya Vidya Bhavan, 1990). While Munshi admits to using his creativity freely in filling what may be gaps in the facts, he remains true to the notion that Krishna-Govinda was a man who eventually became a legend. In his view Govinda was not god, but a (near-perfect) man. I have gratefully followed his lead in beginning with the premise that this is the story of human beings, exemplary ones who are well-deserving of their consequent elevation to divine status. But it is not a story of gods.

Alf Hiltebeitel, a leading Mahabharata scholar, is one of those who speaks of a symbolism-rich Mahabharata; that is, the idea that many expressions in the Mahabharata cannot be literally interpreted ('The Mahabharata and Hindu Eschatology', 1972, *History of Religions*, 12–2, pp. 95–135). Hiltebeitel's *Rethinking the Mahabharata: A Reader's Guide to the Education of the Dharma Kings* (Chicago: Chicago University Press, 2001) also deserves mention for fuelling many ideas; as does James L. Fitzgerald's broad piece covering many topics on the Mahabharata, including the historical evolution of the text itself ('The Great Epic of India as Religious Rhetoric: A Fresh Look at the Mahabharata', 1983, *Journal of the American Academy of Religion*, 51–4, pp. 611–630). Mary Carroll Smith's analysis of the variation in meter, narrative structure, and the subtle moves from Vedic to Classical Sanskrit in the text as we have it today, to identify possible additions and interpolations

('The Mahabharata's Core', 1975, *Journal of the American Oriental Society*, 95–3, pp. 479–482) was central to my reconstruction of the story.

Such a reconstruction also requires political, social and even psychological explanations. For this, I have drawn on ideas from many analytical and creative works, first among them being Irawati Karve's *Yuganta: End of an Epoch* (Hyderabad: Disha Books/Orient Longman, 1991). Karwe is particularly notable for her critical approach to the question of Dharma Yudhisthir's father. Buddhadeva Bose in his *Mahabharater Katha/The Book of Yudhisthir* (trans. Sujit Mukherjee, London: Sangam Books/Hyderabad: Orient Longman, 1986) attributes to Dharma Yudhisthir's character the many frustrations and exasperations that I find likely, and though I am less inclined to glorify Dharma as the protagonist of the epic I cannot deny that I benefitted from reading Bose's book.

Alf Hiltebeitel's work on Panchali (*The Cult of Draupadi: Volumes 1 and 2*, Chicago: Chicago University Press, 1988, 1991) and Pradip Bhattacharya's essay on the *Panchkanyas* of lore ('She Who Must Be Obeyed – Draupadi: The Ill-Fated One', 2004, *Manushi*, 144–Sep/Oct, pp. 19–30) provides deeper insights into her compelling character and even the intricacies of her relationships. Panchali is symbolically and overtly equated to Sri – the consort of Vishnu in terms of the pantheon and the symbol of nature at a deeper level. This clearly places her as the heroine of a story which has Govinda for its hero; an idealized symmetry that is alluded to in Prathibha Ray's *Yajnaseni* (trans. Pradip Bhattacharya, New Delhi: Rupa, 1995.)

The tale, however, unfolds in a different way. The consequent asymmetry, anomaly even, is explained away in canon Mahabharata and its derivative tales (many of which speak of Panchali's preference for Partha) using the concepts of rebirth and divine manifestation. But, if we do away with such interpolated justifications, what might it mean?

I do not have the answer to this riddle, but only a question. Behind the implied and admitted romances, is there a story of affection so obvious that it is easily overlooked? Is it a kind of Freudian transference, whether in the original itself, or perhaps created post-hoc in the interests of sanitizing and legitimizing the epic but nevertheless hinted at by the triangle of three dark-skinned Krishnas – Panchali, Partha and Govinda? Or is the asymmetry itself the story – the tale of a world where many such things are not right? To borrow Govinda Shauri's words: 'The world as we know it would not make sense unless Ahalya were turned to stone.'

ALTERNATE MAHABHARATAS

At this point, I shall admit that I was occasionally surprised, perhaps even shocked, at the alternate theories that seemed to suggest themselves, particularly since I had been brought up on strong doses of canon Mahabharata. The ideas, however, were not as 'alternative' as I had first thought – I discovered the existence of alternate versions of the Mahabharata, many of which were equally canonical in their own right. These included the Bhil Mahabharata and the Indonesian Kakawain versions, both of which I highlight for a reason – The Bhil Mahabharata was (in my view) the nearest I could get to a subaltern version of the epic, and took a very different view of the socio-political status quo (for variations and tales from the Bhil Mahabharata see Satya Chaitanya's blog, based on his research of this folklore: http://innertraditions.blogspot.com).

The Indonesian Kakawain version (http://www.joglosemar. co.id/bharatayuda.html) was equally exciting, since it was possibly shipped out of Aryavarta and to Indonesian islands in a form that was closer to the 'core' or original Mahabharata – that is, an epic with fewer interpolations. A list of resources and essays on the Mahabharata variations across Bengali, Bhil, Oriya, Tamil, Malayalam and Rajasthani cultures (to name a few) is available at A. Harindranath's stunning website: (http://mahabharata-resources.org). Essays on the Oriya *Sarala Mahabharata* are available on B.N. Patnaik's site: http://saralamahabharat.blogspot.com.

BUILDING THE WORLD OF THE EPIC

W.G. Archer (*The Loves of Krishna in Indian Painting and Poetry*, New York: MacMillan, 1957) points to the small but immeasurably important link in the Upanishads that has opened the door to a larger story-world that revolves around the group of scholar–sages known as the Angirasas. With that in mind, the Vedic–Upanishad symbolism in the epic pointed out by Alf Hiltebeitel ('The Two Kṛṣṇas on One Chariot: Upanisadic Imagery and Epic Mythology', 1984, *History of Religions*, 24–1, pp. 1–26) begins to make sense. Many reinterpretations and interpolations fall into place and can be logically identified, keeping in mind the basic symbolic themes, as well as the body of philosophical knowledge that the epic seeks to encompass. Most importantly, the Mahabharata starts becoming a story of technological evolution and the associated social change.

I turned to the broader Vedic and Upanisadic literature in an attempt to decipher what the astra-incantations might have meant in a secular and scientific sense, and to understand the technology that hid behind metaphors. For this, I have relied strongly on Karen Thomson and Jonathan Slocum's work on ancient Sanskrit, available from the Linguistics Research Centre at the University of Texas at Austin; particularly their translations of Barend A. van Nooten and Gary B. Holland's version of the Rig Veda (*Rig Veda: A Metrically Restored Text*, Boston: Harvard University Press, 1994). Also deserving reference are Subhash C. Kak's 'Science in Ancient India' (In *Ananya: A Portrait of India*, S.R. Sridhar and N.K. Mattoo (eds.), 1997, AIA: New York, pp. 399–420); Aurobindo's *The Secret of the Veda* (Pondicherry: Sri Aurobindo Ashram, 1993) and Shatavadhani R. Ganesh's audio commentary on the PurushaSuktam and the NarayanaSuktam (K.V. Raman, *Vedic Chanting*, Bangalore: Sagar Music, 1999.)

The Vedic texts have also been of relevance to understanding the socio-political-economic context of the epic itself. For example, M.B. Emeneau and B.A. van Nooten approach the notions of *Niyoga* and polyandry in the Mahabharata from the broader Vedic context

('The Young Wife and Her Husband's Brother: Rgveda 10.40.2 and 10.85.44.', 1991, *Journal of the American Oriental Society*, 111–3, pp. 481–494). Also deserving mention here is Janet Chawla's feminist reading of the Rig Veda ('Mythic Origins of Menstrual Taboo in Rig Veda', 1994, *Economic and Political Weekly*, 29–43, pp. 2817–2827).

LIFE AND WAR IN EPIC TIMES

In terms of setting the descriptive stage for the story, my first stop was Romila Thapar's *The Penguin History of Early India: From the Origins to 1300 AD* (New Delhi: Penguin Books/Allen Lane, 2002). City descriptions are based mainly on details in the epic narrative, but I also referred to marine archaeologist S.R. Rao's *The Lost City of Dvaraka* (Goa: National Institute of Oceanography, 1999); David Frawley's *Gods, Sages and Kings: Vedic Secrets of Ancient Civilization* (Salt Lake City: Passage Press/Morson Publishing, 1991) and A.S. Gaur, Sundaresh and Sila Tripati's 'An Ancient Harbour at Dwarka: Study Based on the Recent Underwater Explorations' (2004, *Current Science*, 86–9, pp. 1256–60) for ideas on the layout of Dwaraka city, particularly its fortifications and defences. Gaur, Sundaresh and Tripati's 'Evidence for Indo–Roman trade from Bet Dwarka Waters, West Coast of India' (2005, *International Journal of Nautical Archaeology*, 35, pp. 117–127) inspired the notion of Dwaraka as a maritime power.

The military history of India, from the AllEmpires.com historical information website, Sushama Londhe's page on war in Ancient India (http://www.hinduwisdom.info/War_in_Ancient_India. htm), S.A. Paramahans's 'A Glance at Military Techniques in Ramayana and Mahabharata' (1989, *Indian Journal of History of Science*, 24–3, 156–160) and The Sarasvati Web (http://www. hindunet.org/hindu_history/sarasvati) also deserve reference.

GENEALOGIES

In constructing genealogies, I have relied on the texts of the Mahabharata and Harivamsa mentioned above, as well as the Srimad

Bhagavatham. My tables were supplemented and cross-checked against two sources: Desiraju Hanumanta Rao's genealogical tables of the Yadu and related dynasties (www.mahabharata-resources. org) and the tables in Irawati Karve's *Yuganta*. Vettam Mani's classic *Puranic Encyclopaedia* (Delhi: Motilal Banarasidas, 1975) has filled many gaps and provided essential details.

THE CONSTRUCTION OF TIME

My approach to Time has been a mix of the literal and the symbolic. Myth suggests that lifespans were much longer in the previous yugas, lasting perhaps up to three or four hundred years in the Dwapara-yuga – the era of the Mahabharata. However, these figures take on a different meaning if we apply the notion of ashrama or stages of life. K.N.S. Patnaik (*The Mahabharata Chronology*, Pune: Annual Research J. of the Institute for Rewriting Indian History, 1990) compares how childhood (*baalyam*) lasted forty years in the times of the Mahabharata, whereas it lasts approximately 15 years in the current age of Kali. Similarly, youth or *youvanam* lasted till the age of 120 years in the past, as compared to about 45 years in today's age. We are, in essence, dealing with a different basis of measurement of time and age.

Time, in the *Chronicles*, is therefore scaled down to contextualize the main actors as the middle-aged individuals they were, relative to the period of the epic. As a result, the age of the characters is given in contemporary terms.

Interestingly, ancient units of measurements ran by seasonal and sidereal time, along with the common solar. The possibility, therefore, of a year as we know constituting a shorter period of time, cannot be discounted. Subash Kak ('On the Chronological Framework for Indian Culture', *Indian Council of Philosophical Research*, 2000, pp. 1–24) mentions how one of the bases for variation in the dating of the events of the Mahabharata may be the calendar system used (more precisely, the number of stellar constellations in a given cycle).

LANGUAGE

My work would have been near-impossible but for these amazing dictionaries and glossaries, accessed primarily through the Cologne Digital Sanskrit Dictionaries website (http://www.sanskrit-lexicon. uni-koeln.de). Included in this database are the well-known Monier-Williams, Apte and MacDonnell dictionaries, as well as Kale's work on Sanskrit grammar. I also used the simpler but wonderful Spoken Sanskrit Dictionary (http://spokensanskrit.de) and relied on the Sanskrit Heritage Site (http://sanskrit.inria.fr/sanskrit.html) for grammar reference.

Acknowledgements

Shobana: Mother and closet feminist. She taught me to love our rich legacy of spirituality and scripture and to defy the irrational in it.

Sumita Chattopadhyay: Teacher and lover of literature. The mirror that showed me long ago the writer I now am.

Jai: Husband, beloved, best friend and consummate believer in gender equality. If writing be a labour of love, then his is the love that gives meaning to what I write. Without him there would be no words.

Boozo and Zana: My dearest (fur) kids. They showed me the meaning of unconditional affection and compassion, qualities that make epic heroes of us all.

Alvin: Mentor, guide and kindred writer. He taught me the most important lesson in writing – that the stories we tell are our own.

Jayapriya and Priya: Awesome agents and committed friends. They believed in me long before I believed in myself.

Shashi Warrier: For taking the time to read in entirety an aspiring author's awkward first draft and for kind encouragement.

Poulomi: Invested editor, fellow wordsmith. Her passion and vision for the world of Aryavarta moved me to bring it alive in ways I had not dreamt of.

Thanks also to my extended family and close friends, especially my parents-in-law, for their patience and courage in the face of adversity. There are few things more trying in the everyday world than putting up with an obsessed and cranky writer who is, partly, resident of another universe.

Thanks to Chandrika, whose diligence has greatly subsidized my domestic irresponsibility.

My thanks also to the entire team at Hachette India for investing so much in this book, and to Gunjan Ahlawat and Kunal Kundu for the cover.

And last but not the least, my father, A.R. Udayasankar: For my world of words, books and philosophy; for Amar Chitra Katha and Subramania Bharati in equal measure when I was five; for Dumas, Kipling and Adi Shankara at eight; and the Gita, the Upanishads, Hesse and Plato at thirteen. The list goes on. He could not have left me a greater legacy.